Emma Donoghue is an Irish novelist, playwright and historian who lives in Canada. Her second novel *Hood* won the American Library Association's Gay, Lesbian and Bisexual Award in 1997. Her other books include *Passions Between Women, Stir-Fry, Kissing the Witch, We Are Michael Field* and *Life Mask*.

Slammerkin

Emma Donoghue

VIRAGO

First published in 2000 by Virago Press
This edition published in 2001 by Virago Press
Reprinted 2001, 2005, 2007, 2008, 2009

A CIP catalogue record for this book is available
from the British Library

ISBN 978-1-86049-899-2

Typeset by Palimpsest Book Production Limited,
Polmont, Stirlingshire
Printed and bound in Great Britain by Clays Ltd, St Ives plc

Papers used by Virago are natural, renewable and recyclable
products sourced from well-managed forests and certified in
accordance with the rules of the Forest Stewardship Council.

Mixed Sources
Product group from well-managed
forests and other controlled sources
www.fsc.org Cert no. SGS-COC-004081
© 1996 Forest Stewardship Council

Virago Press
An imprint of
Little, Brown Book Group
100 Victoria Embankment
London EC4Y 0DY

An Hachette Livre UK Company
www.hachettelivre.co.uk

www.virago.co.uk

This book is for my agent
and tireless ally, Caroline Davidson.

London in the 1760s

Naked came I out of my mother's womb,
and naked shall I return thither.

–The Book of Job, 1:21

Slammerkin, noun, eighteenth century, of
unknown origin.

1. A loose gown. **2.** A loose woman.

Contents

Prologue

There once was a cobbler called Saunders who died for eleven days. At least, that was how his daughter remembered it.

In the year 1752 it was announced that the second of September would be followed by the fourteenth. The matter was merely one of wording, of course; time in its substance was not to undergo any change. Since this calendrical reform would bring the kingdom of Great Britain in line with its neighbours at last, what price a brief inconvenience, a touch of confusion? London newspapers printed witty verses about the 'Annihilation of Time', but no one doubted the Government's weighty reasons. Nor did anyone think to explain them to persons of no importance, such as Cob Saunders.

He knew this much: injustice had been done. There were eleven days of chiselling shoe leather he'd never be paid for, eleven dinners snatched away before they reached his lips, eleven nights when he was going to be cheated out of the sweet relief of dropping down on his straw mattress.

On September the fourteenth – New Style, as they called it – Cob Saunders woke up with a hammering head and knew that eleven days of his life had been lost. Stolen, rather; cut out of his allotted span the way you might nick a wormhole out of an apple. He had no notion how those days had been done away with, or how he might fetch them back; his head was fit to split when he tried to figure it out. He was a man eleven days nearer to his death and there was nothing he could do.

But perhaps there was. When the Calendar Riots began – though Cob had no part in the starting of them – he joined in with all the breath he had, tossing his rage on to the general bonfire. The cry went up: *Give us back our eleven days.*

The Government was merciful; Cob Saunders wasn't executed. He died of gaol fever.

Christmas came eleven days early, that year. The clamour of church bells pulled the air as taut as catgut, and the cobbler's five-year-old daughter Mary knelt below the window, watching for snow that never fell.

Eleven years later Mary Saunders was back on her knees, herself in gaol.

Like father, like daughter.

The night room in Monmouth Gaol was twenty-two feet long and fifteen feet wide. She'd measured it by pacing, her first night. Four walls and no windows: here the men and women awaiting trial at the Spring Sessions lived like rats. Some were chained up after sunset, but not necessarily the murderers; there was no rhyme or reason to it that Mary could see. Anything, she learned, could happen in the darkness. Rapes, and only a hiss for breath; blows, and no sound but the slap of meat. There was no straw provided, so shit piled high in the corners; the air was as thick as earth. One morning an old Welshman was found face down, unmoving. But nothing could shock Mary Saunders any more; she wouldn't let anything touch her now.

It had been worse back in September, when mosquitoes sang in the night heat and the guards didn't bring any water. Once before dawn it had rained so hard that water leaked through the cracked ceiling, and the prisoners laughed like hoarse lunatics and licked the walls.

Now it was Christmastide, and in the gaol's day room Mary Saunders sat on her feet like a carving, hour after hour. If she didn't move, she wouldn't feel. Her palms rested on the rough brown dress the gaolers had given her three months before; it felt like sacking, stiff with dust. Her eyes latched on to the barred square of window, followed the crows wheeling across the white frosty sky towards the Welsh border; her ears took account of their mockery.

The other prisoners had learned to treat the London girl as if she weren't there. Their filthy songs were inaudible to her; their gossip was a foreign language. Their couplings meant no more to her than the scratch of mice. If thrown dice happened to clatter against her knees, she didn't flinch. When a boy stole the blue-edged bread out of her hand, Mary Saunders only contracted her fingers and shut her eyes. She was going to die in gaol, just like her father.

Until the morning she felt a light tug in her chest, as if her heart were starting to unravel. Gin clouded the air. She opened her eyes to see a purse-snatch with only one sleeve stooped over her, delicately pulling a faded red ribbon out of Mary's stays.

'That's mine,' said Mary, her voice hoarse with disuse. With one hand she seized the ribbon, and with the other she took hold of the old woman by the soft part of the throat. She tightened her grip on the grey jowlish flesh while the thief choked and wrenched herself away.

Mary let her go, and wiped her hand on her skirt. Then she wound the ribbon round her thumb till it made a hard rusty-coloured ring, and tucked it back down her stays where it belonged.

Part One

LONDON

Chapter One

Ribbon Red

The ribbon had been bright scarlet when Mary Saunders first laid eyes on it, back in London. 1760: she was thirteen years old. The fat strip of satin was the exact colour of the poppies that grew in Lamb's Conduit Fields at the back of Holborn, where the archers practised. It was threaded into the silver hair of a girl Mary used to look out for at the Seven Dials.

Mary's mother – known as Mrs Susan Digot ever since she'd remarried, a coalman this time – had told her daughter often enough not to pass through the Seven Dials on her way back from Charity School. *A pond for the worst scum in London*, she called the Dials. But the warnings drew the girl like a hot fire on a winter's night.

Besides, she was never in a hurry to get home. If it was still light when Mary reached the family's two-room cellar on Charing Cross Road, she knew what she'd see through the low scuffed window: her mother shipwrecked in a sea of cheap linen, scaly fingers clinging to the needle, hemming and cross-stitching innumerable quilted squares while the new baby wailed in his basket. There was never anywhere to sit or stand that wasn't in the way or in the light. It would be Mary's job to untie the baby's foul swaddlings, and not say a word of complaint because, after all, he was a boy, the family's most precious thing. William Digot

– the Digot man, as she mentally called her stepfather – wouldn't get home from work for hours yet. It would be up to Mary to stand in the pump queue on Long Acre till nightfall for two buckets of water so he could wash his face white before he slept.

Was it any wonder, then, that she preferred to dawdle away the last of the afternoon at the Dials, where seven streets thrust away in seven different directions, and there were stalls heaped with silks and live carp butting in barrels, and gulls cackling overhead, and the pedlar with his coats lined with laces and ribbons of colours Mary could taste on her tongue: yellow like fresh butter, ink black, and the blue of fire? Where boys half her size smoked long pipes and spat black on the cobbles, and sparrows bickered over fragments of piecrust? Where Mary couldn't hear her own breath over the thump of feet and the clatter of carts and the church bells, postmen's bells, fiddles and tambourines, and the rival bawls of vendors and mongers of lavender and watercress and curds-and-whey and all the things there were in the world? *What d'ye lack, what d'ye lack?*

And girls, always two or three girls at each of the seven sharp corners of the Dials, their cheeks bleached, their mouths dark as cherries. Mary was no fool; she knew them for harlots. They looked right through her, and she expected no more. What did they care about a lanky child in a grey buttoned smock she was fast outgrowing, with all her damp black hair hidden in a cap? Except for the girl with the glossy scarlet ribbon dangling from her bun, and a scar that cut through the chalky mask of her cheek – she used to give Mary the odd smile with the corner of her crooked mouth. If it hadn't been for the jagged mark from eye to jaw, that girl would have been the most gorgeous creature Mary had ever seen. Her skirts were sometimes emerald, sometimes strawberry, sometimes violet, all swollen up as if with air; her breasts spilled over the top of her stays like milk foaming in a pan. Her piled-high hair was powdered silver, and the red ribbon ran through it like a streak of blood.

Mary knew that harlots were the lowest of the low. Some of them looked happy but that was only for barefaced show. 'A girl that loses her virtue loses everything,' her mother remarked one day, standing sideways in the doorway as two girls flounced by, arm in arm, their vast pink skirts swinging like bells. 'Everything, Mary, d'you hear? If you don't keep yourself clean you'll never get a husband.'

Also they were damned. It was in one of those rhymes Mary had to learn at school:

The harlot, drunkard, thief and liar,
All shall burn in eternal fire.

On cold nights under her frayed blanket she liked to imagine the heat of it, toasting her palms: eternal fire! She thought of all the shades a flame could turn.

Mary owned nothing with a colour in it, and consequently was troubled by cravings. Her favourite way to spend any spare half hour was to stroll along Piccadilly, under the vast wooden signs that swung from their chains; the best was the goldbeater's one in the form of a gigantic gilded arm and hammer. She stopped at each great bow of a shop window and pressed her face to the cold glass. How fiercely the lamps shone, even in daylight; how trimly and brightly the hats and gloves and shoes were laid out, offering themselves to her eyes. Cloths of silver and ivory and gold were stacked high as a man's head; the colours made her mouth water. She never risked going inside one of those shops – she knew they'd chase her out – but no one could stop her looking.

Her own smock was the dun of pebbles – in order that the

patrons of the school would know the girls were humble and obedient, the Superintendent said. The same went for the caps and buttoned capes that had to be left at school with the books at the end of every day, so parents wouldn't pawn them. Once Mary tried to smuggle *The Kings and Queens of England* home for the night to Charing Cross Road, so she could read it under the covers by the streetlight that leaked into the basement, but she was caught going out of the school door with the book under her arm and caned till red lines striped her palms. Not that this stopped her, it only made her more resourceful. The next time the teacher forgot to count the books at the end of the day, Mary tucked *A Child's Book of Martyrs* between her thighs and walked out with stiff small steps, as if in pain. She never brought that book back to school at all. Her favourite illustration was of the saint getting seared on a gigantic griddle.

As well as her daily dress Mary had a Sunday one – though the Digots only went to communion at St Martin-in-the-Fields twice a year – but it had long since faded to beige. The bread the family lived on was gritty with the chalk the baker used to whiten it; the cheese was pallid and sweaty from being watered down. If the Digots had meat, the odd week when Mary's mother finished a big batch of quilting on time, it was the faint brown of sawdust.

Not that they were poor, exactly. Mary Saunders and her mother and the man she was meant to call Father had a pair of shoes each, and if baby Billy didn't learn to walk too fast, he would have a pair too, by the time he needed them. Poor was another state altogether, Mary knew. Poor was when bits of your bare body hung through holes in your clothes. Poor was a pinch of tea brewed over and over for weeks till it was the colour of water. Falling down in the street. That smell of metal on the breath of that boy at school who collapsed during prayers. 'Blessed are the meek,' the Superintendent was intoning at the time, and she stopped for a moment, displeased at the interruption, then continued, 'for they shall inherit the earth.' But that boy hadn't inherited anything, Mary decided. All he'd done was fainted again the next morning, and never come back to school again.

Yes, Mary knew she had much to be thankful for, from the leather soles under her feet, to the bread in her mouth, to the fact that she went to school at all. Dull as it was, it was better than mopping floors in a tavern at eight years old, like the girl in the cellar beside theirs. There weren't many girls who were still at school when they turned thirteen; most parents would call it a waste of education. But it had been Cob Saunders's fondest whim that his daughter should learn what he never had – reading, writing and casting account – and as a matter of respect, his widow saw to it that the girl never missed school. Yes, Mary was grateful for what she'd got; she didn't need her mother's sharp reminders. 'We get by, don't we?' Susan Digot would say in answer to any complaints, pointing her long callused finger at her daughter. 'We make ends meet, thank the Maker.'

When Mary was very young she had heard God referred to as the Almighty Master, and ever since then she'd tended to confuse him with the man her mother quilted for. The delivery boy would arrive with a sack of linen pieces every week or so, and dump it at Susan Digot's feet: 'The Master says to get this lot done by Thursday or there'll be hell to pay, and no more stains or he'll dock you tuppence on the shilling.' So in the girl's mind the Mighty Master owned all the things and people of the earth, and at any time you could be called to account for what you had done with them.

These nights, in Mary's dreams, mustachioed Frenchmen knelt before her, and she hid her face behind a stiff fan of lace. The scar-faced harlot from the Dials shook her head like a silver birch in a high wind, and the red ribbon slid right down into Mary's hands, as smooth as water.

'Get up now, girl,' came her mother's cry first thing in the morning. Mary had to empty the Digots's brimming pot into the gutter, and blow on last night's fire, and toast crusts on a blackened fork. 'Make haste, now. Your father can't dawdle here all day.' As if he was any father of hers; as if his kindness to Mary had lasted any longer than it took to court the Widow Saunders. 'Come now, can you not hear Billy boy whinging?' As if Mary cared.

A boy was worth ten times as much as a girl, Mary knew that without ever being told. Since the girl's half-brother was born, though, Susan Digot had not looked more content, but the opposite; her elbows sharper, her temper shorter. There seemed a kind of fury about her sometimes when she looked at her daughter. 'Four mouths to fill, I have,' she muttered once, 'and one of them a great useless girl's.'

While Mary was waiting at the corner for the milkmonger each morning – and especially if he'd bittered the milk with snail juice to make it froth as if fresh – she took refuge in her best memories: the time her mother had taken her to watch the Lord Mayor's Procession, or the sky-splitting fireworks on Tower Hill last New Year's Eve. As she hugged her pint basin of tea and soaked her crusts to soften them, she conjured up a luxurious future. She dwelt on how she would have her maid wind a scarlet ribbon into her plaits every morning; how its gaudy stain would make her hair gleam like coal. The sounds of her future would be foreign ones: flutes, and galloping horses, and high trills of laughter.

All day at school Mary thought of gaudy colours as she copied out Precepts and corrected the spelling of the girls in the neighbouring desks. None of the tasks set demanded more than a fraction of her mind, that was the problem. The Superintendent called her proud, but Mary thought it would be nonsense to pretend she didn't know she had quick wits. As far back as she could remember, she had found her schoolwork ludicrously simple. Now she busied herself with fantasies of hooped gowns with ten-foot trains as she stood – a full head above the younger girls – reciting the Principles of Goodness:

Put upon this Earth to work
None but wicked children shirk.

Mary was so used to these rhymes by now that she could join in with the chorus of voices while her mind was altogether elsewhere. Could chant the Five Requirements for Salvation, for instance, while deciding that once she was grown to womanhood she would never wear beige. She tried not to think about how empty her stomach was, or the Mighty Master in the sky, or what piece-work he was going to hand her, or how long a life she'd have to do it in. That Immortal Soul the teachers harped on so much – Mary knew she'd swap it quick as a blink for the merest inch of beauty. A single scarlet ribbon.

In September, old King George dropped dead and young George was the new king. William Digot said things might take a turn for the better now. This fellow had been born on English soil, which was more than you could say for his dad and his grandad, 'and Lord knows we've had enough of those Germans and their fat wives.'

When he fell asleep in his chair, Mary peered over his shoulder at the newspaper in his lap. She suspected her stepfather couldn't read one word in three; he just stumbled his way through the headlines and looked at the pictures. Under the title 'King of Great Britain, Ireland, Gibraltar, Canada, the Americas, Bengal, the West Indies, and Elector of Hanover' there was a full-length drawing of the young king; his expression a little nervous, his thighs in their velvet breeches as smooth as fish.

Crouched by the window to catch the last of the daylight, Susan Digot nibbled her lip. Mary knew her mother took no interest in politics. All the woman had ever wanted was to be a proper dressmaker, shaping elegant skirts and jackets instead of quilting coarse six-inch squares twelve hours a day for dirt pay from a master she'd never met. She and Cob Saunders had both grown up in a faraway city called Monmouth before they'd come to London in '39. 'What was it brought you and my father to London in the first place?' asked Mary now, softly, so as not to wake the coalman.

'Whatever makes you ask a thing like that?' Susan Digot's eyes were startled, red at the rims. But she didn't wait for an answer. 'Myself and Cob, we thought we'd better ourselves, but we should have bided at home.' Her fingers moved like mice across a hem, stitching as fast as breath. 'It can't be done.'

'What can't?'

'Bettering yourself,' said her mother bleakly. 'Cob didn't know the London cobblers had the trade all sewn up, did he? He never got the work he wanted, the fine skilful stuff. Patching holes with cardboard, that was about the height of it. Here, count these.'

Mary went over and knelt at her mother's knee, lining up the squares stuffed with muslin. She imagined her father as a cross-legged fairy man, tapping nails into pointed dancing shoes with his tiny hammer. But no, that wasn't right, that was out of a story. When she concentrated, she could see him as he'd been: the great bulk of him.

'Cob wouldn't have gone and got himself killed back in Monmouth,' added her mother, her mouth askew. 'There was never such bloodshed there.'

Mary tried to picture it: blood on the London cobbles. She'd seen a riot go down Charing Cross last year: boots clattering past the basement window, and shouts of 'No Popery', and the screech of breaking glass. 'Like the No Popery?' she said now, eager.

Susan Digot sniffed. 'That was nothing to the Calendar Riots your father got mixed up in, nothing at all. The chaos and confusion, you can't imagine it.' She went silent, and there was only the scratch of her needle on the cloth. Then she asked, 'And what about me?', giving Mary a hard look as if she should know the answer. 'Wasn't I as neat a needlewoman as my friend Jane, look you, and here am I wearing out my fingers on squares like some iron machine while she was making costumes for the quality, last I heard!'

That Mary could imagine more easily: *costumes for the quality*, sleek and colourful as fruit on a china plate. Scarlet ribbons threaded through hems, sleeves, stomachers. 'Why can't you be a dressmaker now, though, Mother?' she said suddenly.

Susan Digot let out an impatient sound. 'Such impossibilities you invent, Mary. I never got the skills for more than hemming, did I? And where would I be supposed to get the capital to start up for myself, or the space for a shop likewise? Besides, my eyes aren't what they were. And isn't London choked with dressmakers already? What could possess anyone to hire me?'

Her voice grated on her daughter's ears. Dreariness and complaint, that was all she ever spoke nowadays. Mary tried to remember the last time she'd heard her mother laugh.

'Besides,' the woman added sternly, 'William provides for us now.'

Mary kept her head down so her mother wouldn't see her face.

She was sure there had been better times, when she was small and her mother was still Mrs Saunders. There was a tiny picture in the back of Mary's mind of being weak after a fever, and her mother holding her in the crook of her arm, and feeding her warm ale posset with a pewter spoon. The posset was soft on Mary's throat, going down. The spoon must have been lost since, or pawned maybe. And she was sure she remembered Cob Saunders too, the vast shape of him against the light as he worked by the window, his hammer as sure as a heartbeat. The dark fuzz of his beard used to catch crumbs; after supper he'd lift his small daughter on to his lap so she could comb it with her fingers. Mary couldn't have made up a picture as vivid as that, could she? She knew it was from her father she'd got her height and her dark eyes and hair; all she had of her mother's was a pair of quick hands.

Even the food had been better in those days too, she was sure of it. She thought she remembered a week when there'd been more than enough of everything, after Susan Saunders had made a big sale, and the family had fresh meat and tuppenny ale, and Mary was sick all down her shift from the richness and the thrill of it, but no one got angry.

'How many is that, then?' said her mother, and Mary was jolted back into the present, the fading light of afternoon.

She looked down uncertainly at the pile of pieces on her lap. 'Fifty-three, I think, or maybe fifty-four . . .'

'Count them again,' said her mother. Her voice sagged like an old mattress. 'Maybe's no good when the Master sends for them, is it?'

Mary started again as fast as she could, thumbing the pieces but trying not to dirty them, while beside her Susan Digot bent closer to her sewing. 'Mother,' the girl asked, struck by a thought, 'why didn't you ever go back to Monmouth?'

The seamstress gave a little jerk of her shoulders. 'Cob and I, we didn't fancy crawling home with all our mighty plans demolished. Besides, he wasn't a man to give up hope. He had a liking for London,' she said contemptuously. 'It was his idea to drag us here in the first place.'

'No but afterwards,' the girl said eagerly, 'after my father died.' She could see it like a tale in a book; herself as the little girl in her widowed mother's tender arms, the two of them costumed in black satin, jolting along in a plush-lined coach to the fabled city of Monmouth where the air smelt clean and the people smiled at each other in the street.

Her mother shook her head as if there was a bee buzzing in it. '*You make your bed*,' she quoted, '*and you lie in it*. This is where the Maker has put me and this is where I'll stay. There's no going back.'

And there was never any arguing with that.

One damp November evening Mary had been sent in search of a shell-cart for tuppence worth of winkles when she bumped into the ribbon pedlar coming out of an alley off Short's Gardens. He opened his coat at her like a pair of wings. Mary backed away in fright. His coat was old, blackened at the edges. But there, pinned to the lining, long and snaky and curled at the end like a tongue: the very match of the harlot's ribbon.

'How much for the red one?' The words slipped out on their own.

'A shilling to you, dear heart.' The pedlar cocked his grizzled head sideways at her as if she had made a joke. His eyes were shiny.

Mary ran on.

It might as well have been a guinea he'd asked. Mary had never held a shilling in her hand. And when she stood at the shell-cart tonight and dug into her smock pocket for the two pennies William Digot had entrusted to her to buy the family's dinner, one of them was gone. There was a hole in the cloth, its edges soft as Billy's eyelashes.

What was she to do? A pennyworth of winkles would never

stretch to four people, she knew, so she ran round the corner to the pieman on Flitcroft Street and asked him had he anything for a penny. The ham pie he gave her had a broken crust but it looked filling, at least. All the way home she kept her eyes on the ground to catch the winking of the lost penny between two cobbles or in a gutter overflowing with peelings and turds, but she never caught a glimpse of it. As if a coin would lie long in the dirt of Charing Cross!

She hoped the Digots would be content with the pie, as it was hot and smelt wholesome. Instead, Susan Digot called her a liar. 'You spent the penny on hot lardy-cake, didn't you?' she said, rubbing her sore eyes with the heel of her hand. 'I can smell it off your breath.'

Over and over again, as the hard end of the broom landed on her legs, the girl sobbed out her defence: 'I lost it! I lost the penny, I swear!'

'Oh, Mary,' said Susan Digot, and hit her again.

She'd been thrashed before, and harder, but somehow she had never felt so injured. What good was it to be a grown girl of thirteen, if she could still be put over her mother's knee and beaten for something she hadn't done?

Afterwards she squatted in the corner and watched the Digots eat the pie, feeding the corners to little Billy. Her tears dried to salt on her jaw. Her stomach growled; she hoped they could hear it. Finally she stood up and turned her pocket inside out. 'Look,' she said, her voice shaking, 'there was a hole and I didn't know it.' She pushed her thumb through the gaping seam to show them.

William Digot looked up from his dinner. 'You could have poked that there yourself,' he accused.

His wife stared at the frayed pocket, and for a moment such a peculiar look strayed across her face that it almost seemed she might cry.

'It wasn't thievery!' said Mary, almost shouting.

Her mother's eyes flickered over her. 'Carelessness is just as bad.' Then she held out her tin plate with the crust of pastry on it, like someone feeding a dog.

'She doesn't deserve it,' remarked her husband, eyeing the plate.

'She's my daughter,' said Susan Digot, quiet and fierce.

Was the woman raging against her child, or her husband, or the Mighty Master who had burdened her with such a family, and so little pie to divide between them? Mary would have liked to knock the crust on to the floor, or even better, to look away, quite indifferent – but she was too hungry for dignity tonight. She took the crust between finger and thumb and choked it down.

The lesson she learned that night was not the one intended. The next time she was sent to buy dinner, she knew enough to lie about the price of the half-dozen oysters; she kept that penny, to pay herself back for the beating.

Mary had bled two months in a row now. Susan Digot had wet eyes, the first time, and muttered about this being greatly early for it all to begin, even if Mary was taller than many a grown woman. 'I was a child till I was past sixteen, back in Monmouth,' she added aggrievedly. 'Everything moves too fast in the big city.'

The pointed bones of Mary's elbows were wearing through her grey uniform, and she'd lost a button off the front where her chest was swelling. These days she wasn't paying attention at school. She forgot to join in with the chanted rhymes, even though she knew them all by heart. Her mind stretched and yawned like a tiger. She could read and write and make accounts better than any other girl in the school; what else could she learn here? The other girls her age had all left by now, one to become a washerwoman, another to be apprentice to a stockinger, and three more to hem piece-work. A girl that Mary had almost thought of as a friend was gone into service in Cornwall, which might as well be the end of the world. All these trades seemed to Mary to be wretched.

Other girls seemed unburdened by ambition; most folks seemed content with their lot. Ambition was an itch in Mary's shoe, a maggot in her guts. Even when she read a book, her eyes skimmed and galloped over the lines, eager to reach the end. She suspected ambition was what was making her legs grow so long and her mouth so red. In the gap between day and sleep, when Mary curled her swelling body in the hollow of the mattress she shared with Billy, she was plagued by vague dreams of a better life; an existence where dirt and labour would give way to colour, variety and endless nights dancing in the Pleasure Gardens at Vauxhall, across the river. Sometimes Mary's sense of grievance focused like a beam of light. Before dawn, when she woke up with a start at the sound of the first carts jolting by, or the wails and kicks of the boy lying at the bottom of the bed, it was as clear as glass in her head: *I deserve more than this.*

The earth itself seemed restless this year. There was a quake in February, and another in March, when Susan Digot's last chinaware plate that had belonged to her parents slipped from the shelf and smashed itself to bits on the hearth. People took these to be warnings; some said a great quake was coming which would shake the city of London to bits. Preachers said God in his wrath meant to raise the waters of the Thames and drown all the sinful gamblers, drunkards and fornicators.

William Digot told his family it was all a lot of nonsense, but when the time came and Londoners began to flee to the outlying villages, his wife managed to persuade him that it would do no harm to move the family to Hampstead for the night. They sat on the heath looking down at the city. When nothing had happened by ten o'clock, they sought out the barn floor where they were to bed down in the straw alongside eleven other families. William Digot got in a quarrel with the owner about the exorbitant rates she was charging; she made him leave his best shirt as a surety for the money.

The stink and the raised voices kept Mary awake. Later she got up and sneaked out on to the heath. Wrapped in her mother's shawl, she squatted beside the barn, staring down at the flickering lights of London. Mary thought of the masked balls and the all-night card parties, the satin-shod revellers who laughed in the face of the wrathful Almighty. It was a city full of glitter and glee, and it was all about to be destroyed before she'd had so much as a taste of it.

She waited to feel the earth start to shudder, or the air to fill with the rising reek of the Thames. But there was no punishment, that night, only a long taut silence as the stars came out one by one.

In May of the year 1761, Mary turned fourteen. After school that day she passed through the Seven Dials and caught a glimpse of the back of the scarred harlot. On an impulse, she followed the girl up Mercer Street, past St Giles-in-the-Fields. What was it her mother said? *Every man in St Giles who's not a beggar is a thief.* But Mary scurried on after the white wig with its cheeky red ribbon. When the girl stopped at a gin-shop Mary hung back; then her quarry re-emerged, swinging a bottle.

At the Holborn warren she'd heard called the Rookery, Mary stopped, afraid to go any further. The harlot disappeared between two buildings which leaned drunkenly on each other across a street no wider than the span of Mary's arms. Courts cut the nearby streets, yards cut the courts and yards conspired briefly in crannies. Mary had heard that no one chased into the Rookery by a watchman or even a Bow Street Runner ever got caught. Two Indian sailors passed by then, and one of them winked his white eye at her. Mary ran half the way home.

Susan Digot looked up from her stitching and rubbed her damp forehead with the back of the hand that held the needle. Her coppery hair was turning grey. 'Ah, Mary, at last. I got us a pigeon. It's very high, look you, but in a good spiced ragout we'll hardly taste it.'

The quills were loose in the pigeon's skin. The girl plucked fast, to get it over with, shuddering a little. The big feathers flared in the fire, but the small ones clung to her fingers. Her knife laid the pigeon's entrails bare. She thought of what it meant to be fourteen.

Susan Digot watched her daughter, and licked the thread as if she were thirsty for its flavour. 'You'd have quick fingers for the work.'

The girl ignored that.

'High time you learned a trade, now you're a grown woman.'

Mary concentrated on getting all the dirty innards out of the pigeon. She hadn't thought her mother had remembered her birthday.

'Plain work, fancy work, quilt work . . . A girl won't ever starve as long as she's a needle in her sleeve, Mary.'

The girl turned and stared into her mother's eyes; they had always been the dirty blue of rain clouds, but recently she'd begun to notice the red around their rims. They were ringed as sure as targets and speckled as if by darts. How many more years would they last? Mary had seen a pair of blind seamstresses that lived in a garret in Neal's Yard; you could count the bones in their arms. So she shook her head and turned back to the flattened pigeon. She scooped up its guts on the edge of her knife and flicked them into the fire.

For a moment she thought it was going to be all right; silence would fill up the little room as the last light gave way to evening shadow. When Digot woke for his dinner, the talk would start up again, and Mary knew how to steer it on to harmless topics: the mild air, or how strong Billy's arms were getting.

But Susan Digot pushed her fading hair back from her face and let out her breath as if it hurt her. 'All this reading and writing and casting account is well and good, and when Cob Saunders insisted you go to the Charity School I never said a word against it, did I?'

It was not a question that required an answer.

'Did I stand in your way?' she asked her daughter formally. 'I did not, even though many told me so much schooling would be wasted on a girl.'

Mary stared mutinously into the fire.

'But it's time you thought of getting your bread, now. What do they say about it at school?'

'Service.' The word came from the back of Mary's throat. 'Or sewing.'

'There now! Just as I say! Isn't that right, William?'

No answer from the man in the corner. Mary let her eyes slide over. Her stepfather was nodding, halfway asleep, his head repeating its coal-dust mark on the wall.

'And if it was the needle, couldn't I start training you up myself, Mary?' her mother rushed on.

She sounded fond of her daughter, for a moment. Mary was reminded of the years when there were only the two of them, the Widow Saunders and her child, and they shared one narrow warm bed.

'And if you turned out vastly handy, Mary, and why shouldn't you with those fingers the very spit of mine, well couldn't I get you out of this filthy city? Maybe I could even send you to Monmouth.' Susan Digot's voice had a hint of light in it, as always when she said that word. 'My friend Jane Jones that's a dressmaker, I could write to her. Wouldn't she take you for apprentice in half a minute?'

The pigeon bits clung to Mary's fingers. She shook them into the pot one by one. They didn't amount to the size of an egg. How were they meant to make a nice spiced ragout for four?

'A fine place it would be, Monmouth, for a growing girl,' said her mother longingly. 'Such clean civil people as they are, and the greenness all around, and the quiet of the streets.'

Mary conjured it up in her mind as best she could: a muffled, pristine little city. 'I don't like quiet,' she said.

'As if you know what you like, child that you are!' said her mother, astringent again. 'Besides, the main thing is to find you a trade.' Her voice softened again, and her hands stilled on the cloth. 'Once you're trained you could come back and work alongside of me. Partners, we'd be.'

Mary looked into her mother's shining eyes, observed the dampness of her lower lip. Her guts tightened. So now she knew what was really going on. *A trouble shared is a trouble halved.* Maybe she'd been bred up for this very purpose, to stand as a buffer between Susan Digot and her fate. *Like mother, like daughter.* With ruthless love Susan Digot was offering her child all she had, all she knew: a future that went no further than this dank cellar. Mary would inherit it all in the end: the Digot men, the bent back, the needles, the scarlet eyelids.

'I'm sorry,' she whispered.

For a moment she thought her mother knew what was unspoken between them, the delicacy of their mutual betrayal. For a moment it seemed that they might come to some kind of understanding.

But then she saw that Susan Digot hadn't heard her, would never hear her. 'Or would you rather go into service?' said the woman coldly. 'Speak up, which shall it be?'

'Neither,' said Mary clearly, scraping the knife on the edge of the pot.

A hawking cough from the corner; William Digot was awake.

'Then what'll you do with yourself, so?' his wife snapped. She held her needle like a weapon, aimed at her daughter.

Mary nibbled her lip as she set the cooking pot over the coals. A thin strip of skin came away in her teeth with the sweetness of blood. 'I don't know. They're both wretched trades.'

'And where did you ever get the idea, Miss,' spat her mother, 'that you were marked out for anything better? Such greed! Such wilfulness!'

Her husband roused himself with a hunch of the shoulders. 'Does the girl think we'll feed her for ever?' he asked hoarsely.

Mary looked away so the man wouldn't see her face. She poked at the hissing pigeon pieces with her knife.

'Answer your father,' snapped Susan Digot.

Mary kept her mouth shut, but looked her mother in the eye as if to say that she would have, if her father had been there.

Susan's small slate-blue eyes, so unlike Mary's, blazed back at her. 'What do you propose to make of yourself?'

'Something better,' the girl said between her teeth.

'What's that?' said her stepfather.

A little louder: 'I have a wish to be something better than a seamstress or a maid.'

'A wish!' William Digot roared, wide awake now, his blackened nails digging into his breeches. 'Your mother and I drudge all day to put food on the table, but that's not good enough for Milady Saunders, is it? And what might Milady Saunders have a *wish* for, then?'

She was tempted. She was on the verge of turning and saying: Any smell but the stink of coal dust. Any trade but the cursed needle. Any place in the wide world but this cramped cellar.

Her mother put down her sewing. Her callused hand gripped Mary's jaw before the girl could say any of that. Dry fingers sealed Mary's mouth, almost tenderly. *Save me, Mother*, she wanted to whisper. *Get me out of here.*

'We're each of us born into a place on this earth. We must make the best of it.' The woman's voice had a dropped stitch in it. 'Your father forgot that, and took liberties with his betters.'

'And look what came of it,' said William Digot with satisfaction.

Mary broke away. The door crashed shut behind her. She could hear the boy send up his thin scream.

The sky was covering over with darkness like a rind on cheese. All down Long Acre the lamps spilled tiny circles of yellow; the oil released plumes of smoke. In the distance the Covent Garden Piazza was a dazzle, loud with the sound of violins. But Mary wanted to stay out of the light.

Once she turned up Mercer Street the shadows thickened where the lamps had been smashed. In the parish of St Giles, it was said, the locals didn't like a spotlight shone on their doings. Mary's breath came quick and shallow as she ran along the slippery cobbles. She was glad she hadn't worn her shoes; she told herself that she had nothing worth stealing, nothing worth anyone's while to hurt her for.

At the Seven Dials, there were only a few harlots standing about on this warm May evening; the girl with the scarred face wasn't there. Mary stood against the central pillar and scraped her hands till the grease and down of the pigeon was gone. The stone left lines on her palms. Nobody paid her any attention. Her hollow stomach folded in on itself. Faint light leaked from a nearby cellar, along with the click of dice. The damp air was falling round her; it must be nearly nine o'clock. Round and round the pillar she went, craning up and counting the seven blind dials, until she lost count.

Mary had nowhere to go but home, so she set out in the opposite direction. Her stomach rumbled; she was filling up with rage again. If her mother thought Mary was going to settle for the same sort of gritty-eyed, bleached, half-buried, half-life—

The pedlar was leaning in a doorway off Short's Gardens. Mary only recognised him when she came up close. She was almost as tall as him these days, she noticed with a shock. A reek of gin clouded him, and he made a skewed sort of bow as she came up close.

He lifted his huge eyebrows and took a drink from the dark bottle in his hand. 'The schoolgirl,' he said with a wet smirk.

'Is it still a shilling?' Mary's voice came out hoarse as a crow's.

'What?'

'The ribbon, sir. The scarlet,' she repeated stupidly.

The man opened his coats as if to remind himself of the one she meant, but without a light there was no telling one colour from the next. He pursed his lips; he seemed to be trying to remember. 'One and six,' he said at last.

Mary's eyes stung from straining through the twilight. 'But you said—'

'Times is hard, my dear. Getting *harder* every day.' He leaned on the word. It sounded like a riddle, but Mary couldn't think what the answer might be. 'One and sixpence,' the pedlar repeated, letting his coats fall. 'Or a kiss.'

She blinked at him. He grinned back, his teeth faintly white.

Then the girl Mary Saunders had never known herself to be took a step closer.

The old man's tongue pushed past her lips as if looking for something, a buried treasure. It tasted like a burnt thing. It thrashed like a dying fish and bruised the roof of her mouth. She thought she might choke.

When he backed her against the wall, Mary didn't scream. What surprised her was the dull absence of surprise. 'Hush now, hush now,' he slurred in her ear, and she thought she remembered her father saying the same words, one stifling night when she couldn't sleep. Now the pedlar's hands were full of her skirts and his bristling face was grinding into her forehead as if to leave a secret mark. The darkness covered them like smoke. Mary held her breath so she wouldn't make a sound. Somehow she knew that she'd stepped beyond the point of screaming. Somehow she knew that no one would save her now. 'Hush,' said the old man, more urgently, as if to himself.

She didn't whimper even when a stone in the wall pierced the skin of her shoulder. It was over in minutes. Little pain, no pleasure. Just a sudden vast stretching and the hot black sky above.

She stood and watched the pedlar walk away. She had a wet face, and one sleek satin ribbon in her fist.

When Mary got home at last that night, there was a moment when she might have spoken. Her thighs were slick; they shook under her smock. She thought the first word she spoke might make her burst into tears. She was almost ready to say, 'Mother, something terrible—'

But Susan Digot was raging. A girl of fourteen out past ten o'clock, when decent folk were long in their beds? Hanging round the Dials, no doubt, in defiance of orders, along with every bit of trash the city could throw up? '*If you mix with muck, you'll end up just as brown*,' she quoted contemptuously.

So all Mary said was that she was sorry. She turned her grazed face away from her mother's candle and went to bed in the next room, where Billy was fast asleep, his foot dangling out of the end of the bed.

When she pulled the ribbon out of her mattress, at first light the next morning, it was brown.

The girl stayed away from the pedlar after that, but it made no difference. She'd outgrown ignorance like a skin that had split, and been shed, and crumbled away to nothing. Now she'd never be that child again.

Still, she played her part for all she was worth. Later, she thought it must have been herself she was trying to fool.

As that summer panted to a close, Mary gave no trouble to her mother. When William Digot occasionally stirred out of his weary doze to give his wife's daughter an order or a warning, she never answered back. In September there were raucous celebrations for the young King's wedding, and even more for his coronation a fortnight later, but Mary didn't even ask if she could go and watch the fireworks. She never complained about the meagre food any more, not even during a bad week in October when a bundle of quilting fell on the hearth and got singed, and Susan Digot shrieked loud enough for the neighbours to hear, and had to make it up out of her pay. Some days Mary said she had no appetite, and gave half her bread to the small boy, chewed up soft. She hurried to school along the slippery streets, where the creaking alehouse signs hung low and blocked out the light. She kept her head down over her desk and joined in the chants as if they were gospel.

> *It is a crime*
> *To waste time.*

Her voice, deeper than all the others now, rose above them.

> *The wage of vice*
> *Is fire and ice.*

Once, after a sermon by the visiting chaplain, Mary Saunders was found weeping under the row of coat pegs. When the Superintendent asked what the matter was, all the girl could say was that she'd lost another button off her smock.

For the first time in her life Mary tried praying. *Mighty Master*, she whispered into her pillow, *Mighty Master*. She listened hard, but there was no answer.

She came home one October evening and her stepfather struck her across the eye.

She stared up from the floor, blinking. Black dust moved beneath her knees. The strangest thing was that Susan Digot was not sewing; her linen lay in untidy folds on her chair. Her face was scrunched up like a bag. In her hand, vibrating as if in a draught, was a scrap of paper. The boy whinged in the corner, unfed. Susan Digot brought the note up to her eyes, and began to read aloud. 'Your daughter—' Then her voice drained away. She dropped the note at Mary's feet.

Mary didn't want to touch the letter. She tilted her head and deciphered the words upside down.

Yore dawters a hor. You ony have to look at her bely.

That was all. Mary said it over and over to herself, till the words fitted together. Till she knew for sure what she'd spent five months half suspecting, half denying.

Her mother bent and dragged her to her feet. The two of them were as tall as each other. Susan Digot took the grey school smock in two hands and pulled it to lie smooth against her daughter's body. Such a strange gentle curve, arching above the girl's skinny thighs, nothing anybody would have noticed through her loose smock if they weren't looking. The mother sucked in her breath.

'It's true, Devil fetch her,' said her husband, softly.

Mary's half-brother screamed. 'Milk!' The front of his mother's dress was dark in two places.

William Digot stepped so close Mary could smell the loud tang of coal. 'Who've you been meddling with?'

She found she couldn't speak.

'Who was it, hussy?' He seemed to have come fully awake at last. His fists were bunched like rats. But his wife slid between him and her daughter and wrapped her bony arms around the girl.

For a moment Mary thought it was somehow going to be all right. 'Why?' whispered her mother. Her chin pressed down on the girl's head, almost lovingly. Her sour bodice leaked on to Mary's shoulder. 'Why?'

The girl tried to remember. Her thoughts moved like mud.

'Did he have a knife?' whispered her mother, almost hopeful.

Mary shook her head. She couldn't think of a single lie. 'A ribbon,' she whispered, husky.

The word got lost in the silky folds of her mother's neck. Susan Digot moved back a little, and bent down to hear her. 'A what?'

'A ribbon.' The silence lengthened. 'He had a red ribbon,' Mary added faintly, 'and I had a wish for it.'

That night Mary learned that all she owned in the world fitted into an old shawl. Her mother packed the shifts and petticoats together as if she were mashing a potato; her fists were white. She never looked at her daughter. Her husband had stalked out to an alehouse, and the boy had been sent to bed with the heel of the loaf. As Susan Digot folded and pressed, she kept talking, as if she feared that a moment's silence would weaken her. 'We only get one chance in this life, Mary Saunders, and you've just tossed yours away.'

'But—'

'You couldn't be satisfied with your lot like every other body on this earth, could you? For all my efforts to raise you right, all my long labours, you've sold yourself into the lowest trade there is. For a ribbon!' She spat the word as if it were the name of a sin. 'For a cheap, grubby little scrap of luxury. Is that all you're worth, then? Is that the price you put on yourself?'

'I'm sorry,' sobbed Mary, and at that moment it was true. She would have done anything to reverse time and crawl back into her childhood.

'Answer me this, what did you lack?' asked Susan Digot, twisting the clothes together as if she could squeeze an answer out of them. 'When were you ever starving? What did William and myself and little Billy ever have that we denied you?' Her questions hung on the air, like a fog indoors.

'Nothing.' Mary sounded entirely meek, as if this was the response to a catechism. But the meek didn't inherit the earth, she knew. The meek inherited bugger all.

'We gave you a home, and schooling, didn't we?' asked her mother. 'Didn't we? And the chance of a good living by your needle, if only you hadn't been too proud to take it. We gave you all we could – all we had – but you've ended up in the muck anyway.' She spoke as if her mouth was full of salt, and she tied the last knot so hard that a piece of the shawl came away in her hand.

'I didn't—' But the sentence trailed off, because Mary couldn't remember what she hadn't done, could only think of what she had done or what had been done to her, five months back: the dark, foreign exchange in the alley, in the warmth of a May evening. 'I didn't mean—' But she couldn't remember what she'd meant. Besides, it didn't matter any more. The facts stood up like boulders in a muddy field.

'You're your father's daughter,' said Susan Digot, in a voice so broken that for a moment Mary heard it as the beginning of mercy. 'I see Cob Saunders in you every time you turn your head.'

Mary crept a little nearer. She looked into her mother's reddened, watery eyes, so unlike her own. 'When he was with us—' she ventured.

Susan Digot's face shut like a door. 'You don't remember. You were too young.'

'But I do,' insisted Mary.

'He was a stinking cur,' said Susan Digot, pronouncing the words like an epitaph. 'To go off rioting on a whim, and leave me a widow and a debtor! I rue the day I ever married him.'

Her daughter's mouth was trembling, but Susan carried on, more rapidly now. 'You're Cob's alright, twisted at the root. The bad seed never dies out. You're headed for damnation in a hurry.' She picked up the small hard bundle in two fingers, and stared down at it as if it were verminous.

'What am I to do?' the girl whispered.

Susan Digot's shoulders shrugged as if wrenched out of their sockets. 'If ribbons are what you like, then try living on ribbons!' she spat. 'Try depending on your fancy menfriends instead of your kin. See how far you'll get on your own! And soon you'll be dragging another soul into this world of pain,' she added, her forehead contracting. 'I only hope it never opens its eyes.'

Mary tried to speak but nothing came out. 'What's – what's going to become of me?'

'Maybe you'll wind up in the workhouse, or maybe you'll swing from a halter at the end of the day,' Susan Digot said formally, holding out the bundle. 'I just thank the Maker I won't be near to see it.'

The girl's throat opened. 'If you let me stay a while, Mother—'

'Don't you use that word.' She shoved the packed shawl into Mary's arms.

'One more chance—'

'You've used up all your chances.' The woman strode over to the door and pulled it open, so the October night was sucked into the house and tainted the air with smoke.

'Mother,' repeated Mary faintly.

But the salt-blue eyes looked right through her. 'You have no mother now.'

In all her fourteen years Mary Saunders had never been out past midnight. Gradually it came to her that the night only began when the decent folk barred their doors. There was a whole other festivity of darkness, for which the twilight was only a rehearsal.

She saw an unconscious man dragged out of a cellar on Dyott Street by his collar, and the wig stolen off his head; he had only patches of hair underneath, the colour of dishwater. On High Holborn a drunken boy tried to snatch her bundle but she ran. 'Poxy jade', he called her, and other words she didn't know. Later she hid in a doorway on Ivy Lane, twitching with cold, and an old woman crawled by, her bare breasts hanging down like rags. 'The birds has got under my skin,' the creature screeched, over and over. Mary shut her eyes so she wouldn't be seen. A while afterwards, she heard grunting behind the door and bent down to look in the keyhole; two people were face down on the floor together, juddering backwards and forwards, and both of them were men.

There were puzzles she couldn't begin to solve and horrors she could only guess at. Mary tramped on fast enough to keep her feet from going numb and tried to think of any door she could knock on at this hour of an October night. She had no relatives in London. Cob Saunders must have made some friends in the city, Mary supposed, but he'd never brought them home, and she'd have been too young to know their names.

Her feet automatically led her the way she walked every morning, to school. Its narrow windows were black. Mary stared through the iron gates. Could it have been only this afternoon that she'd passed out through them freely, a child in uniform like a hundred others? There was no refuge for her here. The girls she'd known were all gone from London. And if she stood here all night, the teachers wouldn't take her in tomorrow morning, not even if they found her half-frozen on the step; not once they'd made her tell them why she had no home to go to.

She clung to her bundle now as if it were a dying thing. She was lost; she didn't know the names of these streets. At a dark corner she tripped over something, and crashed to her knees; when she put out her hand, it met the icy hide of a dog, half hollowed out. Maggots between her fingers; she screamed, then, and slapped the hard ground to get them off her.

A lantern, swinging by; in its narrow circle Mary saw a watchman with his club and rattle. It occurred to her to cry out for help – but what would she say? She crouched in the shadows and watched him pass. If she was sunk so low that her own mother wouldn't give her shelter, what use was it to appeal to strangers?

On her feet, moving faster. There was the spire of St Giles again, or was it another church? The moon had fallen out of sight, and Mary was so drunk with weariness she couldn't see where she was putting her feet. *Mighty Master*, she chanted in her head, *Mighty Master, please*. But if he was there, he wasn't listening.

She climbed down into a ditch at last and slept as soon as her face touched the cold ground.

She woke to pain like a long knife in her guts. Her smock was up around her waist and the night had got in. There was something on her back, a beast, its scalding breath on her neck, and laughter far away like the shreds of a dream. When she twisted her head, the beast's teeth met in her ear. Mary screamed then, belatedly, the way she should have done five months before, in the alley. She found her voice, the depth and fury of it, and what she roared was 'No!'

But the man – because now she was awake she could tell that this was nothing but an ordinary man – he hit her in the jaw, harder than she'd ever been hit in her life, and again, and again. This time wasn't quick or simple like it had been with the pedlar. This man didn't want relief; he wanted to crush her entirely. He pulled her head back by the hair and banged her face into the cold ground, then held it there until she couldn't make a sound, couldn't breathe, couldn't do anything but feel his pain inside her.

The laughter, Mary realised soon enough, was coming from the other soldiers, who were leaning on their bayonets, waiting their turn. Afterwards she could never be sure how many of them there'd been.

A lifetime later, Mary woke to fingertips on her eyelids. She cringed, but the hand didn't go away. Light came under her lids like a needle. She twisted, but the probing fingers followed. She bit blindly.

A screech of laughter. 'None of that, you nasty thing!'

Mary was so numb she barely knew she had a body. Only when she began to curl up on her side did she recognise this stiffness as cold. A stranger's silhouette stood above her, blocking the watery sun. Mary tried to sit up, but then the shaking started.

The stranger was sucking her bitten finger. She took off her cloak and dropped it over Mary. 'I'll be wanting that back, mind,' she remarked, as if they were in the middle of a conversation.

The world swayed round Mary as she dragged herself to her knees. Her bundle of clothes was gone. The smock she wore seemed made of mud, stiff and dented as a shield. The spire of St Giles winked down at her. In the morning light everything was laced with frost: the railings, the cobbles, the nettles that edged the ditch. She could feel the print of dirt like a complicated map across her face. And deeper, under her frozen skin, in her nose, beneath her jaw and ribs and above all between her legs, the pains massed like an army.

'Ain't you a sight.' The stranger grinned down and her scar crinkled in the terrible light.

It was her, the harlot with the red ribbon in her powdered wig; the one who was to blame for making Mary think there could be more to life than work and sleep. At that moment Mary felt rage like a spike running through her.

'Fancy a bite of breakfast?'

Mary started to cry.

The harlot was called Doll Higgins. Mary followed her up stair after stair, half-dragged by the girl's hot hand, to a dark room at the top where Mary lay until the mattress beneath her face was soaked through. There was a pain inside her that moored her to the floor. She tried to say where it was but her voice came out like a rook's caw.

'Been made a woman of, ain't you?' said Doll.

Mary woke and thought the room was on fire. The light was dim, but colour poured down the walls. She blinked until she had convinced herself that these were only clothes, hanging on rusty nail-heads that protruded from the walls. Only gauzes and silks; nothing but jade and ruby, amber and aquamarine.

A warm, yeasty smell beside her. A face on the pillow, softened in sleep and obscured in brown wisps of hair. At first Mary didn't recognise Doll without her silver wig. Finally she managed to open her dry throat and whisper, 'Where am I?'

'My room, of course,' yawned Doll with her eyes shut, 'in Rat's Castle.' Her breath made a cloud on the chilly air.

'But where's that?'

'The Rookery. Where else?'

At first these words made Mary's heart pound. The Rookery was a lawless place where a girl could be robbed, beaten, raped. But then, with a little tremor like mirth, Mary realised that the worst was over and she had nothing left in the world to fear.

Doll sat up on the straw mattress, and stretched her hands above her with a great creaking of muscles. Up close, she had rough edges, dusty hems, but still the loveliest face Mary had ever seen. 'Now then,' she said, all business. 'Where's home?'

Mary shook her head, and felt tears press behind her eyes. She squeezed her lids shut. She'd be damned if she'd cry for the Digots.

'You must have come from somewhere,' Doll pointed out.

Mary let herself imagine the way back to the basement on Charing Cross Road. Ten minutes' walk, and an impossible distance. Today Mary was not the same girl who'd whimpered, *Help me, Mother*. Her soft stuff had been fossilised into something stony during the night in the ditch. Never again, she swore to herself, would she beg so feebly. Never would she let herself be thrown out like trash.

'Well?' asked Doll impatiently.

'I can't go back,' she whispered.

Doll shrugged. 'Any friends, then? Any kind gentlemen?'

Mary shook her head vehemently.

'Well you can't stay here, Miss, so don't give it a moment's thought!' said Doll, almost laughing as she clambered out of bed. 'I'm as good a Christian as the next girl, and I don't hold it against you that you near bit my finger to the bone, but I don't go picking up strays.'

Mary stared into the harlot's eyes.

'It's every girl for herself, you understand?'

She nodded as if she understood.

The fact was though that Doll Higgins made no immediate move to evict Mary. Not that day, nor the next, nor even the next.

Mary lay limply in her sleeveless shift, wrapped in blankets to ease the shivering. Her bruises were red and blue and purple. Her broken nose looked monstrous in Doll's triangle of mirror. 'A clean wholesome break,' the girl assured her; 'it'll heal with barely a bump.' Mary stared into the mirror and waited to see what her new face would be.

As for her belly – surely what the soldiers had done to her would have disposed of that. She thought it seemed a little flatter already. Besides, there were signs. She knew it was all over for sure when she investigated the pain between her legs on the fifth morning. 'I'm leaking, Doll,' she whispered in the ear of the woman who lay snoozing beside her. 'Strange stuff.'

'Yellowish, greenish?' asked Doll, rolling on to her back with a great heave that sent up a cloud of warm perfume.

A shamed nod.

'That'll be the clap.'

The girl's eyes prickled at the word. She didn't know what it meant exactly, but she'd heard it before.

'Comes to us all, sooner or later,' said Doll merrily. 'Just about every rogue in London's clapped or poxed or both, the dirty hounds! But your luck's in, if it's Madam Clap. Compared to the pox, you know, the clap's a doddle.'

A tear slid down Mary's jaw. She blinked hard.

'You'll live!' said the harlot, passing over her gin bottle.

Mary stared though the brown glass at the oily liquid, then raised it to her lips. It went down her throat like a knife, and at first she choked. After a few more swallows she felt better.

Doll Higgins was always saying brutal things as if they were jokes. But for all her talk about *every girl for herself*, she did let Mary stay in her room for a fortnight, sharing her mattress, and brought her the occasional plate of bread and Yarmouth herrings, and the odd basin of icy water with a rag to clean herself as best she could. Mary took everything gratefully. She had nothing of her own; she had lost her grip on the world. *A girl that loses her virtue loses everything*, repeated her mother like a wasp in her head.

Rat's Castle was the biggest, most ramshackle house in the strange world that was the Rookery. There were four small rooms in the garret, and Doll's was the one with no lock. While Doll was out on the town, Mary lay curled up on the mattress and waited for her to come home. Down below, the third and second floors were occupied by a rabble of porters, chandlers, brandy merchants and small-time thieves. The best rooms, on the first floor, were rented by bully-men who ran a stable of a dozen Misses each, Doll said. One of the dark ones, Mercy Toft, was a very civil girl, who'd been brought back from India by a Company man and abandoned when he went off to Holland. Down in the basement were thirty Irish, squeezed in with their donkey.

It was a wizened Irishwoman who owned the whole lodging-house and twenty like it; half the parish of St Giles drained into Mrs Farrel's red hands. The rooms were always dim. When Mary asked why the windows were filled with balled-up brown paper, Doll explained it was because the old bitch Farrel was too cheap to glass them, 'and I'd rather the dark than the howling winds. Besides, night air is well known to be noxious.'

'So does Mrs Farrel . . . is it to her you answer, then?' asked Mary confusedly.

'What, does she pimp for me, you mean?' Doll's smile was scornful. 'Not at all. All I owe her is the rent. I'm a free agent, I am; I answer to no one.'

The Indian girl, Mercy Toft – who put her head in the door once in a while to say good day to the newcomer – thought Doll Higgins was mad. 'It's a hard life without a madam or bully-man to drum up trade and keep you out of trouble!'

Mary nodded weakly, as if she understood, and watched the inky tendrils that kept slipping out of Mercy's hair-knot. 'Have you lodged here long?' she asked hoarsely.

'Half a year in Rat's Castle, and another six years hereabouts. But mind, the worst rogues in London are to be found in the Rookery,' Mercy warned her with a grin that showed her white teeth; 'they'll rob your legs if you stand still long enough!'

How perverse, then, that Mary was coming to feel almost at home here, surrounded by the people her mother used to call *riff-raff*, or simply, *scum*. She spent her days dozing on Doll's stained mattress, her fever rising and falling like a flame in her spine. She sensed herself to be strangely safe, as if she were floating far above the ordinary world.

She could hear Doll's thumping feet on the stairs long before the door opened. Doll might stalk in at any time of night or day and let herself fall on to the thin mattress. She smelt like a fishmonger's and her pockets clinked, fat with shillings. 'Devil ride me,' she'd declare, 'if I ain't giving up this nasty trade.' But when Mary pressed her, she seemed unable to remember a time before *strolling* – that was her word for it – or any possibilities beyond its reach. It was like a country she lived in. To hear her describe life on the streets, everyone – man, woman or child – prostituted themselves one way or another. When drunk on her favourite gin – *blue ruin*, she called it fondly – she'd breathe perfume in Mary's face and swear that there was no trade like a Miss's. It required no training, capital nor premises, and the supply of customers would never run out till the end of the world. 'I defy you,' she would slur, 'I defy you to name me any other trade so merry.'

Mary sometimes had to remind herself: she wasn't a harlot. Only the friend of one. Only a girl fouled and in trouble.

After a fortnight, Mary's fever had died down, and the pains with it. Doll, who'd been most impressed to hear that Mary was a *scholar*, as she called it, sometimes got her to read pamphlets aloud in the long winter afternoons. Mostly they were bawdy political doggerel that bewildered Mary, about what Countess P—m got up to at B—h with the Honourable Member for W—r, but they made Doll cackle and roar. Sometimes she'd take the trouble to fill Mary in, telling her lurid and improbable tales, like the one about the King's old tutor carrying on with the King's own mother.

One morning Mary felt strong enough to get up, and asked for her smock, but Doll let out an alarming laugh and said, 'That filthy thing? Gave it to the ragman and got no more than ha'pence for it.'

'But I have nothing else.' Mary's voice began to quiver at the thought of going down into the streets with nothing but a linen shift to cover her.

Doll waved expansively at the clothes hanging on the nails. 'Take your pick, my darling.'

Mary stared over each shoulder. Such clothes, such colours, on her? She wouldn't know herself.

Doll let out an impatient puff of breath. 'You can start with my spares,' she said, bending to root in a corner.

The stays were stiff and stained. As Doll tugged the strings tight at Mary's back, the girl began to gasp with fright.

'Ain't you ever laced before, then?' asked Doll.

She shook her head and bit on her lower lip. She thought her ribs would crack.

'Fourteen years old, and never in stays!' Doll marvelled. She loosed the strings infinitesimally, and Mary sucked in a mouthful of air. 'High time you learned to dress like a grown girl. A female without boning ain't nothing but a sack of corn.'

Doll lent Mary two petticoats and a pair of steel improvers, which sat like buckled birdcages over the girl's narrow hips. Mary picked the least outrageous clothes: a pale blue skirt, a pink bodice and a pair of sleeves to match the skirt, buttoned on tight at the shoulders. Doll showed her how everything fitted together, and how the pockets hung down from the waist seam. Then she stepped back and thrust a triangle of mirror in Mary's face.

Mary stared at this festive bruised creature, a child in the clothes of a woman twice her age. She didn't recognise herself, not even when she tried to smile.

She could walk upright on her own, but when they went downstairs she still leaned on Doll's broad milky arm, gasping for breath. Mercy Toft's door was shut, and from behind it came a repetitive groan in a deep bass; Mary knew what that meant, even before Doll nudged her.

As they stepped out of the cracked front door of Rat's Castle, the noise of the city hit her as hard as the cold wind. The improvers made her vast skirt surge and sway like a boat in rough seas.

Doll was her sainted saviour and her only friend in the world. She told everything and asked nothing. She brought Mary all over the city, that day and many other days, as October gave way to a chill November. Doll had no sense that there was any border to her territory. She even marched Mary into the new white-stone squares of the West End, where the locals were so rich they hired linkboys to walk ahead of them with flaming torches so they'd never step into a pile of dirt. Ladies had themselves carried round in sedan chairs, with their tasselled skirts spilling out of the sides.

On Carrington Street in Mayfair, Doll pointed up at a fresh-painted apartment and said, 'That's the famous Kitty Fisher's.'

'What's she famous for?' asked Mary.

'Don't you know nothing yet?' Doll gave a pleasurable sigh. 'She's only got six lovers in the House of Lords, that's what for!'

'Six?' repeated Mary, staggered.

'They say one night she was entertaining Lord Montford, who's a shrunken little man, you understand – when up the stairs marched Lord Sandwich. So how do you think Miss Kitty smuggled the pygmy out?'

Mary shrugged to show she had no idea.

'Under her skirt!' shrieked Doll with mirth, slapping Mary's hoop to make it hum. 'They say her fee is a hundred guineas,' she added more reflectively.

'A year?'

'A night, you dupe!' crowed Doll. 'And once, at breakfast, when a gentleman gave her nothing but a fifty-pound note, she took such offence, she put it between two bits of bread and ate it.'

Mary stared up at the high rectangles of glass, hoping for a glimpse of Kitty Fisher, the famous mouth that could eat money. But the footman at the arched door was giving her and Doll a frozen stare. Mary dropped her eyes, suddenly seeing what he saw and knowing what he thought. To him there was no difference between the two of them. *Harlots*, she thought to herself, trying out the word. *Seven-Dials strollers, Misses, trulls.*

But Doll blew the footman a fat kiss. Doll never minded who looked at her or how.

'Why did you take me in?' Mary asked her on the walk home that evening. Then she wished she could swallow the words again, because she feared they would make Doll turn cold and scornful, or tell her that her time was long up and she owed a pretty penny, by the way.

But Doll gave a peculiar smile, almost sheepish. 'When I stopped to look at you in the ditch, that morning, I was just curious,' she began. 'I was all set to walk on to the Cheshire Cheese in Fleet Street for my breakfast. But then you bit my hand, and I liked that.'

'You liked it?' asked Mary, bewildered.

'Showed some spirit,' said Doll with satisfaction. 'That's what I'd have done myself.'

But Doll never said if she'd ever been there herself: face down in a ditch, left to rot. She never said much about the past at all. It seemed she'd always been and always would be what she was: a Miss. That was their favourite word for themselves, Doll said, though *whores* would be more honest. The men who hired them were called *cullies*. Men came in all shapes and sizes but they all wanted much the same thing, Doll explained to Mary.

The girl was amazed to learn the Misses were not a distinct population, set apart from the mass of womanhood. A stroller by night might be a herring-seller by day. As well as the *half-timers*, as Doll rather scornfully called them, there were many others – especially the wives – who'd only stay in the trade for a year or two, while times were at their worst. 'Your whores for life, now, like myself, we're as rare as black swans,' she boasted; 'the aristocracy of the trade, you might say. I was even in Harris's List, back in '55.'

'What's that?'

Doll rolled her eyes, as always when Mary displayed her ignorance. 'The *List of Covent Garden Ladies*, don't you know. It's a sort of circular, published every year for the gentlemen's benefit.'

'And do you know what it said about you?' asked Mary.

'Every word. I paid a boy to read it out to me till I'd learned it by heart. *Miss Dolly Higgins*,' Doll quoted, '*fifteen and full-fleshed, of a cheerful disposition. Application should be made at the Sign of the Moor's Head.*'

So Doll was still only twenty-one, Mary calculated, appalled. That face looked so lived in.

'*She is guaranteed to please the discerning beau*,' Doll went on, '*who need have no fear of consequences.*' She let out a hoarse laugh. 'Of course, I was clapped to the hilt already, no less than yourself. It sounded well, though.'

'But I think I'm clean now,' Mary told her.

'Ah, once it's in your blood it never quite leaves you,' said Doll professionally. 'A visitor for life, is Madam Clap. Next time you lie with the fellows, wash in gin first, if you can spare it, or in piss if you can't.'

'I won't be lying with any fellows,' said Mary coldly. Her hands began to shake at the thought of it, and she folded them behind her.

Doll let out a hoarse ripple of laughter. 'How d'you mean to get your bread, then?'

'I'll think of something.'

Now that Mary was getting to know the wider city, she could tell that there were more trades for women than she'd ever heard of. Not every girl had to end up a servant or a seamstress. There were cooks and milkmongers, fishwives and flower hawkers, washerwomen and gardeners and midwives and even the odd apothecary. Women kept schools and asylums, pie stalls and millinery shops. Mary made herself ask questions of strangers, everywhere she went. All she needed to know was, how could a girl of fourteen make her own way in the world?

But the answer in every case was that Mary was too young. Too ignorant. Lacked a cow, a barrow, a shop. Had no money to buy an apprenticeship, no husband to inherit a business from. Lacked knowledge of the world, trades, customers.

On her own, Mary would have clawed herself a little piece of some market in the end, she knew that. If she'd had to, she could have sold dripping, old newspapers, used tea-leaves – the detritus that never went to waste. On her own, she would have learned how to live off ha'pennies and made herself wear plaincloth all year round – if only to defy her mother's prediction that she would end up in the workhouse.

But she wasn't on her own, of course. She had Doll, strolling along in silks at her side and laughing at the notion of any trade honester than her own. Under her tutelage Mary tasted rum from Barbados, French wine, lemons from Portugal, and a pineapple so sweet she thought her head would explode. 'That came from a glasshouse out Paddington way,' Doll told her, 'and do you know what it grew in?'

'What?'

'Our shit!' Doll howled with laughter. 'I swear to the Maker, they buy fresh London shit from the night-soil men and grow pineapples in it!'

With Doll came gin and merriment, a great randomness, a feeling that you never knew what the day might hold. Decisions edged out of Mary's reach; the future slid out of her grasp.

And there was another thing: her belly. Mary felt its contours every morning, and for all her bleak hopes, she had to admit it now: the swelling had never gone down. Somehow what was growing inside her had survived the soldiers, and the ditch, and even the dirty fever. It was a little bigger every week. At night she lay in her shift with her back to Doll. She crossed her arms and pressed down on the bump till she thought she might burst.

But a fishwife she got talking to about the oyster trade gave Mary's borrowed bodice a knowing look and remarked, 'You could always put yourself out to nurse, if your own didn't live.'

Mary was too shocked to answer. She walked away without a word.

She knew she had to tell Doll. It was just a matter of finding the moment, and the right words. But when did Doll ever need telling about anything?

'High time you rid yourself of that,' she remarked to Mary one morning with no preamble, as she staggered in the door of their dark garret.

Mary stared up from the straw mattress, unblinking. Her hands were joined across her stomach. 'You mean—'

'Lud, didn't they teach you nothing at that school?'

Mary stared down at her belly.

Doll let herself down on the mattress with a vast sigh. She smelt like a fire in a gin-shop. 'Now don't turn spleenish,' she yawned. 'I'm only saying what's sense, devil take me if I'm not. You can't tell me you want to bear it?'

All Mary knew about childbearing was gleaned from her brother's birth, when her mother had kept her shut up in the second room. All she remembered was a terrible panting, and stained sheets hung over the dresser to dry afterwards. And William Digot, blind drunk, roaring, 'A boy! A boy! We're a proper family now!'

'Any case,' added Doll, 'it'll be born clapped. Had you thought of that?'

Mary's eyes were wet with panic, but she blinked until she

could see. She hadn't known that. She let herself think of a baby, pushing out from between her legs, diseased before its first breath. Nausea rose up in her throat. 'Tell me, then,' she said rapidly. 'Tell me how to stop it.'

Doll let out a massive yawn and pushed herself up on one elbow. 'Well, looks like it's too late for coffee berries, though I've known a brew of tamarisk to work at a pinch . . . Sit up,' she ordered.

Mary sat straight; her belly pushed out in front of her, now she wasn't trying to hold it in. They both stared at it.

'When did you get it? July, August?'

'May.'

Doll counted on her fingers and tutted. 'Six months! You're such a skinny thing, I didn't reckon you were so far gone. Well, you'll have to pay a call on Ma Slattery, that's the only thing for it. But she charges a full crown.'

'I don't have it,' said Mary after a few seconds, wetting her lips with her tongue. 'I don't have a—'

'I know that,' said Doll. 'But don't keep letting on you can't think of a single way to get it.'

Mary turned her head away.

'Listen,' said Doll in a hard voice, 'if you intend to keep laying about here for ever—'

'I don't,' interrupted Mary. 'And I'm vastly grateful—'

'Gratitude's not needed. And besides, it won't pay the rent.'

The silence lengthened.

'You got anything else?' asked Doll softly. 'Anything to pawn? Any friends you haven't mentioned?'

'No.'

'Then use what you've got, I say. Sell it while you're young and the market's high.'

Mary's head swung from side to side like a pendulum. 'I can't,' she said. 'I just can't bear the thought of it.'

There was a long silence. Doll Higgins seemed to be looking at her from a great distance.

'Maybe,' Mary began pathetically, 'if you could possibly see your way to lending—'

But the rage had flamed up in the older girl's eyes, and Doll's hand thumped the mattress between them, making the dust leap from the straw. 'So it's all right for me to go out whoring, but not for the Charity Scholar?' she bawled. 'I'm to dirty my hands to keep Madam's clean? Well, let me tell you, little Miss Precious: in this world, what you need, you pay for. You lost your virtue at the end of an alley like any common slut, and it ain't ever going to grow back. You're clapped and carrying, in case you hadn't noticed. You're one of us now, like it or not.'

After Mary had cried her eyes dry, and said how sorry she was, for everything, and, 'Yes, all right, yes, yes,' then Doll was very kind to her. She wiped her face with a handkerchief dipped in Hungary water, and the sharp lemony smell cleared Mary's mind.

'Young thing like you, fresh as lettuce,' said Doll, 'virgin goods, practically – you should get two bob a throw.'

Mary tried this new mathematics. Two bob by three *throws* – she didn't let herself think what this harmless word covered – meant a crown plus a shilling left over. (And she had done it before, she reminded herself. It couldn't possibly be as bad as what the soldiers did to her in the ditch.) 'Just this once,' she muttered at last.

'That's right.'

'As soon as it's all over' – glancing at her hard belly – 'I'm going to find another trade, even if it pays less.'

'Of course you will,' murmured Doll.

She was already pulling on Mary's stay-strings; she tugged them so tight that Mary cried out. But Doll was already leafing through the layers of clothes that hung on the walls. 'No, no,' she

said under her breath, 'too quiet by half.' Finally she plucked out
something in orange silk.

'But it doesn't even button up.'

'It's not meant to, dolt. It's a slammerkin.'

Doll hustled her into the long dress, tying it at the waist. 'Look,
it cuts away and shows a mile of petticoat. The cullies love an open
gown. And see how the train flares out behind you! Ever noticed
the words for us all sound drunk?' Doll put on an intoxicated slur.
'Slovenly, slatternly sluts and slipshod, sleezy slammerkins that
we are!'

Mary realised Doll was trying to make her laugh, to relieve her
panic, but she still covered her face with her hand.

Doll ignored that, and threw her a pair of worn red shoes. 'A girl
needs to stand out, on the streets. No use fading into the wall!'

'But I don't know how to do it.'

'What's to do?' asked Doll, slapping dust out of the orange
slammerkin's skirts.

'The words,' stammered Mary. 'What do I say?'

'The clothes will speak for you, won't they?' said Doll cheerfully. She found a carved wooden busk and slid it down the front
of Mary's ribboned bodice where it narrowed cruelly, tapering to
a point.

Mary stared at herself in the bit of mirror she held and
blushed scarlet. Her small breasts poked out on top of her
stays, as white and hard as elbows. The gaudy silk ruffled
at her neck and shoulders; grubby blue lace dangled at her
forearms. She looked half dressed. She looked like the whore
she was tonight.

'See,' said Doll, giving her bodice a lewd tug, 'these lines lead
the fellows' eyes directly down to the spot. And your big curved
flounces,' she added, snatching at Mary's skirt, 'they're meant to
make them think of tits and arses. We loop one bit of the train up

to your waist, see, and that's a sign that you're in the trade – in case they haven't guessed!'

'My face is still wrong,' said Mary gruffly, looking in the mirror. 'I look like a bony child.'

'But the gentlemen like 'em young, don't you know? And you have your assets,' said Doll professionally. 'Good dark eyes, and you can wear your own hair, if we comb it high; black's very *à la mode* these days. That bump in your nose is no worse than the one I was born with. And the cullies like a wide mouth; it reminds them of the other one!' She let out an obscene laugh.

Mary tried to join in.

'Now all you need is a dab of powder' – Doll pulled out a box and puff, and set to work on Mary's face – 'and a lick of ribbon red.'

'Ribbon red?'

Doll let out that little sigh that meant exasperation, but also a delight in her own knowledge. 'Quicker than carmine,' she said, 'and cheaper too.' She pulled down the end of her own scarlet hair ribbon and spat on the limp strip of satin, then sucked it. She rubbed it hard against Mary's lips as if polishing the tarnish off a teapot. She moved on to Mary's cheekbones and the warm pink spread, like a flush of health: magic.

In the mirror Mary watched the mask take shape. This wasn't her any more; this was some vivid, fearless puppet. She tried a smile.

Doll stuck out her tongue at Mary: it was as red as a devil's from the ribbon.

The girl laughed aloud. She was a quick learner, as Doll kept saying. Already she was picking up the language: words of spite and laughter, words she'd never heard at school or in the cramped rooms on Charing Cross Road.

That night Mary stood at the Dials with one hip pushed out the way Doll had shown her, and tried to mimic her friend's crooked smile. Grease and powder lay like armour on her face, but her knees trembled under the petticoats revealed by the gauzy orange slammerkin. The bell shape of her skirt was full of icy air. She kept the fur muff over her stomach so her bump wouldn't show. Doll would have been with her, except that she'd passed out cold on the mattress after half a bottle of gin.

Mary had only had a few gulps. The drink washed around in her stomach, warm and queasy. She remembered her instructions: *coyness gets you nowhere*. She would have to learn to think of every passer by in breeches as a cully. How bold the other Misses were, accosting a stranger or laying a hand on his thigh. 'What d'ye lack, gentlemen?' called one woman in a felt bonnet.

'Need of company?' asked another, linking arms with a soldier as he passed, but he shook her off.

'A shilling for a glimpse of Eden!' cried a girl in a brown wig. Alice Gibbs, that was her name, Mary remembered; she was rumoured to let cullies go in her mouth. Mary was revolted by the thought, and looked away.

She cleared her throat as a man in fine plush breeches hurried by. 'Fourteen and clean, sir,' she whispered.

He gave her a brief stare, but kept walking. The corner swallowed him.

That's what Doll had told her to say as her come-on. *Fourteen and clean*. Only half of it was a lie. It could have been a child's skipping rhyme. What was the one Mary had learned at school?

Spick and span without, within,
Soul and body cleansed of sin.

'Trade's ever so slow tonight, ain't it?' said a fair-skinned girl in a silver-edged sack gown, and Mary nodded back. 'Have I seen you before?'

'No,' said Mary nervously, and gave her name, before it occurred to her that now might have been a good time to change it.

The Miss was called Nan Pullen. By day she was a maidservant on Puddle Dock Hill, she told Mary rather proudly, but as soon as she was sure her mistress was asleep, she borrowed a handsome dress from the oak wardrobe and walked the streets half the night. The fine clothes worked a treat; she was rarely short of trade. 'Quilting keeps the worst of the cold out,' she said professionally, slapping her heavy underskirt. And she always got home by four in the morning, to snatch a little shut-eye. 'Saving my shillings, don't you know.'

'Are you?' said Mary.

'Someday I'm going to have my own lodging-house,' boasted Nan, 'and be beholden to nobody.' She left soon after that, saying she had an instinct the cullies were all hanging round the Piazza at Covent Garden tonight. 'I follow my nose,' she said, tapping it. She waved at the other Misses as she swept off, her fine gown scattering the dust.

A while later, a man hurried by with his hands in his pockets. 'Take me under your cloak, my dear,' bawled the red-haired woman who was leaning against the shutters in the shadows that hid her age. According to Doll, Mary remembered, she was the wife of an Indian footman who'd crushed his fingers and couldn't work any more. A scrivener's clerk with his sleeves full of papers came up the street now. The redhead pulled her skirts up as far as her garter. 'How does Mr Cock stand tonight, sir?'

Mary blushed at the words, but the clerk passed the woman as if he hadn't heard. He walked by Mary too, then paused, and looked back at her.

She stood a little straighter, pushing out her small chest but trying to suck in her stomach. She began to shake. Just this once, she promised herself, just this once. When all this was over, she'd find another way to earn her bread: there had to be something to make, or mend, or sell.

Now the clerk had taken hold of her sleeve and was pulling her into the light. She wanted to turn her hot face to the wall. She wondered whether he'd start with a compliment, or a request that she might not understand. She wondered when to mention that her rate was two shillings.

'Ninepence.' The man said it calmly, as if he were standing at a gingerbread stall.

And though she could feel tears pricking her eyes, what could Mary say but yes? If she refused this cully, who was to say when she'd get another?

They stood in the shadows. It was all very peculiar, Mary thought. It wasn't like the other times. This was no rape; she was letting it happen, making it happen, in fact. She helped the clerk unbutton his thin breeches; she wanted it over fast. His long sleeves full of papers creaked awkwardly. He looked down at his yard, and so did she. It was the first time she'd actually seen one close-up; the thought started a giggle in her throat. Such a pale, peeled thing it was. The clerk put her hand on it so she started to rub it, as if cleaning a plate, and all of a sudden she felt it growing like a marrow in her hand. Such power she tasted, then!

But he hauled up her skirts as if he was running out of time, and kneed her legs apart, and pressed himself into her, and all at once Mary was a helpless child again. It didn't hurt, exactly; it was just dry and heavy, like a weight she had to carry inside her. The worn papery smell of the man surrounded her. She held on to the shoulders of his plain coat; she bore his thrusts, staggering a little on the cobbles. When panic rose up in her throat she kept her mind on the goal: the crown for Ma Slattery – five shillings, ten sixpences, sixty pennies.

Then with a scalding gush inside it seemed to be over. The clerk leaned his head on her shoulder for a moment, and his legs buckled and swayed. Mary despised him, and almost pitied him too, until he pulled away, straightened up and reached for his purse.

Nine pennies; she dropped them into the pocket that hung inside her waist seam. There; she'd done it. It wasn't the end of the world. She'd got paid for the thing instead of having it snatched. Her head suddenly ached with tears.

After the clerk came a carpenter, very sawdusty, and then a soldier in an old uniform, and then an old fellow who smelled as if he'd never had a bath, and thanked her afterwards. What they all had in common was a terrible, rutting need. Like that saying of Doll's when she was drunk: *Cunny draws cully like a dog to a bone*.

Between customers there were long stretches of waiting. Mary's thighs were sticky. Her stomach ached. By midnight she'd earned three shillings and she was beginning to acquire a stroller's arrogance. She could do it; she had something any man would pay for.

But then the girl in the brown wig stalked over. 'Treating time, my dear,' she announced.

Mary stared at her. Inside her muff, her hands knotted round each other.

'Didn't Doll Higgins tell you our custom?' said the girl pleasantly. Behind her, the others were lining up, arms crossed. 'First-timers always treat.'

They took every penny she had in her purse; she didn't dare hide any, because she had a feeling they would know. She didn't cry either, in case it left lines in her painted face. She managed a sort of grin. It was their beat, after all, and she couldn't afford to make enemies. Not that they were spiteful; the brown-wigged girl invited her along to the Bull's Head for a sup of negus to warm her up, but Mary said she thought she'd stay on for a bit.

'Youngsters these days,' remarked a fat older woman; 'don't know where they get the strength.'

Mary was the only girl at the Dials now. When she'd finished with one man she turned away from the wall and there was another waiting, watching her. Somehow that was the worst thing, being seen. The man waiting had his breeches half-unlaced already, so as not to waste any time.

He was the biggest so far, and the roughest. Mary didn't protest. She kept her eyes shut as much as possible. Inside she said a word she wasn't meant to say any more: *Mother*. She thought she was bleeding a little, after that man, but it was hard to tell because of everything else that was running down her thighs.

Between each cully now her feet started taking her home to the Rookery, but she turned back to the pillar at the centre of the Dials, and folded her arms and pressed down on the treacherous curve below her ribs, to remind herself what this was about. The killing she had to pay for. This was the only way.

Please. Mighty Master. Somebody. Let it be over soon.

A few hours before morning, Mary dragged herself up the stairs of Rat's Castle. She felt divided from herself. The ache sounded in her stomach like a drum. The milk of eleven or twelve strangers – she'd lost count – brewed to a poison inside her. She could smell it through the petticoats, through the limp orange slammerkin: dark and yeasty. Of course, she realised; that was what Doll smelt of.

But Mary had survived, and the men's faces were blurred already. And locked in her fist were the many small and greasy coins that amounted to a crown.

'One of us, ain't you now?' said Doll, half-asleep, giving her a one-armed hug.

Doll saw to it all, the next day; it was she who bought the big bottle of gin, and only took a mouthful for herself. Doll knew which cellar on Carrier Street was the right one. It was she who held Mary's head against her own perfume-drenched bodice, so the girl only caught glimpses of Ma Slattery. When the old woman took out a rusty knife to sharpen the stick, a wail seemed to start up from Mary without her knowledge, but Doll covered her mouth and whispered nonsense in her ear. She stood at the end of the stained mattress where Mary lay; she pulled the girl's wrists over her head and gripped them hard enough to break. She chattered on, describing a fine lavender trollopee she'd seen going cheap on Monmouth Street – a trollopee was like a slammerkin, and how vastly it would suit Mary – and the new tigers on show at the Tower, and a riot over the price of mackerel all down Billingsgate, and how soon it would be Christmastide. She kept talking all the way through, while the speechless old woman did things to Mary that the girl had no words for, things that made her twitch and buck like the mad dog she'd seen on Holborn last summer. It seemed ten years since last summer, when she'd been a child in uniform, trailing home from school. Now the cramps took this new Mary Saunders and shook her like a blood-spattered flag.

It was Doll who wiped the vomit from Mary's mouth with the back of her hand. In the end it was Doll who took the pot away to empty it into the gutter, but not before Mary had glimpsed what was in it. Just a pale shape swimming in the red; a worm, a parasite, a demon expelled from her body. Nothing, really; nothing that made any difference.

Mary bled for a week. But as soon as the rent came due she went back on the town, bracelets of blue marks round her wrists. *What d'ye lack, gentlemen, what d'ye lack?*

Chapter Two

Magdalen

Because of course this was the only trade. Her eyes had been forced open. The fact was, there was nothing else a fourteen-year-old girl could do that would earn a fraction of what Mary was making, now she was hardened enough to stand up to the cullies and set her price. The world was vastly unjust, she recognised that now – with the rich born to idleness, and the poor like the mud under their carriage wheels. But here was a way for a girl who had already lost everything to seize her chance. Why scrape an uncertain living by wearing out her hands, her feet, her back or her eyes, when, as Doll quoted with a coarse chuckle, *Cunny beats all*?

It was the way the world was. It was the bargain most women made, whether wife or whore, one side of the sheets or another. 'Don't you see?' slurred Doll one night on Oxford Street, seizing the bottle from Mercy Toft and draining it. She chucked it at the fresh-painted door of a four-storey house, and clapped her hands with glee to hear it smash. Then she remembered her point, and turned on Mary. 'You've got a thing, ain't you, that any man, from a beggar to a baronet, will pay to lay his hands on.'

She started hoisting up her skirts for illustration, petticoat by petticoat. Mercy Toft was laughing so hard she couldn't stand upright. Only Mary saw the door of the great house open; she grabbed Doll's skirts before she could show her snatch to the whole neighbourhood, and shoved her into the road.

'It's true, frig you!' bawled Doll. 'You can take his own weapon – see – and turn it in his face.' That mime was even more obscene. Mercy's laugh turned into a violent cough. They never noticed the pair of footmen hurrying down the marble steps to investigate the matter of the broken glass. Mary had to hook her arm into Doll's and Mercy's and haul them off down Soho Street before they all got their heads broken. They giggled all the way to St Giles.

The winter was a wet and cold one, but Mary and Doll bought fourth-hand fur-edged muffs to keep them warm, when ale and wine and gin wouldn't do the trick. Most of the girls picked a beat and worked it, but Doll said that was tedious stuff. 'The whole city's our bawdy-house, my lass,' she crowed. Mary was coming to learn that men were easy, in the end; not worth being afraid of. Doll showed her where to find them, and when they were ripe for the picking. Mary took strangers against walls, in taverns, in rented rooms; clerks blind with drink on the Strand; rich Bishopsgate Jews restless after sunset on Saturday; young bucks reeling out of Almack's after losing hundreds at brag.

Mary was a free woman now, with more money in her pocket than she'd ever seen in her life before. She dressed in the brightest colours she could find on the stalls of Monmouth Street – pinks and purples and oranges – and never cared if they clashed, so long as the cullies kept looking. She knew herself to be wanted. She wore her rouged face like a carnival mask.

One grey morning she thought of the Mighty Master for the first time in months. 'Are we going to hell?' she asked her friend, suddenly doubtful.

Doll let out a dry chuckle. 'I'm a Roman, ain't I?'

'A what?'

'You know, a Papist, same as my parents before me. I take

the sacraments every Easter, rain or shine,' Doll added proudly. 'When I reckon my hour's come, all I'll have to do is send for a priest and get myself absolved.'

'What's that, then?'

'Scrubbed clean, soul-wise.'

Mary considered this image. 'But what about me?' she asked, troubled.

Doll shrugged. And then, more kindly, added, 'They ever told you about the Magdalen in that school of yours? Mary the Magdalen?'

The girl thought she remembered the name.

'Well, she were a whore, and she did all right in the end, didn't she?'

At Twelfth Night Doll took her to the Theatre Royal in Drury Lane, 'to teach you how to cheek the fellows in the grand style,' as she put it. They paid a shilling each to squeeze into the gallery – the price of a fuck, Mary thought, trying out the new word in her head. Doll gazed round critically and guessed there were no more than a thousand and a half in the house this afternoon. The hum of talk rose like bee song.

Mary felt sick with anticipation. The play was said to be a new one, adapted from the French: *The Game of Love*. Her mother had always kept her away from the theatres, told her that no good would come of folk pretending to be what they weren't. The air was so hot, she felt her shoulders released as if by the touch of the sun. The curtain didn't go up till ten past six, and at first Mary was so dazzled by the set that she could see nothing else. There were great trees that slid on and off the stage, and gilt sofas, and a full moon shining without any visible means of support. The lights stank like burning hair.

But then Mrs Abington came on in a white flowered gown with

scalloped flounces and a ladder of increasingly tiny bows on her stomacher. Mary forgot everything else. 'Does the manager let her pick out what she wants to wear?' she asked Doll.

'Pick it? She owns it,' said Doll. 'The actresses all have to furnish their own clothes.'

Mary watched Mrs Abington with a sort of tender envy. Imagine owning such dresses and walking out on the stage for thousands of people to stare at you.

'No wonder they need rich keepers!' said Doll with a dirty laugh.

Mary looked at her hard, to see if that was a joke. Then she stared even more closely at the woman who was floating across the stage as if she'd never seen a male member in her life. It puzzled Mary, how a girl could wear such a face after entering into the trade. Maybe it was different for an actress; maybe she could reach into a pair of breeches while all the time pretending to be someone else.

The speeches were hard to follow, above the shrill commentary of the audience, and the swish of fans, and the swell of gossip whenever some viscount or duchess showed themselves in a box. But soon Mary had got the gist of the play. Mrs Abington was a lady who had switched clothes with her maid, as a sort of joke. It was astonishing, the difference a hat made, or an apron, or a gilt buckle. If you looked like a lady, it seemed, men bowed to you a lot, and if you dressed like a maid, they tried to kiss you behind doors. But what the maid and mistress didn't know was that the gentleman coming to court the lady had done the same swap with his manservant. So they were all liars, and none of them knew who they were flirting with, which made it very funny.

Doll nudged Mary in the ribs whenever a riposte got a laugh. 'There's the old repartee for you, Mary!'

'If you shut your mouth for a minute I might be able to hear it,' said Mary, elbowing her back.

There were folk they were acquainted with – and some they were friendly with, like Mercy Toft and Nan Pullen and Alice Gibbs and the Royle brothers who ran the cider cellar round the corner from Rat's Castle – but when it came right down to it, Mary was coming to the conclusion that she and Doll had no one but each other. Even when they lost themselves in a crowd – they joined in half the peltings and 'rough music' that went on that winter, even helped to burn an effigy of a silk-master who wouldn't raise wages – Mary and Doll always kept one eye out for each other. No one else quite spoke their language, got the joke. They might be seven years apart in age, but they could finish each other's sentences.

There was an old song Doll used to sing, late at night:

Ribbon red, ribbon grey,
Men will do what they may.

By now there was hardly a corner of the city where Mary hadn't turned a trick, from the pristine pavements of the West End to the knotted Cockney streets where Spanish Jews, Lascar seamen from the Indies, blacks and Chinamen all mingled like dyes in a basin. She'd had coopers and cordwainers, knife-grinders and window-polishers, watchmen and excisemen and a butcher with chapped hands. In the crowd that gathered to watch the famous Mr Wesley preach at the old foundry in Moorfields, Mary had done three hand jobs and earned two shillings. She'd taken on an Irish brickie in Marylebone, a one-legged sailor back from the French wars, a Huguenot silkweaver in Spitalfields, a planter gentleman back from Jamaica, and an Ethiopian student of medicine. She'd charged that fellow double, expecting him to hurt her with his monstrous yard – such were the rumours – but it turned out he was no bigger than an Englishman after all. So now she knew. She was acquainted with the whole city, from a coach trundling along Pall Mall, to the back wall of St Clement Danes, to a room upstairs at the Lamb and Flag on Rose Street. It was a drover down from Wales who hired that room. 'Lie still,' he'd said afterwards, with his soft lisp; 'lie still a while, Miss, and I'll pay another tuppence.'

She'd had a few bad nights, but she didn't let herself dwell on them afterwards. When she came home once with the marks of a cully's nails on her neck, Doll called her a ninny, and taught her how to knee a man so hard his bag would ache for weeks.

Mary knew she'd never starve, now; she could be sure of that much. *Cunny draws cully like a dog to a bone.* What she had between her legs was like the purse in the old story that was never quite emptied.

Ribbon grey, ribbon gold,
You must dance till you be old.

Mostly the men blurred together in Mary's mind, after the first two months in the trade, but there were a few who stood out. A greasy-haired jack on Queen Street, for instance, who'd taken her against the side of a cart and – she found afterwards – reached under her skirts with his knife and snipped her pocket in the act. She should have known he was a thief from his crooked eyes.

One regular was a young Scot the Misses all called Mr Armour – laughing behind his back – because he insisted on wearing a thin sheath of sheepsgut. 'What's that, then?' asked Mary in alarm as he drew it on, the first time.

'A cundum,' he said, digging her breasts out of her stays. 'Reasons of health.'

She held him at bay with one hand. 'Which reasons would those be?'

The Scot shrugged. 'It armours me against venereal itches and fluxes.'

'What, you wear this cundum thing every time you do the business?'

He tore at her laces in his haste to loosen them. 'Well, not with ladies, that goes without saying. Only with women of the town.'

Mary let out a screeching laugh. She sounded like Doll, it occurred to her. 'And what about us?' she asked as Mr Armour buried his face in her breasts and tugged up her skirts. 'Are we not as likely to get clapped or poxed by you cullies as you by us whores?'

He looked up, wild-eyed, as if he hadn't been expecting argument. He gripped the sheath at the root to hold it on. 'Such', he panted, 'would seem a necessary risk of your trade.'

He was nudging her knees open, but she had one last question. 'Couldn't I buy one of these cundums myself?'

'Why, yes,' he said, straight-faced, and then, with a smirk, 'but I can't imagine where you'd wear it!' And with that he was up to the hilt in her, and the time for talk was over.

Soho Square at five in the morning was a good hunting ground; that was when the lords were finally turfed out of Mrs Cornelys' Select Assemblies. Once Mary went into the bushes with a nob who turned out to be a Parliamentary Member. He kept talking about a Monsieur Merlin who'd performed for the Assembly in shoes that went on wheels. 'Wheels, I tell you!'

'Never!' murmured Mary, as she rubbed the swelling in his breeches, noting the flawless pile of the velvet.

'Dashed along like some bird – until he came a cropper and

smashed through Mrs Cornelys' mirror. Blood and glass all over, I declare, the poor Frog.'

'Poor Frog,' Mary repeated, addressing the lopsided prick she was lifting out of the velvet. 'Poor, poor little Froggie.'

'Not so very little, surely?' he asked, half-forlorn.

Mary thought the lord must have been drunk, or dreaming, to make up a story like that one. But the image stayed in her head as she straddled him: a little Frenchman, flying along the ground like a swallow, towards disaster.

Another day Mary met a chair-man with a worn-out spine, who carried sedan chairs for a living and suffered with every step. He paid for a room in a bagnio so they could do it lying down. She climbed on top and promised not to shake him. What a luxury that was, to fall asleep afterwards and dream that she was riding through town in the King's State Carriage with its carbuncles of gold.

Ribbon gold, ribbon brown,
What goes up must fall down.

Not that she was very picky. Street Misses couldn't afford to be, 'not like those bawdy-house bitches on their velvet sofas', as Doll put it. Mary lay down with prizefighters with broken faces and a sailor with one ball poxed off. (He swore the disease was long cured, but she would only give him a hand job.) It took a lot to disgust her, these days. She went with flogging-cullies who wanted to play mother and wicked son – strange, she thought the first time, for a man to want to be hurt rather than to hurt – and even a freak who offered her two shillings to let him spit in her mouth. The only kind of fellow Mary wouldn't touch was a coalman, because the smell of the dust took her back to the cellar on Charing Cross Road.

She'd never seen any of the Digots since the night she'd left home last November. Once in Lincoln's Inn Fields she stared after a woman hurrying by, her head bent over a huge bundle of cloths, but it couldn't have been Susan Digot, not so far from Charing Cross. 'Decent folk don't wander like we do,' as Doll said with a curl of her lip; 'decent folk stay in their place.'

It did occur to Mary to wonder if the woman had ever made any attempt to trace her. Asked around, kept one eye out, even? Surely where once there'd been love, something had to remain, some scraps, leftovers? Or was it possible for a mother to cut a daughter out of her life as if she'd never been born?

Not that it mattered. Mary wouldn't have gone back now, she told herself, not even if Susan Digot climbed up the groaning stairs of Rat's Castle to beg her on hands and knees. Mary could barely remember her old life: the narrowness of it, the poverty not just of goods but of spirit; the hours of weighty silence, as they'd all sat round the shivering fire. No, it was too late for return, or even forgiveness.

> *Ribbon brown, ribbon rose,*
> *Count your friends and your foes.*

With Doll life was never dull. There were no reproaches, or sermons, or tasks. The two of them slept in their paint, which left their pillows streaked and gaudy. They paid an Irishwoman in the basement of Rat's Castle to do their laundry. Every few weeks they went to a bathhouse and soaked themselves clean in scalding water. They got their dinner from a chop-house or went without, depending on their purses, but they never cooked so much as a bit of toast. They bought cups of tea and coffee whenever their hands were cold. They drank whatever liquor they could lay hands on and never thought more than a day ahead.

Lovers of liberty, Doll called the two of them. They got up when they wanted, and stayed up all night if they fancied, and at any hour of the day they could climb back up the stairs to bed. For the first time in her life, Mary had time for idleness. Few cullies ever had her for more than a quarter of an hour. She was free to choose one fellow over another, or walk away from the lot of them if her stomach turned at the thought. Sometimes she and Doll took an evening off to sit by the fire in a gin-shop and share a pipe. The drink blurred the edges of everything, turned boredom to hilarity.

One crisp February night she met a sweet-faced apprentice playing cricket in Lamb's Conduit Fields. He couldn't have been more than twelve. 'Please, Miss, how much?' he asked, like Jack the Beanstalk at his first market.

'More than you've got,' she said, not unkindly, chucking him under his chin. It was as soft as a cat's.

'I've a shilling,' he said sternly, producing it from deep down in his pocket.

Mary knew he'd probably nicked it from his master to pay for his fleshly education. She took it all the same, and led the boy by the hand behind a spreading holly bush. The ground was soft and barely damp.

She felt almost sad, afterwards, and hoped she hadn't passed on the clap. She thought she was clean, these days – she had no fever or flux, and she always washed in gin when she had it, or piss when she hadn't – but a person could never be sure.

'So now you know,' she told the apprentice, as he struggled with his buttons.

He flashed her a grin.

'Find yourself a girl,' she told him, 'and don't be wasting your money.'

He blew her a kiss before he ran off.

That night she and Doll lay on their leaking straw mattress in their dark room and talked till the poet who'd moved in next door battered the wall with his fists.

Ribbon rose, ribbon white,
Each day ends with a night.

Many a Miss was a purse-snatch too, which gave the trade a bad name, and was dangerous besides. 'Nobs can stand being poxed much sooner than being picked,' Doll advised. Besides, Mary had her principles. She'd only robbed a man the one time, and he was a lying dog who wouldn't pay the half a crown he'd promised her if she'd let him beat her with his shoe before the act. She waited till he'd drunk himself to sleep on the tavern table, then she ran off with two fine Pinchbeck shoe-buckles and a silver watch. 'Fair dues,' as Doll said.

Mary had yet to figure out why any woman would do it for free. There were some who did it to get children, she knew, and others for pleasure or what they called love. Doll occasionally did it for nothing, mostly with a soft-skinned journeyman carpenter. 'It's comfort, ain't it?' she argued. Not to Mary. And Mercy Toft was sweet on a bookish Frenchman who was as pale as she was dark; she snuck him up to her room sometimes when her bully-man wasn't around. Mary found such longings unimaginable.

She'd never yet felt this thing called lust, but she knew enough about its signs to copy them. She'd learned the knack of dirty talk. It wasn't so much the words she used – though foul terms did excite some cullies – as the tone. If her voice was sufficiently arousing, she could be talking about porridge for all it mattered. The trick was to pretend to be excited herself. An intake of breath, a catch in the voice: it fooled the cullies every time, and speeded them up like nothing else.

The odd night she lay beside Doll and her carpenter, pretending to be asleep, while they moved together like fish. Doll rolled her head back as if in pain, but her mouth was tender, and her cheeks were wet. Mary stared through the darkness.

She'd never yet opened her legs for her own body's sake, but only for what it had earned her: money, shelter, bargaining time. It wasn't herself Mary sold, she was sure of that much. She just hired out a dress called skin.

Ribbon white, ribbon green,
Some grow fat, some grow lean.

In the months since Ma Slattery's cellar, Mary hadn't had her courses, which was just as well, she supposed. Safer. She'd thought at first that it was just a temporary reprieve, but by now she'd come to the conclusion that her bleeding days were over. It was a peculiar sensation, to know herself finished with all that at fourteen. But not uncommon, among the Misses, Doll said. And, all in all, wasn't it handy for a girl in the trade to get the belly business over and done with?

Mary had the impression that Doll had dropped a couple of brats in her early days. There was no point asking about them, she knew. They wouldn't have lived.

She itched to know her friend's story, but she had to get it by guile, a line at a time; direct questions got no answers. One day they were passing a wig shop on Monmouth Street when Doll mentioned that her first was a perruke-maker.

'Who's that?'

'My first. The man my old folks sold me to.'

Mary gave her a wary look. She was still never sure if Doll was joking or not.

'He'd heard a virgin was a sure cure for the pox,' said Doll, walking on. She let out a laugh like a pebble in a jar. 'Money down the drain!'

Mary ran to catch up. 'How old were you?'

Doll shrugged.

Did this mean that Doll didn't remember, Mary wondered, or didn't think it mattered?

The older girl said nothing more about it that day, but when Mary asked, another time, Doll added, 'I was young enough to know naught. I was so green, I reckoned the fellow was making water in me!' And that terrible laugh came from the very back of her throat.

Ribbon green, ribbon red,
The tale's not told till you're dead.

One night in March Mary came on to a pair of tars behind St Mary-le-Bow singing 'The Cunts of Old England'. 'Evening, my dears,' she called, but they didn't seem to hear her. The taller one's voice was rapt with nostalgia.

Then, then, we were able
to fuck or to fight,
our swords always drawn
and our pricks always right –

His friend burst in then, almost jolly:

but now we're a parcel
of shittle-come-shite –

They joined in harmony for the sweeping refrain.

Oh! the large cunts of old England,
and oh! the old English brown cunts!

Mary stood nearby, smiling as she waited for the end of the song. Finally, one of the sailors turned around with his breeches gaping and his yard in his hand. She stepped closer, and he punched her in the breast. 'Wouldn't take you with a pitchfork, my darling,' he crowed.

She backed away, clutching herself, but he pissed all over her, soaking her best violet overskirt. His friend tried to join in but was laughing too hard to aim.

'Rot you for a pair of sodomish arsers!' she shrieked.

She'd learned how to say what she meant, but it wasn't much comfort. Back at Rat's Castle, she sponged her skirt. Doll swore it was good as new, but Mary could still smell their sourness on it.

Not that she'd anything against doing it arseways. There were more than a few cullies who couldn't stand for it any other way. Some Misses declared they'd rather have their throats slit than submit to such filthiness, but Mary couldn't see that it much mattered. Arse and cunny were only an inch apart, after all. It was a clockmaker that taught her how to bear the thing, and though she'd left her teethmarks on his fingers, she was grateful to him for the lesson in the end. She wasn't ready for it, that first time; she didn't understand why he was spitting on himself. She let out a scream when he pushed into her. But she soon learned the trick of it, that night and other nights. If she thought of a door creaking open, or an orange with its peel coming off, it hardly hurt at all. Clearly there was nothing in Mary Saunders that couldn't learn, couldn't bend, couldn't open if it could turn a penny.

One morning she was up an alley with her hand down the stained breeches of a saddler, when she happened to turn her head and recognised the gates of her old school. It gave her an odd sort of feeling, to see the little figures in their grey buttoned smocks lining up in the yard. What a wet-eared innocent she'd been, only a year ago!

Mary and Doll were on King Street one night, sharing a pigeon pie and licking their burnt fingers as they broke it apart between them. Mary nodded at the fresh-varnished door of the brothel opposite. 'D'you think they're hiring?'

Doll blew out a contemptuous puff of air. 'All the street-cullies ask is a pair of open legs, my dear. In the bawdy-houses, gentlemen are paying so high, they expect a girl to roll her eyes in bliss.' She snorted at the idea.

'How d'you come to know so much about it?' asked Mary.

'Worked two years at Mother Griffith's, didn't I?'

'I didn't know that.'

Doll's lips formed into a sneer. 'You don't know everything, then. Reckon you know a bit more than when I picked you out of the ditch, but you still don't know much.'

'So tell me about Mother Griffith's,' said Mary lightly, refusing to fight.

Doll shrugged and spread her hands. 'What's there to tell? You lie on sofas waiting to get fucked, that's about it. So after two years I ran away, for a bit of liberty.'

Mary grinned at her.

'But the stinking bawd sent Caesar after me, to learn me a lesson.'

'Who's Caesar?'

'Aren't you the innocent,' said Doll fondly, 'not to know Caesar!'

She pointed him out to Mary the next day, down on the Strand. The man was an African, dressed all in white velvet, with a wig

like a snowdrift; the polished yew of his face stood out against it.
His skin had the high shine that only money gives. 'You'll know
him next time.'

'Yes,' said Mary, staring.

'They say he was in a mutiny,' said Doll impressively.

'Where?'

'On a slaver, don't you know, in the Indies. The blacks all
upped and massacred the masters, so they say. Imagine!'

Mary gazed at the man called Caesar, who stood talking to a
pale girl, one hand resting lightly on his hip. He wore immaculate
doeskin breeches: a thrill flickered through her. To think that this
fellow once lay in chains, and now here he was, lording it up and
down the Strand. It wasn't true, if it ever had been, what Susan
Digot used to tell her daughter: that people had to stay all their
lives in the places allotted to them.

'She must be one of his whores, and there's another over
between the columns, as well as those two flirting with the
Grenadier Guard,' Doll added, pointing. 'Caesar runs this whole
beat, from George Court to Carting Lane. Not a soul gets in his
way. They say he has a protection on him.'

'A protection?'

'Black magic, don't you know.'

It was true that no one came within a yard of the pimp and
his girl; the crowds parted round them like water. When Mary
walked near enough to see the length of the knife in his glossy
belt, she knew why. The heavy scent of Caesar's pomaded wig
hung on the air, and he was grinning. She didn't meet his milky
eye. She hurried back to Doll, and a terrible thought struck her as
she looked her friend in the face. 'I don't suppose it was him—'

Doll fingered her scar as if appraising its value, but her eyes
still rested on the stately African. 'Aye. Caesar was Mother
Griffith's own bully-man in those days, before he struck out

as his own master. Mind you, he let me off easy, I'll give him that.'

'Easy?' Mary put out a hand to her friend's jagged face, but didn't quite touch it. How could Doll speak so lightly, as if it was someone else's story she was telling?

'You know that card-sharp with half a nose we saw the other night?' asked Doll.

Mary nodded.

'And there was a girl found in Pig Lane with no face at all, that was the bastard's work too; they say she'd run off with some money that was owing him.'

Mary covered her mouth. She imagined the great knife descending.

'Well, they wouldn't hire him if he weren't the best, would they?' asked Doll reasonably.

There was no answering that.

'So really it might have been worse. I call this my lucky scratch,' said Doll, tapping her scar with one long grimy nail. She slung an arm around Mary's shoulders and they walked on. 'Let it be a lesson to you, dear heart, never to pay poundage to any idle pimp or bawd. Every girl for herself, remember? Here's the first rule *Never give up your liberty*.'

So this was liberty. Mary was beginning to recognise the taste of it in her mouth: terror salting the sweetness.

Doll could read anyone by the cut of their cloth, from Lyons velvet right down to grubby fustian. One night at the cold end of March, she and Mary were on their way home from Cock Lane in Smithfield, where they'd paid halfpence each to see the famous ghost of the Poisoned Lady, but she hadn't appeared. Doll pointed out a girl on the corner of Maiden Lane, with a thin, pleasant face, a torn shift, and one petticoat. 'That one won't live till summer,' said Doll, as if commenting on the weather.

Mary peered at the girl, as if to distinguish the hand of death on her. 'Will she freeze?'

'Starve,' explained Doll. 'Unless she begs or borrows or steals a good gown, no cully's going to waste a look.'

'She's a pretty thing, though,' Mary objected, glancing back at the diminishing figure at the street corner.

'It's not us they want, you dolt!' said Doll. 'In those rags, the girl can't let on to be anything but herself. Remember, sweetheart, you should go without a week of dinners sooner than pawn your last good gown.'

That was rule two: *Clothes make the woman.*

Dawdling outside Almack's, another night, they saw a phaeton fly up, and its door bend back like a wing.

Mary elbowed Doll. 'Who's that dazzler?'

'Her?' Doll's smile was broad and wet; it creased her scar. 'Nothing but a painted whore, no better nor you nor me, and ten years older.'

'No! She's quality, surely.'

'What a fool you are for a spangle, Mary Saunders.'

They watched from behind a pillar as a thick-waisted gentleman ran round to hand the lady down.

'What about that underskirt?' objected Mary. 'It's figured satin, ain't it?' She was beginning to pride herself on her knowledge of these details.

'Only in the crack,' said Doll with scorn; 'the rest of it's plain muslin. And those diamonds in her ears look like paste to me,' she added gleefully, 'and when she undoes those stays, I bet her bubs fall on her stomach.'

Mary gave her friend a shove. 'Jealous old trull!'

Doll sighed, hands on hips, making her white bosom swell like a wave. 'Mark my words, she'll get another few months out of him, and a few more presents, but never an annuity. And another thing,' she said, watching the couple hurry into the club, 'there's pocks as deep as your nail under those starry patches.'

'How do you reckon that?'

'I'd say she's barely over the fever; pale as puke, she is.'

Mary was learning everything Doll had to teach. She committed to memory that night's lesson: *Clothes are the greatest lie ever told.*

One mild afternoon in April she and Doll were strolling down Charing Cross Road. The younger girl began to tremble a little as they passed the door that led down to the cellar where she used to live, but Doll never noticed and Mary didn't say a word. She glanced down the steps, but she couldn't see anything through the dusty window. The place could be full of strangers now, or derelict for all she knew.

It came to her that she was utterly changed. What she had between her legs was not her only goldmine, she'd discovered; there was one in her mouth as well. Once she let loose, Mary was a cheeky thing, as skittishly rude as any man could fancy. It gave her great satisfaction to say sharp pointed things and call them merriment. If she wasn't careful, she sometimes thought, she'd end up a shrew.

Not that she'd have anything to say to the woman who used to be her mother, if she met her coming along the street. Anyway, Susan Digot wouldn't likely recognise her child-as-was, all gussied up in a flowered jacket-bodice and a worn silk skirt buoyed out by a pair of improvers. Mary looked like a woman of the town, these days. She smelt different, even, with the mouth-watering lemony reek of Hungary water.

What a fool Susan Digot had been, to think everyone in gold

braid her better, and the wider the skirt, the higher the breeding! Mary had seen commoners walk as queens on the stage in Drury Lane. Doll was opening Mary's eyes to all life's shortcuts, back alleys, gaps in the walls. In these uncertain times, Mary was learning, a duchess was sometimes just a stroller who'd picked the right honourable cully.

In a four-storey house in Golden Square lived a lady who'd once been known in the trade as Angel Arse. On the corner of Hyde Park was a new mansion the Duke of Kingston was building for Miss Chudleigh, who'd been his mistress for a dozen years already and he still hadn't tired of her. The famous Kitty Fisher was said to be about to swap all her lordly lovers for a rich husband from the Lower House. A bit of loveliness, a bit of luck; that's all a girl needed.

On long bright evenings, Mary sat on the grass in Lamb's Conduit Fields behind Holborn and watched the courting couples meander by. The air was full of the sounds of leisure: the archers' arrows hitting the target, the click of balls on the bowling green, or the distant roars of a dogfight or wrestling match. She was reading again for the first time since school. She bought crack-backed romances and memorised all the long words, in case she'd ever need them. *The History of Pamela Andrews* was her favourite. The crafty wench, to fend off her master all those times, then squeeze a proposal of marriage out of him in the end! She'd swapped her maid's apron for bridal satins and ended up as good a lady as any other, hadn't she? It all went to show, Mary thought. If a girl had her wits about her, nowadays, she could rise as high as she wanted, as sure as cream through the milk. Anything was possible.

In May, Mary turned fifteen. Doll gave her a cap with a soaring feather in it. Between her new life and her old one flowed a wide river.

There was one morning every month when the whores got up early: Collar Day.

It was hot July and the city smelled of vengeance. The Metyards were to swing at last, and evil women always drew a crowd. Mary and Doll had to pick up their skirts and push and shove in order to join the Newgate cavalcade when it passed the Rookery on its way to Tyburn. As always the bellman stood on the wall of St Sepulchre's, exhorting repentance, but it was hard to hear him over all the festivity. Mary had grown even taller this summer, but still she couldn't see the prisoners as well as she wanted. She stood up on a barrel and craned her long neck. 'Lord have mercy on you!' came the bellman's faint cry as the mob moved up Holborn after the cart. Mary elbowed her way up until she was close enough to see the criminals' faces, and their pale necks, already circled by rope. They bumped along, backs to the horse, their hands knotted in their laps.

The cart was heavy. 'Six thieves to be collared today,' Doll bawled in Mary's ear, 'three forgers, a runaway soldier, a sodomite and a girl that stifled her babby.' There sat Thomas Turlis the famous hangman, marked out by his little black mask. And in front of him, as if under special guard, those had to be the Metyards. No sign of penitence; the daughter seemed indifferent and the mother shook as if having a fit. Mary had a sharp stone in her pocket, and aimed at the daughter as the cart rattled on, but she missed.

Then the crowd surged on past. As Mary walked, she tried to imagine the two Metyard women as they'd once been, without the wild hair, squinting eyes, nooses and tied hands. Without all the marks of Newgate. She pictured them as respectable haberdashers – *decent folk, by all appearances*, she thought in Susan Digot's grudging voice – who for years had earned the gratitude of the authorities by taking children off the parish and making apprentices of them.

Of course, what the Metyards had made of Nanny Nailor was minced meat. Mary had memorised every detail from the newspapers she read aloud to Doll in the drowsy afternoons. Nanny Nailor had run away from the Metyards the summer she reached thirteen, but she never got the chance to tell anyone what conditions she was running from. She never found a Doll Higgins to take her in. Instead the Metyards had tracked her down, brought her back to that attic and tied her up in the heat without water. After three days they had started telling the neighbours that they couldn't imagine what had become of poor little Nanny Nailor. Then they had chopped her in pieces and dropped them in a gully-hole.

Mary craned her neck for a glimpse of the Metyards in the cart now: mother and daughter, both limp, bumping along in their noose necklaces like puppets loosed from their strings. It made her laugh, really. They thought they could do what they liked with girls like Nanny Nailor; that such creatures were at the disposal of their mistresses – body and soul, quick or dead. As the years had gone by after Nanny's death, the Metyards had counted on the other girls being too fearful to say a word. They'd assumed they were unassailable.

'A glorious day, eh?' said Doll as they sweated and panted through the crowd at the cart's tail.

Mary grinned back.

'Still, this crowd's not a patch on the one for Earl Ferrers. The procession took three hours to go three miles, with the lord chewing tobacco and waving out the window all the way. White satin, he wore—'

'Yes, I know, and silver lace, you've told me often enough,' said Mary. Doll had never quite got over the excitement of watching a peer of the realm hang. But nothing could irritate Mary on a day like this, when every street, every balcony, every barrow for half a mile around was full of riotous faces waiting to see Nanny Nailor's killers swing. She could smell ginger cake and hear a baritone snatch of 'A Soldier Met a Silly Lass'. She was struck with amusement to see how the West End was growing around the brutishness of Tyburn. To think that the nobs kept shifting a little westerly every year, only to find their streets filled up again with mob every Collar Day! Mind you, some of them had a taste for it themselves; she could see three curtained carriages beside the stands, parked for a better view.

For a penny each, she and Doll squeezed into the top bench of Mother Proctor's Pews; it was worth splashing out on such an occasion. The hangman's men had wheeled up the huge black triangle of the Tree already. 'It used to stand there all year round, you know,' shouted Doll in Mary's ear, 'but it blocked the traffic something awful.' There stood Thomas Turlis, masked and orderly, directing the men to hammer the scaffolding into place. 'A vastly educated fellow, so they say,' remarked Doll, 'though he's been known to squabble over tips.'

The minister was saying a psalm now, but it was quite drowned out by the chants of the crowd. Mary joined in: 'Let them swing! Let them swing!'

At last Turlis had checked that every rope was knotted to the Tree and every criminal sitting on the cart was bagged. The Metyard mother was stretched out in fits; he had a struggle getting the white bag over her head. Mary could feel her own stomach tighten like a sheet. It wasn't sympathy she felt, or not for the Metyards, at least. It was more like the feeling she got sometimes when a cully moved back and forth inside her for a long time, till she wanted to spit in his face.

The hangman laid his whip to the horses then, and the cart began to trundle off. The ropes stood out like skeletal sails; bodies began to slide. And suddenly there was a disturbance: the younger

Metyard woman had leapt off the side of the cart and broken her neck. Her body swung as heavy as a sack of potatoes.

Turlis roared at his men, and the crowd growled. 'Damn her,' screamed Mary in Doll's ear, close to tears. 'That was much too easy!'

Doll slung an arm around Mary's waist. The Metyard mother and all the others were dying now according to the slower, traditional method. As Turlis hauled on each rope in turn and fastened it tight, it seemed to Mary like a peculiar mummers' dance: the heads masked in sacks, the jigging legs, the sudden stink of shit, the friends and relatives and hired 'hangers-on' hauling on the feet to hurry death – but no one was let near the Metyard mother – and the carrion crows wheeling overhead. Mary fixed her gaze on the jerking limbs of Mrs Metyard for as long as it took, till her eyes watered.

As the bodies had to stay up for an hour, now was the time for the bringing out of picnics. Doll produced a sweetbread pie, and Mary ate her half with a good enough appetite, though she kept glancing over her shoulder at where the Metyards hung, over the stained sawdust.

When Turlis's men cut the corpses down smoothly – one man to support each around the hips, another to saw through the rope – there was the usual squabble. Bodies sprawled on the dusty ground, with ruby necklace-prints around their throats. The surgeons' boys, being entitled by law to all Tyburn cadavers, ran in while Turlis and his men beat the families off with sticks. Those in the crowd afflicted by warts snatched at the still-warm hands to rub them on their faces.

Mary didn't want Collar Day to be over. She pushed through to where the Metyards had been cut down, and on a joyful impulse paid sixpence for an inch of the mother's rope.

'Half a fuck, that cost,' said Doll with mild reproach.

'As if you don't drink twice that every day of your life, and piss it out the next!' But Mary did stare at the coarse fibres in her hand. Which half had paid for the rope, she wondered – the pushing in or the pulling out?

On the way home she realised she'd no money left for supper, and Doll was skint again. So Mary looked out till she found a country fellow with hay in his seams. She brushed against him in the crowd. 'Looking for a sweetheart?' she said, smiling like an angel.

His eyes bulged; he was too embarrassed to say yes or no. So Mary led him behind some railings on Oxford Street, and convinced the poor blockhead afterwards that the going rate in London was three shillings. She got rust marks all down her pink sack gown, but Doll assured her they'd brush out.

That long steaming summer she and Doll saw all the sights. They took a party of Dorsetmen to a club Mercy Toft knew where the dancing girls were all Africans or Indians – just to see the fellows' faces, really. The girls moved as fluidly as water. They were called things like Cleopatra, Cocoa Betty, Dusky Sal. Mary wondered what their real names were.

Other times, Mary and Doll strolled past all the print shops on the Strand to look at the new pictures, laughing at the filthy ones. 'That'll come to naught,' Doll might say, tapping the glass; 'he'll never get it in from that angle.' They went to drink chocolate at Bedlam, and put their faces to the grates to see the lunatics dance. Another night, they watched a house burn in Cheapside, till a maid jumped out of a window on the third storey and died of the fall.

Some nights, some cullies left a foul taste in the mouth, but the answer to that was simple: drink another bottle. Gin blurred all the edges, perfumed all the foulness. 'This life's the only life, ain't it, Mary?' Doll would slur.

'Yes, my dear,' Mary always replied, 'there's none other so merry.'

One of the few men Mary ever felt hatred for was the barber who lived downstairs in Rat's Castle. When she begged him to draw out a tooth that was hurting her, that July, he insisted she lie down and pay him before he'd so much as take out his tools. She shut her eyes and squeezed tight to hurry him on. When he tried to kiss her she thought she would gag from the pain.

By August, London was one great stinking armpit. At St James's Palace a son was born to Queen Charlotte, 'a bare eleven months after Young Georgie set to work on her!' as Doll put it crudely.

One sticky afternoon, Mary saw Mr Armour on the Strand, arm in arm with a fat old fellow, and thought she might as well have a go. 'Three shillings for the pair, gen'men,' she murmured as they passed.

The young Scot stared straight ahead as if he'd never seen her before in his life, never bent her backwards over the Bridge in broad daylight with the gulls egging him on. It occurred to Mary that he was ashamed; she could have laughed in his face. But the older gentleman turned around. His plump fingers were ink-stained, and he shook his heavy head. 'No no, my girl,' he said, 'it won't do.'

Mary took two steps closer, as if she were about to curtsy, and gave him the finger. His face registered pain before Mr Armour pulled him away. She watched the two of them hurry off. She was oddly shaken.

What else was she meant to do, she should have asked the old fellow? What else was she good for?

After Bartholomew's Fair in September, the heat began to drain out of the sky. It occurred to Mary that she never wanted to see a man drop his breeches again. 'Time for a holiday,' said Doll. 'Let's go to Vauxhall.'

That evening a Westminster waterboy who couldn't have been more than ten rowed them across to the south bank in their best gauze slammerkins. Mary had never seen the Gardens before. There were neatly boarded walks, and seats with scenes from plays painted on their backs. Fiddle-players sat hidden high up in the trees, and lemon ice melted in glass troughs, and Mary and Doll strolled about and sat slurping their tea in an arbour swathed in honeysuckle, making much play of the ugliness of various lords and ladies. They recognised three purse-snatches from the Rookery, keeping their hands in, as it were. When the organ in the high wooden gallery blasted out its triumphant chorus, the crows lifted from the trees and wheeled in shock through the navy-blue sky.

Much later, after the music was over, the night turned chilly. Mary found Doll with her head in a uniform's lap, helpless with gin, laughing so violently she seemed in danger of choking. 'Excuse us, soldier. Time we were getting home,' said Mary, hauling on Doll's hand.

Her friend yawned and grinned guiltily. 'Got the fare for two, ducky?' she slurred. 'Because I must admit—'

'Oh, Doll! Not again!' Mary looked pointedly at the soldier, but all he managed was to turn out his pocket, which held nothing but crumbs.

So much for a holiday. Mary left them on the bench and went off down the long gravel walk, to where the lights ran out, and the path branched into a sort of maze, and gauzy figures stood around waiting. Trade was poor; it took her half an hour to find a cully. He had lace cuffs that hung to his fingertips, and a clammy, unhealthy look to his neck. But she got two shillings off him, which took herself and Doll safe home across the river with drinking money to spare.

When Mary tried to be witty, these autumn days, it came out

sour. Doll had taken to calling her Miss Crab. 'Have a go at Miss Crab here, but mind her claws,' she'd say, shoving Mary into some cully's arms; 'you might wake up missing a bit!'

These days the pair of them didn't stroll the whole length of the river just for larks any more. Instead, they'd taken to meeting for a snifter and a gossip in a dead-end alley behind Rat's Castle. There they could rest their bones on a heap of bricks and pebbles someone had hidden and never come back for. Mary and Doll ducked down that alley whenever they got word that the Reformation Society had sent out their men.

The strollers had no fear of the city constables, who spent their time in exhausted pursuit of thieves and murderers, and rarely bothered a girl at her honest trade. But the Reformation bullies were hired by their Society to do nothing but stamp out vice, as they called it. One night in early October Mary didn't move fast enough. When the cry around Seven Dials turned into a chorus – *Reformers, it's the bleeding Reformers!* – she was engaged in finishing off a buttonmaker by hand, in a doorway in Neal's Yard. She tried to run, but the men cut her off at the top of the yard. They had sticks with metalled ends, and they were fast runners. They shouted at the cullies, calling them sinners and whoremongers, but they arrested only the girls. Mary was one of about twenty Misses rounded up; she went quietly, wary of the sticks.

At the Dials, she couldn't see Doll in the crowd; she knew she should be glad of her friend's escape, but she could have done with her company. The rumour was going round that they were all to be committed to gaol. Panic locked Mary's throat. Some of the drunker Misses were whimpering already.

Mary heard her friend before she saw her. 'Get your base paws off me, you scurvy rogues!' Doll Higgins was being dragged up Mercer Street, struggling in the grip of three Reformation constables like a sail in a rough wind. Her bodice was torn open, showing one creamy breast, and she had a fresh cut on her jaw, but she was enjoying herself hugely. 'Call yourselves Christians?' she bawled. 'Don't make me laugh!'

Mary was afraid for her and wanted to make her stop, but Doll was in full spate. 'There's girls here not thirteen years old,' she raged, sweeping her hand over the crowd. Her finger alighted on Mary, and she gave her a wink. 'That skinny thing there, for instance; twelve years old and barely a week on the town, poor wench. Would you drag her off to Bridewell too, you filthy dogs?'

The head Reformer stepped up to Doll, almost respectfully, and backhanded her. Mary heard the crunch of his knuckles against her cheek. Doll subsided into silence. She winced, and spat out a bit of tooth.

Mary did get to go home that night; all the younger girls were let off. But those the Reformers called the *hard cases* were put in fetters and led off to the Bridewell, down at Blackfriars.

For two nights Mary didn't go out on the streets except to ask for news, but there was none. She stayed in the garret and waited, chewing the skin off her thumb. Sometimes, she knew, girls came back from the Bridewell with slit noses as a perpetual mark of their crime.

On the third morning in stumbled Doll Higgins, her back all scabby from the lash but her nose as pert as ever. 'You missed a bit of an adventure, my girl,' was all she'd say. Mary washed her friend's stripes with gin.

All in all, Doll was the worse for wear these days. She gave every sign of running out of jizz. That scar that had once stood out bold and brash – when the child Mary used to watch out for the beautiful harlot at the Dials – now sank into her cheek like a furrow. Mary tried to get her to eat a good dinner, but Doll only had a taste for the old blue ruin. Mary feared her friend might end up like that woman they'd seen one night, staggering down Fleet Ditch in search of her children, too addled to remember where she'd left them, skidding on scraps of offal left behind by the tripe men. Last winter, Doll had stood between Mary and all harm, but now more often than not it was the younger girl who had to keep an eye out for the elder, if there was any trouble, and help her up the shaky stairway of Rat's Castle at four in the morning, the boards groaning as if they'd collapse any minute.

Worse than that: Doll had broken her own rule. She'd started pawning her clothes. She was often short, on rent day. 'I haven't your head for figures,' she'd complain. If Mary hadn't the money to cover for both of them, Doll would haul herself out of their fusty garret in the late afternoon with a bodice or shawl, go down to the stalls on Monmouth Street and stroll back boasting she was rich again. She claimed she had enough in the way of silks and satins that surely she could trade a few in, at this stage in the game. Mary had never heard anything stupider. Even the sailors knew how much clothes mattered; that's why, if they wanted to punish a Miss for poxing one of them, they docked every scrap she wore with their knives.

Sometimes Mary bought Doll's things back for her from the pawnbroker's the next week, at twice the price. Her friend barely noticed. 'A girl's clothes are her fortune, Doll, isn't that what you've always told me?'

But Doll only laughed and said she looked better naked.

One night, in the Royle brothers' cider cellar, Doll let slip that she had just turned twenty-two. 'When?' asked Mary, suspecting she was lying so the Royles would buy her drinks.

'Yesterday.'

'You said nothing.'

Doll shrugged. 'I was soused; I've only just remembered.'

Nick Royle was a cheapskate, so all he did was propose a toast and lift his glass high.

'No toasts,' said Doll, wrenching at his arm.

Nick got cider all down his sleeve. His brother squeezed the cloth and sucked it like a baby. Mercy Toft laughed, lunatic-style.

'What's the matter with you?' hissed Mary to Doll.

'No toasts,' said Doll grimly. 'Forget I said a word. Aren't we all dying fast enough?'

In candlelight she stood as magnificent as ever, but at noon her face hung like pale leather. There were tuppence bunters on the street as old as thirty, Mary knew; one of them was half mad from the mercury she'd taken to cure her syphilitic pox. If you were still there at forty, it was under the ground, not over it. Mary wasn't going to stay past the age of twenty; she promised herself that much.

That gave her five years. In the meantime she was spending every spare penny on clothes of her own. It seemed to Mary these days that there was nothing else you could place your trust in. Clothes were as lasting as money, and sweeter to the hand and eye; they made you beautiful and others sick with envy. On Sundays she went off to Hyde Park to see what the quality were wearing these days as they rode about showing themselves off; her eyes sought out the tiny details of pleats or buttons, the altered curve of a set of new hoops. Once she'd dragged Doll out of bed to come with her, but Doll had ended up making a scene and frightening a baronet's horse.

Mary could hardly remember that she herself had ever been a shy girl. Now she could haggle with the best of them at all the stalls from the Seven Dials down to the Piazza at Covent Garden; the traders knew not to try their tricks with her. At night when she couldn't sleep, she consoled herself with the inventory of her possessions. She had sleeves, bodices, ruffles and embroidered stomachers, a brown velvet mantua and a cardinal cape. She owned a spray of silk daisies and a black ribbon choker, one silk slammerkin in violet and another in dark green. Doll had taught her all she could, but Mary's taste was finer. She was saving four yards of oyster grosgrain she'd got cheap from the pawnshop; someday she'd have it made up into a wrapping gown any duchess would give her eye-teeth for.

Something would turn up, for her and Doll both. You never knew. There was no use worrying over a future that might never happen, because the end could come as quick as a wink. The other night a warm wind had blown up and the sign of the Blue Lion fell down on Tilly Denton's head. Caesar had been her bully-man; he buried her handsome enough, as the girls agreed, and they all made sure to be at the graveside, as a mark of respect. (Not to poor Tilly, so much as to her pimp; you wouldn't do him an insult if you valued your skin.) But a decent burial wouldn't be much consolation, Mary thought, if you were snuffed out as quick as a taper.

The cough came with the first frost in October. Mary ignored it. Soon it was her constant shadow, pressing on her chest when she walked uphill, nagging at her on and off all day, raising its voice at night. 'Shut your mouth,' moaned Doll, tugging the edge of the mattress round her head.

Mary's voice had always been deep but it was huskier and darker now, with a hint of a growl. It made some cullies nervous. She tried to smile instead of speaking.

It was going to be the worst winter in years. All the signs said so: birds, berries, the fortune-tellers' coffee-grounds.

The Magdalen was Doll's idea. Weren't they all? 'Mary, old muck-mate,' she remarked one day, 'you'll not last the winter.'

They were walking the Drury Lane beat, curtsying to gentlemen actors and pursing their lips at everything in breeches. Where Mary's skirts were tucked up on one side as the mark of the trade, cold wind dug in. She doubled over with a whoop and hawked up blood, red and yellow against the slithery mud of the street. Ugliness covered the world. She stared down at the mess, as if divining her future.

Doll stood over her, hands perched on hips like hungry birds. 'You ought to take that to the Magdalen Hospital, so you should.'

'I'm not so sick I'd risk my life in a hospital, thank you,' gasped Mary.

'It's not a real one, lack-wit,' said Doll with a snort. 'That's just the name. It's meant for getting young chits off the town before they end up raddled old jades like me.'

Mary grinned back at her, wet-mouthed.

'Think of it!' said Doll. 'Free bed and board through the worst of the winter. Liz Parker went in like a bag of bones and came out fat as ham.'

Mary tried to speak, and started coughing again. When she finally caught her breath she said, 'Doll-Doll, I'm no penitent.'

Doll's eyes rolled, and she jerked her thumb over her shoulder at the theatre behind them on Drury Lane. 'So you ain't picked up nothing about acting, all those times I took you to the play?'

The wind rose, and Mary pulled her taffeta scarf over her mouth. She turned for home.

Doll ran along beside her. 'You can't say I'm not right.'

'I'll think about it,' whispered Mary, holding in her cough.

'You'll do it. I'll see you do. If I don't, may my next sleep be my last,' finished Doll triumphantly.

Mary stopped and looked at her hard. 'And what about you?'

'What about me, then?'

'What about the rent?' Mary didn't know how else to put it.

'Mrs Farrel's no liking for Misses. She'd put you out soon as look at you, if you fell behind.'

Doll's gaze was icy. All of a sudden her face was an inch from her friend's. Mary tried not to look at the scar, frilled like lace, dusted with powder. 'Don't you fret about Doll Higgins, dear heart. Never needed you in the first place, did I?'

So on the first Thursday morning in November, Mary wiped off every trace of paint before she set off – her stomach in a reef knot – to walk right across the city to Whitechapel.

'Night-night,' mumbled Doll from her pillow.

Mary didn't know what to say. She stood in the doorway, and waved her hand, but Doll's eyes were shut.

Mary had never gone quite so far out of her home beat before. She had to ask the way to the Magdalen Hospital three times, and she imagined the East Enders who gave her directions looked a little askance. What an odd thing, that posing as a Penitent shamed her more than walking the streets ever had.

The Magdalen Hospital was an imposing block of stone. Hours after the line of Petitioners had formed, it still stretched along two sides of the building. There had to be forty girls here, Mary reckoned, and she was about halfway along. The downstairs windows were all shuttered – to stop the Petitioners from seeing what went on inside, maybe. A man in some kind of uniform walked up and down to keep them in order. He seemed like a servant, but they all bobbed their heads to him just in case he turned out to be important. Mary pulled her shawl so tight her shoulders turned in, and edged a little nearer to the railings. Was that Con March from the Rookery? Mary gave her a tentative nod, but the other girl avoided her eye.

Mary shifted from foot to foot in the cold morning air, her breath like a cloud around her. A huge cough went through her like an earthquake. It was lucky that she was used to standing round on street corners; how well she knew that feeling of sending down roots between the icy cobbles. Hadn't she often taken on a cully standing up against a frozen wall, or let herself be bargained down to ninepence just to get indoors?

She amused herself now by eyeing the other Petitioners. That tiny girl in carmine and a torn lace-edged trollopee, she was definitely your Covent Garden stroller. The one beside her looked poxed to Mary. If they spotted the disease, Doll claimed, they'd send the girl off to the Lock Hospital, where the food was the worst.

Mary's eyes moved down the queue, picking out Misses from Ruineds. ('That's what the good girls are called, Ruineds,' Doll had said derisively. 'Tell anyone who asks, you was pure as snow till some gentleman took advantage.') The Ruineds had a bruised, bewildered air about them. One wore a little pearl cross around her neck, and clutched it as if at any moment she might be transported to a better world.

By now the thin November sun was high in the sky, drilling into Mary's eyes. She should have worn a straw hat, but the only one she had was red, with a broken feather, and Doll said they'd never let her in with that on, so Mary had had to leave it behind in the garret with all her other favourite things. It wasn't that she didn't trust her friend, exactly; what troubled her was the thought of robbers, a fire, or any of the thousand things that could steal away her stock of glad-rags.

Dressing, this morning, Mary hadn't been sure whether it would be better to look like a respectable Penitent, or a wretched one. She'd put on the plainest jacket and skirt she had, but she knew she still had the mark of a Miss on her. Was it the satin shoes, with their worn points? Or just the way she stood, a little too practised, her hip too far out? She couldn't remember what innocence looked

like. She tried to conjure up a memory of herself as a charity
schoolgirl, her face blank as paper. No use: all gone.

A stir in the ranks; the tiny Miss in the torn slammerkin had
keeled over in the gutter. Mary craned to see. After an uneasy
moment, five women rushed to pick her up. Were they trying to
prove their kind-heartedness, Mary wondered? Two porters in fat
grey wigs walked out with a padded stretcher. They carried the
little girl along the whole length of the queue. Her lips were blue.
The great doors shut again behind her.

'That one's a sharper and no mistake,' muttered a sunken-
cheeked woman in front of Mary.

Mary grinned and began to answer, but the cough doubled her
over and took all the air from her lungs. That was a neat trick,
fainting in the gutter; why hadn't she thought of that? Doll would
have. Mary would have had nothing to fear if only Doll Higgins
were with her. 'Why don't you come along too, then?' she'd
complained, as she got up before dawn.

But Doll had lain back on their lumpy straw mattress and let out
one of her cackles. 'Catch me letting them lock me up in there!'

Mary tried not to think about the locks. She tried to remember
why she was here. For medicine for her cough. For food she
wouldn't have to earn. For shelter in the worst of what was
shaping up to be a brutally cold winter. The Magdalen was the
only place in London a girl like her would be taken in, and all
she had to do was persuade some do-gooders she was ashamed.
That was all they asked.

Her mouth filled with sour water. It occurred to her at this point
to walk off, to give up the place she held in this four-hour queue
and make her way back across the city to the Cheshire Cheese on
Fleet Street for a pint of small beer. Only the thought of Doll's
face twisted with rage kept her feet frozen to the ground. 'All you
have to do is keep your head down for a couple of months and

save your damn skin,' Doll had told her, towards the end of their argument. 'You ever heard of a better bargain?'

A rumour came down the line now: 'They're not taking but one in five.'

Mary's mouth set in a hard line.

Another message passed from ear to ear, faster this time: 'They like you barefoot.' Girls started plucking off their shoes and throwing them in the gutter. The woman in front of Mary was barefoot already; her toes stood out like worms on the hard ground. Mary glanced down at her own satin pumps. Five shillings she'd paid for them, at Bartholomew's Fair; they'd been practically clean, then. She was damned if she was going to throw them away before they had so much as a hole in them.

As the queue inched its way between the high panelled doors, Mary listened hard. It was important to have a story, she realised; something for the clerks to write down, something that sounded well. Three women in a row ahead of Mary – Drury Lane Misses, the lot of them – all claimed to be ladies' maids whose masters had tricked them with promises of marriage. Others lifted their stories from ballads, French romances, and even a recent trial. Mothers were all dead in childbirth, it seemed, and fathers all at sea.

The only honest words Mary heard were spoken by the woman just in front of her, who Mary reckoned was toothless from a mercury cure. Mary bent closer to hear what she muttered. The woman didn't bother acting. She told the clerks she'd always walked the streets, but at her age she couldn't earn her dinner any more.

The younger clerk gave her a chilling look. 'Is that all you have to say for yourself?'

She nodded tiredly.

The older clerk wiped his pen. '*Application refused*,' he recited, writing in a huge leather-bound account book. '*Petitioner too hardened to reclaim.*'

The woman pushed past Mary blindly. She spat on the doorpost on her way out.

Mary's chest was hammering. Her turn. She tried to cough, to exhibit her neediness, but she could only produce a faint clearing of the throat.

'Name?'

'Mary Saunders,' she said, before it occurred to her to lie. Her deep hoarse voice made the younger clerk glance up at her. She curtsyed, to soften the impression. She watched the older clerk scratch the words in the right column.

'Age?'

'Fifteen,' she said softly. It was true, but it sounded like a lie. Maybe fourteen would have been even better.

'Reason for application?'

'If you'd be so good as to put down whatever you think fit, sir,' she whispered.

A pause. Then it worked; the words rolled out like a prayer. '*Most Gracious Governors*,' the Clerk murmured as he wrote, '*this Petitioner has been guilty of prostitution and is truly sensible of her offence. Her penitence is equalled only by her resolution to begin a better life.*'

The worst of it was the surgeon. Behind a thin curtain he laid Mary flat on her back and stuck his fingers in her privates, 'to discover your state of health,' he claimed, not paying a penny for the privilege. Nasty fingers, too, studded with warts.

'Any itch? Any whitish running, or yellow?' he asked. 'Any stoppage of urine?'

'None, sir,' she said, trying to sound as if she had no idea what he meant.

He didn't believe her, she could tell. He went on peering between her legs and muttering. She didn't think there were any marks of her old ailment, though. She was tempted to kick him in the face, but she supposed that might damage her chances. Then he stood up and looked in her mouth, for mercury scars, she presumed. Thank God she'd never been poxed; that was harder to hide than the clap.

Mary had a feeling they were going to take her. She could smell her luck turning.

One week later, she lay in her narrow bed in the ward and reminded herself what a lucky slut she was. So why did she keep wanting to cry?

If she had stretched out her arm she could have touched the sharp back of Honour Boyle in the next bed. Honour was a Devon girl; the Piazza used to be her beat till she had a child born half-formed, and she sickened of the trade. She wasn't a bad sort, but she was no Doll Higgins. This ward was the one for Misses of some education. They could all write their names, in here; not that they'd much call to.

Steps in the corridor; Mary recognised Matron Butler's pacing feet. The Matron had sad eyes and such a high hairline, her forehead seemed to bulge with the burden of her knowledge. She didn't trust any of the Misses, which in Mary's book meant she was no fool. The Matron reserved her mercy for the hapless Ruineds, who got the occasional basket of fruit from Lady Subscribers and had the best ward at the top of the Hospital, with a view all the way across Goodman's Fields to Tower Hill.

Mary had missed the Guy Fawkes bonfire. She hadn't been outside for seven days. She hadn't felt sun on her face except through glass.

The Magdalen was the biggest building she'd ever lived in, and the cleanest. No matter how long she lay awake and listened in her bleached sheets in the scrubbed ward, Mary couldn't hear so much as the scurry of a rat. None of the clutter and filth of the city could get through the Magdalen's great doors. None of the news, even; none of the noise. This was a silent world of its own, sealed off from the real one. A convent, or a cage.

The Penitents knelt in chapel every day and twice on Sundays, being preached at by the Reverend Dodds. As for their costume, Matron Butler explained that there was to be nothing in excess, nothing for beauty's sake, nothing to which any visiting Sub-scriber could take exception. Every girl wore the same low-heeled shoes, the same worsted stockings; even the dull green of their garters had to be hidden by the roll of stocking over the knee. Two quilted linen petticoats and one under-petticoat apiece; no more, no less. Their gowns were all thin shalloon wool, the colour of dust; their aprons were bleached to muttonbone. The sleeves they buttoned on in the morning all had the same lawn ruffles at the elbow – one row only, for fear of vanity. Their long, fingerless mittens, their stocking purses, their needlecases, were all absolutely uniform. Decency, above all: the linen neckerchief had to be tucked into the stays so as to cover every inch of skin, and the cap had to seal off the hair dressed low in a bun, without a curl.

The greyness appalled Mary's eyes. It left a taste of ash in her mouth. At night she squeezed her eyes shut and dreamed of walking the Strand in her reddest quilted petticoat. When she woke and put her hand to her unpainted face, it felt dry as old paper.

But she knew enough to be grateful. Meat and greens at nine and one every day in the clattering refectory; nothing too tasty, 'nothing spiced high enough to inflame the female constitution', as the Matron put it dryly, but it was all solid food, and all for free. The Penitents had to say prayers before and after meals, but Mary was used to that from school; she'd have chanted the almanack if she'd been told to. The tea was only powdered sage, but at least it was hot. When they were served collops of beef, that first afternoon, Mary's plate held as much as her whole family would have dined on, back on Charing Cross Road.

She kept her eyes half-shut and got through the first days like a sleepwalker. She ate, she slept; her cough began to ease. Even her chapped lips grew smooth.

Matron Butler constantly had to remind the Penitents not to glory in telling tales of their former lives. What Mary found so silly was that they were expected to forget the trade, while living cooped up with dozens of other whores! The Matron's eyes darkened with concern as she addressed them before breakfast: 'This is your great opportunity to shed the past and start afresh.' Otherwise the rules were simple: *No drink, lie-a-beds, swearing, gaming, quarrelling, or indecency. No one is kept here against her will*.

It was the drink Mary missed most. After a week without so much as a pint of burnt wine to warm her stomach, she felt always on the point of running away. The water they were given smelled fresh, but it was like drinking nothingness; Mary felt even emptier afterwards. The idea was to wipe the Penitents clean like slates, she knew, and to make them start again from scratch. The plan was to make them forget who they were.

But she had promised Doll to give it a try, and strings of ice were hanging from the eaves outside; the winter was proving just as bad as the fortune-tellers had predicted. Mary burrowed under the blanket and thought of the other Petitioners: the ones turned away for being too old, too poxed, too bad at faking repentance. She wondered how many of them had a roof over their heads tonight. Not that she'd spare a tear for them. *Every girl for herself*, as Doll always said.

What was that other line of Doll's? *Never give up your liberty*. How grand it sounded. And now, on her advice, here was Mary Saunders, a Magdalen fallen and lifted, lost and found, undone and restored – and locked up tighter than any bawdy-house girl.

The workroom had fallen silent. Matron Butler held out the needle, point up.

'I don't sew, madam,' repeated Mary, a little louder. She coughed violently against the back of her hand.

'You must understand, Saunders,' said the Matron gently, 'that there is nothing else for you to do.'

The girl tightened her folded arms.

'It is certainly unfortunate that you've not been taught this most useful of female skills,' Matron Butler went on, 'but it's never too late to make a new start, as Reverend Dodds likes to remind us.'

Mary glanced up. Was that a hint of irony?

'The Governors,' the Matron said in her official voice, 'wish the Penitents to acquire the habit of industry by means of shirt- and glove-making for persons of quality who are kind enough to extend the Hospital their patronage.'

Mary nodded, bored.

Matron Butler leaned her pale fists on the table and spoke, soft and urgent. 'It's also a chance for you to earn honest wages by honest work for the first time in your life.'

Mary could hear the anger sing in her blood. As if she didn't know what work meant. How easy it would be to cause a minor riot now, in this over-packed chicken coop! She could break a few heads, tear a few skirts, get herself kicked out and be back in Rat's Castle with Doll before nightfall.

But the thought of Doll steeled her: she had promised to stay till her cough was gone. So, after a long minute, Mary took the needle between finger and thumb. Its tip was sharp. She thought of what damage it could do.

The Matron set to teaching her plain-stitch. Mary thought of a plan: she would be such an incompetent needlewoman that after a day or two the implement would be taken away from her for good. She meant to scratch her thumb and cover her square of linen with brown smears.

She never anticipated that halfway through the morning, as she watched her needle duck in and out of the cloth like an otter in a stream, she would feel pleasure like heat in her fingers. Out of the corner of her eye, she thought she caught Matron Butler smiling, but when she glanced up, the Matron's head had turned away.

By the end of the month Saunders was the deftest seamstress in the Magdalen, and Matron Butler smiled at her every other day. The Ruineds tossed their heads, and Mary was generally disliked. It wasn't the meagre wages that kept her going, but the satisfaction of the stitching itself. It was a most peculiar thing.

Thread seemed to obey Mary; cloth lay down obediently at her touch. She couldn't imagine what the other girls found so difficult, or how they were so often waylaid by snags and knots. She cut out white kid for gloves, knowing without being told how the leather should lie against the curve of the thumb. She liked the challenge of the more complicated stitches she was learning from the Matron, but even the simplest hem, perfectly done, gave her a rush of delight like gin in her throat. How proud Susan Digot would have been if she could have seen her daughter – as was – biting off the thread as she finished edging the pew cloth for the Magdalen Chapel. And how Doll Higgins would guffaw.

Mary would have written to her friend, if she hadn't known that the Matron opened all correspondence, in or out. Doll wouldn't have grudged the ha'penny to the forger in Rat's Castle to read her a letter from her old muck-mate. *Doll*, Mary would have liked to write, *you'll never believe it. I've worked my way up to Presidor*

*of my ward. That's like a mistress. The others have to treat me
civil or I'll report them for moral backsliding. Only the Presidors
get real tea to drink instead of that sage muck.*

She was keeping her promise, wasn't she? Getting well, getting
through the days, right up till Christmas. Not that Christmas
differed much from any other day, behind the shutters that
kept passers-by from peering into the dark parlours of the
Magdalen. Honour Boyle had her pander come all the way out
to Whitechapel, got up like a man of the cloth. He brought
her a cone of sugar. He kept lamenting, 'Niece, niece, what a
pass have you come to!' as he fondled her ankle under cover of
her skirts. Honour was laughing so hard she had to pretend she
was in tears.

But no one visited Mary. Of course, no one knew she was
there but Doll. On Christmas afternoon she went into the needle
room and carried on with the lace she was tacking round a cuff.
She tried to imagine the man whose arm would fill it. Would he
notice the repeated rose motif, or would he wipe his nose on it?
She wondered how long it would take her to lose her mind, locked
up in this doll's-house where every day was the same. There was
a girl in the Ruineds' ward who was said to have been here three
years. Maybe you could get so used to obeying orders that you'd
never leave.

On New Year's Eve, Mary Saunders was on her knees. She'd
held that position for two hours, and every muscle in her body
was aching. Darkness draped the high chapel windows.

Her eyes were shut. It had filled her with rage to pull on her
grey bodice this morning. There was no call for looking-glasses in
the Magdalen, where seventy-two bodies reflected her own. Like
mantua-makers' poppets, the girls knelt in rows in the chapel,
displaying their uniform virtue to the visitors' gaze. Each wore a

flat straw hat – as if to shade her eyes from the light, but really to hide her face – bound on with a royal-blue ribbon. It was the only splash of colour permitted, and a shade Mary had never liked. The Penitents even smelt much the same as each other, it occurred to her now, and no wonder; the same stewed beef, the same sweat, the same whiff of ash soap on their necks.

The opening hymn brought the congregation to their feet with great rustlings and creakings of whalebone. Mary leaned her numb weight on her hands and clambered up. Looking round covertly, she counted five Governors at the back, with their white ceremonial staves catching the light from the sconces. The Lady Subscribers wafted their fans.

The Magdalens were known for their singing, the obedience of their divided harmonies.

How many kindred souls are fled
To the vast regions of the dead

Mary's fingers were icy; she flicked through the prayer book to find the words. Her voice came in with a caw in the third line.

Since from this day the changing sun
Thro' his last yearly period has run?

As the organ crashed between verses, the cheap print blurred for Mary. Who might have died this year, without her knowing? She gave a brief thought to Susan Digot in Charing Cross, quilting squares for petticoats at sixpence a piece; too skinny to live to a great age, surely? Mary wondered if Billy had thrived, or whether he'd swallowed a needle yet. And William Digot; when would he buckle under his load of coal? Strange that they could all be rotten in their graves and Mary wouldn't know of it. And wouldn't much care either.

Was that hard-hearted? Well, so what if it was. She'd been through enough to harden anyone. It was none of her choosing; all she'd done was clung on to her life like a spar from a shipwreck. Better to be hardened than crushed to nothing.

A wintry glance from Matron Butler made Mary bend her head and join in the 'Hymn on the New Year'. Tomorrow would be 1763; it had a new and alien ring to it. Who was to say Mary herself would live to see another Christmas? Her voice died away again in the middle of the verse. She felt an intolerable need to get out of this building. She held her thumbs tightly, like triggers.

Back down on her aching knees, Mary tried to keep her balance. She swayed a little forwards, a little backwards on the stone floor, like a giddy kite tethered to the ground. High in his walnut pulpit stood young Reverend Dodds, announcing the theme. '*Can the Ethiopian change his skin,*' he quoted impressively, '*or the leopard his spots*?'

Mary thought of leopards. She'd paid a ha'penny to see one at the Tower last winter; its spots were huge and lush, and it was the angriest creature she'd ever set eyes on. Sometimes it paced back and forth through her dreams.

'The thirteenth verse of the Book of Jeremiah,' Dodds went on, 'is a *vastly* suitable text for this, the last night of the year of our Lord seventeen hundred and sixty-two.' His cauliflower wig dipped over his bright cheeks. Mary eyed the puce breeches that embraced his thighs without a wrinkle: they must have cost five pounds if a penny, she reckoned. Her fingers itched to test the pile of the velvet.

The sermon-tasters in the front rows nodded along like pigeons, as if Jeremiah 13 were the very verse of the very book they would have chosen themselves. An ostrich feather nodded in the gallery, light as foam. A good house, thought Mary: a sprinkling of nobs, and plenty of country cousins up for the Twelve Days, seeing the sights, and none prettier than bad women made good.

The Reverend could be relied on not to weary the visitors with too much hard thought. He turned now to the distresses of the vulnerable young women of London, 'how like straying sheep,' he moaned, 'they fall prey to the ravening wolves of avarice and vice.' The Lady Subscribers sucked in their white and red cheeks. The gentlemen looked into the distance, as if they had never heard of such a phenomenon as 'the slavery of prostitution', thought Mary with dark amusement.

Now Dodds began his rhapsody on the most humane, most merciful Magdalen Hospital. 'A hospital not for the body, no! but for the *character* – where these young women may return to the natural state of female virtue, and learn to grow the fruits of honest toil.' As his cheeks turned to juicy cherries in the heat of the packed chapel, Mary could almost see why the little girls swooned for the Chaplain-in-Extraordinary, which was his full title. Dodds rose on his toes now and extended one long white hand in the direction of the Penitents, shaking back a triple ruffle. Belgian lace, Mary reckoned, peering past the brim of her hat. And a fat diamond on the finger that pointed now at a girl in the front row, little Amy who'd fainted in the gutter on Petition Day. 'Though the Ethiopian will be black for ever, according to the Divine plan, *you*, Amy Pratt, may yet be washed clean of your manifold sins!'

It is a sin
To steal a pin.

Mary's head was full of detritus; the rhymes nailed into it at school were the hardest to shake out. Amy Pratt leapt to her feet, now, swaying with excitement. It occurred to Mary to join her, as an excuse to straighten her legs. Had the Reverend picked Amy quite at random tonight, or was it for her pink oval face, exposed now as she raised her eyes to merciful heaven and her hat swung back like a straw halo? The gentleman in the pigeon-wing wig seemed to approve of the choice; he passed his spy-glass to his blond friend – who was too modish to wear a wig at all. The blond stared down as if at the opera-house. Now where had Mary seen him before?

'Here before us,' proclaimed Dodds with a tender wave at Amy Pratt, 'we see a woman – nay, a very child – stripped by penury, enfeebled by hunger, and lured into depravity at an all too tender age.'

Sell it before you lose it, chanted Doll in Mary's head. Mary exchanged a tiny grimace with Honour Boyle, who was picking her nails with a splinter from the pew.

'But as Jeremiah instructs us, *Then may ye also do good, who are accustomed to do evil*,' the preacher recited in the rolling bass he kept for the Prophets.

Matron Butler, pinned on her knees at the end of the row, knitted up her lips as if she doubted that, somehow. Mary could sense the Matron's cool eyes on her, and she had to pretend to be looking at a painting on the wall. Mary's namesake in dusty oils, the Virgin, six months gone, stumbled across an arid field into the curved arms of her cousin. Mary imagined their big bellies meeting with a thump.

Dodds was bouncing up and down on his shiny toes as he recited one of the Hospital's own hymns.

Flee, Sinners, flee th' unlawful Bed,
Lest Vengeance send you down to dwell,
In the dark Regions of the Dead,
To feed the fiercest Fires of Hell.

He relished the rhymes; Mary suddenly suspected him of writing poetry in his spare time.

But Amy Pratt's faint sobs were swelling now. She burst forth in lamentation, gulping the air like a fish. Honour Boyle was giggling; she could never stop once she got started. Mary avoided her eye. The girls next to Amy Pratt were climbing to their feet one by one, infected by her shame, their tired legs shaking.

'Embrace the light,' Dodds urged them, gripping the glossy edge of his pulpit. Jill Hoop, eleven years old and unused to metaphor, cast an appalled glance at the chandelier that hung near the pulpit; she was clearly reckoning the distance. The older girls quivered in their pews. Who would be the first to faint tonight? Sixteen or seventeen, most of them, years older than Mary; ought to know better, she thought coldly. A bowl of proper tea to steady the nerves, that's what they needed. Or better yet, a slug of gin.

The Reverend managed to look distressed and gratified at the same time. Were those tears in his eyes, or just a glitter of candlelight? 'Be of good cheer,' he told the girls now in a buttermilk voice. 'Through the grace of God and his Son, you have been lifted from the *Hades* of the streets into this *Elysium* of sisterhood.' Upturned faces stared at him, bewildered by the allusions. 'This is no grim house of correction,' he carolled. 'It is a safe refuge from your miserable former circumstances – a happy home at last.'

But the girls had picked up grief like a fever; whimpers passed down the rows. The Ruineds were the most sentimental, Mary thought scornfully. Jane Taverner stooped down, heavy with tears; she was a vicar's daughter. Was it acceptable for a Presidor to remain dry-faced, Mary wondered with a slight start? She knotted her hands on the hard rim of her stays and dipped her chin, as a halfway measure. Her neck began to throb in time with her knees.

When she glanced up next, the velvet-coated blond man was whispering a joke in his friend's ear. She wished she could remember who he was; a lawyer, maybe? He was looking down most eagerly at the Magdalens. At least let him pay for it, thought Mary furiously. Why should we kneel here and let him gawk for nothing?

The lady with the ostrich feather was craning over the rail. Over a dark blue petticoat and bodice she was wearing a loose slammerkin in cream shirred silk; the light of every candle in the chapel was lost in its flounces. Her hair was dressed in such a heavy, flower-studded egg, it was always possible she might topple over the edge of the balcony and keep Honour Boyle laughing all year. Her pearl-ringed hands squeezed the pew cloth. Three of the Ruineds had worked the ivy leaves on that one, Mary remembered; a fortnight it took them, going all out.

Dodds plucked at his throat to loosen his black ribbon. He opened his arms to the gallery. 'You see before you, most honourable Subscribers, a poignant display of true penitence. Do not the salt tears these lovely outcasts shed testify to their abhorrence of their crime?'

It is a crime
To waste time.

Mary shook her head, to clear it of the childish words. Think how much time she'd wasted, kneeling in this chapel, every day and twice on Sundays, and all for the sake of a roof over her head. And here she was penned into a herd of snivelling girls, while the sermon dragged on and on, and this the best night in the city's calendar. Mary's eyes strayed to the western window. What wouldn't she give to be out there tonight in London's familiar dirt, the streets strung with lamps as if for a perpetual holiday?

Suddenly the city sounded like a story, believed for a moment, then fading away. Mary remembered the huge swollen dome of St Paul's as if from a dream. How could it be less than two months that she'd been cooped up here like a hen?

The Reverend Dodds slammed his white hand on the pulpit. Mary jumped and almost fell, but there was no room where she knelt in the press of bodies. She couldn't feel her knees; she had the illusion that it was her hollow petticoats that bore her up. The preacher's cambric handkerchief was fluttering in his hand like a badge of surrender. His excitement reminded Mary of a cully's last thrusts before the moment of spending. 'Though the leopard or the Negro cannot change the colour of their skins,' cried Reverend Dodds, 'each of *you* can alter the hue of your heart, and this very night. Heaven', he urged them in a cracking voice, 'is within your grasp.'

There might even be a riot, tonight, in the city; New Year's Eve was always a good time for trouble. Mary could black her face with chimney-dust in half a minute. She and Doll were liberal in their tastes; it didn't matter to them whether they were chanting 'Old Prices' or 'Dutchies Out', forcing landlords to stand toasts or householders to light up their windows in honour of Hallowe'en. They'd once helped chase a pair of pickpockets all the way to Shoreditch.

Yes, that's where she knew that blond fellow from. Not a lawyer but a merchant; Mary had picked him up in Shoreditch one night last summer. Now she remembered: he couldn't keep his sail up, and she had to stuff it in by hand, and he splashed through her fingers and then tried to bilk her of her shilling. 'It's no fault of mine if you can't hold your liquor,' she bawled at him. He threw fivepence at her feet before weaving his way off in search of a carriage, the milk still dripping from his breeches. Mary waited till he was out of sight before she picked the coins out of the mud.

She stared up at him now; no chance of him recognising her in this Quakerish gear. Such a sleek look he had, with the gold seals hanging from his pocket and the snuffbox he passed to the lady beside him. Shoreditch was only a moment to him; it would have slipped from his memory by now. No doubt he had gone home to a house, a bed, a wife. A whore's life was made up of fragments of other people's.

He must have paid at least ten times fivepence for his ticket tonight, which amused Mary, until she remembered she wouldn't see a penny of it.

The Reverend Dodds was reaching his crisis. 'It only remains for these young women to choose life for ever. *Choose*, therefore,' he cried, turning to face them, flinging out both pink hands: 'choose for yourselves!' He held the moment. Then he took a reviving sniff at the nosegay pinned to his waistcoat, and bowed to the gallery before trotting down from the pulpit as the applause rained on his head.

Mary's hands clapped automatically. She discounted most of Dodds's remarks as sanctimonious nonsense, but she did try to remember the last time she *chose, chose for herself.* Had she chosen to kiss the pedlar, to be kicked out of home, to go on the town? Maybe not, but she hadn't stopped herself either. She struggled to think of one day in more than fifteen years of life when instead of drifting along like a leaf on the river she'd simply grabbed what she wanted.

The ostrich feather bobbed, high above her. Mary had put such a feather against her throat once, in a milliner's; its touch had made her shiver all over. She stared up now at the Lady Subscriber who sat wiping a tear from her eye with a square of lace. Her skirt filled up the pew like a bank of snow. Every line, every button, every shadow was beautiful. Mary spoke aloud inside her head: *That's what I choose. That's who I'll be. Everything you have will someday be mine, I swear it.*

Meanwhile, it occurred to her, life was much too short to while away on her knees. She pressed down on her hands and lifted herself to a sitting position. Her knees throbbed with pain and relief. She was the only upright body among the Magdalens; she registered the shock all round her, the eyes skidding sideways. She felt like the Queen, and smiled to herself.

Her eye caught that of Matron Butler, in the aisle, who made an unmistakable though tiny gesture with her finger: *On your knees.* Mary considered the matter, then let her eyes unfocus as if she hadn't seen the Matron. She sat back against the bench, luxuriating in the support of the firm mahogany. The prayer book slid down into the curve of her skirt. They'd be letting off fireworks at Tower Hill in a couple of hours, bright enough to splash against the scrubbed windows of the Magdalen.

'Why such indecent haste?' Sitting in her wainscoted office, Matron Butler was an owl staring at its prey.

'My health is quite restored. I think I've stayed here long enough, madam. And the offer is such a good one—' Mary's voice was jerky. She used to be a better liar than this. Overhead she could hear the dull thumps of the other girls going to bed with the remains of their bread and butter.

The Matron let out a long sigh, and for a moment Mary was somehow sorry for what she had to say. Then the Matron folded her long arms like barricades on the desk. 'If you are indeed so fortunate as to have a place with a dressmaker in Monmouth, far from the wickedness of this city,' she said, 'then I see no reason to dissuade you. It only remains for me to inspect the letter.'

Mary wet her lips. 'The letter?'

The Matron held out her hand for it. 'The letter, Saunders, in which your late mother's friend makes this generous and, if I may say so, extraordinary offer. The letter', she went on acidly, 'that reached you without passing under the eyes of myself, the Assisting Matrons, or the Porter.'

Mary stared at the panelling; ugly wood, for all its expense. 'There wasn't – there's no need for a letter.'

Matron Butler's arms folded back into place. 'Indeed?'

'Mrs Jane Jones, as I said, she was so devoted to my – my poor departed mother,' Mary stumbled on, 'she always said, she always used to promise, she'd take me on any time if I wanted to leave London.'

'Take on a girl who must own herself to be fouled?' The Matron said the word as if she could taste it.

Mary was surprised to feel herself blush like a coal. 'She said she would. Mrs Jones, I mean. She always said she would, whatever happened, for my mother's sake.'

Matron Butler made Mary wait while she straightened her linen apron. '*If* this woman Jones is still living,' she said thoughtfully, 'and *if* she still resides in Monmouth, and *if* her family happens to be in need of a maidservant – what persuades you that her husband would be willing to let into his house, among his children, a known prostitute?'

Mary couldn't remember why she had ever had even a half-liking for this bitter old sow. She had run out of answers, now she bit on her bottom lip till it hurt. She heard a clatter upstairs. Hunger was a stone in her stomach. And then she looked up into the Matron's grey eyes. Words floated out of her mouth. 'You have to let me go.'

'I beg your pardon?'

'I've a right to my liberty,' said Mary softly. 'I remember it from the rules; I was listening, all those times. *No one is kept here against her will.* It's not a prison; it only feels like one.'

Matron Butler's eyes suddenly reminded Mary of her mother's, on the last night in Charing Cross Road. She looked away, unable to bear their weight. A long moment, and then the Matron's voice vibrated like the string of a violin. 'In the space of a month or two, Mary Saunders, when you are lying broken and naked in Fleet Ditch—'

'I'm not a whore any more,' said Mary. The vehemence of her own words startled her.

The Matron's eyebrows lifted infinitesimally.

'That's all over,' said Mary, almost pleading. 'I want . . . a better life.'

Those stony eyes softened a little. The Matron pulled her chair nearer and leaned over the desk. 'Mary,' she murmured as if imparting a secret, 'I know you to be a young woman of great capacities. Your education is solid, your wits are original and your will is strong. In less than two months, with my own eyes I have seen you blossom into a seamstress of remarkable skill. But still the shadow hangs over you.'

Mary looked away.

'If you truly mean to escape from your former degradation, and your former so-called friends, then you must stay here with us until all your old habits are broken.'

'They are,' said Mary shortly.

Matron Butler shook her head sorrowfully. 'Not yet. You're still restless and perverse. I've seen you pick up work and then throw it down a minute later. Your face shuts up like a safe whenever you hear the Holy Word of God. You tell lies, such as this nonsensical story about Monmouth. The seeds may be planted, my dear, but it's not yet harvest-time.'

Mary stared at the wall, traced the pattern of the wainscoting.

'Just a few months,' coaxed the Matron. Her hand slid across
the desk and enclosed Mary's chilly fingers. 'To prepare you for
a truly better life, you need to remain a little longer here in the
safety and sanctity of—'

'I can't,' the girl interrupted, throwing off the Matron's hand.
The words broke out of her throat. 'This is no life!'

The Matron watched Mary as if across a great gulf. 'Very well,'
she said, almost coolly. She got up and turned her back, lifting
down a huge leather-bound volume and placing it in the dead
centre of the desk. She pressed her hands flat on its cover. 'You
are among the third.'

'The third what?'

'Ever since this institution was founded,' said the Matron, 'It
has been our experience that we cannot expect to save more than
two of every three.'

Mary was struck between the ribs by something like regret. 'I
truly mean to better myself,' she mumbled.

The Matron ignored that. She opened the huge volume with two
hands as if it were Scripture, and read in a low voice: '*Sarah Shore,
restored to her friends by the grace of God, placed in service as a
washerwoman in Glasgow.*'

God help Sally, thought Mary; bleeding from the nails by now.

'*Betty Vale, sent to St Benet's Hospital.*' The Matron ran the
words together under her breath. Mary remembered Betty, who
somehow hid her belly till her waters broke in Chapel. How the
Reverend Dodd's extemporised!

'*Moll Gatterly, dismissed for irregularities.*'

Was that the word for it? Moll had threatened the smaller girls
with her needle till they handed over their puny wages.

'*Jessie Haywood,*' the Matron murmured, '*restored to her
friends by the grace of God, married a journeyman of good
character. Lucy Shepherd, died contrite.*'

Died raving about worms, more like, remembered Mary. Did this book contain the full list of destinies, ever since the Magdalen had opened its gates?

'And *Mary Saunders*,' said the Matron at last, slowing down as her quill marked an inky path across the page, '*discharged at her own request*.' She looked up, her eyes as dry as salt. 'What reason?'

'Uneasy under confinement,' suggested Mary gravely.

The Matron paused a moment, then wrote it down. 'You will leave at the end of the week.'

'No,' breathed Mary, 'tonight.'

Chapter Three

Liberty

The rocket cracked a mile above her head. Mary felt the jolt in her spine; her eardrums crackled and itched. Another, and another; the yellow-tailed stars fell as slow as leaves on the heads of the watchers. Spiked high on the wall of the Tower, a Catherine wheel spun like a soul in hellfire. Squibs moved like snakes, straining to escape across the sky, before they too coughed out their guts of light. Dark-white smoke against the black night, drifting like fog, and the glitter of the fireworks caught in it, gold rain.

Mary couldn't believe how cold the air was tonight; it lit up the inside of her mouth like a bunch of spearmint. It didn't make her cough, though; her lungs were strong again. Grit fell in her eyes; she covered them, then bared them again, peering round her hand. Colours she'd never seen, had no words for, were lavished on the hard sky. She couldn't imagine how this magic was done, how the air exploded without killing the watchers, how the stars were made to come out all at once in every colour of the rainbow.

At the base of the Tower, men bared to the waist ran up with tapers, sweating in the cold, then dashed to a safe distance. 'Last year one of them run the wrong way, and stumbled on a rocket,' commented an old man to his neighbour, just in front of Mary.

'I remember,' the woman said in satisfaction. 'I heard there was a hole burnt clear through him!'

Silver lights plummeted and faces appeared again all round Mary, hundreds and thousands of them, thick-set like primroses all over Tower Hill. No one was looking back at her; their eyes were all on the extravagant lights. In the crowd she saw a child with his face to the sky, his mouth an O of wonder. Then she noticed his small hand picking the pocket of the gentleman beside him, and she laughed out loud. It felt like the first time she'd laughed all winter.

The white fog of smoke rolled over the crowd and the bodies surged backwards. The woman in front of Mary stood on her foot; Mary shoved her away. Burning ash landed on wigs and bonnets; screams went up. People pressed against Mary from all sides, squeezing the breath out of her. She won herself a space with her elbows.

The smoke sank. Was that the last of it? 'More,' bawled the crowd. A silence; that plaintive sound of something whizzing up into the sky, and every mouth in the city seemed to hold its breath. Then a crack like a gun, and the darkness split again. Rockets exploded like blood jetting from a dozen cuts. A Roman candle spat out stars. Mary's neck was stiff from watching the world turned upside down. She could almost believe those preachers who claimed earthquakes were a sign of God's wrath. How could the Mighty Master not be irked by such a stealing of his thunder?

When the show was finally over and the sky cleared, the crowd began to stretch and thin. Mary stumbled; she couldn't feel her frozen legs. She was seized from behind by an old fellow with one arm. 'Sound of war, that is,' he boasted fearfully in her ear.

'As if you'd remember!' said Mary, not unkindly.

She picked out a small coin from the sewing wages the Matron had given her, and bought a cup of hot gin from a barrow-woman to warm up her insides; its harsh perfume mixed with the smoke on her tongue. If she kept moving she'd be all right. She spent another few pence on a small pot of rouge and applied it to her mouth and cheekbones. Glancing in a shop window, she saw her reflection, her old familiar red-lipped harlot's face.

Rounding the corner to Billingsgate she crashed into a man with his waistcoat hanging from one shoulder and his shirt billowing. 'Give's a kiss for luck then.' He wrapped himself round her like a flag.

She thrust him away.

'Can't say no tonight, m'dear.' He breathed pure brandy in her face. 'Nobody can't say no on New Year's.'

His mouth was warm and liquid. Mary let him dip his tongue in for a minute before she pulled loose and walked on. She tripped over a stick that was still smoking. It shocked her to recognise it as a firework; all that glory come down to a blackened skewer. How much all this had to cost! They might as well toss banknotes on a fire, like leaves at the end of summer.

Such a hard icy night she'd picked to make her grand exit from the Magdalen. Still, Mary had no regrets. She walked faster, taking the liberty of her legs after two months cooped up like an old hen. The cold made her gasp. Her clothes, which Matron Butler had passed over to her at the door of the ward like soiled bandages, were so much thinner than she remembered. However had she survived in them before? Now her cotton pocket-hoops thrust her pink skirt over her hips, swinging it as she walked, scooping up icy air around her legs. The sheen of her jacket-bodice delighted her fingertips after their long starvation, but underneath, her skin was hard with goose-pimples.

The street lamps gave off the familiar stink of oil. She breathed in deeply, though it made her eyes prickle. The city was a frozen puddle of mud, and Mary was an exile come home. She remembered its dangers but none of them could touch her tonight. Even the names of the streets thrilled her, because she was free to stride down any she pleased. Clement's Lane, Poultry Street, Cheapside . . . The sounds of the midnight bells swelled across the city. She picked up speed as she came in sight of St Paul's.

Around the towering dome the streets were black with revellers. Guisers went by in fox and rabbit heads; St George was busy saving the Lady at two different street corners. A red-eyed young gentleman in cream brocade tossed coins high in the air, barking with laughter as the beggars scrabbled for them. On the steps of the Cathedral, a fat man was wrestling an old bear; they embraced like Cain and Abel.

Buying whisky and an oatcake to toast the New Year, Mary kept one eye out for Doll, who surely had to be on the town tonight. It would be very merry to surprise her. 'Evening, old muck-mate,' Mary would call out, as if she'd seen her only the other day. Was that Doll there, under the apple-laden kissing bough lashed to a lamppost? No, it was another girl, with an unmarked face, baring her breasts to the sharp night air, a man at each nipple.

Mary's legs were beginning to give way; she felt as brittle as an icicle. Deep in her stomach, the whisky fought the gin. Time to head for home.

Hurrying by the vast blank fortress of Newgate she spared a thought for the prisoners inside. Surely the sounds of pleasure taunted them; how they must have longed to be set free for one night. Mary tried to imagine what it would be like to sit and wait for your fate, whether the noose or the Americas. In the back of her mind she saw the great dark bulk of her father, squatting in the straw. What had Cob Saunders's last days been, before the gaol fever took him? What had he seen in that delirium?

There were times in her childhood when Mary had almost believed what her mother said about Cob Saunders: that he was a fool who'd thrown himself away like a bit of paper. But then all at once would come a memory of pale arms like the branches of an oak wrapped around her, and a thick black beard standing between Mary and all harm. She couldn't see his face; it was blurred like a coin worn flat from handling. But she knew he'd never have thrown his daughter out on the street, no matter what she'd done. And it occurred to her now that he must have been some kind of hero, her rebel father – to join a riot and wager all the years he had left in him, for the sake of eleven stolen days.

They'd never even given his body back, after the fever had left him cold. He was somewhere behind those high Newgate walls in the locked Burying Ground, his bones scattered in the general pit. When the authorities laid hold of you, Mary thought with bitterness, nothing was your own any more, not even your body. She would have liked it if there'd been a grave. She could have gone there tonight, and knelt for a moment on the iron earth, as if to say she'd come home.

She let the broad frosted river of humanity that was the Strand take her all the way, up Aldwych and Drury Lane. From a basement door she heard the sharp chatter of the dice, the roars of winners and losers. Two mollies slipped by in taffeta skirts, arm in arm; their stubble showed through the powder. Men of their kind weren't safe on the streets, but who could stay home on New Year's Eve? Down High Holborn, and Mary was nearing her own parish of St Giles now; she knew every stinking cobble of it. The Seven Dials at last: the spinning centre of the world.

The Misses were out in force tonight; *Some whores just don't know how to take a holiday,* laughed Doll in Mary's head. There was Nan Pullen in one of her mistress's well-made silk mantelets, pacing to ward off the cold; she nodded back at Mary and covered a yawn with thin fingers.

What was Alice Gibbs doing here, so far from her beat on Downing Street, in such a faded old wrapping gown? 'Will you give me a glass of wine, sir?' she called out to a passing lawyer, shrill as ever, but he turned into Short's Gardens instead. Mary nodded at Alice as she passed, but the older woman's eyes had unfocused already.

A stumbling baker, flour-dusted, paused to look Mary up and down. He pursed up his mouth as if to guess a price. She'd forgotten the manners of the trade; she almost blushed. For a moment she was filled with an absurd regret for the plain brown gown and apron she'd left crumpled on her bed in the Magdalen Hospital; for the wide straw hat that had sheltered her from strangers' eyes, and the unpainted face, which was its own kind of mask. It seemed years, not months, since she had been a stroller, and all at once she began to doubt whether she could take up her old life where she'd left off. Maybe what she'd told the Matron was true; maybe she wasn't a whore any more.

The moon was full over St Giles-in-the-Fields, spiked on the gold weather-vane like an apple. Tiny spears of ice frilled the high railings, and the trees were covered in soft white spines. Mary took gulps of the frozen air; it weighed on her lungs like stone. She was shuddering with weariness; she couldn't think of anything but her bed, hers and Doll's. The merriment and stale warmth of it. She wanted to share her first fingerful of snuff in months and tell Doll all about the Magdalen, shake off the weight of the place at last. She planned to show her friend what penitence looked like, and how to behave as a Presidor should; she'd make Doll laugh till she clutched her stays and gasped with pain. If anyone could remind Mary why a harlot's life was the only true liberty, Doll could. If anyone could restore her to herself, it would be Doll Higgins.

Mary crouched to look in the ice-pocked window of the cider cellar. A few pickpockets she knew, or knew of – Scampy, Huckle, Irish Ned and Jemmy the Shuffler – as well as a handful of St Giles blackbirds with their ebony faces glowing against white shirts. No sign of Doll playing a game of brag in her usual corner. The door spat out a pair of sailors, and a song leaked into the street, in a rumbling bass.

> *My thing is my own*
> *And I'll keep it so still,*
> *Yet other young lasses*
> *May do what they will.*

Mary hurried on, past the night-soil men, who wheeled their foetid barrows with blank faces. Maybe, she thought, in time you grew accustomed to your toil, whatever it might be. She ducked through an arch. Rat's Castle was a good name for the worst pit she'd ever called home, but how glad she was to reach it. And a little surprised to find it still standing, its stained timbers clinging together like drunkards. Every time she'd ever climbed these stairs, she'd wondered when they were going to splinter under her.

Without a candle, she had to feel her way up the damp walls. As she passed Mercy Toft's door, she could hear the funereal thump of one of the girl's cullies. At that pace he'd never finish, Mary thought professionally. On the third floor a door hung open, creaking in the icy draught; that forger whose name Mary could never remember was asleep on his papers, his wig half off. She stumbled through a pile of rubbish. In the rot she smelt something peculiar: an orange? She was no longer accustomed to dirt; the clean vinegar-rinsed floors of the Magdalen had softened her senses, left her open to every passing stench. She bent her head as she mounted higher and the walls closed in.

The garret seemed empty, filled with a greasy darkness. There was a long lump on the mattress, and Mary bent to touch it lightly, but it gave under her fingers: not Doll, only a knot of blankets.

Mary had come a long way. She lay down and was asleep before she could shrug off her shoes.

She dreamed the best dream she'd ever had. She was on horseback, cutting through the crowd, her heels higher than their heads. The pale back of the stallion moved under her like fresh cream; plaited in its mane were ruby ribbons. Mary's powdered wig was topped with a tricorne; her cheeks were untouched snow. The white velvet of her riding-habit flared from the side-saddle like a river in spate. A balladeer began a song about her, but she couldn't make out the words. She pretended not to hear; she smiled to herself, and stroked the pulsing neck of her horse. Now the whole crowd was shouting out her name: *Lady Mary! Lady Mary!*

It might have been the cold that woke her, or the skittering of a rat in the corner. It was still dark – about four in the morning, she guessed – but now her eyes had adjusted to the darkness, and she could see that the room was absolutely bare. Disgust rose up in her stomach. At least in the Magdalen there were chairs to sit on; here the floor was sticky with nameless dirt. This wasn't a home, but a sty. The nails stuck out of the wall, but there was nothing hanging on them. It occurred to Mary now to wonder where all her things were – her bit of looking-glass, for instance, and her clothes, that Doll had promised to keep safe. Could the greedy jade have pawned them? Gambled or drunk them all away?

Mary stumbled to her feet; her thin shoes felt full of stones. She wrapped a blanket round her and clambered downstairs through the silent house. Cold hit her a blow as she stumbled into the dark street. Only as she caught a stale whiff from the chop-house on the corner did she realise how hungry she was. The last thing she'd eaten was dinner in the Magdalen: boiled buttock of mutton at three o'clock yesterday.

She stuck her face in the window of the gin-shop where four

or five men nodded over their mugs; no sign of Doll. Then Mary remembered the alley behind Rat's Castle. If Doll was working all night, there was a good chance of finding her there, having a rest between cullies.

Mary's steps quickened as she reached the alley. 'Doll?' Her voice was hoarse with sleep. No answer from the bottom of the alley, but the moonlight caught something. Mary strolled down, a smile beginning to twist her mouth. The walls were furred with frost, white as mould. 'There you are, old slut,' she called out.

The woman sitting on the heap of rubble against the wall didn't stir. Her feet were drawn up under her gauzy blue overskirt which shifted in the night breeze. The tops of her breasts stood out like wax pears. Her hand was curved around a bottle of gin. The scar on her cheek caught the moonlight.

It must have been the cold that was slowing Mary's thoughts. She stared at the small movements of the sky-blue gauze. Her mind dragged along like a mule on a tether. First she thought, what a blunderbuss was Doll Higgins to snooze on stone on a night like this.

Dead drunk, probably.

Only then did it occur to her: *dead*.

She stepped close enough to register the signs, the blue showing through the lead-whitened skin. There was no stink; it was too cold for that.

Mary swayed as if a sudden gale had filled the alley. She tasted blood, salty on her tongue. What she did next shocked her a little, afterwards. She stepped forward until she was near enough to touch her friend, to say the word that would wake her. Instead she reached for the bottle. It came away from the dead hand with a twist and a tug. Mary heard a little cracking sound like an icicle dropping from the eaves. Eyes shut, she put the bottle to her lips. Its rim was scaly. The perfumed gin made her gag but she swallowed it down, and kept swallowing until the bottle was empty. When she could bear to look again, the hand was poised, cupping air, like a guest at an imaginary banquet.

Breach in the hull; all hands to deck.

Mary wouldn't be sick; she'd never had any time for pukers. She set the empty bottle down, and the glass clinked against the stone. She made herself look. No blood, no fresh bruises on those crimsoned cheeks, nothing out of the ordinary. The silver horsehair wig, ornamented with a limp red ribbon, was only slightly askew; from underneath, a strand of pale brown hair escaped over one ear. The broad lips were flaking under their traces of scarlet. Doll leaned back against the wall as if taking a little breather, snatching a moment's tête-à-tête with Madam Gin, as on any other night of her life.

And it could have been any night during this long cold snap when she'd fallen asleep and never woken up. There was nothing to tell Mary how long Doll had been here, waiting with this ironical curve to her lips. Had she been hungry? Feverish? Too drunk to remember to go home at the end of the night? Too cold to feel how cold she was, or too old to fight it off any more? Had she not a friend in the world to come looking?

Mary could have bawled, but she feared Doll might laugh. *What's to do, lovey?*

Mary had to try to be the clever one, now. But she didn't know how to begin. This much she remembered, that when a body was found in the streets of London, it was put on a hurdle and dragged to the nearest churchyard and thrown in the Poor Hole. Not a scatter of earth went over it till the pit was full up with nameless corpses at the end of summer. *Mary, my sweet*, Doll once said, holding her nose, *never go within sniff of a churchyard till the first frost.*

How strange to see her sit so still now, Doll Higgins who

couldn't even sleep without heaving and thrashing, who moved along the Strand like a posture girl would dance on tables, all legs and jutting breasts, jiggling at the punters. There was a curious kind of modesty about her last pose: her azure skirt pulled well over her ankles, her carmined mouth wearing only the ghost of a smile.

Mary shut her eyes for a moment and pictured the excessively splendid coffin she would buy, if she were a lady, and the milky horses that would pull Doll to her marble tomb. She knew this much: it was no use to run screaming for the parish men. Doll Higgins would never agree to lie on her back in the crowded Poor Hole. Mary would have to leave her here for a few more days, just until she'd earned enough to buy her friend a decent burial.

Her stomach was lurching with cold. Her lips moved but no sound came out: *Won't be long, dear heart.* It occurred to her to kiss the taut scarred drum of Doll's cheek, but she found she couldn't. The lightest touch might keep Mary there, rooted in this frozen alley. Instead, she stretched out her hand to the worn red ribbon in Doll's wig. Was it the same one, she wondered, the first one, the ribbon the child Mary had set her eyes and heart on at the Seven Dials, three long years ago?

After a moment of resistance, it released its bow and slid free. Its edges were stiff with frost. Mary stuffed it down her stays. It made her shudder.

In exchange she pulled off her blanket and laid it over the dead woman. It covered the hump of her head, the bulge of her empty hand. Surely no one would disturb her before Mary could come back.

From the top of the alley, the blanket looked like a sack, tossed on a pile of stones.

Mary ripped balls of frozen paper out of the garret window, letting in grey dawn and sharp air. There was no sign that anyone else had ever lived in this room. Not a scrap of clothing, not so much as a crust of bread. It was as if Doll had wiped away all marks of her presence before walking out into the night.

But there was that gap under the cracked floorboard where the two of them used to keep their money in a little tinder-box, when they had any. On her knees, Mary prised up the wood with her filthy nails. Relief, like Canary wine flooding her mouth: not the box but her clothes. Folded still, lying in layers and rolls between the rafters, starched with cold. She began wrenching them out. It was all here, Mary's whole stock of bodices, sleeves and stomachers. There was her bag, crammed with linen, petticoats and trinkets. Her snuff-brown mantee was as good as ever; that length of oyster grosgrain still flowed like cream. She touched them shyly, like old friends after a long absence.

There was that bit of mirror she'd got from the house that burned down in Carrier Street. She powdered her face till it looked back at her from the glass, as white as chalk; she needed the full mask today. She reddened her lips and two spots high on her cheeks. Little worms of black hair escaped from her cap. Only cullies had ever called Mary beautiful. *Come here, me beauty*, they mumbled. And why should she have believed them, since they were only spurring themselves on, convincing themselves that this girl was worth the shilling? Mary was handsomer than some though, she knew that much. And she was only tired, today; she couldn't be losing her looks yet, not at fifteen. She pulled on her crumpled felt slouch hat, breathed in to puff up her cleavage and tried a dirty smile. But her dark eyes wouldn't join in.

Between the layers of damp cloth she found the little tinder-box. Not a brass farthing in it; Doll must have been down to the bone. Had the woman been starving, then, by the end, and would she still not pawn any of her friend's clothes? Mary felt her throat swell up as if she'd swallowed a stone. She should have known to trust her. And she should have seen past Doll's bluster about needing no one, her fine talk of liberty and *every girl for herself*. Mary should never have gone off and left her alone.

She replaced the box in the hole, though she couldn't have said why. The thud of boots on the stairs; only when the door crashed open did she turn. Mrs Farrel's nose was even smaller than she remembered. The landlady shook her nest of keys like a rattle. As always, she was in full flow: '. . . and you can be telling your scar-faced crony that no one bilks Biddy Farrel and lives to boast of it!'

Mary gave her a cold stare, and then bent to scoop up her clothes.

Mrs Farrel snatched a bit of lace from her hand. 'D'ye hear me, hussy? The cheek of ye, to come sneeviling in here in the night, removing property, with so much owing on it!'

'I owe you nothing.' Mary seized the lace.

It ran taut between them. 'Then the other hoor does, sure.'

Mary let go of the fabric. 'What's that to me?' she said after a second.

'Five days running she's after giving me the slip now, but I'll sniff her out, wherever she's hiding herself, so I will. You can tell her she pays up or I'll have the rest of her face cut off of her.'

A wave of nausea started in Mary's stomach. She had a feeling she was going to take this woman by the throat and press her thumbs in hard. 'Go look in the alley for your rent,' she could tell her then. But no, Mary wouldn't let anyone find Doll before she'd scraped together the price of her burial. She folded her arms tightly. 'What's the reckoning?'

A flicker of hesitation in the purple face. 'Ten shilling.'

'Damn me if it is!'

'Not a farthing the nasty drab give me for a fortnight. No, nor a month past,' added Mrs Farrel, smoothing her oxblood skirt over her bulky improvers.

Was the woman lying? Please let her be lying. The thought of Doll, hungry for the whole month of December— 'Half a crown for your trouble,' offered Mary coldly, reaching into the waist of her skirt to pull up her pocket.

'Half a crown up your arse.' There were specks of froth on the older woman's lips.

Mary shrugged and began stuffing her clothes into her bag, on top of her linen.

'Leave all that down where you found it now.'

'Every shred of it's mine,' said Mary softly. She kept packing at top speed. 'Whatever wasn't, you've flogged already, ain't you? Bet they're scattered across the stalls of Monmouth Street, all Doll's clothes.'

'Little I got for them, then, if they are,' spat Mrs Farrel.

'What about her cameo bracelet? And her French cloak with the fur robings?' Mary edged across the room.

Mrs Farrel extended herself across the door like a spider. 'There was nothing worth tuppence. Put down that bag now or I'll call thief.'

Mary let out a contemptuous puff of air. 'And what good would it do you, in this part of town? D'you think you'll get Bow Street Runners racing into the Rookery?'

'I've a fellow in my pay that'll put manners on you,' said Mrs Farrel, her voice rising to a whine.

Mary put her face very close to the other woman's. 'Get out of my way, old bitch.'

For a moment she thought she'd won. Mrs Farrel scuttled away – but only as far as the window. She stuck her head between the bars. 'Caesar?' she shrieked down, loud enough to be heard at the Dials.

Not him.

'Caesar!'

It couldn't be. There had to be other men with that name. The Caesar Mary knew of was his own master, wasn't he? Surely he wouldn't hire himself out as a hunting dog to Mrs Farrel? Not even for the kind of wage that only the richest woman in St Giles could pay?

'Come up this minute, man!' Mrs Farrel bawled down.

But he'd worked for Mother Griffith once, hadn't he, the time he'd come after Doll with his long knife?

'There's a girl wants cutting, so she does,' Mrs Farrel screamed with satisfaction.

Oh, Christ Almighty. It was him.

Mary crossed the room and shoved Mrs Farrel so hard her head cracked against the window-frame. The two of them stared at each other in shock. A trickle of blood zigzagged down the Irishwoman's wrinkles.

'I'll have him slice the lips off of you,' gasped Mrs Farrel.

Mary seized her bag and bolted for the door.

'Caesar!' came the long wail behind her.

Mary got as far as the second floor before she heard the front door crash open. For a moment she paused on the balls of her feet. The bag of clothes hung like lead from her arm, and she felt her life like a thread stretched to breaking. She was turning to run back the way she'd come, when her eyes fell on Mercy Toft's door, and she remembered that the silly slut never locked it.

Mercy's room was empty. Mary shut the door with quiet, shaking hands and flattened herself against it. She stopped breathing.

On the other side of the thin wood, Caesar's feet hammered by. The African could run like mercury. Mary counted one, two, three, four, until she reckoned he was on the third floor. Then she ripped her shoes off and opened the door. The stairwell was empty. A trace of his sugary pomade hung on the air.

Ducking barefoot through nameless courts and yards and alleys of the Rookery, her bag clutched to her chest like a baby, Mary found she was still holding her breath. She turned sharp left, and headed for the Dials, hoping to lose herself in the throng. As she thudded down Monmouth Street, weaving between the garish clothes stalls, she was reminded of something her mother used to say: *When I was a girl in Monmouth, there was none of this running about.*

She turned again, doubling back along Mercer Street and up St Giles's Passage. Before she reached the church she could hear its bells; their clamour rebounded between the tight-packed houses. There was no room to think, with her head full of bells and her ribs full of terror. A wind came up, and the golden bird spun on its spire. High on the chiselled gate, sinners with dirty stone faces crawled over each other to evade the gaze of God.

At noon Mary was sitting over a bowl of strong tea in the Cheshire Cheese. Her heart had stopped banging in her chest. She wasn't letting herself think about Caesar for a little while. In her head, Doll chuckled. *You can't let the fact that someone wants you dead put you off your tea, lass.* But Mary wasn't going to let herself think about Doll either.

In one of the spare shoes in her bag, rolled up to look worthless, was a single gold-clocked stocking; she'd lost the other one long ago at a gin party on Bow Street. She emptied the rolled-up stocking into her lap discreetly, now, and counted the money all over again. Two months of sewing hems, and this was all she'd got to show for it: one pound six shillings and a penny. So much for the fruits of honest toil. She raked the small coins in her lap like sand.

When a voice hailed her, she scooped the money back into her makeshift purse. (*You can never be too careful with whores, duckie*, said Doll in her head.) It was Biddy Doherty, a Cork girl who walked St James's Park. Her words were fragrant with ratafia, a reek like almonds. Mary had to keep repeating that she'd been away, and no, she hadn't seen Doll Higgins lately. Something in her throat wouldn't let the story come out.

She stood Biddy a quart of ale, for the sake of the news, and old times. The river was frozen solid at Richmond, according to Biddy; a gang of Misses had gone down for the skating and the bonfires. Trade had been sluggish all winter; Biddy blamed the mollies. 'Sure, they do it for free, half the time, the filth!' And in this cold spell, cullies feared to unbreech in the street in case they'd freeze their bags off, and the war didn't help; Biddy blamed the Frenchies. Oh, and there was a thing: Nan Pullen got arrested.

'But I saw her last night, at the Dials,' said Mary, bewildered.

'Sure, it was only this morning they picked her up.'

'For whoring?'

'Not at all,' said Biddy with a snort. 'For borrowing her mistress's clothes, don't you know. They're after saying she stole them. It was a fine taffeta robe they caught her in, so she'll swing for it, so she will.'

Mary's head was buzzing. The Tyburn Tree rose up in her mind's eye, the bodies dangling like flies in a web. 'God help her.'

'Well, Nan should have known, the poor eejit. Thievery's the one thing they never forgive.'

Mary sat back against the greasy oak settle and let Biddy ramble on. She knew what she should do, what Doll would have done in her place. *Biddy, dear heart, let me kip with you for a night or two* . . . But the thought of lying next to this skinny, spirituous body repelled Mary. Maybe she could do without a bed for a few nights. Maybe she could walk the streets from dusk to dawn in her violet slammerkin till she made a bit of cash. Enough to bury Doll. Mary was sure she could bring in the cullies despite the weather, if she offered a cut rate of sixpence a throw. (Doll tut-tutted in her head. *Never go below ninepence, sweetheart. For the dignity of the trade.*) Mary knew the best thing would be to work all day and night, standing against a wall till her legs buckled, till her guts numbed, till the memory of Doll's frozen hand was wiped out of her head along with everything else.

But Caesar. Mary's heart was thumping again, as if she could smell him, the spiced aroma of muscle under the rich waft of his vast white wig. If only it had been anyone else but him. She covered her mouth with her hand as if to shield it from the knife. She tried not to imagine what she'd look like with her red lips carved off.

She had to think practically. How much would it cost to pay Mrs Farrel to call off Caesar? Now that blood had been mentioned, and his victim had slipped out of his grasp by means of a trick; now that it was a matter of the pride of his trade?

Mary couldn't sit still. The man might walk in any minute, pristine and calm, with his long knife pointing right at her. Was there anyone in the room who'd stand in Caesar's way? She'd never heard of anyone who defied him and lived to boast of it. She scrabbled to her feet now, and left Biddy Doherty behind in the chop-house, still chattering into her cup.

On the Strand, Mary met nobody's gaze; she bent her head over her bag as she broke into a run. Old snow moved like lard under her wet shoes. Wherever she turned, she kept an eye out for Caesar; once she thought she saw him, and ducked into an alley so fast she fell down and wet her skirt through to the top petticoat, but it was some other black fellow, a footman in gold livery.

If she were Doll Higgins, Mary knew, she'd be laughing at danger, greeting old customers, drumming up trade. If she were Doll Higgins she'd pick up her old life like a stained skirt and turn it inside out. But she was only Mary Saunders, and a man was hunting her through the slippery streets of this city, and all she could think to do was run.

She remembered Mr Armour's companion, the old man with inky fingers. *No no, my dear, it won't do*, he repeated in her head. The words tapped like delicate hammers.

It is true.
It won't do.
It is true.
It won't do.

She couldn't be a Miss any more, Mary suddenly decided, not without her friend to turn it into a lark. Not after sleeping two months on clean sheets. There had to be something better. This was no life at all, without Doll.

She crept along by the river, keeping out of sight of anyone who might know her, and might feel like earning sixpence by telling Caesar where she was. In her bag she found a muslin scarf to pull over her head and face. The water slid along like ale down a giant throat. The cold bent her knees; one false step and she might topple into the freezing waters. Every Londoner who'd seen the boatmen hook a corpse bobbing arse-upwards and draw it in – laughing, as you had to laugh when you hooked that fish, or you'd howl – every Londoner knew that life need last no longer than you could bear it. But Mary wasn't sure it would work today, the water being so thick with ice. If she jumped in she might be held up, snagged like litter, borne slowly away.

'Excuse me, but they say you go to the city of Monmouth.' The near horse threw up its tail and released a dollop of shit. Mary pulled back her skirts just in time. This blue holland – that she'd bought from a stall and changed into down a narrow alley – was the only sober gown she'd got; everything depended on keeping it clean.

The driver withdrew a pipe from his blackened mouth. 'What if I do?' He pushed his crumpled hat out of his eyes and looked her up and down.

Mary stood very straight. Did he know what she was? How could he spot her for a Miss, when she'd got a broad handkerchief tucked into her stays, and a clean white cap under a brand new straw hat? Her face was scrubbed like a child's, without a trace of paint, not even a rub of ribbon red. But was there some sort of brand on her, even now she had left it all behind?

'Where *is* Monmouth, exactly?' she countered after a moment in her deepest voice, nerves making her sound angry.

He grinned back at her. No, he had no idea that she was anything other than what she seemed. That's the one thing the Magdalen had done for Mary, it occurred to her now; where else would she have learned to play this part?

'France,' said the driver at last.

Mary's forehead contracted. France was over the sea. Surely her mother would have said if she'd ever crossed the sea? 'That's not in England,' she said warily.

He let out a great laugh as if it'd been stuck in his throat for some time. 'Naw,' he said, 'it's in India.'

She turned away.

'No more jesting, sweetheart.'

She glared over her shoulder. 'I doubt you could find Dover in a storm.'

'Monmouth', he said equably, 'is in the Marches.'

'The Marches,' she repeated, as if she knew what that meant and didn't believe him.

'The Borders. Wales, nearly.'

Mary felt a little sick. Her mother wasn't Welsh, surely? She should have listened more closely to Susan Digot's stories. *Myself and my friend Jane*, they began, or *Back in Monmouth*, or *When I was the age that you are now* . . . 'Wales is not in England, is it?' she hazarded.

'Naw, my dear,' said the driver. 'Wales is where England runs out.'

Soon she was shivering in a corner of the wagon. She should have spent her money on a blanket instead of a dress. The driver called this thing a coach, but Mary wouldn't dignify it with the name. She'd never been in a coach except for trade – 'Twice round the park, fellow, and mind the potholes' – but she knew exactly how it should be. Velvet was essential; seats should be sprung and padded; bevelled glass should catch the flare of the street lamps. This thing Mary found herself in now was nothing but a great box on wheels, with eight sluggish horses waiting to haul it. A crack in the frame to her left let in a whistling wind, and the windows held feather-fans of mud.

The driver's name was John Niblett; she hadn't told him hers. This coach was the only one for a fortnight. 'Your luck's in, ain't it,' he remarked, 'to find anything going your way on New Year's Day.'

But Mary thought this might turn out to be the worst idea she'd ever had in her life.

She knew this much in her bones, she couldn't outrun Caesar in London. To stay out of range of his whetted blade for half a day already must have used up what was left of her luck. If she wasn't past the city gates by nightfall, she was sure, she'd be found in some corner of the Rookery, carved up like a Sunday joint, with her limp lips in Caesar's pocket for a souvenir. If she stayed to bury Doll, there'd be two of them stretched together in the Poor Hole. *Forgive me?* she asked in her head, but there was no reply. She simply had to get out of this city. Escape from who she'd been and who she might have become, from the future awaiting her at the end of an icy alley.

Till a few hours ago, the last place it would ever have occurred to her to go was the city her mother came from. What Mary had told the Matron at the Magdalen last night about a job waiting for her in Monmouth had been a lie, plucked out of the air. She only meant to spin a touching story of the welcome always kept warm for her in the household of her mother's best friend. The Jones woman could be dead and buried for all Mary knew, or she might have forgotten the very name of Susan Saunders. Who'd take in the daughter of a friend she hadn't seen in twenty years? What kind of fool would open her house to a stranger?

But it was this simple, when it came down to it: Mary's old life had slipped through her fingers. She couldn't think of anywhere else to go but Monmouth, nor anyone else in the world who might take her in but a woman she'd never laid eyes on.

'All aboard,' bawled John Niblett to the passers by. 'All aboard for Hounslow, Beaconsfield, Burford, Northleach, Oxford, Cheltenham, Gloucester, Monmouth.'

Along the Strand the coach crawled in the fading light of the afternoon, more slowly than the strollers and their cullies. Traffic had clogged where a gang of apprentices were playing football, their stockings muddy to the knees,

Niblett had said the journey would take nine days. Mary hoped that this was another of his jokes. He wouldn't laugh so loud if he knew how little she had in the rolled-up stocking she used as a purse; a bare fifteen shillings, after buying the blue holland gown. She had no idea how her money was going to stretch to food and lodging on the road, as well as Niblett's fare at eightpence a stage – but she couldn't afford to worry about that now. Her numb fingertips felt for her bag under her skirts. Niblett had offered to put it up behind, but Mary wouldn't hear of it. She'd weighted it with two cobblestones to make herself seem like a woman of substance, but she feared he might hear the stones lurching about beneath her folded dresses.

The wagon jerked feebly. Opposite Mary sat a merchant, his belly bulging out of the front of his fur-edged coat; he planted his knees on either side of hers and grinned. A pair of farmers, husband and wife, were folded together like nutcrackers, beside a runny-nosed student and three underfed journeymen. Riding up top with Niblett, saving his pennies and freezing his arse off, was a fellow with the lean chalky look of a schoolmaster.

As the coach turned up Pall Mall, a sedan chair cut across its path, borne by two footmen sweating into their liveries. Shoppers lingered on the street as if they'd forgotten what they needed, and blinked and stepped aside only when Niblett cracked his whip. And there, outside a milliner's, was the carriage of Mary's dreams: a butterfly in green and gold, resting on gigantic wheels. She pressed her face against the window to catch a glimpse of the rouged, wide-skirted creature descending from the step. She stayed in that position, though it made her neck ache.

Through the thick muddy glass she caught fragments of arches, grassy squares, pale columns and marble window-sills. The merchant cleared his throat and pointed out new houses off Piccadilly. 'They say the Duke of Devonshire's is the *nonpareil*.' He leaned forward to point out Berkeley Square, and his other hand hovered just beside her knee, brushing against it when the wagon hit a stone. Mary shot him a frozen stare. He withdrew it, as if a mousetrap had snapped his fingers. It worked, she thought with amusement, this acting the prude.

As they creaked past Hyde Park, Mary glimpsed frozen water, and a pair of lady riders in tricornes trotting along its rim. When they passed the Tyburn Tree she made sure to observe it blankly, as if she didn't know what it was; as if she'd never bawled and cheered, never bought an inch of hangman's rope for the price of half a fuck.

'Madam?'

The merchant was speaking to her. Mary tried to remember if she'd ever been called that before in her life: *Madam*. He was leaning forward again with a sheepish smile, offering a small green bottle. Mary flinched. Had she let the mask slip? Had he guessed what she was?

'A sup of port, to ward off the chill?' he said.

She shook her head before the words were out of his mouth. And then she sat there with her eyes shut, taunted by the warm whiff of wine on his breath. She could have drained the bottle in one go.

Even when the road was clear in front of them, the wagon moved at the pace of an old man; this was clearly the best these spavined animals could do. She'd be quicker walking all the way, Mary thought grimly. But when she opened her eyes next, London was beginning to ebb away. She'd always had the impression that the city went on more or less for ever, but already there was nothing left but a quilt of muddy gardens. The villages they passed were puny: Paddington, Kilburn, Cricklewood. Mary shut her ears to the merchant's chatter about population and trade, and kept her eyes on the world outside the brownish windows.

One day she would come back. She was sure of that much. One day when she'd nothing to fear from Caesar or hunger or the freezing night air. She'd ride into London again, not in this filthy cart but in her own gilt coach behind a pair of black mares to match her hair, with her own liveried men running alongside with torches, and trunks full of finery lashed on top. She'd live in a brand new pale-faced house in Golden Square; she'd look down from a window so high that people in the street would have to strain their necks to catch a glimpse of her.

'My dear Lady Mary,' he'd call her. A Jewish merchant, maybe, like the one in *Harlot's Progress* prints; they were said to make the most civil keepers. (The first time Mary'd had a Jew-man, she'd laughed out loud in surprise to see his yard all bare-headed.) Or she might have a husband by the time she got back to London; you never knew. She tried to imagine herself on the arm of a husband. Somehow she couldn't see it. But one thing was sure: she'd never have to empty her own pot.

Idle fantasies kept Mary going for the first few days, as the roads began to crumble and the wagon shook its passengers as if they were falling into fits. As the smell of bodies filled up the air, Mary shut off all her senses and breathed through her mouth. She lived in a dream of classical colonnades. Beyond the window the mud stretched away in silence, streaked with ice. On the third afternoon they passed a gibbet on a hilltop. Mary peered through the glass at the tarred body swinging in its iron cage, and tried to work out which bit had been its face.

Every morning she expected some hint of thaw; the passengers talked of little else but when the weather would break. Never in her life had Mary known such cold. Always before she'd been within reach of a source of heat: a tavern hearth, a cup of hot negus, a handful of roast chestnuts even. But this wagon inched across the country as naked and unprotected as a cow. Mary couldn't walk around or stamp her feet; she could only sit still. Her legs went numb from the toes up, till she had the impression they'd disappeared, and if she lifted up her skirts there'd be nothing there.

A peculiar memory nagged at her. When Mary was a child, in the worst of winter, her mother used to heat a stone in the embers, wrap it in a rag, and give it to her to take to bed. Once the child put it between her thighs, and after a moment bliss began to fill up her body like water in a cauldron, and a tiny fish leaping. But she must have made a sound, because her mother asked what she was doing, and she said, 'Nothing', and shoved the stone down to her feet.

Occasional fliers clattered past the wagon, now; Mary watched them speed into the distance.

'It's well for some as can change horses every sixty miles,' said a journeyman sourly.

'If Niblett put the whip to his,' muttered Mary, 'we might move a bit faster.'

'You should rightly be on the other coach, then, if you're in a hurry.'

'What other coach?'

The journeyman let out a laugh that showed his browned teeth. 'The one as gets to Monmouth in three days.'

Niblett always took the slow road, Mary learned, to her immense irritation. And not because of the age of his mares, but his itch for trade. Stuffed under that sacking at the back of the wagon was London ware: patent cordials, printed cottons, ballads and books. The fellow stopped to haggle in every petty town along the way. He always bent and roared in the window to tell his passengers where they were, but the names meant nothing to Mary. She sat in the corner and chewed her lip furiously. Her money was draining away like water in a sieve, and it was all that buffoon's fault for taking the slow road.

She queried the tavern bill at Northleach and got two shillings knocked off it; she stopped handing out the usual tips to cooks and chambermaids. In consequence she slept on damp pallets and ate lukewarm dinners. At Oxford the silent student gave his nose one final wipe on his black cloak and got down. The inn there was the dirtiest Mary had ever seen, and when she asked – in a discreet murmur – for whatever was cheapest, they served her a leg of fowl so grey that she was running to her pot all night. The maid who came to empty it in the morning held out her cupped hand pointedly, but Mary stared right through her.

These towns were handsome enough, Mary supposed, but they were only specks in a wilderness of heath and marsh and waste, ruled over by the occasional tar body hung up in its iron gibbet. Her problem was, she didn't believe in anywhere but London. Even having to name the city she'd left behind was new to her. When she'd lived there, it was simply where the world was, where life took place. London was the page on which she'd been written from the start; she didn't know who she was if she wasn't there. Not that she bore any sentimental attachment to the city, any more than she might have expressed a fondness for the mud on her boots, the air she breathed – or, rather, used to breathe. She didn't know what she was breathing these days, and she didn't know how she was to live on it.

Late one January afternoon Mary's lashes lifted, blinked away the cold dust. The coach had slowed to a standstill. She rested her temple against the icy glass to see what the matter was. Yet another top-heavy cart of grain, pulled by a pair of oxen, and, in front of the tangle of vehicles, rounding the curve of the narrow road, another cattle drove on its way to the fattening fields round London. It might take an hour for the hundreds of skinny cows to thrust past. She shut her eyes again, preferring not to meet their hungry gaze. The smell of fresh dung strengthened around the wagon; at least there was something that was the same as home, thought Mary, with a shadow of a smile. The animals were all around them now, bumping into the sides of the coach. The drovers made hoarse, incomprehensible bird calls. All the world seemed to be taking the slow road, but in the other direction, pushing down this stinking track towards the green pastures of the south. Mary couldn't shake off the feeling that she was going the wrong way, perversely pushing north-westwards against the tide.

Night was closing in now. She hadn't seen a street lamp since the Strand. The smell of that singed oil was fading from her memory already. Out here, in what Mary was beginning to realise was the real world, the greater part of this godforsaken country, the day came to an end as soon as the sun fell behind the flat horizon. All you could do was find shelter before the day's lamp was snuffed out and the walls of the sky slid together. All you could do was keep close to those around you, for fear of the wild things outside whose names you didn't know. Even the snoring farmer's wife, who in sleep let her elbow sink into Mary's side, and occasionally drooled on to the shoulder of Mary's good blue gown, had come to seem almost like a friend.

Darkness thickened. Mary tried to remember what she was doing here, wherever here was. There was no name that she knew of for this particular wasteland, almost a day's ride from the lights of the last inn. Mary could no longer believe that she was on a journey between two cities; she was simply journeying. And for what? A memory not even her own, but stolen from the woman who used to be her mother. The faintest possibility of shelter. Perhaps Mary had lost her wits, like that Covent Garden Miss who'd got taken bad after lying-in one time and had run away across the Heath. The baby had failed for want of milk, but no one ever heard what became of the girl. No, Mary wasn't that far gone yet. But what on earth had possessed her, to take a wagon this far beyond nowhere?

When the cattle passed and the coach finally moved on, it was through dung knee-high; the wheels squeezed and clogged. Mary wanted to sleep and sleep and wake up out of this.

'Fourteen shilling you owe so far, Miss Saunders,' mentioned John Niblett as she climbed into the coach that morning.

Surely it couldn't be that much? Mary gave him a stiff smile to cover her fright. 'That's right,' she said lightly. 'I'm going all the way to Monmouth; that's where you'll be paid.'

He shrugged equably. 'Most folks clear account at the end of each day, that's all.'

She did a little roll of the eyes. 'What a waste of time, all that making change!'

'Aye,' admitted Niblett, 'it's not entirely convenient. But I once had a low rogue leg it at Gloucester and leave me eighteen shilling the worser!' He let out a hoarse laugh.

Was he giving her a warning? She shook her head as if she could hardly credit there was such wickedness in the world.

In the back of the coach she slid her hand into her bag and checked the coins in her rolled-up stocking purse by feel alone: they amounted to half a crown and an odd penny. Silently she damned herself. What was the use of her having spent half her savings on a sober costume if she couldn't pay her bills? The blue holland was grubby at the hem by now; her kerchief was set in jagged creases. Oh, very respectable she was going to look when she was thrown into the debtor's cell in Monmouth Gaol!

All day in the coach she plotted. Running away was out of the question; Monmouth was her only hope of refuge. If she could get off this foul wagon long enough to find a buyer for some of the finery in her bag—

But when they stopped at the inn in Cheltenham, it was pitch dark already. The merchant left the party there; he was taking the waters for his dropsy. Mary lay awake on stale sheets, her mind racing. What if she rushed out first thing the next morning and found a market with a clothes stall?

But by the time she'd gulped down her cup of tea and emerged into the yard, John Niblett was already hitching up the weary horses. 'We'll make good time today,' he remarked, flashing her a grin.

'God willing,' said Mary, her stomach plummeting.

At Gloucester there was no sign of the thaw yet; frost made the cathedral windows wink and dazzle. A Welshman got on; he smelled like a publican. His eyebrows were tufted like an eagle's and his wig was a little askew; his eyes watered in the sunlight. When he felt the weight of Mary's gaze on him he stood a little taller. What did he see when he peered into her corner of the wagon, she wondered? A lady's maid, maybe, very respectable except for her wide mouth, which needed no paint to redden it. She could tell he wasn't a moneyed man, but under the weight of her eyes he tossed John Niblett a shilling for the first stage and waved away the change.

Fish on the hook, as Doll used to murmur, catching a cully's eye.

Mary hadn't eaten all day; she couldn't bear to see her last few coins trickle away until she knew how she was going to replace them. She'd pretended to be ill, but she suspected Niblett could see right through her. In the old days, she and Doll could have gone half a week on a few pints of wine and a dozen Essex oysters, but the Magdalen had softened Mary. She'd forgotten how to get by without food. And now she'd forgotten something else: her recent resolution of giving up the trade.

At midnight Mary was sitting on the creaking edge of a bed in the Swan Inn at Coleford. Twelfth Night echoed through the building: drums and bells and dirty laughter. She was taller than the Welshman, now his wig was off. He had to look up at her. Not a married man, she could tell; brown streaks all over his shirt tail. Mary shivered; the room was so damp that she hardly had to fake it. Her small breasts shook in the hollow where her white handkerchief was uncurling from her stays. Her eyes traced the dirty cracks in the floorboards. Her hair was beginning to fall out of its scarlet ribbon.

How she whimpered, how she swore that nothing but the last pitch of desperation would have made her approach a gentleman with whom she was so utterly unacquainted. 'If only I hadn't lost my mistress's purse or had it lifted maybe – if only Mr Niblett weren't too mean to give me credit – if only you'd consider lending me the fare, sir, I'll give you my word to repay it as soon as ever I get home, may the devil fetch me if I don't . . .'

So easy; too easy. Mary stared into the Welshman's hot wet eyes under his tufted brows. She almost wanted to hit him when his hand floated around her, hovering on the stained counterpane behind her skirt. How could a grown man be so easily gulled? It must have seemed to him that all his ships had come in at once. This girl of such a tender age, alone and unprotected. In the tightening loop of his arms she sat so warm, so safe, she might not even protest . . .

But Mary knew how good girls behaved. At the first touch of his thick fingers on her stays she inhaled as if to let out a screech. The Welshman was obliged to press his hand over her mouth. She let her breath scorch his fingers. He wouldn't have meant to push on so far, but now the girl's handkerchief had come quite undone and her breasts leaped like frightened rabbits. He planted his shiny head between them, just for a minute.

It was clear to Mary that the man hadn't done this in years. She'd have to be careful not to kill him. In the barrel of his ribs his ageing heart was butting like a fish. Her skirts heaved in protest; her petticoats frothed in his lap. 'But sir!' she hissed through his fingers. 'But sir!'

It took him three puffs to blow out the candle.

The Welshman weighed on her like a sack of coal, but Mary let him sleep awhile. She'd have liked to check his purse – to know how much to demand – but she couldn't reach it. Two floors below, she heard the refrain of a song about what the Three Kings kept in their saddlebags, and a crash, and whoops of laughter. Last year she and Doll had spent this evening at the Theatre, then went on to the festivities at the Exchange, stopping for a Twelfth-cake at every stall. But she wouldn't think about Doll now; she wouldn't let herself begin to shake at the thought of leaving her friend unburied in the alley behind Rat's Castle. Instead she'd think about the breakfast she was going to order this morning.

As dawn lightened the grimy window, Mary's stomach let out such a growl that the Welshman half-woke. He twitched and burrowed like a dog. Mary started to weep. The sobs were dry, at first, but she widened her eyes till they watered, and thought of Doll, and now she was crying up a storm.

The man's face was grey with worry. Mary wrenched herself out from under him and got to the edge of the bed. No, she wouldn't stay a moment longer; she wouldn't tell him her name, even. Watching him through her fingers as he buttoned up the flap of his breeches, she scorned his first offer of half a crown. 'I'm ruined, I tell you!'

'Hush. Hush now.'

'How dare you try and buy me off?' she screamed in a whisper. Then, slipping into tragic mode, 'See what you've reduced me to! And all because I trusted in a Welshman's honour.'

That hit home. As he was fumbling for his purse, Mary spotted a reddish stain on the sheet. It had to be wine, because she hadn't had her courses since Ma Slattery's. But this fool mightn't know the difference. She pointed one trembling finger and burst into fresh tears. He'd give ten shillings for a virgin, whether he meant to or not.

The man seized her wrists. 'I swear I'll make it up to you, if you'll only be quiet.'

Mary writhed in his grip. 'And what if there should be a child?' The word came out like a whip.

His white eyebrows almost met.

Mary left the room with a pound, and a giggle in her throat.

All day in the coach she played red-eyed. The Welshman sat cramped in between two dusty masons, staring at his boots. His scratch wig was on crooked, and stubble covered his cheeks.

Today the roads were as rough as fields. They passed a pothole so deep that the farmer insisted on getting down to look at it. Climbing back in with wet boots he reported that there was a donkey drowned in its hollow. 'What an ass,' he said to Mary, working for a laugh. She pretended not to have heard him. She had money in her pocket and a bag full of clothes; she glowed all over.

John Niblett's face appeared upside down in the window. 'Only an hour to Monmouth, now,' he called cheerfully.

But this didn't look to Mary like the sort of landscape a city could emerge from. She'd always thought of the world as flat, but this countryside rose and fell, rumpled and wrinkled, as if a restless giant were sleeping under a blanket of frost. Apart from the track of other wheels under their own, there was no human mark on this hill they were skirting. What troubled her most was the crows. Mary could hardly believe there were so many of them in the world. The outskirts of a city should have been speckled with sparrows, should have echoed with the shriek of gulls, but for the past hour Mary had seen and heard nothing but the choking cries of crows.

As the wagon lurched past a field of stones, before the light quite faded, she let out a painful sniff and asked to borrow the Welshman's writing things. He handed over his box of quills, ink and paper at once. Was he surprised she knew how to write? As Mary began her laborious task, leaning on her knees which heaved when the wagon did, she was aware of the Welshman's uneasy eyes. *My deer old frend*, she wrote. Let him sweat. Let him chew his fingers over the possibility that she was going to swear a rape against him. He'd been hot enough and no questions asked last night; let him do his fretting now.

The road was more like a ditch, really. Niblett got off to lead the horses down a woody hill; the coach leaned over to one side, and Mary feared it might break through the trees like a hunted animal. She clung to the pen. *My deer old frend Jane, I rite you this leter on what may be my death bed.* Mary could spell pretty well, but she doubted Susan Digot could, and it was as her mother, her imaginary, dying mother, that she wrote now. She felt queasy from the motion and lifted her head. A skinny doggish sheep was nosing at a stream that ran across their path; the water was brown.

She returned to her letter. *The favor I ask of you for the sake of frendship is not small.* As they edged down the valley past a number of furnaces, the smell of hot metal thickened. They overtook a shepherd, huddled in his sheepskin cloak; man and beast clearly wore the same cover in this part of the world. The wagon jerked towards a solid bridge of stone arches over a rushing river; this was the Wye, the farmer told Mary. It was almost twilight now, that bare hour before darkness when the last brightness was sucked out of the sky. On the far side of the bridge she could just make out a cluster of houses, seamed with whitened wood. This had to be the very edge of the city.

She squinted at the paper in the gloom. The ink had better dry fast; she'd no sand for blotting. As the coach lurched from side to side she gripped the quill like a knife and tried to think what a mother would write on her deathbed. *My dimise I fear will leave my onlie girl alone in a cruel world and quite frendless.* The words blurred as Mary scribbled. For a moment, she almost believed her own story. She thought of a mother who'd never see her only girl again.

'Monmouth,' bawled John Niblett.

Thank the Mighty Master for that much. At last Mary could get out of this chamberpot of a wagon in which she had spent the longest week of her life. She pressed her cheek to the window, and something fell inside her.

Monmouth? This wasn't a city, nothing like a city. It was barely a town. What had she done?

The Welshman was holding out his hand for his writing things now. As she scribbled her mother's name at the bottom, Mary suddenly registered the fact that he was getting down here too. Pox on the man; could he be a local? Of all the stinking towns on the fringes of England, did he have to come from this one?

She should have thought of that before bedding him. She should have paid more attention. She would just have to hope that his house was far out in the country and that their paths never crossed again.

Mary handed the man his box and averted her eyes.

Downstream of the bridge, trees rose from several muddy islands in the river. Crows were gathering at the tips of the highest branches. One let out an imperative cry and set off for the next tree, flapping heavily, its feathers set apart like blunt fingers. Restlessness infected another, then another. Shapes Mary had taken for leaves came to life and flew in circles. Soon they were all whirring from tree to tree, like needles darning the torn sky.

The wagon creaked across the bridge. At first glance, Mary took in a few pitiful rows of houses; a single spire. This was all there was to Monmouth, clearly. She'd come all this way to end up in a crow town, where there were more birds than people.

Part Two

MONMOUTH

Chapter Four

The Whole Duty of Woman

'See the mark of her tears here.' Mrs Jones passed the letter to her husband.

He held it towards the candlelight for a moment, then handed it back and edged around the bed.

'To think of Su Rhys's little child grown up into such a tall, handsome girl, and her not here to see it.' A sigh whistled in the little gap between Mrs Jones's front teeth. 'There was no lingering, though, thanks be to the Maker. The girl told me the fever took dear Su off quick as lime in the end.'

Mr Jones nodded soberly, sat down and hoisted his leg to remove his single red-heeled shoe.

'Listen, Thomas, there's one part that wrings my heart.' She read through the letter in a rapid mutter. *'The larning she has from the charity school is reading, writing, sowing . . . can cut out a fine shirt and hem cuffs and set her hand to all maner of plain work . . . my poor Mary will make a good sarvant being quick and industrous of a humbel disposition without gall or guil.'*

'What's heart-wringing about all that?' he asked, pulling his nightshirt on over his head.

'I'm coming to it.' Mrs Jones leaned closer to the narrow candle. *'If you, old frend, perform so Christian an act as to take my poor motherless dauter into your servise, I have no apprehension that she will do anything to forfet yor trust, and yor reward will be in heaven.*' Her voice grew muffled. '*Pray dear Jane let my spirit rest easy, knowing my onlie girl is safe in your hands.*' She brushed her knuckles against one eye.

'Come to bed now, my dear,' he said, arching his tired back.

'Aye, presently. You know, the girl's not got a penny. She hadn't eaten since Cheltenham! I told her to order chops at the Robin Hood and say the Joneses would be good for it.'

He nodded again, fitting his nightcap over his stubbled scalp.

His wife held the letter stiff, poring over the uneven lines. '*Yor obedient sarvant and eternal frend Mrs Susan Saunders, Rhys as was,*' she murmured. Then she folded it up very small. 'Such an awkward scribble, for her that was the neatest of all us girls at dame-school. Do you remember how neat in her person Su Rhys was, my dear?'

He nodded.

'Saunders, I mean. How fine she looked on her wedding day, do you remember?'

'I wasn't one of the party,' he reminded her. 'I didn't come home from my apprenticeship in Bristol till the year after.'

'Of course.' Mrs Jones smacked her temple. 'I have my memories but they're jumbled up like laundry.' She looked down at the folded note, and shut her hand over it. 'I wrote Su a letter when I heard she was widowed, I think, and then another to tell her about her father passing on, but nothing since. I kept forgetting, in the press of business. There's always so much to be doing—'

'Aye, that's true,' he said gently. 'The years pass faster than a person can count.'

'She didn't make the bargain I did, poor Su.' Mrs Jones's voice was quivering again. 'To think of that clown Cob Saunders leaving Su to scrape a living from shoddy piece-work!'

Her husband let out a little grunt of contempt. 'She picked a weak beam there.'

'But how fast a body can come down in the world! Never married again, it seems, just wore herself out tending the little girl. Just exactly six months my junior, Su was, remember?'

'Was she?'

'And bones in a London churchyard now.'

Mr Jones watched his wife, bent over the candle. Was she crying, or was it only the light that wavered? He smoothed the cold blanket over the clean line of the stump below his left hip.

'Only think of it, though, Thomas.' His wife's voice shook like a rope. 'To feel your dying come upon you, and your child to be cast adrift on the world. That must be near as bad as, as—'

He couldn't let her go on. 'Maybe it's time you had someone to help you,' he remarked, 'now our busy season's coming on us.'

Her face turned towards him, outlined in yellow light; he couldn't see whether it was wet.

'Has she Susan's hands?' he asked, for something to say.

Her voice brightened. 'She has. Fine thumbs for a needle, I took particular notice. But surely, Thomas, we can't afford a fourth servant?'

'We wouldn't have to pay her till the end of the year,' he improvised, 'and by that time we ought to have got some very profitable orders. The Morgan girl's coming-out trousseau, for instance.'

'Oh, tush!' said his wife shyly, 'they might go to Bristol for that.'

'But Mrs Morgan looks very favourably on your work. Besides, my dear,' he added with a small shrug, 'if we're ever to expand our trade and attract the attention of even greater names than the Morgans, we must take a chance or two. *He who would succeed must first aspire*,' he quoted.

Mrs Jones sucked in her breath with pleasure. Her cheeks were the faint tinge of apple-flesh. At times like this, the decades fell away and he caught sight of her old unobtrusive loveliness. As if her hoity friend Susan had ever been a patch on her!

Privately, Thomas Jones thought it was Cob Saunders who'd made the fool's bargain. In their boyhood Cob had been the champion of the schoolyard, but it was his crippled friend Thomas who'd come top of the class. Cob was a pleasant fellow, but he never could tell a wormy apple from a whole one. Any man who'd pick Susan Rhys over Jane Dee could be said to have deserved what he got: blundering into a riot and dying of gaol fever. A quarter of a century ago, when Thomas Jones had come back from Bristol a new-made tailor, and found Jane Dee unaccountably still single, he'd been convinced it was an instance of the Divine Plan, and he held to that belief today. It was yet another way the Maker meant to reward him for the loss of his left leg.

His wife had that fretting look on. 'And if we found we couldn't afford the girl after all, but?'

'We could pay her what she's owed and turn her off at once.'

'To be sure. How right you are, Thomas, as always. Shall I send Daffy to the Robin Hood tonight, so, to tell her to come in the morning?' she added in a rush.

Mr Jones inclined his head. 'It will benefit the trade.'

'Do you think so?'

He never answered questions twice. He smiled slightly.

His wife knotted the strings of her nightcap under her pointed chin. 'I feel badly now, that we told Daffy we couldn't take his cousin.'

'But Gwyneth is a farm girl.'

'That's true.'

'What would we have done with her?' he asked patiently. 'Haven't we Mrs Ash for the child, and Abi and Daffy for everything else? Whereas this Saunders girl, she could sew for you and lend a hand with the patrons. An educated London girl will give an air of *bon ton*.'

His wife could always hear when he was trying out a new phrase, picked up from the *Bristol Mercury*. And he could never deceive her, he knew, when he did her a favour and called it reasonableness. She smiled over her shoulder, forgetting to cover the gap in her teeth. 'You won't regret this, husband.'

He patted her place in the bed. She blew out the candle and took off the rest of her clothes in the smoky darkness.

He lay beside her, very still. It was safer not to touch his wife. He knew he couldn't put her through all that again, not six months after the last catastrophe. There was a limit to what the frailer sex could endure. So he stretched his leg out very quietly and listened to his own breath. Gradually Thomas Jones was getting the mastery of himself.

Then his wife turned over and laid her soft hot hand on him.

The light of a frosty morning silhouetted the Robin Hood. In the yard of the inn, Daffy Cadwaladyr introduced himself. 'Short for Davyd,' he said pleasantly.

The Londoner looked as if she'd never heard a sillier name in her life.

He heaved the bag on to his shoulder; its contents rumbled. 'What have you got in here then, cobblestones?'

Now she stared at him as if she'd been kicked. Her eyes were black as mineshafts, and her face was all angles. She was too bony to be handsome, he decided; a man needed a bit of flesh to get a hold of.

'Only asking a civil question,' he muttered.

Mary Saunders made no answer to that. She followed a few paces behind, all the way up Monnow Street, as if she feared he'd make off with her precious possessions. The worn soles of Daffy's boots skidded on the icy stones. He'd been saving up for a new pair for Christmas, but then he'd come across an encyclopaedia in ten volumes, going cheap. Boots might last ten years, at best, but knowledge was eternal.

It was Mrs Jones who'd sent him down to carry the stranger's bag, though why a servant should start off by being treated like a lady, Daffy couldn't tell; if she hadn't the strength to hoist her own baggage she wouldn't be much use in the tall skinny house on Inch Lane. Nor had anyone informed him why there was suddenly to be a new maid in a family where none had been needed, a fortnight back.

Scraps of meat and paper were frozen to the cobbles. Pedlars were drifting in, bent under their loads. There were cages of old goats and six-week kids, and the fishmongers who came every Friday to sell salmon to the Papists were setting up their stalls already. 'Market Square,' he said over his shoulder, without stopping.

'This?' Mary Saunders's voice was deep and hoarse.

'Aye.'

'It's not a square,' she protested, 'it's a crude sort of diamond.'

Daffy turned to stare at her. Did London folk all talk in such a croak? Her dark hair was pulled back under a cap and her creased kerchief was tucked up to her neck, as tight as a noose. She had the look of a prude about her, except for that gash of a red mouth. 'It's only a name,' he said coolly.

'Also, I was wondering,' she called after him, 'why is the water so brown?'

'It's from the coal pits,' Daffy told her; 'they stain the streams. But it won't do you a tittle of harm.'

She looked as if she doubted that very much; as if there were poison creeping through her veins already.

Daffy hurried on down Grinder Street. He was mightily tempted to carry on to the Quays, duck between the piles of sacking and the wine barrels, and lose her there. Instead he turned down between the narrow walls of Inch Lane and stopped under the blackened sign that said *Thos. Jones, Master Staymaker* on one side, and *Mrs Jones, Purveyor of Fine Clothes to the Quality* on the other. The Roman letters were splendid, if he said so himself; he'd copied them out of *The Signmaker's Sampler* – borrowed from a painter friend down Chepstow way – and burnt them on with a poker.

The girl's lips were pursed as she stared up at the sign.

'Can you read, then?' he asked, with a spurt of fellow-feeling.

'Can't you?'

The snobbish vixen! 'I'll have you know, I own nineteen books fully bound,' growled Daffy, 'as well as parts of many others.'

'So that's how you get those sunken eyes,' observed Mary Saunders.

He decided not to resent that remark, because it was true. He reached one numb finger under his wig for a scratch. 'So have you any books in this weighty bag of yours?' he asked as he mounted the stairs before her.

'Reading's for children who've nothing better to do.'

Daffy decided to pretend he hadn't heard that. In the attic, he dropped her bag with an almighty thump at the foot of the narrow bedstead. 'You'll share with the maid-of-all-work, Abi.'

The girl nodded.

'I should warn you, she's a blackie,' he remarked, moving towards the door. 'No harm in her, though.'

The girl looked down her pointed nose at him. 'You forget I'm from London, fellow. We have all shades there.'

Again, she made the temper flare up in his chest like a pain. 'So what brings you to Monmouth, then?' he asked pointedly. He was sorely tempted to suggest that Niblett's coach could take her straight back tomorrow, and he'd even throw in a shilling of his own to speed her on her way.

'My mother came from these parts.'

'Who's that, then?'

'Susan Saunders,' she said unwillingly.

'Born Rhys?'

A wary nod. 'You knew her?'

'I'm only twenty,' Daffy protested.

She gave a little shrug, as if to say it mattered little to her whether he were nine or ninety.

'No, your mother must have gone off to the City years before I was born,' he added, 'but I've heard my father mention her. There are no more left of the Rhys line now, I think? Nor the Saunderses?'

'No,' she said decisively. 'None living.' And then the girl sat down on the very edge of the bed, and her eyes were so hard, like a gull's, that he realised she was trying not to cry.

That was a tactless thing he'd said, reminding the girl that she was alone in the world, with not a soul to acknowledge her as kin. He tried to think of a civil way to change the subject. 'Was it a bad journey you had from London?' he asked.

Mary Saunders blinked once, twice, then sat up straighter. 'Vastly uncomfortable,' she said. 'Your roads don't deserve the name.'

Daffy gave up. He wiped his hands on his loose nankeen jacket and turned to go.

He'd reached the door by the time she went on – as if she couldn't bear to be alone – 'We almost drove into a hole that was ten feet deep. There was a horse and rider drowned in it. The man was all green, still sitting in the saddle.'

Daffy nodded briefly before he turned away. He wouldn't call her a liar, not on her first day.

Mrs Jones had always known she wasn't a lady. Her patrons – as her better-born customers preferred to be called – would probably have described her as a very good sort of woman. *Most genteel for her station, all things considered.* Today she was a little breathless. She showed her friend's daughter round the narrow house, trying to remember all the things a mistress should say to a new maid.

Winter light pried into the girl's dark irises, and her breath made a little cloud on the air. She must have got those eyes from her father, thought Mrs Jones, and her height too. She had her mother's neat ear lobes, though, as well as the seamstress's thumbs. Her dusty blue gown and broad neckerchief suggested she didn't expect to be looked at, but she drew a person's gaze all the same.

Mrs Jones tugged her apron straight, and in a moment of weakness wished she'd worn the one with the lace edging. Just to make an impression on the girl. To make her authority felt from the start. If she and her husband were ever to rise in the world, she had to learn how to be a good mistress, kindly but firm. 'Ten pound paid at the end of the year,' she told Mary, 'and a suit of clothes every Christmas, with bed and board too. Are you a great eater?'

Mary Saunders shook her head.

'Not that we'd wish to starve you,' Mrs Jones added hastily. 'You look a little sickly.'

Mary assured her she was only pale from the journey. 'It was vastly cold.'

'Why, this is nothing!' said Mrs Jones merrily. 'The winter I turned twenty, the birds were frozen to the branches. The price of bread was so high we had to . . .' Then she recollected herself, and folded her hands on her stomacher. She should have worn her good brocaded one. Oh, Jane, for mercy's sake! 'You know how to wash and get up fine linen, I think, Mary, and do plain-work? I seem to remember your mother said that in her letter.'

'Yes.'

Mrs Jones thought a maid should have said, 'Yes, madam.' But it was only a little thing, and the girl was new to service. 'Any household affair you may be ignorant of,' she swept on, 'I can soon instruct you. You have only to ask. For now you'll help our maid Abi with cleaning and such, as well as working with your needle alongside of me. All I require is that you be diligent, and neat, and . . .' She strained for another word. 'Honest,' she finished with satisfaction.

The girl inclined her head.

Mrs Jones remembered a line from one of her novels that had an impressive ring to it. 'I can't abide deceit or any such nastiness,' she assured the girl, 'for if I catch a servant in a lie, you see, I can never depend on them again.'

Another nod.

'Oh, and I was forgetting, I have a book for you—' She scrabbled in her hanging pocket, and drew the worn volume up through her waist seam. '*The Whole Duty of Woman*,' she pronounced, putting it into the girl's hand. 'Most improving.'

Before Mary Saunders could thank her, a small child ran through the doorway, and Mrs Jones scooped her up. Briefly she dipped her face into the child's buttermilk hair. 'This is Hetta, our darling,' she said, and then regretted the word.

The new maid smiled guardedly.

'Muda?'

'What is it, child?'

'Can I go out in the Meadow?'

'Not today, Hetta. It's still thick with snow. I named her Henrietta for the heroine of Mrs Lennox's romance,' Mrs Jones confided, turning to Mary Saunders and shifting the plump child to her other hip. 'I was reading it all through my confinement. The full of a fortnight in bed I was . . .' But then she remembered she was speaking to a girl of fifteen; she blushed faintly, and rested her chin against her child's hot round face. Hetta struggled in her arms; Mrs Jones let her slither down her skirts. She straightened up and pressed her fists into the small of her back. 'Say good-day to our new maid Mary, *cariad*.'

At four, Hetta was generally wary of strangers. But when the London girl bent and extended one hand, Hetta seized and shook it. Mary Saunders's mouth loosened into a smile, and for a moment she was the dead spit of Su Rhys.

'You must be a good girl for Mary, my dear,' Mrs Jones told her daughter gently, 'since she's just lost her mother. Can you imagine that?'

Hetta's grin slid away; she mirrored her mother's grave face.

'Gone off to heaven, the poor woman has,' added Mrs Jones.

'In a chariot, like my brother?'

Mrs Jones winced imperceptibly. 'That's right, my dear.' Turning to Mary she lowered her voice and asked, 'Your mother didn't suffer long, did she?'

The girl shook her head, mute.

Mrs Jones covered her mouth with her hand for a moment. Listen to her, harping on the girl's grief. 'Well, my dear, if you be half as worthy a creature as poor Su, we shall get on very well together. Let you come downstairs now and meet Hetta's nurse. Mrs Ash is . . . a very Christian woman,' she added uncertainly.

The girl's thick eyebrows lifted; there was something almost ironic about them.

On the stairs, Mrs Jones racked her brain for any further advice suitable to the occasion. 'Oh, and snuff, Mary.'

'Snuff?' repeated the girl.

'I must warn you against it. A very costly habit and pernicious to the health.'

The girl assured her she never touched snuff. Was that the ghost of a laugh, behind those strangely familiar lips?

Mrs Jones always heard her knees creak on the steep staircase. She moved faster. Forty-three wasn't so very old.

'Hetta is your only child?' asked Mary.

Had the girl read her mind? 'That's right,' answered Mrs Jones lightly.

She still bled, sometimes. Forty-three wasn't impossible. There had to be the kernel of another child inside her. There had to be a son.

It was the longest morning of Mary's life. Dogged and straight-backed, she moved through her tasks in the order allotted. She'd never lived anywhere like this. Everything in the high, narrow, terraced house was to be cleaned over and over, it seemed, week after week. Susan Digot had never managed to ward off dirt this way, in their basement on Charing Cross Road where ants came up the walls every summer.

Not that Mary told Mrs Jones that. She let the woman assume that Mary and her widowed mother had lived together in a quiet, respectable way until a sudden fever had carried off Su Saunders before she could make any provision for her dearest daughter except the letter she wrote her old friend. Whenever Mrs Jones's questions probed too far, that first morning, Mary bent her head as if grief were welling up inside her.

The wretched woman seemed to feel that the best cure for a motherless girl was to be kept busy every minute of the day. There were so many petty rules to learn. At nine o'clock – after they'd all been up and working for two hours already – Mary was to ring the little bell for breakfast. She couldn't see the need for it, in such a small house, but 'the master prefers it,' Mrs Jones explained; 'he says it raises the tone.'

On Mary's way to breakfast Mr Jones overtook her in the passage, moving as lithely as any man. He swung into the tiny parlour and took the head of the table, next to the Chinese tea-kettle bubbling over its tiny flame. His oiled birch crutches lay under his chair like dogs. Mary had never eaten with a one-legged man before. She had to resist the temptation to bend down and look under the table at his stump, as if she were at a freak-show.

Brown curls escaped from the edges of the little manservant's short wig. At least Daffy was less unpleasant to look at than the dried-up wet-nurse Mrs Ash, who hunched over the table to examine the newcomer. Mary glanced down nervously at her blue holland gown; she'd brushed the dirt out of it as best she could.

'Do maids wear hoops, then, in London?' enquired Mrs Ash.

Mary swallowed her tea with difficulty. 'I was never a maid in London.'

'I see.' The words appeared like frost.

Mr Jones tapped the table with his fork. 'Now, now, good Mrs Ash.'

Good Mrs Ash's grey skirts sagged as much as her breasts. Her chest resembled a salt-barrel, Mary decided. She couldn't be more than forty, but she had the manner of an old woman.

'We must all make Mary welcome,' the mistress added quietly. 'She's never set foot in her own town before, can you imagine?'

Mary tried to look grateful. *Her own town*; what nonsense. As if this misbegotten spattering of streets meant anything to her. And she'd be damned if she'd give up wearing her improvers, just to fit in with these country-dwellers!

Abi brought in the porridge, moving like a sleepwalker. Hetta babbled on about wanting toasted crusts instead, but the maid-of-all-work didn't seem to hear the child. She gave no sign of understanding English, in fact. How strange for her to have ended up here in Monmouth; hers was the first dark face Mary had seen since the Strand. Mary watched Abi sideways as she served them, the coal gloss of her standing out against the whitewashed walls. She had cheekbones you could cut butter with. She disappeared back into the kitchen as soon as all the porridge was ladled into their bowls. Would she eat afterwards, alone?

'Is Abi an African?' asked Mary, once the door had shut.

'Oh, I don't think so,' said the mistress, sounding a little alarmed.

'On the contrary, my dear,' said Mr Jones to his wife between two spoonfuls of porridge, 'Angola is in Africa, you remember?'

She slapped her head in reproach for her forgetfulness.

'We believe Abi's origins are Angolan, you see,' said Daffy, addressing himself to Mary, 'but she was brought up a Barbadian.'

What a strutting little scholar he was! What was it Doll used to say about bookish men? *Much learning, little prick.* Mary had to hide her smile. She tried to clear her mind of the thought, in case it might show on her face. All that was behind her now, she told herself. These days she had to think like a maid, in every sense of the word.

'Barbarian,' said the nurse suddenly.

'I must correct you, Mrs Ash,' said Daffy politely, 'the word is Barbadian. From the land of Barbados.'

'And I said barbarian,' Mrs Ash repeated. 'I've said it before, but it's no less of a sacred duty to say it again. No good can come of keeping a heathen at such close quarters with a Christian child.'

Hearing herself mentioned, Hetta bounced in her chair. As Mary watched, Mrs Jones's face suddenly sagged with fatigue. 'Please, Mrs Ash—'

The nurse interrupted her mistress. 'It's not my place to

complain, madam, but I can't help but observe it causes perplexity and confusion. The child is all eyes and ears. She ran in to me the other day, asking what colour our Lord might be!' Mrs Ash's pale eyes stood out in her face.

Mrs Jones's lips moved as if formulating an answer, but her husband put his hand over her own.

'I compassionated the woman at first, as was my duty,' Mrs Ash ran on, 'but when I heard Daffy's father had offered to baptise her, and she'd stood out against it—'

The door opened and Abi drifted in with a tray to take away the bowls. The silence tingled. 'We do appreciate your concern, Mrs Ash,' said Mr Jones thoughtfully after a minute, 'and we'll speak of this again.'

Mary checked Abi's face to see if she had heard anything, but the maid's lashes were lowered.

'Yes, sir,' said the nurse, almost meek.

There was silence, then, after Abi had gone back into the kitchen. Mary watched the family avoid each other's eyes. It was like sitting down to a game of brag where she was the only stranger, and had no idea what cards were in play.

Mrs Ash took out a tiny dog-eared Bible now. It was just like the ones given out at the Magdalen, but Mary pushed that memory to a distance. Her eyes caught those of the master. (*Is the leg all he's lost?* Doll wondered lewdly in Mary's head.) He smiled, but she didn't trust herself to smile back, in case it looked flirtatious. She made a mental note to practise the smile of an innocent orphan in front of the mirror.

The porridge sat on her stomach like stone.

A new rule of the house was that no matter what task Mary might be engaged in, she had to answer the door. Having a London girl in a lace-edged apron to greet the patrons clearly delighted Mr Jones: 'It'll give such a genteel impression that no one will raise an eyebrow at our prices!' So even if he happened to be right behind the front door when he heard a knock, he would call in to Mary and duck back into the Stays Room.

But the first time she answered, that morning, it was not a patron at all, but a crowd of farm boys. They made the most peculiar noises as they dragged a dirty great machine, decked with white ribbons. Mary's first instinct was to shut the door on them, but Mrs Jones hurried along the hall to stop her. 'It's Plough Monday, my dear; had you forgotten?'

Mary stared at her.

'Didn't your mother ever tell you about it?' said the mistress amazedly.

Mary watched Mrs Jones hand a farthing to every stripling who had his muddy hand held out. One of them was done up in a skirt and apron, and was that rouge on his cheeks? What a strange part of the world this was, where mollies walked the streets in broad day! Another boy called the painted one Bessie. They started singing some bit of nonsense and pushed the molly-boy forward to give Mrs Jones a kiss. Stranger still, it seemed to Mary – she let him.

When the door was shut Mrs Jones turned to Mary. Her colour was high, against her high-necked black jacket; she looked like a girl. 'It's for the harvest, don't you know.'

'The harvest?'

'The plough must go round all the houses for a blessing before the spring sowing starts, you see, or the grain won't thrive.'

Mary couldn't help letting out a little giggle. 'You don't really believe that, do you?'

'Well,' said Mrs Jones, stiffly.

Mary knew she'd gone too far; she was going to lose her place on her first day. Her stomach sank.

'I couldn't say, for sure, if it does much good.' The mistress fiddled with the string of her apron like a child, then her small eyes brightened again. 'But it does no harm, surely!'

'Surely not,' echoed Mary. She went back to the parlour where she'd been scrubbing rugs with damp tea-leaves. There was no reasoning with country folk. They would hold to their charms and customs till the Last Trumpet. Now she thought of it, Susan Digot always used to throw salt over her shoulder, even when they couldn't afford to buy more. And once, Mary remembered, when she'd dropped a tiny mirror and cracked it, her mother had knelt down on the floor and wept for the *seven more years' bad luck.*

The world was changing, Mary was confident of that much; already it was not the same one as her mother had grown up in. But in a backwater like Monmouth they'd clearly never heard about the changes, and wouldn't believe in them even if they had.

Her breath rose as she scraped up the dirty tea-leaves; her ribs protested against her tight-laced stays. Mrs Ash was right about one thing: hoops were a hindrance when you were down on your knees. But since when did a young woman dress just for comfort, like any dog or cat?

She shook a stray lock of hair out of her eyes, and saw Abi in the doorway, standing like a pillar. She hadn't heard her come in; the maid-of-all-work moved from room to room like a ghost. Perhaps she was only newly arrived from the plantations? She seemed a mute lump of a creature.

'Mistress send me for help you,' said Abi at last. She had a heavy accent but at least she spoke English. Her voice was not a girl's, Mary realised; she had to be thirty at least.

'Very good,' said Mary with a civil smile. It was best to take charge from the start, she decided all at once. This woman was twice her age, and might prove difficult. Mary saw herself as a higher sort of maid – an apprentice dressmaker, really – and even if some of her duties overlapped with those of the maid-of-all-work, there was to be no confusing them. So she pointed to the biggest rug, a brown square heavy with dust.

There was a pause. Abi's lip curled a little, and then she knelt down at the edge of the rug.

The two laboured away on their hands and knees in silence, but sometimes when Mary turned her head to ease her stiff neck, Abi was watching her with those huge white eyes. Her stays were leather; Mary could glimpse them through a hole under her arm. The maid's skirt hung so flat, she mustn't have so much as a petticoat under it, the poor wretch. Her left hand had a pink gash in the middle of the brown, Mary noticed – right through from front to back. 'What happened to your hand?' she asked.

No answer.

Mary tossed her head. She wasn't so desperate for conversation with this sulky creature anyway.

Back in the scullery, Abi immersed her hands in the basin of kettle water and let out a slow gasp. The relief of the heat filled her like a pain, from the knuckles up. She'd been more than eight years in this country, but she would never get used to the cold till the day she died. Already this month the mistress had started talking about the whiff of thaw in the air, but Abi couldn't smell it. All her nostrils caught was snow and dirt outside, fire and bodies in the house. At each daybreak, Abi was too immersed in work to notice what the air smelt like, and before she got around to looking out of a window, it seemed, the afternoon's portion of light was used up and it was night again. As far as she could tell, this country was locked in perpetual winter. Even in the season they called summer, the sun was thin and watery; it never soaked into her skin.

'Abi?' The mistress's voice on the stairs. The maid tipped the hot water into the slop bucket and went into the tiny pantry for the bacon.

Abi wasn't her real name, of course, only the sound she answered to in the house on Inch Lane, except for the times she pretended she hadn't heard. She'd had as many names as fingers, over the course of her thirty years. When she was an baby in Africa she'd had an infant name. Then when she'd started turning into a woman the old ones had picked her a name that meant *bush heavy with berries*. She hadn't heard another mouth form the sounds of that true name since she'd been hoisted on to the ship – clinging to her mother's fingers – at nine years old. On the voyage to Barbados she'd had no name at all; she'd been all at sea, slipping down a gap between the old self and the new.

The Joneses called her Abi because it was short for Abigail, which meant a maidservant, according to Mrs Jones. Abi remembered other names that other masters and mistresses had given her, back in Barbados. Each of them hovered round her head for a year or two: *Phibba*, *Jennie*, *Lu*. They made no difference. She had cast a name off like a shift, every time she'd changed hands.

Mrs Jones ran in on light feet. 'Abi? Don't forget to rinse the lettuce well this time, won't you?'

Abi nodded mutely, and carried on trimming the bacon. Lettuce! You might as well chew on the grass of the field for all the good it would yield up. But it wasn't her place to comment. She'd learned the first rule of survival, back on her first plantation. *Keep your head down, child*, her mother had told her before she died of the yaws; *don't ever meet nobody's eye*.

The bacon was purple, like a bruise. It had taken Abi years to learn to cook this food. Even the names were peculiar and unappetising: *milk pottage, mess of dried pease, chine of mutton with egg-sauce, quaking pudding*. None of this pallid food had any sun in it; even the dried pepper and cinnamon kept in jars on the chimney piece were only ghost spices. When Abi sat down to her own food in the kitchen after each meal – she ate alone and preferred it that way – her plate of leftovers tasted of nothing; her mouth never even began to tingle.

There was the newcomer, the London girl, standing in the doorway with a slightly uneasy look. Hoping to find the kitchen empty, was she? Abi carried on carving hard rind off the bacon and pretended not to notice the girl's presence.

'Ah, Abi,' said Mary Saunders as if she were the mistress, 'I just came down for a cup of small beer.'

Abi let her head swing like a bell, meaning no.

The girl drew herself up. 'All I want—'

'Nothing till dinner,' Abi interrupted. 'Is rules.'

Mary Saunders chewed her upper lip.

'Anything go missing, I get blame,' added Abi levelly.

'Quite so. But those dusty rugs have given me a dreadful thirst; I'm sure Mrs Jones would agree that it's a special case—'

'You nobody special,' pronounced Abi, looking the girl in the eye.

A long pause. The Londoner's pupils were black as cinders. She turned on her heel without a word.

Trouble: Abi could smell it like something gone bad under a floorboard. That was foolish, what she'd just done. She'd let her temper rise. The day had gone wrong from the start; it was that Ash woman's fault for looking skew-ways at her with those colourless eyes at breakfast. Just now Abi had been provoked into forgetting another rule of survival that her mother had taught her: *whatever white folks says, is so*.

By one Mary's stomach was grumbling. Dinner was at two, in the parlour. Salt bacon in pottage, with raw leaves; Mary lifted them with her fork, to check for slugs. She'd never eaten anything so green in her life.

'You won't be used to fresh salads, Mary?' said the mistress. 'They're a gift from Mrs Ha'penny's own greenhouse, imagine!'

Mary smiled back as if she were grateful. She folded a leaf into a tiny parcel and washed it down with weak beer.

Conversation was mostly a matter of 'Pass the pepper-pot, would you, Daffy?' or 'Pickles, Mr Jones?' Occasionally the master expounded his views on corruption in His Majesty's Government, or the Dutch interference with trade. Mrs Ash didn't say a word out loud; when she wasn't whispering orders to Hetta, her lips moved silently in prayer, like a lunatic. The Joneses let the child steal titbits from their plates, as if she weren't plump enough already. There must have been more than one that died, Mary realised suddenly. To be married twenty years, and only have one child living – that wasn't much of a score.

Well, if they lost this one, it wouldn't be for want of feeding. Mary watched the child's mouth stretch around a vast lettuce leaf, and found herself grinning. Hetta caught her eye, and froze. Mary screwed up her nose. Hetta did the same, and laughed silently, open-jawed, the leaf hanging out. This child had a bit of wit, then, Mary decided.

But as soon as Mrs Ash noticed their little game, she shut Hetta's mouth with a snap of her hand and announced to the table, in apocalyptic tones, that a crow had stolen her wedding ring off her window-sill.

Mary's eyebrows went up. 'I didn't know you had a husband,' she said in congratulatory tones.

The nurse flushed darkly.

'Mrs Ash is a widow,' murmured Mrs Jones. Mary hid a smile. To think of any man brave enough to lift that woman's dank skirts! No wonder he hadn't lasted long.

Her own sympathies lay with the crow. It should have known a gold ring was no use to it, but it clearly hadn't been able to resist the glow, the hint of hot sunlight in the depth of January.

Later that day Mary was washing the stairs – *like any old skivvy*, Doll mocked in her head – when the manservant passed through the hall under a gigantic bale of coarse linen. Any interruption was a chance to straighten her sore back, so Mary got to her feet and tugged her hoop back into the right shape. 'Where does Wales start, then?' she asked him, pressing a hand into the small of her back.

'Just over thataway,' said Daffy, jerking his head over his shoulder. 'The Black Mountains. It's mostly Welsh spoken beyond Abergavenny.'

'So this is England?' Mary felt a distinct sense of relief.

'Not at all,' said the man, sounding injured. 'It's the Marches. We're Marchermen.'

She let out an impatient breath. 'Which country are we in, then?'

'Both. Or neither, you might say,' Daffy added slyly, shifting the weight of the bale on to his other shoulder.

He headed for the door into the Stays Room where Mr Jones worked. 'How can you people not know where you live?' she said to his back.

She thought at first that he hadn't heard. Then his head turned. 'You don't know the first thing about us,' he threw over his shoulder.

There was the mistress coming downstairs, drawing up her improvers on their iron hinges to squeeze past Mary with a smile. The girl pulled back her scrubbing brush and watched Mrs Jones's shoes pick their way through the suds. The red heels were worn down at the back, she noticed; the family business mustn't be too profitable yet. It gave her a tiny prick of amusement to see the edge of one under-petticoat trail in a soapy puddle.

'Oh, Mary, you haven't even seen the shop yet, have you?'

Mary shook her head.

'What was I thinking of?' cried Mrs Jones. 'Let you leave all this for now' – carrying the bucket and brush down to a corner of the tiny hallway – 'and come with me this minute.'

'Very well.'

But the mistress paused then, in the hall, so Mary bumped into her from behind. 'Ah, yes. My husband—' Mrs Jones began awkwardly.

Mary waited, her arms folded.

'Mr Jones thinks perhaps, that is to say, it might be best if you were to call me madam, Mary.'

'Very well.'

Purple suffused Mrs Jones's cheeks. 'For instance,' she said, as if remarking on the weather, 'there you might say, "Very well, madam."'

'Very well, madam,' said Mary. Her mimicry was barely audible.

The shop was a small space, peopled entirely by clothes. A lady's embroidered bodice, laced up with silver, hung from hooks set in the ceiling. Ruched under-petticoats swayed in the icy draught from the door; Mary had the impression they'd just stopped dancing. A quilted petticoat in swanskin flannel was tasselled in ten places. A French sack dropped voluminous pleats of yellow and white silk. 'Stripes, on a sack gown?' asked Mary.

Mrs Jones put her hand under the hem to catch the light. 'My draper in Bristol assured me it's the very latest thing. This one's promised to Mrs Fortune for the Shrove Ball. She says if I sell stripes to any other lady in Monmouth, she'll see me ruined!'

Mary joined in the laughter a little absently. She walked up to a riding-habit in fine green wool and brushed it with one finger. Her mouth watered as at the smell of a cut lemon.

She turned to Mrs Jones. 'You made all these? Madam,' she added belatedly.

'Aye, but not the hats,' said Mrs Jones modestly. 'Them and the gloves I have sent down to me from Cheltenham.'

Mary tried to remember what she'd made her mother say in that letter about the poor orphaned daughter's sewing skills. She'd never seen finer work in the shops of Pall Mall. Her eyes took the measure of a jacket in blue watered tabby. 'This'll be a casaquin, I suppose?' she said casually.

'Lord bless you, no, you innocent!' laughed Mrs Jones. And for the next hour she explained the difference between a fitted casaquin and a caraco like this one, and a pentelair which was really a cross between a jacket and a sack gown but shorter, and a palatine and a mantelet and a cardinal and, most importantly, between a round gown and an open gown, not to mention a wrapping gown, and a nightgown (which was worn only in the day). Mrs Jones had strong views on what was *à la mode*, what was *démodé*, and what was likely to be *the coming thing*. The first rule of cut was, *Be true to the cloth*. The first rule of business was, *Give the customers what they want*.

As she spoke, Mrs Jones unfolded a length of brown silk so thin Mary thought it would feel like the wings of a moth. Mary kept nodding, but she was too distracted to take it all in. She watched the chintzes, satins and damasks eddying in the draught.

'And this is Mrs Morgan's slammerkin, or some would call it a trollopee; a loose sort of morning gown. She's wife to our Member of Parliament, you know.'

Mary hid a grin. The harlots all wanted to dress like ladies and the ladies returned the compliment, it seemed. Mrs Morgan's unfinished dress was white velvet; it hung from a hook in the ceiling as if it were being poured out. 'Is she beautiful?' she asked, on impulse.

'Mrs Morgan?' The dressmaker's mouth pursed in mild distress. 'Well, no. I'd be telling a falsehood if I said so.'

'A pity,' murmured Mary. Above the flaring scalloped edge of the gown's train a tiny pattern had begun to spread. She looked closer: apples and snakes, in silver thread.

'I've been flowering it for a month already,' said Mrs Jones, with a tiny sigh. 'If I do a very good job and it's finished by August, Mrs Morgan might be persuaded to come to us for her daughter's first season, don't you know!'

Looking up into the silvery folds, Mary promised herself something: she would learn to make clothes like these. And what's more, someday she'd wear them. Her fingers closed on the ice-white hem; the pile felt as deep as fur.

'Have a care,' said Mrs Jones.

Mary pulled her hand back as if she'd been burnt.

She knew she wasn't trusted, yet. It was only to be expected.

After tea that afternoon, for instance, Mrs Jones locked up the little chest and pocketed the key. As if Mary would nick a scoop of her cheap China tea!

The first thing Mary did when she finally reached the attic room, late that night, was to pull *The Whole Duty of Woman* out of her pocket and drop it into the stained pot under the bed. The last thing she wanted was a book to tell her how to be a good maid. She could rip out the pages one at a time to wipe her arse.

On the flat pillow, Abi's face was blank with sleep. She wore no nightcap; her hair was a bristling storm cloud. The bones of her face caught the faint starlight. She looked older now; something about the set of the jaw.

Mary slid in beside her and lay at the edge so as not to wake the maid-of-all-work. Sharing a bed was a delicate business, and she was in no hurry to make an enemy, even if the woman had been intolerably mean about the beer, this morning. How strange, to lie down beside someone who wasn't Doll, and not exchange a word. Mary held herself still, feeling she'd lived through a day that had lasted all year. It seemed impossible that she'd ever be allowed go to sleep.

Thick frost coated the black window, and snow was beginning to drift down. Abi's breaths came slow and sibilant, like the ocean. It was so silent outside, Mary couldn't believe there was a town out there at all. It seemed to her that this tiny house was adrift on a white sea.

Then she must have fallen asleep, because in her dream she was in the Piazza at Covent Garden, dancing with a bear. All round her, people were selling things out of barrels: frogs, and lit fireworks, and babies, and cups of gold. A tiny man opened a walnut and pulled out a skirt the colour of the stars. Carriages and carts dashed through the square, and two of them collided. A keg of blue water was overturned, and fish gulped and writhed on the cobblestones. But in the centre of the Piazza, undisturbed, fingers and claws barely touching, Mary and the bear maintained their stately gavotte.

Abi woke in the night with that crawling feeling that told her she was not alone. The Londoner lay beside her, snoring lightly; she had a reek of perfume about her, something acidic. Abi wrapped her arms tightly round herself to make sure their nightshirts didn't touch.

'You'll be company for each other, won't you?' was what Mrs Jones had said, with her nervous little smile.

What she needed, Abi realised, was an obeah woman. These

things were simpler back in Barbados. On the island, if some chit of a girl moved in, and tried to boss you around, and slept on your mattress without asking your leave – taking up nearly every inch of it with her pale sharp elbows – you'd naturally turn to obeah. That girl would know to be afraid. Even after the longest day in the fields, if you had a sore grudge in you, you could find relief by walking over to the old woman's hut with a gift of some corn mush or a tot of rum and simply saying, *That new girl's a thorn in my foot, won't you put some good strong obeah on her for me?*

Of course, the problem with thinking about Barbados was that every sweet memory had ten evil ones hanging on its tail. Scratching her shoulder blade just now, for instance, Abi's fingertips met the S in the word *Smith*. Smith was her first owner; he had bought a job lot of them off the ship, eighty-six women and girls all polished up with palm oil to look healthy. The branding-iron was red gold, she remembered, and when it descended a smell went up like fried chitterlings.

Most nights Abi said her name to herself – her true name, from Africa – over and over, to draw herself back into the arms of sleep. But now her bed was occupied by a stranger, she'd have to be sure not to whisper it, not even to think it secretly in her head, in case it slipped out.

All quiet on Inch Lane. Nothing stirred in the house.

In her narrow room, Mrs Ash crawled on to her back. Moonlight slipped its blade between the shutters; it made her breasts ache. Times like this, in the awful accuracy of the night, she knew what she had become: a dried-up bitter thing of thirty-nine.

She always seemed to start out on the wrong footing. This London girl, for instance; Mrs Ash had had the civilest of intentions, but somehow she'd taken an instant dislike to the creature, sitting at table all pert and bright-eyed in her stylish hoops. Mrs Ash knew she herself lacked the gift of making herself liked. She was always on the edge of things.

Once upon a time there'd been a woman of twenty-two called Nance Ash; a new wife and mother in the tiny village of Abergavenny in the Black Mountains. She had no Welsh, so her husband spoke English to her, tenderly enough. She kept to herself, by and large, but she did no one any harm. *Kind enough*, her neighbours would probably have said, for all they knew of her. Kind enough, at any rate, to keep the baby in bed between her and her husband on a cold January night. She wouldn't have left him to freeze stiff in a cradle, as too many did. She kept him lovely and warm between her breasts, didn't she?

Could've happened to anyone, as they said to her husband. *The will of the Maker, and no use fretting over it.*

If only Owen Ash hadn't been stupid with drink and rolled on to his back, not feeling the soft bundle crushed under him; if only his wife Nance hadn't been sleeping so sound, or if she'd woken to check the infant in the night, if only the creature had been a bit stronger, cried a little louder—

An overlaying's nobody's fault. That was what everyone said.

The thing was, though, that baby had been Nance Ash's only chance. Without her knowledge, on that one long night all the hope was pressed out of her life. The next day her tiny boy was put in a coffin no bigger than a hatbox, and her husband, blind with gin, called her terrible names and stumbled out into the lane. After three days she knew he was never coming back, no matter how long she waited.

No longer mother, no longer wife. Her parents were dead and she'd been their only child. She had no relatives left alive. She'd never possessed what you might call friends. The neighbours offered what they could, but in Abergavenny in wintertime, that wouldn't be much; certainly not enough to keep flesh on a grown woman's bones. Her only skills were those that would have fitted her to be a wife and mother. Nance Ash was reduced to beggary, with her own milk dribbling away through her stays.

Which is why she would always owe the Joneses a proper gratitude. When she'd jolted into Monmouth on her neighbour's cart, all dusty from the road, Thomas Jones had nodded approvingly at her swollen chest and hired her on the spot. She hadn't been able to speak, at first, she remembered now; she'd just nodded her head. Mr Jones had told her quite gently that she should stop crying. 'It might sour the milk for our little Grandison.' Then he'd asked whether her husband was gone for good. She'd quite understood the question. For a wet-nurse, a widow was best; seed spoiled the milk.

It was in those days that she'd first turned to the Good Book. Before that she'd assumed life was going to be a pleasant enough business, and thought little about it. But in the first years of what everyone called her widowhood, Mrs Ash had felt a terrible hunger to make sense of the whole story. And in the Scriptures – troubling and enigmatic as they could be, at times – she had learned to see a pattern. For all the days of this life the evil might triumph over the good, but in the end the sinners would be cast down and the clean souls would be lifted up. The Lord's was the only company in which Nance Ash could really feel at ease, because she was convinced He loved her, no matter how she snapped or no matter how many lines there were on her forehead. He was her one true friend. And she knew she had His written promise: in the end He would wipe away all the tears from her eyes.

In return, she gave thanks regularly. The Joneses had offered her a home, hadn't they, when there was nowhere else to go but the workhouse, or the bare ditches? And in return she had fed their children well. When Grandison was weaned, Mrs Ash had clung on in the family; she'd even taken in some other babies to keep the milk flowing. She'd nursed all the Jones children, and it wasn't her fault if they'd died, all except for little Hetta. These things happened. It wasn't as if she'd blighted them. She'd given every drop she had for thirteen years, all told, right up until the day Hetta turned her face from the wrinkled nipple and screamed for bread and dripping. There were plenty of other wet-nurses in Monmouth by then, and no one asked Mrs Ash to take in their child. Her worn-out breasts hurt for a while, but soon dried up. Strange, to have them lie flat against her ribs, after so many years of fullness.

She had to give Thomas Jones full credit. The man might be missing a leg but he had more than his share of principle. Another father might have lacked understanding of the sacred bond between nurse and child; a lesser man might have told her that her job was over once Hetta was weaned. The family could have turned her off to save the price of her wages, and few in Monmouth would have thought any the worse of them. But Mr Jones had kept Mrs Ash on to rear the girl so his wife could spend her days cutting and sewing in the shop. Oh, Nance Ash never lacked gratitude.

She knew how much, above all, she had to thank her Maker for. She went to church twice a week, but most of all she read his Holy Word, and puzzled over it, and tried to live it, and every night she stayed on her knees by the bed until they were bruised. But when the moonlight came in the shutters, on nights like this one, Nance Ash couldn't help thinking of how she'd had her single chance and lost it as easy as a leaf might be blown from a tree, simply because she'd slept sound one night seventeen years ago this January, dreaming of God alone knew what. She'd never slept right though a night since. She just wished, now, she could remember what she'd been dreaming of, all those years ago: what was it that had been so sweet she hadn't wanted to wake?

It was still pitch black out; Mary decided it couldn't be later than half past five. The second day of her new life.

'Mary!'

There it was again, from somewhere downstairs. Mrs Jones: her voice had that strange lilt to it – like Susan Digot's, it occurred to Mary now. But this wasn't Mary's mother or Mary's house. This was a mistress waking a hired maid.

All at once Mary knew she'd wandered out of her own story into another, and was lost. She pressed her face into the pillow and stopped breathing. *Service*. The word sounded so harmless, so everyday. Folk went into service all the time. *I've found a very proper place*, they said; *I mustn't lose my place*. But whatever place this was, it wasn't Mary's.

She conjured up Caesar's impassive plum-coloured mouth to scare herself. She couldn't show her face back in London yet, she knew. *Monmouth's a hidey-hole, that's all*, said Doll in her head. *Like that stinking ditch we crouched in when the bread riot ran amok, remember? Anything can be borne for a while.*

'Mary Saunders!'

Nan Pullen had once said a strange thing about her mistress, the same woman who would one day hand Nan over to the magistrate. Masters and mistresses were only cullies by another name, according to Nan. You pretended to be satisfied, or grateful, even. You served them, but they never knew you. You robbed them of whatever you could, because whatever they paid, it was never enough for what they asked.

Mary hauled herself off the pillow and sat up. Abi was lying beside her like a figure on a tomb, arms folded. Mary almost jumped. She had thought the maid-of-all-work would have been up hours ago, starting the fires and boiling water. 'Good morning,' she said warily.

Abi said nothing, only stared up at the ceiling.

'Aren't you needed, below?'

'I sick.'

Mary gave her a closer look. No flush or sweating, not a shiver. 'What ails you, in particular?' she asked pointedly.

'I sick,' repeated Abi, and turned her face to the window.

As Mary hurried down the stairs past the Joneses' bedchamber, the mistress called her in. 'Do you need any help dressing, madam?' asked Mary.

'Oh no,' said Mrs Jones, flustered, tugging the cage of her hoop up around her narrow waist, 'I only wished to ask if you slept well.'

'Well enough, madam. So Abi's been taken sick, it seems,' said Mary neutrally.

'Ah, yes, so she told me when I looked in, first thing this morning.' Mrs Jones worried at a knot in her hoop strings. 'She's not as strong as she looks, you see.'

Meaning – Mary took her to understand – that Abi was a shamming malingerer, but the mistress didn't want a fight today.

'Perhaps you could help me serve breakfast?'

'Of course,' she told Mrs Jones, taking the tapes of the slim hoop and pulling them into a neat bow in the small of her mistress's back.

'Why, thank you, Mary.'

The master took no more notice of Mary than if she'd been a cat. It was a strange sensation; most men had been in the habit of taking their breeches down at the sight of her, but Mr Jones carried right on dressing. Out of the corner of her eye, she watched him get his wrinkled linen drawers on under his flowing shirt. She had a childish longing to see his stump, but it was hidden in the folds of linen. She supposed he must have a yard and balls like any man; there was Hetta to prove it. Now he unrolled a woollen stocking precisely along his pale calf and fastened it with a garter over the knee. Mr Jones's leg was hairy and massive; did it have the strength of two, Mary wondered?

She held the wide black skirt over Mrs Jones's head – quality grosgrain silk, though dull, she noted – and helped her mistress wriggle into it. Then she picked up the matching sleeves and started buttoning them on to the bodice.

'Oh, Mary, you're very deft.'

'Thank you, madam.'

Her eyes slid back to the master. For a moment, when he stood up in his single leather shoe, the empty leg of his breeches swung. Then he snatched it up behind with one hand, and fastened it to his waistband with the little button his wife sewed on all his clothes. After that he dressed like any other man. The old-fashioned skirts of his frock-coat, stiffened with buckram, flared around his knee.

Mr Jones's fuzzy head looked odd once the rest of him was dressed. He raised a cloud of blue powder when he clapped on his dishevelled wig.

'Should you like to have Daffy up to dress your peruke, my dear?' asked his wife.

He shook his head, sitting down at the mirror and taking up a comb.

Mary suspected the master would always see to his own wig, even if he had ten thousand pounds a year. She'd never yet heard him say the words *I need*.

After a week Mr Jones decided that the new girl was settling in well. She had a slightly bold manner, at times, but that was only to be expected in a girl who'd grown up in the streets of the great city; impudence was endemic there, he'd heard.

As a rule Mary Saunders was to be found cleaning the house

or helping his wife in the shop, but every now and then his wife sent her through to the stays room with a message or a query. The girl was acutely aware of his missing leg, he noted with amusement; sometimes she'd offer to fetch things so he wouldn't have to get up, dreading perhaps that he might trip on the edge of a floorboard! At such times Mr Jones swatted her away, hopping across the room with his arms piled high with unfinished stays, his head almost touching the ceiling. 'Find someone who has need of you, girl,' he liked to say.

Once Mary Saunders came in when he was cross-legged at his work, the translucent plates of whalebone laid out in front of him on the little low table which was scored as if by a wild animal. He cut strips of bone with his knife, then whittled them down. Laid out in rays around him on the rush mat, they reminded him of the articulated skeleton of some star-shaped fish.

'How many bits of bone do you need?' Mary asked. 'Sir,' she added, a half-second too late.

He glanced up at her. 'Forty pieces,' he answered pleasantly. 'Forty at the least.'

She watched over his shoulder for a few minutes. He could feel her gaze on his hands. 'I thought they'd all be the same shape,' she remarked at last.

Mr Jones looked up from his blade and laughed. 'Girl! Is the human form a rectangle?'

Mary blinked at him. Did she understand the word, he wondered? It was only female schooling she'd had, after all.

'Am I a mere box-maker?' he asked, more simply.

She smiled uncertainly.

He gave a little sigh, but the truth was, he loved to explain his trade. He took up the new stays for Mrs Broderick that hadn't been covered yet. 'You need strong verticals to press the stomachs in, and diagonals across the ribs,' he told the girl, stroking the double lines of backstitch that went up either side of each ridge. 'Then these thin horizontals are required at the back to flatten those unsightly shoulder blades. Not forgetting the wide shaping bones across the front, to plump up the breasts.'

She looked away, at the word; suddenly he remembered that the girl was only fifteen.

'Such are the whims of fashion,' he rushed on, 'that the neckline sinks a little lower every year. Some staymakers use steel across the top,' he added, 'but in my view whalebone is just as efficacious, and more genteel.'

Mary still wasn't meeting his eye; perhaps she was one of those modern young girls who were martyrs to their modesty? 'How many seams are there?' she asked softly.

'Oh, some lax fellows get by with five or six,' said Mr Jones, 'but I'd be ashamed to go under ten.' His hand caressed the shoulder-straps of the stays he was holding. 'I bone the straps too. It's these little touches that make a set stand out from the crowd. The great staymaker Cosins, of London—'

But she'd interrupted him. 'How can they stand out when nobody sees them?'

He gave her a tiny smile. 'Those with an eye can see the shape through no matter how many layers of bodices and jackets.'

'As if the cloth were glass?' asked the girl, fascinated.

'Exactly. The French call us *tailleurs de corps*, tailors of the body,' he added crisply. 'We are artists who work in bone. Though whalebone is in truth a sort of giant fish-tooth.' He dropped a splinter of it into the girl's hand. 'Some cheap staymakers rely on goose quill and others on cane, but in my view there's no substitute for the true Greenland *baleen*.'

She looked at him blankly.

'Have you never seen a whale, Mary?'

'No, sir. There were none in London.'

'Nor in Monmouth,' he said with a chuckle. 'I meant a whale in a picture. Here—' With the help of his hands he lurched to a standing position. The girl stepped backwards, clearly afraid they would collide. With two hops he had reached his little bookcase and unlocked it. In an old gilt-spined periodical he found what he was looking for: an engraving of a fat monster ploughing through the waves. He tapped the lines that represented the coast. 'Greenland,' he said. 'Three months from here.'

The girl peered at the picture. Only when his callused finger pointed out the boat with the tiny men in it did she seem to realise what size the whale was. He could hear her suck in her breath.

'They say his teeth are fifteen feet long, Mary.'

'Is that true?'

'I don't know.' He stared at the picture. 'I do hope so.'

She offered to go, then; she hadn't meant to disturb the master, she said. But he assured her he could do with some assistance, since Daffy was out delivering stockings. So he had her hold a long strip of whalebone bent like a bow while he backstitched it into its narrow sheath of linen. Her hands were surprisingly steady.

It was in the afternoons that Mary felt most restless. Sometimes the mistress seemed to notice this, and sent her out on errands on the pretext that 'Abi seems tired today, don't you think?' The black maid appeared to be working to rule these days, going about the bare minimum of tasks with a mulish manner that Mary interpreted as: *Let the Londoner do it*.

But Mary was glad enough to get out of the house. Today the long list she had to memorise ended with 'a half pound of coffee from the chandler's, look you now, and ask them all if they'd be so kind as to put it on the slate till Friday.' *Look you now*. That's what Mary's mother used to say. But unlike Jane Jones,

Susan Digot had usually been pointing out some disaster: a spill, a breakage, another ruined day.

Dirty snow was piled up against the houses. In the weeks since Mary's arrival, Inch Lane had narrowed to the width of her skirt. Was this winter going to last for ever?

There were no pavements here, as there were in much of London; you had to pick your way along the street through all the rubbish and dung that stuck up out of the snow. Coming out of Inch Lane, Mary found herself smack in the middle of Monmouth, halfway between the genteel houses of Whitecross Street and the stink of the small docks. The cramped quality of the place still amazed her: nobs and mob not two minutes' walk apart. Everywhere she turned, the walls were lime-washed; the small doors glared.

Since the first day she'd stepped outside the house, she'd kept one dreading eye out for that Welshman from the inn at Coleford, the man she'd bilked of a whole pound for what she'd claimed was her lost virginity. But she'd never caught a glimpse of him in Monmouth. He had to be a farmer from beyond the mountains, she decided.

By now Mary had learned the names of the dozen streets, and that was all there seemed to be to this little knot of a town, snowbound between two rivers. Over there in the curve where the tiny Monnow met the fat Wye lay Chippenham Meadows; folk walked there on summer evenings, according to Daffy. But summer seemed to Mary like another country. Time stood still in this part of the world; in the house on Inch Lane, the Christmas evergreens were still nailed to the walls.

The wind made her eyes run; she pulled her scarf across her face and tugged the open ends of her mittens over her fingertips. Her thin boots skidded on the packed snow. She couldn't remember why she'd longed to get outside today. She had two shawls knotted round her shoulders, over her cloak, and she was still freezing. The air was so peculiarly clean, it smelled of nothing at all.

She bought a twist of salt in paper from the grocer's; a stoppered jar of green ointment from Lomax the apothecary for Mrs Ash's mysteriously ailing legs; a slice of fresh butter from the stall by the bridge. An hour later Mary trudged back along the Wye with a heavy basket. The half a crown in her pocket was Mrs Jones's change. No chance of losing it; ever since the night her mother had beaten her for the lost penny, Mary had never put her hand into her pocket without checking her seams for holes.

Be sure and always carry half a crown to prove you're not a whore.

How does that prove it, Doll?

It pays off the Reformer constable, lack-wit! Said Doll Higgins, who'd always kept a half a crown in her shoe, and never drank it, not even when she'd pawned the cloak off her back. Doll, who'd had a mortal dread of losing her liberty, and thought a half a crown would stand between her and all harm.

A woman stumped by through the snow with three children at her skirts. 'Idle hands!' she barked at Mary.

The girl jumped. At first she didn't understand the words, the woman's accent was so thick. She stared into the dull brown eyes of the woman who carded wool as she walked, scraping the muddy shreds into place. Behind her the hurrying children worked away on smaller combs.

'I've a basket to carry,' Mary protested, her voice coming out too shrill.

The stranger never broke her stride. She called back over her shoulder, 'Carry it on your elbow next time, why don't you, and put those fine fingers to use.' Her children scurried after, still clacking their combs like untrained musicians.

Alone on the road, Mary stared down at the fingertips emerging from her mittens, purpled by cold where they gripped the basket. She could hardly feel them. But she saw now, with a malicious pleasure, how smooth they were compared to a real Marcherwoman's. In her old life, the only job of work these hands had ever done was hold her skirts up out of the mud, or rub the occasional old fellow's tool to life. She snorted aloud at the thought. What would the locals call her if they knew that?

At the chandler's, the women were gossiping as loudly as geese, but they fell silent as soon as Mary came in. She still wasn't sure whether it was Welsh they spoke among themselves, or English with a thick Welsh accent. But the chandler was a friendly fellow. 'Su Rhys's daughter, in't it?' he asked, wrapping up Mary's parcel of ground coffee.

Mary nodded, startled. 'Can you tell by my face?'

The chandler laughed like a monkey, and a few of the woman joined in. 'Not at all, dear. We've had word of you, that's all.'

'Welcome home,' added one of the customers.

Mary thanked her stiffly, and got out of the shop as fast as she could. *Home*, indeed! Were they mad?

As she hurried down Monnow Street, wind lifted settled snow like dust before an unseen broom. The road cleared and filled again, white dust moving like muslin, gathering and smoothening along the air. It was snowing upside down now, from the ground up, swirling into her face. She looked up at the sun over the spire of St Mary's, a white ball swathed in cloud. Sheds in the distance were the same dim brown as the trees. It was a world without colour; Mary couldn't shake off the impression that she was gradually going blind.

A flick of blackness drew her eyes upwards. Crows were gathering in a skinny beech, bouncing in the branches, shifting their heads from side to side as they cawed, as if looking for trouble. Mary craned up and tried to count them.

Five for riches,
Six for a thief.

Her neck hurt as she let her head drop back and her mouth open. There was another, in the next treetop. And another.

Seven for a journey,
Eight for grief.

Others wheeled overhead. Her eyes were watering. The birds' croaks were fusing into one great excitement. She blinked snow off her lashes. Scores, hundreds of crows, all homing to this skeletal tree; shaking away from it in a wide arc, then doubling back as if constrained to return. Some waited on the very ends of the branches as if preparing to migrate, but she knew that couldn't be so. It wasn't as if they had anywhere else to go.

Now she was paying attention, Mary realised that the air had been full of the crows' rapid grumble all morning. Such a sore cawing; a shallow abrasion of the throat that seemed to expect no acknowledgement, no answer, certainly no consolation. She wondered what was grieving them. The scarcity of worms? The long wait for spring? The fact that they hadn't been born peacocks? The dark beaks repeated the birds' resentment as if they had to, as if they'd forgotten why they ever began but now knew no other sound to make. The heavy sky shook with their complaint.

Across the river the men were going up and down the white fields with barrows; a dark stench drifted through town. 'What are they doing in the fields?' Mary asked Daffy when she squeezed past him in the little yard.

'Dunging,' he said between blows. The log split apart under his axe.

She repeated the word, derisory.

His breath came out in a cloud. 'They spread dung out to be ready for the plough, see. To fertilise and fructify the soil.'

Him and his words! Mary pursed up her lips. 'What'll they sow, then?'

'Coltsfoot,' he said, leaning on his axe for a second. 'Hogweed. Maybe crow garlic.'

Mary laughed out loud. 'Don't think to fool me with your nonsensical names.'

'As if a city girl would know one leaf from another!' he said.

She believed him now, but she wouldn't say so. She dawdled on the icy doorstep. As the man lifted the axe high in the air, his shoulders were thick as a terrier's. 'That's what you all call me, the Londoner, isn't it?'

Daffy's axe paused; he glanced up.

'I've heard you in the Stays Room, with the master, and with Abi too.'

He split a log cleanly. 'Here's another little quaint country saying you may not know: *Those who listen at doors won't hear any good of themselves*.'

'Do you bear me a grudge, then?' Her voice was merry.

His blade stuck; he had to batter the log against the stump before the axe cut through. He spoke gruffly. 'All I say, and I'll say it to your face, is you got a place that should have gone to another.'

So that was it. This wretched job! At once Mary went on the attack, as Doll had always taught her. 'This other you mention,' she began sweetly, 'I don't suppose she's that little brownish girl I've seen you dawdling with in the market?'

Daffy straightened up. 'My cousin Gwyneth,' he said through narrowed teeth, 'is the finest woman who's ever walked the earth.'

He'd bared his throat to her blade; he knew it and she knew it. 'I do beg your pardon,' said Mary softly. 'I must have been confusing your fine cousin with some ragabones I saw begging for heads and tails round the back of the fish stall.'

She wouldn't have been surprised if he'd hit her, now, but his hands stayed wrapped around the shaft of the axe, and his eyes rested on the log-pile. The man's silence impressed her. Perhaps he was wondering how she came to be such a shrew before the age of sixteen. Mary occasionally wondered that herself.

Finally Daffy glanced up at her. 'One day, when you're reduced in your circumstances, you'll regret your uncharitable talk.'

Mary regretted it a little already. Sometimes words were like glass that broke in her mouth.

For Abi, the last Monday of each month started hours before dawn. The washerwomen, hired for the day, gave her the stick to churn the sheets while they measured out the lye. Only bent over this cauldron in the scullery did she ever begin to feel warm. The women were always glad when Mrs Ash sent Abi to help them; she could face the steam twice as long as any Christian, they said. 'Leather in place of skin, that's for why.' They thought she didn't understand them, just because she never bothered to engage in foolish chit-chat. Sometimes, Abi had discovered, it was useful to be thought a halfwit – or a half-ape, more likely.

They set up a tub on the kitchen table for the white small-clothes and poured in fresh boiled water. 'Bestir yourself now, Abi,' said the younger washerwoman loudly, tipping a load of clothes into the froth.

The maid-of-all-work smiled with her lips shut, having learned that the sight of her bright teeth could cause outbursts of nervous laughter among white folk. Lye stung the pink cracks in her hands as she immersed them to begin the scrubbing. Abi could read volumes off the folds of cloth as they moved in the water; every stain told a story. The child Hetta, for instance; her woollen bodice was tiny and easily scrubbed between fingers and thumb. Her petticoat was rimmed with dust and splashed with yellow. What was the polite phrase the mistress liked to use? *Like takes out like.* Meaning, that petticoat would need boiling in a pot of fresh piss after the first wash.

The washerwomen in the scullery were laughing like drunkards. She'd have to check the level of the beer after they were gone.

The Londoner's sleeve ruffles had waxy grease on them; clearly Mary Saunders wasn't used to trimming and snuffing the candles yet. Abi would have to melt the tallow off with the end of a hot loaf later, and she'd get no thanks for it either. The girl's shift smelled of her lemony scent. She was said to be fifteen, this Mary Saunders, but her eyes were twice that. Where had she picked up that hard stare? Maybe folk were all like that in London.

Abi rather regretted that she'd never made it to the great city. After the long voyage, eight years ago, her master the doctor had come up from Bristol to winter at Monmouth, and commissioned the Joneses to make him a new suit for the season, from hat to shoe-buckles. When he set off the following March, he still owed them six pounds ten, so he handed over Abi in lieu of the cash. She had cried without a sound for three days – not because she missed the doctor, but because everything was alien to her in England.

The Joneses hadn't quite known what to do with her, at first, but they'd soon found her useful. In this chilly house on Inch Lane, she'd learned how to make soap from ash and lights from reeds, when to curtsy, how to say *yes, sir, yes, madam*, who not to annoy (above all, the Ash woman). Daffy

the manservant had offered to teach her to read, but at first she'd
distrusted his motives – since when did a white man ever want
nothing for something? – and even when she did allow him
to show her a page of his book, the scratchings on the page
repelled her. They were some form of magic she didn't want
to touch.

'Abi?' The London girl, her arms piled high with lawn. 'The
mistress sent me in to wash this batch of new handkerchiefs,
if I may.'

The maid-of-all-work cleared her throat. 'Wait a while. This
water dirty.'

'Very good,' said Mary Saunders with conspicuous civility,
depositing her load on the table and drawing up a stool.

Abi worked on, uneasy under the stranger's gaze.

After a few minutes' silence, Mary Saunders leaned her chin
on her hands like a child. 'Hardly a chatterbox, are you?' she
murmured.

Abi scrubbed harder.

'Don't they speak English in the Indies, then?'

'Pick sugar cane, mostly,' said Abi coldly. 'Not much call
for talk.'

'I like a bit of conversation when I'm at work, myself.'

Who did this brat think she was, Abi wondered? She called
this *work*, as if a bit of light laundry bore the least resemblance
to toiling in the cane fields. Abi threw the men's small-clothes
into the pot now: flannel drawers, muslin shirts, worsted stockings
and garters, all cut much the same.

'Is this the master's?' asked Mary, snatching at a breeches cuff
before it went below the water.

Abi shook her head.

'Ah, yes, the nap is low, and here's a little hole; it must be
Daffy's. Too busy studying to sew on a patch, I suppose. He's an

odd little fellow, don't you think? Daffy, I mean,' she repeated, as Abi hadn't heard her the first time.

The maid-of-all-work gave a slow shrug and carried on rubbing the clothes together in the soapy water.

'Has he been here many years?'

A shake of the head.

'Three or four?'

'Maybe one year,' said Abi reluctantly.

'And where was he before that?'

'I think he work in his father's inn.'

Mary Saunders nodded her head, storing the information. 'Yes, I can just see him as a drawer-boy, with cider stains down his front!' She pulled a pair of old velvet breeches out of the pile. 'Now these must be the master's; the cloth's not worn at all, on the side where he buttons it up. How did he lose his leg, tell me? Or was he born that way?'

Abi shrugged to show she had no idea. She had never thought to ask. It was easy to lose a part of your body, it seemed to her; there were so many ways, it was a wonder anybody reached their death intact. She punched the swirl of clothes with her stick now, watching dirt rise to the surface. Hot water slopped over the side. She might not work fast, but she never quite stopped. That was the first thing she'd learned when she joined the field gang at ten years old: *Keep moving. Never look idle.*

Mary was examining a pair of Nottingham stockings. 'Very nice,' she said professionally, testing the delicate pattern with her thumb. She was about to drop them into the tub when Abi stopped her. 'Those go in cold,' she said, gesturing to a basin.

'And these lace ruffles? They must be the mistress's too.'

'No wet at all. Only dust with bran for take the grease out.'

Mary nodded and went for the bran tub. 'I never did any laundry in London; we had a neighbour do it for us. It's vastly complicated. I don't know how you keep it all straight.'

Recognising flattery when she heard it, Abi ignored that.

The Londoner plucked up a cambric shift now. 'This must be Mrs Ash's,' she murmured, sniffing at it. 'Smells as sour as her face.'

Abi found the corner of her mouth curling with amusement.

Mary was plucking long grey hairs out of the nurse's nightcap. 'If she goes on at this rate she'll soon be bald as an egg. So what did the husband die of, then – being preached at?'

The washerwomen were busy wringing out the sheets in the scullery; they couldn't hear a word of this. Abi muttered, 'Didn't die. Ran off, I hear.'

The girl's eyebrows went up. 'That explains a lot. Would you blame the man?'

Abi pursed her lips so as not to smile.

'When did this happen?'

'Twenty years back, I hear,' said Abi, bending a little closer.

Mary covered her laughing mouth and whispered through her fingers, 'So no one's laid hands on the old bitch since . . . 1743!'

A yelp of laughter escaped from Abi's mouth. And then the washerwomen came through, so she straightened up and began hauling clothes out of the tub. The London girl worked by her side.

That afternoon Mary and her mistress sat sewing in the shop, not two feet apart. 'I was wondering,' Mary began mildly, 'is Abi a slave?'

'Not at all.' Mrs Jones looked up at her, shocked. 'We'd never do such a thing as sell our Abi.'

'What is she, then?'

'A servant,' said Mrs Jones uncertainly. 'One of the family.'

Mary mulled this over. What a multitude of oddities the word *family* could cover. 'But she's not free to go, is she?'

'Go?' Mrs Jones's lips pursed. 'Where would the creature go? I think we treat her kind enough.'

'Does she get any wages?' suggested Mary.

'Well, no, but what would poor Abi do with wages?' Mrs Jones looked at her in such confusion that Mary said no more about it.

Here in the Marches, she was coming to realise, folk had no idea that things could ever be different.

After three weeks in the house on Inch Lane, Mary could hardly remember any other life. The Seven Dials gauzes and taffetas she kept hidden in the bag under her bed seemed like relics from a former life, limp costumes from a play. She didn't recognise herself in her scrap of mirror. How shockingly respectable she looked, with her boiled white caps and her plain wool stockings and only the discreetest hint of carmine on her lips; how young! And how the St Giles strollers would howl to see Mary Saunders now, scratching a living without opening her legs.

Her mistress intrigued her. Mrs Jones seemed to have no vanity at all. Her face was only a little haggard; its lines were sweet, especially when she smiled. But the only time the dressmaker ever looked in the long mirror in the shop was when one of her patrons was standing in front of it, posing critically in a half-made gown. 'Why do you always wear black?' Mary asked Mrs Jones now, teasing slightly. 'Is it for simplicity, or as a foil for the patrons?'

'Really, I couldn't say, Mary,' the mistress murmured over a difficult stitch. Then she looked up, into space. 'I went into mourning for my last boy, and I suppose I never thought to change back . . .'

It was the first time she'd mentioned the other children, the dead ones. Mary wanted to know more – their number and names – but something prevented her from prying into such a painful subject.

Mrs Jones rarely stopped moving all day, and nor did Mary. Their window-lit corner of the shop was a chaos of fabrics, ribbons, spools and scissors, but Mrs Jones claimed to know where everything was, even if it sometimes took her half an hour to find it. For the whole month of January the two of them had worked on fat Mrs Fortune's enormous riding-habit, made of grey wool so deep Mary's fingers sank into it. All the girl had to do was hem, but perfectly; it would clearly never occur to Mrs Jones to let a little flaw pass.

The girl only got a chance to rest when she lingered for a moment in the passage between the stays room or the shop, or went out to use the necessary behind the house, her arms wrapped round herself to keep out the frigid wind. At such times she sometimes felt like leaving the back door to swing, and running down Inch Lane to find the nearest way out of this narrow town.

One morning hail fell from ten till half past eleven. Mary had never seen the like of it. There was no limit to weather, in this part of the world; there was nothing to contain it. She stood at the narrow window and watched the icy hail smashing down on the roofs. Daffy came home from market with blood all down his neck; his ear had a gash in it half an inch long. He told them about a rumour going round that a crow had fallen out of the sky with its head split open.

'I hear you used to work in your father's tavern,' Mary mentioned to the manservant at dinner. 'But I thought he was a curate?'

Daffy gave her an unreadable look.

Mrs Jones chipped in to fill the silence. 'Oh, Joe Cadwaladyr could never be expected to keep body and soul together on what the vicar allows him.'

'That's right,' added her husband. 'If the poor fellow hadn't his inn as well he'd have starved by now!'

Mrs Ash looked up from her tiny Bible, her mouth turned down. 'Ecclesiastes says,' she began, '*Better a crust with a quiet conscience than two hands full along with vexation of spirit.*'

No one had an answer for that.

'Crow's Nest,' remarked Hetta.

'That's right, my clever,' said her mother, reaching down to part the child's milk-white hair, 'Daffy's father owns the Crow's Nest Inn.'

The manservant was squirming, so of course Mary couldn't let the subject rest. 'If you had a job in your father's tavern, what made you come to work here, then?' she asked lightly.

Daffy shoved back his chair and stood up. 'I'd best deliver those hats,' he told Mrs Jones.

When the door had shut after him Mary looked round with wide eyes.

The master reached down for his crutches. 'It's as well for Daffy to be with us, learning a clean trade,' he added gravely, 'but I don't like to interfere between father and son.' He said no more before going off down the corridor to the stays room.

'What did I say?' Mary asked her mistress.

'Ah, there's bad blood there,' murmured Mrs Jones, shaking her head.

Some afternoons Mary sneaked upstairs and lay on her bed for a few minutes, just to get away. She couldn't bear to be so thickly set around with people who knew her name and could make demands of her. In the shifting crowds of St Giles, it had somehow been easier to be alone. She lay on her side on the narrow bed and turned the greasy pages of the *Ladies' Almanack* she'd paid ninepence for at the last Bartholomew Fair. On the cover, young Queen Charlotte looked out glumly, despite her fur-lined cape. Mary shut her chilly eyelids for a moment and conjured up that exquisite fur around her throat.

'Mary?' The mistress's voice, like the sharp cry of a blackbird. 'I've need of you.'

The girl remembered London as a place of infinite freedom. Now it seemed she'd rented out her whole life to the Joneses in advance. Service had reduced her to a child, put her under orders to get up and lie down at someone else's whim; her days were spent obeying someone else's rules, working for someone else's profit. Nothing was Mary's any more. Not even her time was hers to waste.

'Coming, mistress.' She stamped down the stairs.

Whenever Hetta managed to escape from her nurse, she liked to follow the new maid round, clutching at her skirts. The child's questions followed each other like waves. 'What colour is this called?' 'Is it dinner time yet?' 'How old are you?'

'Guess,' panted Mary, shovelling ash out of the grate.

'Are you . . . ten?'

'No. More.'

'Are you a hundred?'

'Why, do I look it?' said Mary, laughing despite herself as she wiped ash off her cheek with the back of her hand. 'I'm fifteen, and that's the truth.'

'My brother was nine. My brother Granz.'

'Was he,' said Mary, casting the little girl a curious glance.

'He got skinny and went to heaven in a chariot.'

'That's right.'

'I'm not skinny,' Hetta remarked, a little guiltily.

Mary swallowed a smile. 'I should hope not.'

'Mrs Ash calls me a porkish little glut.'

This made Mary laugh out loud, despite herself.

'Do you really have no mother?' asked Hetta suddenly.

Mary stopped laughing. 'That's right.'

'She's gone to heaven?'

'I hope so,' said Mary grimly, picking up the bucket of ash.

The afternoon was the longest stretch of work, but at least Mary was generally sitting down in the shop. She snoozed over her needle, hemming the skirts and bodices of the better families of Monmouth. Tannery owners, cap merchants and iron-masters, that was all; not a viscount among them. Beside her, Mrs Jones used her great curved scissors to cut confident shapes in silks and brocades, turning every now and then to consult one of the pattern dolls John Niblett had brought her last week in the back of his wagon. Their aprons were two inches long; their skirts were no wider than cabbages. With their twiggish arms and thick necks, Mary thought they looked liked rats dressed up as duchesses.

Mrs Jones could go on for hours about the latest romance she was reading. Sometimes she even talked about the boy she'd lost the previous summer, her Grandison – named, of course, for Mr Richardson's best novel. Privately, Mary thought it just as well the boy hadn't had a long life, bearing the weight of such a name. Now, to hear Mrs Jones talk, you'd have thought he'd been the kindest, cleverest young fellow that ever reached nine years of age. But when Mary had asked Daffy about him, the manservant had admitted that he'd once caught the boy holding a cat's tail in the coals.

Now she let out an enormous yawn.

'You're not used to working such hours, are you?' asked Mrs Jones with a hint of amusement.

Mary shook her head. 'In London I was often idle,' she confessed.

'But you said you went to school?'

'Oh, yes,' she answered, her tongue dry. *Careless, ducky!* said Doll in her head. 'I only meant, the last few months, before Mother . . .'

Mrs Jones clucked sympathetically, pins between her lips. Plucking them out a minute later, she said, 'I suppose you gave up the school when poor Su needed nursing?'

Mary nodded mutely, as if the memory were too painful for speech.

When the light started fading, around four o'clock, Mrs Jones had Mary switch to the simpler chemises and seamed stockings that she sold ready-made to the lower sort; now it wouldn't matter so much if a stitch wasn't perfectly straight. It occurred to Mary – sitting sewing by the side of Mrs Jones – that this was just what Susan Digot had always wanted for her girl. Mary pressed her teeth together hard. The beggarly luck of it, to end up obeying the cold bitch who'd thrown her on to the streets in winter! Well, at least her mother would never hear the end of this story, if Mary could help it. Susan Digot would eke out her days wondering whether her only daughter had given birth in a frozen gutter. She'd go to her grave not knowing, and good enough for her.

'Mary?'

She glanced up, afraid her thoughts were showing on her face.

But Mrs Jones was smiling in concern. 'You've pricked yourself.'

She hadn't felt it. Bright blood flecked the hem of Mrs Jarrett-the-Smith's winter petticoat.

'Let you run and rinse it out in the kitchen. Ask Abi for cold water, and a rub of lemon.'

'It's plain cheap cotton,' muttered the girl.

'Then let it be clean, at least,' said Mrs Jones.

'Why can't I be steaming that taffeta cape of Miss Barnwell's?'

'Because this is our bread and butter, Mary.'

When the girl came back from the kitchen she stood staring out of the little window of the shop, where twilight was settling on the roofs of Monmouth. 'Did my mother like it here?' she asked abruptly.

Mrs Jones looked up with startled eyes. 'Why, Mary, what a thing to ask!'

'But did she?'

The mistress bent over her sewing. 'It wasn't a question Su would have put to herself.'

'Why not?'

'We none of us would have. This was home. Is,' she added confusedly.

'And will you stay here for ever, then?' asked Mary, curiously.

Mrs Jones thought for a moment before asking, 'Where else would we go?'

Mary had always had a feel for clothes and what they meant. But these days she was learning to read a costume like a book, decipher all the little signs of rank or poverty. She was developing a nose for vulgarity; much of the stuff she'd paid out her earnings for, at the stalls of the Seven Dials, now struck her as shoddy tat. Fine cloth, that was what mattered, according to Mrs Jones, and clean lines. And the very best dresses weren't the brightest and gaudiest but the ones that contained months of hard labour: edges stiff with hand-sewn lace or knobbed with beading. There was no way to cheat or skimp on it: beauty was work made flesh.

Something else Mary was learning: what mattered just as much as what someone wore was how they carried it off. The best silk sack gown could be ruined on a stooping, countryish customer. It was all in the gaze, the stance, the set of the shoulders. Mary set herself to learning how to move as if the body – in all its damp indignity – was as sleek and upright as the dress.

Whenever she heard a particularly sharp rap at the front door, she knew it would be a footman knocking on behalf of his mistress, and she would run to clear the little sofa in the shop, straightening her apron as she went. Most afternoons the household on Inch Lane was as busy as a hornet's nest. Patrons plagued Mrs Jones with last-minute requests.

One Saturday, for instance, she was sold out of yellow ribbon by eleven o'clock, and had to disappoint Mrs Lloyd who wanted some specially to bind a silk chrysanthemum on to her wheat-straw hat. Then Mrs Channing ran in to have the hem of her new *robe à la française* taken up half an inch, having got the notion that she might trip on it when walking into church. Mary knelt down to pin up the mauve silk. 'We have a black ourselves, now,' Mrs Channing carolled, catching a glimpse of Abi going through the passageway with a pail of dirty water. 'A footboy, only half as big as your maid. He's a very handy little mannikin; I've named him Cupid. My husband picked him up in Jamaica where they go for only sixpence a pound.' She released another of her shrill laughs. Her knees shook, the flesh on them like pudding.

Mary could tell if a visiting patron was true quality by the fact that they managed to follow her through the narrow hall without giving any hint that they had noticed her existence. The effect was quite crushing; at least in the old days, cullies had looked her in the face. True ladies and gentlemen, it seemed, had eyes only for their own images in the glossy looking-glass.

The patron Mrs Jones was most proud of was Mrs Morgan, wife to the Honourable Member. 'Why, the Morgans of Tredegar have always sat in Parliament for Monmouth,' the mistress told Mary, marvelling at the girl's ignorance. Flat-faced Mrs Morgan wore a black fur cape in all seasons and was carried everywhere in a sedan chair, preceded by a large Frenchman called Georges who held her purse and ushered loiterers off the street in front of her with sweeps of his great ivory fan.

The day Mrs Morgan brought in her youngest daughter for a fitting, Mrs Jones turned remarkably silly, Mary thought. 'And I believe this will be Miss Anna's very first season?' The dressmaker was practically squeaking as she knelt down, brushing the dirty snow from the girl's boots.

A stately inclination of the head from the mother.

'Well, now. An open half-skirt over a petticoat quilted in this rose satin would, dare I suggest, be perfect for one of the many London routs or balls to which I must imagine Miss Anna has been invited.'

Mary bit her lip, embarrassed for her mistress. Mrs Morgan rubbed the satin between two fingers as if feeling for a flaw in the weave.

The mistress turned to Mary and smiled with her lips closed over the gap in her teeth. 'Our new maid has come to us all the way from the capital, have you not, Mary?'

'Yes, madam,' muttered Mary. It galled her to be shown off like a new bolt of paduasoy.

'I do not go there myself, you know, madam, owing to family obligations,' said Mrs Jones, turning back to the Honourable Member's wife, 'but I have my intelligencers! Oh, yes, Mary tells us of all the wonders of London city.'

'What wonders?' piped the girl with the long neck who was holding a spotted bodice up against herself; it was much too pretty for her.

All eyes turned on Mary. She briefly examined her memories. She couldn't decide which to drag out for Miss Anna Morgan, whose eyes were as blue as cheese. Mobs ripping doors off their hinges? That maid who had jumped out of the blazing window in Cheapside? Doll, frozen in the alley, white as whalebone?

'There are fireworks, didn't you tell us once, Mary?' prompted her mistress with an edge of desperation.

Mrs and Miss Morgan stared.

'Yes, madam,' admitted Mary grudgingly. 'Several times a year.'

'As if the stars have plummeted down for the convenience of the *beau monde*!' carolled Mrs Jones. 'And might I venture to suggest perhaps that Miss Anna might wear a cape of this green palatine to Vauxhall Gardens?'

'Ranelagh,' Mrs Morgan corrected her, bringing a handful of the palatine close to her narrow eyes, then letting it down again. 'We don't frequent Vauxhall.'

'Of course,' murmured the dressmaker.

Not that poor Mrs Jones would know the difference, thought Mary, remembering Vauxhall at midnight, dew on the grass where she had earned her fare home.

'We don't see you at church, Mrs Jones,' commented the Honourable Member's wife, breaking in on Mary's memories.

'No, madam.' Mrs Jones hesitated. 'My husband's health, you understand . . .'

'Does not stop him from hopping along Wye Street as fast as any man.' The woman's voice was like sand.

'No, madam,' murmured Mrs Jones.

Any minute now her ladyship would be asking them to lick her heels. The old school rhyme chimed in Mary's head:

May I know my lowly station
At the doorstep of creation.

Now Mrs Morgan examined her white velvet slammerkin, the

few inches of its hem embroidered with silver apples and snakes. 'The work goes slowly, Mrs Jones.'

'My dear madam, I assure you, I expect to make great progress in the next month as the days begin to lengthen.'

'Your London girl embroiders?'

Mary had opened her mouth to say no, when her mistress rushed in with, 'Of course. She knows all the very latest effects!'

A stately nod. Now Mrs Morgan was interrogating a tiny butterfly cap in the long mirror. Mrs Jones went up on her toes to pin it on to her patron's greying head. 'How the lace sets off your hair! Just down from Bristol, this is.'

'I think Mrs Fortune has the same.'

'Madam!' protested the dressmaker. 'Hers is nothing like. Not half so dainty. This is the very pattern of the one Mrs Cibber wears as Juliet on the Drury Lane stage, Mary tells me.'

Mrs Morgan frowned at her image. 'You're sure I won't be put out of countenance when I meet Mrs Fortune at the Shrove Ball?'

'Heaven forbid,' prayed the dressmaker. She was rooting in a trunk now; her voice was muffled. 'And if I can furnish madam with any other little necessaries . . .' She came up, panting, with a shred of lace in her hand. 'You might like to cast your eye over this vastly pretty handkerchief, painted with the Peace of Utrecht—'

Mrs Morgan's eyes didn't leave her image in the glass. 'I'll take the cap,' she cut in. She lifted it off as if it were a miniature crown and gestured to Mary to bring her black fur-trimmed cape. 'You may put it to my account.'

Mrs Jones ran to help the Honourable Member's wife on with her cape. Georges the footman was waiting in the dark hall in a superb quilted jacket with pockets a foot wide. He opened the door for his mistress ceremoniously.

When it had closed behind the Morgan party, Mary let out her breath in a hiss. 'So she stays the full of an hour,' she protested, 'and all she spends is half a crown on an inch of cotton and lace, and gets it on credit too?'

'Mrs Morgan's not always in the buying humour,' said Mrs Jones tiredly.

'And what did you go telling her I could embroider for?' asked Mary, then smiled to soften the impudence.

'Because you'll pick it up in no time, I'm sure,' said Mrs Jones. She took Mary's fingers in her own warmer ones and examined them. 'It's in your bones. Besides, I'll never find the time to get it done on my own, Mary,' she added plaintively, contemplating the great white waterfall of Mrs Morgan's velvet slammerkin.

By the end of that week Mary had filled her practice square with violets, fronds, scrolls and ribbons. The mistress had been right about her: she could flower like a natural. Her fingers were firm, and her eyes were sharp; she never confused her colours.

The day soon came when Mrs Jones laid the hem of the white slammerkin in Mary's lap and threaded her a needle with silver. The woman's eyes were shining; she was on the point of tears, Mary realised with a prickling of embarrassment. 'What's the matter, madam?'

'It's only . . . if your mother could only see you now!'

Mary managed a tight smile. For a moment she joined in the fiction. She imagined a true mother, tender in white wings, looking down on her from heaven and weeping with relief. She pushed her needle into the cloth; it was as soft as a rabbit.

Some afternoons there was a knock at the front door every half an hour. No matter how busy she and Mary were, Mrs Jones always offered the ladies of Monmouth a dish of tea; she wouldn't dream of giving offence. One or two patrons were accompanied by lady's maids, who were much too grand to wait in the kitchen, but stood behind their mistresses' chairs with hands folded, scanning the furniture for dust.

Gossip was the local currency. 'There were two left dead after that football match last week.'

'Terrible.'

'Terrible!'

'There's a new family lodging in St James's Square, I hear, acquaintances of the Philpotts.'

At such hints, Mary could see her mistress's mind whirring like a spinning-wheel. Perhaps they should call early at St James's Square and leave a card offering Mrs Jones's services?

'The Owen widow's daughter's looking very poorly.'

Mary knew what that meant, for all their pious nods. Miss Owen wouldn't be requiring any fancy gowns this spring, or ever.

'A funeral next week at St Mary's?' repeated Mrs Jones with animation. 'What was the crest on the carriage?'

'Two martlets.'

'No, it was three.'

'That'll be the Hardings of Pentwyn.'

Mary met her mistress's eyes. The Hardings would have need of mourning. Maybe they'd be in too much of a hurry to send to London for it . . .

It was Mary who carried in the big China tea-kettle Mr Jones was so fond of. He wouldn't let Abi touch it, and even Mary had to submit to his instruction. The visitors sugared their tea in the saucers, blew on it, and drank with little genteel slurps. Mary watched them thirstily.

Mr Jones had taught her to make a curtsy when leaving the room. He demonstrated on his single leg.

'Even if they're not looking my way?'

'Ah, but if you omit to do it,' he said, with a bark of a laugh, 'they'll be sure to see.'

And indeed, it seemed the ladies of Monmouth could not bear not to know what to make of Mary Saunders. 'Your maid is not from these parts, I understand? But her mother was?'

Hearing her fictional story told and retold in Mrs Jones's tactful undertone – Susan Saunders's deathbed scene becoming more and more affecting, like something out of Mr Richardson's novels – Mary almost felt ashamed. Sometimes she was troubled by an irresistible urge to laugh, as on one occasion when she was pinning up a hem for the Widow Tanner, who owned houses and coppices all over Monmouth. Seeing fat Mrs Tanner's eyes bulge at her in concern, at the story's tragic climax, Mary had to run from the room with a muttered excuse about fetching more pins.

She stood in the passage, fingers sealing her mouth, and shook with guilty mirth. In the shop she heard their voices, hushed a little. Mrs Jones wondered aloud if she had upset Mary. The Widow Tanner was of the opinion that it didn't befit a servant girl to be sensitive, who would have to make her way in the world.

Daffy Cadwaladyr knew he was only a stub of a man. With his short thick arms, and eyes sallow from night-time reading, he was nothing much to look at. But when he walked down Monnow Street with his cousin Gwyneth at his side, he felt like that statue of the young David after beating Goliath that he'd seen engraved in the *Gentleman's Magazine*.

She wouldn't take his arm today, however. There was something weighing on her spirits, he could tell that much. He didn't press her.

Despite the hard times Gwyneth had seen since her family had lost their holding down near Tintern, her cheeks were still the pink of fresh-cut logs, and her wrists were round where they emerged below the frayed ruffles of her sleeves. The line of hair below her limp mob-cap was creamy blonde. She had the kind of looks that put bony dark creatures like that Mary Saunders to shame, and she was as sensible as girls with twice her education. Not a very talkative creature today, his Gwyneth, but he was happy just strolling along beside her down the street where anyone could see the couple and draw their own conclusions.

He didn't care who called her a beggar. The era of such snobberies was drawing to an end. The light of reason was spreading round the world. In the coming times, he felt sure, what would matter was not your birth or upbringing, but what you managed to make of yourself. A woman had no rank of her own, besides; she could rise to the level of whomever she married. He watched his beloved's old pink shoes, and the tide-marks of slush on them.

'Daff,' she said at last, 'you know . . . what's between us?'

A grin crinkled every line on his young face. 'Say no more.'

'No, but—'

'Gwyn,' he said, and he took her left hand into the two of his and held it, for all her squirming. 'You need have no fear.'

She sucked in her rosy lips.

'We reached a sort of understanding two years ago come St John's Day,' he said, 'and to my line of thinking we have that understanding still.' Her mouth opened and shut again. A narrow ray of sunshine hit the wet cobbles of Monnow Street, and Daffy's voice unrolled like a flag. 'I won't be a servant for ever. One of these years, I'll be my own man – my own master, I should say – and I'll have a threshold to carry you over.'

She blinked her pale blue eyes at him. He rushed on before she could speak. 'And I tell you, my dearest Gwyn,' – and here he squeezed her hand between his like a leaf – 'the present misfortunes of your family make not a whit of a difference to my intentions. It's only a matter of patience.'

She withdrew her hand from his damp embrace. 'Daff,' she said, with a constriction in her throat, 'I'm truly sorry.'

He stared at her.

'It weren't . . . quite an understanding that we had, was it? Mean to say, we did talk things through, but to call it an understanding—'

At last it was clear to him why Gwyn was acting so oddly. Oh, the heart this girl had, as sound as an apple! She feared to keep him to his promise, to drag him down with her. As if there was anything in the world he wanted more than to marry her and keep her in comfort. A smile began to spread itself across his cheeks.

'I'm promised to Jennett the Gelder,' she said, dropping her eyes.

Daffy's legs kept moving down the street, like a rooster after its head had been cut off. He watched her, to see why she would say such a thing.

'October, it's to be, after the harvest.'

Finally he was able to speak. 'But our understanding—'

'It were rash of us,' she said, wet-faced.

'Rash?' he repeated, dazed. Then he gathered his forces. 'But you'd wed such a man as Jennett, who cuts the balls off hogs for a living?'

Gwyneth flushed, whether at his coarseness or from shame at her own treachery, he couldn't tell. She spoke even more faintly. 'He's taken my father on as a partner, see.'

Daffy saw.

'Father said he likes you well enough, but we must face facts, see.'

Facts? He had always been the one in charge of facts, before.

He'd been the one who had taught her how to make a reasoned argument.

'At present you're a servant,' she murmured, 'and a servant can't marry.'

'I have ambitions—' he burst out.

'Hopes,' she said softly.

He turned his scarlet face away from her. All at once he saw himself as others must see him: a man-of-all-work on ten pounds a year, whose wig was a little too small.

At dinner Mrs Ash contemplated Daffy, who sat studying his plate, his cheeks sunken. So much for the beneficial effects of reading, she thought. All his education didn't bring him the consolation she got from her one Good Book.

Hetta's plump arms were wriggling out of the nurse's grasp. Her mother spoke mildly. 'Sit still by Mrs Ash now.'

'But I want to go to Mary.'

The Londoner looked up from her plate, all innocent, as if she hadn't been playing wink with the child for the past half an hour.

Acid pooled in Mrs Ash's stomach as she picked at the salt cod, and reminded herself how much the Joneses needed her. Didn't she possess the wisdom of years, the experience of life, the safeguards of piety – everything this new girl lacked? She stared right through Mary Saunders's neckerchief at the pert small breasts hiding in her stays. They'd never fed a child; never felt the absolute greed of a baby's mouth at the nipple. This girl had never known what it was to be necessary.

Hetta slithered down under the table now. Her blonde head emerged on the other side, gleeful. She sat up on the bench between Mary and Daffy. The man didn't even look up. Children were traitors all, thought Mrs Ash. They gave you soft Judas kisses on the cheek, but they were always glancing over your shoulder.

'Such nonsense, Hetta,' murmured Mrs Jones.

'Why do you prefer to sit by Mary?' asked the master disinterestedly, peeling his potato.

The child's smile showed her baby-teeth. 'She smells better.'

'Hetta!' Her mother was on her feet, leaning over to slap the child on the hand. A long wail went up.

Mary Saunders looked down and gave the child beside her a slow, dazzling smile. Mrs Ash could catch a whiff of the maid's perfume from where she sat: spoiled fruit, and spirits, and all manner of wickedness.

The nurse spoke impersonally through Hetta's sobs. 'What will happen to the eye that mocks a father and scorns to obey a mother?'

The Londoner looked across the table at her as if she were mad. Clearly not versed in the Scriptures, Mrs Ash noted.

'Well, Hetta? What will happen to the eye?'

Hetta gulped and screwed up her face with the effort of remembering. 'Crows?'

'*It will be picked out by the crows of the valley*,' intoned Mrs Ash with a nod, '*and eaten by the vultures*. Proverbs, Chapter Thirty, Verse Seventeen.'

'You'd think the crows would eat it themselves, not give it to the vultures,' murmured Mary through a mouthful of salt fish.

Mrs Ash shot her a look.

'Not much of a meal for a pack of vultures, one little eye.'

Mrs Jones let out a tiny involuntary snort. Open-mouthed, Hetta laughed uncertainly. The Londoner's eyes met her mistress's over the cooling dinner.

Mrs Ash knew when she was being scorned. They were making mock of the Scriptures and laughing in her face. She'd given the best of her life to this family; they had quite literally drained her dry.

'Any news of the war with France in the newspaper, sir?' Daffy asked the master blandly, not even troubling to hide the fact that he was changing the subject.

'Oh, you know how these things go on,' said Mr Jones, rather grim. 'Win one battle, lose the next.'

Mrs Ash sat frozen as the Saunders girl took Hetta up in her smooth arms and whispered in her ear. She watched the pair, and gripped her knife. She imagined an axe descending over and over on those slim shoulders, leaving the Londoner armless, spouting blood from her stumps like the maiden in the old story.

The candles used to be Mrs Ash's job, but now it was Mary who lit them and trimmed them. It gratified the girl to feel she was usurping the bitter old Bible-thumper, even in such a little thing. *It's not so bad to make an enemy*, as Doll used to say; *it helps a body feel at home*.

Mary had come to know exactly how much wax it would take to ward off night for an hour longer. Light was a clear badge of rank, she'd learned. The Joneses could stay up a little later than most of their neighbours on Inch Lane, live a little more of each day, not let the darkness drag them down quite so soon. Below in the town, in the squalid alley called Back Lane, families went to bed supperless at six o'clock, because what else could they do in the dark? If you couldn't afford any kind of candle, Mary thought – even the stubs and rush-lights Daffy read by in his cellar room – you were little better than a beast. Someday, she promised herself, someday she would have a house full of candelabras and light them all at once, even in rooms where no one ever went. She'd sup at ten, drink claret at three in the morning and spit at the darkness.

The Joneses ate supper at seven in the little parlour, very hungry but proud to have waited until such a genteel hour. Turnip soup or a poached egg apiece with toasted crusts, but never both. After Abi had cleared away the dishes, the family drew their hard-backed chairs closer to the fire and listened to the wind. Mrs Ash muttered over her Bible, just loud enough to annoy but not loud enough to be understood. If there was darning for the family, Mrs Jones took it out now, and Mary felt obliged to help her. She'd never seen a woman work so hard, except maybe her mother – but Mrs Jones never wore Susan Digot's martyred look. Was it London that soured people, Mary wondered? If lots had been reversed, and the Joneses had gone up to the great city and the Saunderses had stayed behind, would it have been Mrs Jones who grew hard lines in her forehead? Would it have been she who'd have thrown her only daughter out in the street?

Only after supper did the master let the cares of the day slip from him. Mr Jones liked to tease Daffy about his reading. 'What's that you've got there – a storybook, is it?'

The manservant cast him an injured glance and showed it: *A Compleat Geography of the World.*

Mary smirked to herself over the stocking she was darning. Let him look at pictures all he liked, the fellow clearly hadn't the stomach to get him any farther than Abergavenny. He'd had a face like a basset-hound for a fortnight now; he was beginning to get on her nerves.

The master gave a respectful whistle at the title. '*Compleat*, eh? Not a South Sea island left out?'

Mrs Jones made a little clucking with her tongue.

'Quite right, my dear, whistling's a vulgar habit,' said her husband. 'I must leave it behind me if we're to advance in the world. You won't grow up to be a whistler, will you, Hetta?'

The child shook her head and writhed on her mother's knees.

Mrs Jones bent over the child to neaten her tangled white curls and sang under her breath:

Migildi Magildi hei now now,
Migildi Magildi hei now now.

'What does that mean?' asked Mary.

Mrs Jones's eyes went wide as if reading the words on the air. 'I couldn't rightly say, Mary. I had it from my mother.'

Nothing had a reason, in this part of the world, Mary thought irritably; things were as they were simply because they were set that way a hundred years ago.

Hetta pulled free of her mother's fingers and climbed up into her father's asymmetrical lap. 'Fafa,' she began conversationally, 'where did your leg go?'

Mary pricked up her ears.

'It's here in my breeches,' Mr Jones told Hetta with perfect gravity.

'No Fafa,' the child squealed, pounding his thigh, 'your other leg.'

'Mercy on me, it's gone!' Her father tugged at the fold of soft cloth in shock. 'I must have dropped it in the river.'

'You didn't.' She let out her soprano laugh.

His face furrowed in thought. 'Well, maybe I left it behind a hedge and it was gone when I came back for it.'

'No.' Hetta crowed in delight.

'Well then, it must have come off when your mother pulled off my boot last night.'

'Is it in the boot still?'

'I suppose so.'

'Where's the boot then, Fafa?'

'I must have dropped it in the river.'

Hetta squealed again.

She was still wide awake at eight, after her father had gone off with a lantern to his Tradesmen's Club. ('Gossip and cheap port upstairs at the King's Arms,' confided Mrs Jones to Mary.) The child pulled at Mary's sewing, and kept asking to try a stitch, till the older girl itched to stick her needle into the creamy-blonde head.

'Come here now, *cariad*, till I tell you a story,' said Mrs Jones, pulling the child out of Mary's way. Hetta sat down on the end of her mother's skirts. Daffy, snoozing glumly in his chair, moved his feet to make room for her. 'There was once an old couple—'

'What were they called?' demanded Hetta.

'Huw. And Bet,' said Mrs Jones, licking her thread into shape. Mary, watching her over the hillock of darning on the little table between them, wondered if the woman was making it all up as she went along. 'And they went to the winter fair at Aberystwyth, so they did, and hired themselves a serving girl.'

'What was—'

Mrs Jones interrupted her daughter's question. 'Elin.'

She sounded so sure of that name, Mary began to wonder if this were a true story.

'And a very good maid she was.'

Mary's lip curled. She hated stories about good maids. At school the teachers used to talk about virtuous servants whose rewards awaited them in the Hereafter. They made the Mighty Maker sound like the kind of master who was always years in arrears on the wages.

'And the three of them', Mrs Jones went on, 'lived happily all through the winter in their farm in the shelter of the hills.'

How did anyone know they'd been happy, thought Mary? How could anyone be sure that Elin wasn't dreaming of the city, with its lights so vivid she could taste them on her tongue?

'When summer came,' Mrs Jones went on, 'every evening Elin used to take her spinning-wheel down to the meadow and sit beside the stream, singing as she worked. The master and mistress were delighted that Elin spun so much, and they used to count up the bales of wool and cry out, *We have indeed been fortunate in choosing so good a maid.*'

Mary covered a yawn with her thimble. She began to suspect the mistress of telling this particular tale for Mary's benefit, more than Hetta's.

'Now, what Huw and Bet didn't know,' said Mrs Jones, her voice going deeper and livelier, 'was that all the while it was the Little People that were helping her spin.'

Mary's mouth twisted. She might have known. This place was riddled with superstition. Countryfolk couldn't tell the stuff of their dreams from real life. 'Do these fairies ever help anyone to sew, then?' she murmured through the pins in her mouth.

'Never that I heard of, only to spin,' said Mrs Jones with a quick smile that showed the gap in her front teeth. Did she know Mary was poking fun at her? Her voice reverted to the dramatic as she turned back to the child. 'Now, Elin was in the habit of carrying a sharp little knife in case the Little People ever tried to take her away with them.'

Hetta nodded soberly.

'But one day she forgot her little knife.'

The child sucked in her breath.

'That evening she didn't come back from the stream,' whispered Mrs Jones dramatically, 'not the evening after, nor the one after that. All that winter Huw and Bet waited for their maid, but she never came home.'

Hetta pressed closer on the black curve of her mother's hooped skirt.

'Now the next spring,' Mrs Jones went on softly, 'as soon

as it thawed, Bet went down to the stream to look for the girl.'

As if she would, thought Mary sceptically. As if she'd take the trouble.

'Bet looked up and down, that day, and went back the next day, and the one after that. And at last when she was walking along the bank she fell down into a great cavern under the water, and who do you think she found there?'

A broad grin split Hetta's face. 'Elin. Was she—'

Her mother put a finger to the child's mouth. 'But no matter how hard Bet tried, she couldn't save the girl and bring her home.'

Hetta chewed on her upper lip.

'Elin was now wife to an evil fairyman, see, and she'd had his baby, and she could never come back to the mortal world no more.'

There was no sound but the crackle of the flames.

'What a fool of a girl,' remarked Mary at last, 'to forget her little knife.'

Mrs Jones gave her a sorrowful smile. 'It could happen to the best of us.'

Hetta was still lost in thought. 'And were Huw and Bet left all alone then?'

Mrs Jones was about to answer when Mary butted in sardonically. 'Not at all. They went to the next hiring fair and got themselves a more sensible maid.'

Daffy cleared his throat, startling them all; he'd seemed asleep. 'You don't know the story,' he told Mary gruffly. 'So why don't you just hold your damned tongue?'

Mary stared across the room. In the shadows his expression was unreadable. She stuck her needle through a double fold of linen. 'I'll go to my bed, so,' she said stiffly, getting to her feet and dropping the darning on the pile.

Mrs Jones came back from putting the child in her cot and found Daffy still staring into the dying fire. He nibbled at a callus on the side of his thumb. It wasn't like him to cause unpleasantness; she'd always thought of him as an easy-natured fellow. She could see the girl had got under his skin.

A prickly burr on the outside, was Su Rhys's daughter, but that was only her armour. So much would be obvious to anyone who looked into those dark, searching eyes. A bare fifteen, and lost her mother as fast and brutally as a baby abandoned in a gutter! Mrs Jones didn't like to dwell on it. When she thought of her friend Su's life in London, she shuddered. She thanked her Maker for giving her a husband she could rely on through all trials, and a solid trade, and a house to raise her daughter in, and maybe even a son to come.

She picked up her darning as she sat down across from the manservant. It would be easier to say nothing, and safer, but sometimes it seemed to Mrs Jones that she'd spent her whole life choosing the easy and the safe, and saying nothing.

But it was Daffy who began. 'I'm sorry for cursing.'

'Oh, it's not that, Daffy. You were very sharp with the girl, that's all,' she said softly.

'If I was, it was no more than she deserved.' His voice came out like a roar. What was the matter with the man?

'But—'

'You must admit she's a sullen hussy, that Saunders girl,' he interrupted. 'Swanning round the house with her cityfied airs and her clacking tongue—'

'She's a stranger among us, Daffy. She doesn't know our ways.'

'She knows enough to carp and gibe!'

Mrs Jones let out a long tired breath. Authority had never come naturally to her. Living alongside her servants, she found it hard to think of them as anything other than family: her own adopted flesh and blood. 'You were never acquainted with Su Rhys, were you?' she asked instead.

He stared at her, as if she'd made a feeble effort to change the subject.

Mrs Jones clucked her tongue at her own stupidity. 'What am I talking about? She'd have gone off to London when you were only a boy. What I meant to say was, Su – Susan Saunders, as she became – was a very fine woman.'

'Is that where the girl gets her eyes, then?' he asked neutrally.

She made a little amused note of that: he was not immune to the newcomer's eyes. 'No, Daff, I don't mean handsome, I mean good. Su was the best of friends to me till her husband took her off to London. And for Mary to grow up with such a mother, living as close as two females can be, and then to have her snatched away in the blinking of an eye—' Her voice trembled. 'And for Mary to come back here to her native place, but not to know its ways any better than a stranger – well, is it any wonder the girl should be a little spleenish at first?'

'I'm sorry for her loss,' said Daffy coldly.

Exhaustion covered Mrs Jones like a blanket of snow. 'No but try to understand her, would you now? After all the books you've read, you must have a power of understanding!'

He shrugged a little, watching the embers. She should have known better than to try flattery.

'Grief can do peculiar things to a person, you know,' said Mrs Jones, very low. 'The heart can get all twisted.'

She hadn't meant to call attention to her own losses. The last thing she was angling for was this young man's pity. But he looked at her as if she'd said the one needful thing. He stood up all at once and grinned down at his mistress. 'I'll do my best.'

'Thank you, Daffy,' said Mrs Jones.

When he went up to bed she was still darning in the last of the firelight.

That night Mary Saunders lay on her side, too tired to sleep. Beside her in the dark, Abi was as still as a corpse. The chime of eleven sounded from St Mary's around the corner; another icy night. Soon Mary would shut her eyes, and sooner than seemed possible she would open them again on another icy day.

This had all been an appalling mistake.

How could Mary have thought of going into service, even for a short while, a girl like her who'd known what liberty was? Less than a month in this narrow house had taught her that she had no talent for it. She could play the part of a grateful, obedient maid for an hour or two at a time – but sooner or later her wicked tongue showed itself.

Well, now she knew. She couldn't face another wagon journey in the deep snow, but as soon as the weather broke its grip, she'd be on her way, on the run again. She knew London wasn't safe for her yet – Caesar would still have his knife out for her – but there had to be somewhere else she could go in the meantime. Bristol, or Bath, or Liverpool maybe; anywhere with a bit of room for her talents; anywhere you could call a city.

As always, when she couldn't find her way to sleep, Mary buried her face in the pillow and began to dress herself, in her mind's eye. A shift of white silk, next to the skin; a pair of stockings, silver-clocked. As she weighed up the rival merits of a flowered green bodice and a ruched pink one, she felt her limbs grow heavy and luxurious.

Soon her time in this purgatorial place would be up. But till the thaw came she had to stick it out, wear the mask. It was only a matter of a few weeks more in this unlikely town where nothing ever happened and nothing ever would. For now, she had to act as if this was her life.

Abi was awake; Mary could tell by the quietness of her breathing. The maid-of-all-work shifted now, and her hand lay across the blanket, its old scar catching the faint starlight. 'Abi,' whispered Mary, 'what happened to your hand?'

The silence was so long, she'd almost given up on getting an answer. She didn't know why she persisted in trying to coax conversation out of this woman, but it wasn't as if she had a choice of company. Besides, she liked the challenge.

'Got a knife stuck through,' said Abi at last.

'Really?' said Mary encouragingly. Another interminable pause. 'How did it happen?' she whispered.

A slow shrug from the body in the bed beside her, then Abi muttered something Mary didn't catch.

'Beg pardon?'

'Was on my arm,' said Abi, with a little sound that might have been a chuckle or a cough. Then with a heave of blankets she turned her back, but not in a particularly unfriendly way. They lay back to hot back, waiting out the long night.

Chapter Five

Thaw

February came in as bright as an apple. The snow shrank back; the Wye and the Monnow ran full. Everywhere Mary turned her eyes was wet green. She'd never known the ground to look like velvet.

Mrs Ash said it would take more than a week's sunshine to fool her. She quoted darkly:

If Candlemas be fair and clear,
There'll be two winters in the year.

But in spite of her prognostications, the air stayed soft as a feather. Every day there was a little more light for a few minutes longer. Mary hadn't realised how much the darkness had been weighing on her spirits till it began to lift.

'My family,' Mary caught herself saying, as she chatted to a scullerymaid at the pump on Monnow Street, 'my family are the Joneses of Inch Lane.'

'The Roberts sisters were the first in these parts to keep a carriage,' Mrs Jones murmured, so the driver wouldn't hear. 'They've never asked for me before. How good of them to send the driver!'

Mary was rummaging distractedly through the trunk on the

floor of the carriage. 'Shall we show them the burgundy gros-grain?'

'And the pink. They like a bit of brightness.'

The thick mud of Monnow Street slowed the carriage wheels. The bridge at this end of town was an ancient stone enclosure, grey tinged with pink. The traffic slowed to crawl through the narrow passage; packhorses jostled cornbarrows in the gap. Mary caught a glimpse of a tiny door; clearly someone lived in the stonework over their heads. Once on the other side of the gate, something unlocked in her chest, and there seemed more air. This, she realised, was the first time she'd left the town limits.

'Are they handsome ladies, these sisters?' she asked as the carriage jolted up the drive, and the thick shrubs closed around the muddy windows. She stared up at Drybridge House's painted shutters and the crumbling carvings above the door. She pictured a pair of heroines from a genteel comedy, one fair, one dark.

'Once, perhaps,' said Mrs Jones, amused by the question.

Mary had never seen such antiquities close up. Miss Maria Roberts was stringy as a bean, with a face like a pickled walnut. She wore a wrapping gown in orange lace. Her sister, Miss Elizabeth, shuffled out to receive them in a pair of stained French mules. A green silk sack gown drooped from her shoulders. It was old, but finely made; Mary stared at it and thought, *I'd turn heads in that*.

A pleading look from her mistress reminded her to curtsy; she made it a deep one. All she had to do was hold things, tie things, unfold and fold, while looking profoundly respectful. It was up to Mrs Jones to provide the reassurance. Flattery rose up and filled the air like incense. 'For a winter ball? How delightful. Not at *all* unsuited to a lady of your years, Miss Maria, how could you think so?'

A vast confection in rose taffeta. 'See how it brings out the pink in Miss Elizabeth's complexion!'

Mary knelt on the thick Oriental carpet to fasten the gold-braid garter around the old woman's thigh. The fat rolled like satin. 'A little too tight,' fretted Miss Elizabeth.

'Your maid pinches my sister,' barked Miss Maria.

The maid was so very sorry. The mistress was even sorrier. The room was getting hotter. The pink stockings, clocked with gold thread, wrinkled in Mary's fingers and wouldn't stay up.

'Fetch my sister's pannier, girl,' said Miss Maria. Mary ran to the closet and emerged with the most enormous hoop she'd ever seen, from thirty years ago. Between them, she and Mrs Jones stretched it out for Miss Elizabeth to step into. They fastened it with tapes around her waist; it bobbed, it swayed, it bulged a little on one side. Finally Mary abased herself on hands and knees and crawled inside.

Encased in the odorous canvas, she fought with a knotted tape. How ugly were the inner workings of elegance, she thought. The voices came through very muffled. When Miss Elizabeth shifted from foot to foot, the whalebones creaked like a ship. Jonah, thought Mary, remembering her schooldays.

At last she heaved up the edge of the hoop and wriggled into the air. Miss Elizabeth was grinning at herself in the long glass like a child. Mary dusted herself down unobtrusively.

'Vastly vulgar,' pronounced Miss Maria.

Her sister's face plummeted.

'Take it off, Elizabeth. You know I'm right.'

Ladies couldn't be expected to think of the time, Mary knew, as they didn't dine till six. Her stomach growled like a captive animal. But she watched, and listened, and curtsyed every chance she got, and did everything the Misses Roberts asked and other things before they'd thought to ask, and finally she won a little soft smile from Miss Elizabeth.

'Your maid is a capable girl,' Mary overheard Miss Elizabeth tell Mrs Jones.

'That's the truth, madam. I don't know how I ever managed without her.'

That bit was spoken in Mrs Jones's ordinary voice; there was no gush or falsity to it. Listening, with her back turned, Mary felt her skin tighten and glow.

'Might madams be pleased to bespeak any clothes today?' suggested Mrs Jones.

They would not. Nothing quite suited. But they might send for her and her maid again.

'He's a good man, right enough,' Mrs Jones told Mary as they sewed their way towards each other round the four-yard hem of Mrs Harding's new lavender *robe à la française*. 'He's never raised his hand to me, you know, not like' – her voice went down to a murmur – 'Jed Carpenter, who takes a *horsewhip* to his wife.'

'So how did he lose his leg, madam?' asked Mary.

Mrs Jones smiled at her. The fact was, this was one of her favourite stories, though she never told it outside the family. 'I tell you this, Mr Jones is the bravest fellow. He was only a wee boy of nine years old, see?' Her eyes never lost their grip on the tiny stitches. 'He was helping the ostler down at the Robin Hood for thrupence a day. This coach and four came through on the way to Gloucester, and the gentleman, he hopped down outside the inn, and didn't poor Thomas run in to take the reins, and the near horse trod on him.'

'Kicked him?'

'No, no, just lifted up as gentle as you please, and stood down on the boy's bare foot.' Mrs Jones could see the scene as clear as an engraving, with the colours put in by hand: the glossy brown of the flank, the red mark in the snow. 'Mashed it to mush he did.'

'Pugh!' said Mary, her mouth wrinkling up.

Mrs Jones's hands had stilled on the linen. 'It rotted black as your boot, I don't mind telling. Up to the knee the next day, and along the thigh the next.' She marked out the stages of putrefaction on her dusty black skirt.

'Does it go that fast?'

'Like mould on fruit,' said Mrs Jones with relish. She resumed her sewing, faster than before. 'So Dai Barber came to cut it off. But Thomas's mother – a good woman, our neighbour she was – we heard her tell Dai, "Put away your saw. My boy'll die with all his limbs on."' She paused to thread her needle again, squinting against the dregs of the afternoon light. Her eyes weren't what they were.

'And what happened next?' Mary Saunders stretched her cramped hand out in front of her.

'Well. The lad within on his truckle bed, he bawled out so the whole street could hear, "Look you, Mother, I'll not die yet, not for a long while. Bring me in the axe and I'll chop it off myself!"'

There was that disbelieving look in the girl's eyes again. Where had such a young creature picked up such an expression? London had to be a very hardening place. 'I tell you, Mary,' said Mrs Jones urgently, 'you've heard nothing like the sound, outside a sawyer's yard.'

'So Mr Jones cut off his own leg?'

She shook her head impatiently. 'Dai Barber did it, with his saw. He put Thomas out with gin, but the boy still screamed through his dreams. None of us on Back Lane got a blink of sleep that night.'

Mary, bent over her needle, looked revolted. Then, in a curious tone, she asked, 'You used to live down Back Lane?'

There was no use pretending any different. Nothing could be hidden from servants, Mrs Jones knew that much. 'Oh, aye,' she said lightly. 'Thomas and I both grew up there, only two doors apart.'

She could see Mary absorb the new knowledge and store it away. At such moments the girl had the same thoughtful look as Su Rhys used to wear. 'But go on about the leg,' said Mary.

'Well, they dipped the stump in salt water, and it healed up clean as your elbow. Within a month the boy was hopping along like a one-legged rooster.' Mrs Jones let a smile crease her face.

They stitched their way along another foot of ruched silk. Mrs Jones released her breath in a little puff, blowing tiredness out of her way.

'So he didn't die of it, then, for all his mother's fears,' observed Mary.

'No, thank the Maker,' said Mrs Jones with a shocked laugh, 'or where would I be now?'

'Here.'

She stared. Sometimes this girl gave the most peculiar answers. 'Monmouth, maybe, I grant you, but I wouldn't be Mrs Jones.'

'What if you'd married Ned Jones the baker, madam?' asked the girl in a sly murmur.

'Ah, what indeed?' Mrs Jones gave the girl's arm a little shove with the heel of her hand. 'I wouldn't be *this* Mrs Jones, would I? Up to my eyebrows in flour I'd be then, so you wouldn't know me.' She rather liked this image of herself: unrecognisable, chalky white. She sewed on, faster.

It struck her that anyone seeing the two of them together would think them friends, or mother and daughter. Mrs Jones knew she lacked the carriage of a mistress. It wasn't that she was ignorant of how to behave. All the advice books warned about keeping a proper distance, and a romance she'd been reading only the other night illustrated the dangers of befriending the lower orders. *Intoxicated by any Degree of Familiarity, they soon fall into Impertinence*. The heroine ended up being compromised by a duke.

But what was Mrs Jones to do? She forgot all the advice once she and Mary sat down with their needles and fell into conversation. The girl might be penniless, because her shiftless father had died in gaol, but wasn't she Su Rhys's daughter still? Couldn't she read and write and cast account better than Mrs Jones herself, if it came to that? The mistress shifted a little uncomfortably on her stool. It struck her as strange, suddenly, that she who'd grown up shoeless on Back Lane was now lording it over the daughter of her best friend. How arbitrary were the ups and downs of the world. And how could she not grow a little familiar with the girl, while they bent together over the same piece of silk, which pulled back and forth between them like a bird on warm air?

'Does it hurt him still?'

Mrs Jones was startled out of her reverie. Mary was staring at her own bare elbow, its curious knob emerging from the grubby lace.

'The leg? Only the old itch in the winter. Thomas always says it did him good.'

'Good?' Mary's voice was appalled.

How could she explain it to this girl, who was only fifteen years old, whole in body and spirit, with her life spread out in front of her like an untouched feast? 'He knows he's been through the worst,' said his wife gently. 'He's nothing more to fear.'

Mary's private plan of leaving with the thaw had been put to one side, as it were. She had pumped Mr Jones about Bristol, where he'd done his apprenticeship. He claimed it was the next to

greatest city after London – not that he'd ever seen London himself
– but nothing he'd described to Mary made it sound much better
than Monmouth. She'd asked Daffy about other towns within
a few days' ride, but all he'd offered was a history of their
settlement from the Romans on, and a list of their principal
exports. They sounded a shabby lot. If Mary couldn't yet risk
returning to London – and Caesar's knife – it seemed to her that
she might as well stay where she was, for the moment, and eat
her fill, and earn a wage.

Waking in the night, she was soothed by the faint lines of the
attic room. At least she had a share in a bed instead of just a straw
mattress. At least the blankets had no fleas. There weren't any
holes in these walls for the wind to whistle through. No landlady
to thud up the stairs; no killer hammering on the door. Mary was
clean now; no one touched her. She lay motionless, conjuring up
the worst of London, to make herself grateful. Here on Inch Lane
she could watch the moon through glass, instead of following its
naked light down an alley where in all likelihood Doll still sat,
blue and ruined, crumbling with the first thaw.

Mary rolled over, with her back against Abi's steady heat. She
wouldn't think about Doll. She wouldn't dwell on what was past.

Abi was in that state between waking and sleeping when the girl's
voice came out of the dark, beside her ear. 'Abi,' in a whisper. 'Are
you awake?' She heard Mary Saunders's head shift and thump the
pillow into place. Then the hiss came again. 'I can't sleep. I'm
too tired.'

Abi groaned and tucked her face into her cupped hand, which
lay between them.

'It's not right, how the Joneses keep you,' remarked Mary.

Abi pulled her head off the pillow like a turtle. She weighed
the remark: not just what was said, but why.

'A friend of mine', Mary remarked, 'used to say, *Never give up your liberty.*'

Abi brooded over the phrase.

'You know what liberty means? Belonging to yourself?'

'Never had that,' said Abi finally.

'You must have,' said Mary a little impatiently. 'Before you were a slave, I mean. When you were a child back in Africa.'

Abi stretched out on her back and considered the matter. 'No,' she told Mary slowly, 'I belong to king then.'

'What, King George?'

'No, our king,' Abi said. 'Me and my mother and many – hundreds – children and wives, we all belong to king back then.'

'What,' asked Mary, disconcerted, 'you were a slave, back in Africa?'

Abi shrugged uncomfortably. 'Well. It was family. He was father.'

'What, your own father kept you as a slave?'

This girl didn't understand the first thing. Abi yawned hugely. 'Not a bad life there. Little work, plenty food.'

'But he sold you to the whites?'

Abi tucked her face into the crook of her arm. She never liked remembering this bit. Her words were muffled. 'He needed guns.'

The silence lasted so long that she was almost beginning to slip into sleep, when the girl spoke up again. 'Why does it say Smith on your shoulder?'

'That was a master.'

'The one who brought you to England?'

'No. Another one.'

'How many masters did you have, in Barbados?' said Mary curiously.

'Don't remember.'

'In London, you know,' remarked Mary, 'there's a great many people like you.'

'Like me?' Abi repeated hoarsely, lifting her head.

'Black in the face,' said Mary. Then, with a tiny giggle, 'All over, I mean to say.'

This was news to Abi. She cleared her throat; it sounded too loud in the slumbrous house. 'How many?' she whispered.

She could feel the tug in the blankets as the girl shrugged. 'Lots.'

'But how many?' Since the day the doctor had brought her to Monmouth, Abi had counted no more than three dark faces, and they were all footboys to visiting gentry; none of them lived in the town.

'How should I know?' answered Mary with a touch of asperity. 'Two in any busy street, I'd say.'

Abi let herself savour the image. 'Their masters let them out on the streets?' she asked after a minute.

'Oh, the greatest part of them don't have masters,' said Mary. 'London's full of runaways. The East End is crawling with free negroes. Some of them have English wives, even.'

'But free women, too?'

'Indeed. I knew an Indian girl whose master left her behind, to save the price of her passage to Holland. Oh, and there's a club where all the girls are black.'

'Club?' Abi pictured the little gathering of tradesmen upstairs at the King's Arms.

'You know,' said Mary impatiently, 'a place where girls dance.'

Abi pictured it. 'For white men?'

'Well, yes, mostly. For whoever pays to see them,' said Mary, a little awkward. 'But they're not like you, these girls,' she added. 'They get wages, don't you know.'

Abi shut her heavy eyes and tried to imagine such an extraordinary place. What were they wearing, these girls so like her yet not like her at all? How did they dance? Like back in Africa, or the slave dances of Barbados? Or did they skip in complicated patterns like the English? She spoke at last. 'How much wages?'

'Oh, don't ask me,' said Mary. 'But the thing is, they're free to come and go.'

Abi thought of it: the coming and going. 'Do whites spit?'

A heave, as the girl went up on one elbow. 'Do they what?'

'Sometime,' Abi said neutrally, 'when I go on message, folks spit.'

'Country boors,' said Mary scornfully after a few seconds. 'What can you expect of Marchermen? They're just frighted at the sight of you. Give them a year or two and they'll get used to your face.'

'Eight,' said Abi, very softly.

'What's that?' Mary leaned a little closer.

'I been here more than eight years already.'

There was a pause. The girl seemed to have nothing to say to that. She lay down with a thump, making the bed shake.

'Tell me more,' whispered Abi in the darkness.

'About London?'

She nodded, forgetting Mary couldn't see her.

The girl let out an enormous yawn. 'Well, I don't remember much spitting at blacks, there. Londoners save their spit for Frenchies! The blacks keep to themselves and give no one any trouble. They all seem to know each other,' she added. 'If one is thrown in gaol, you may count on it the others will come and visit him, with food and blankets and such. Once I even heard of a supper party, a sort of ball,' she added with another yawn, 'and only blacks were allowed in.'

The older woman didn't ask any more questions. Her head was

too full already; it clinked like a jar full of pebbles. She lay by Mary's side until the girl's breaths lengthened into sleep.

Oh, child, what kind of foolishness is this?

Mary Saunders had slid into routine like slipping into deep water; she'd tasted the dull sweetness of knowing what to do at every hour of every day; of being sure there would be breakfast, for instance, and what that breakfast would be.

The moment she liked best was teatime, if there were no patrons visiting. Then she and the mistress could put down their work for a quarter of an hour and take tea together in the shop. At first the brew was hot enough to scald Mary's whole body from the inside, but it cooled rapidly in the saucer. She took small sips to make it last, holding the porcelain rim between her teeth. It would break so easily if she bit down. She was still plagued with occasional thoughts like that, images of destruction. Surely someday, by a word or a sign, she wouldn't be able to hide who she was – or at least used to be.

'Another drop, Mary?'

'Yes please, madam.'

One day Mrs Jones leaned across the teacups as if she had a secret to impart. 'You know—' she began, then broke off. 'That is, my husband was quite right about the principle of the thing.'

Mary waited.

'I mean to say, that you should call me madam, whenever we have company and such. But when we're on our own, you know,' she stumbled on, 'then it's not so necessary.'

The girl smiled into her tea. Victory, sweet as pineapple.

Why hadn't she been born to Jane Jones instead of Susan Saunders, it occurred to her now? She didn't want to have her mother's hands. She didn't want to be her mother's daughter. In this house, Mary was coming to realise, stains wore off and lies came true. Mary was indeed a hard worker and embroidered like an angel. She could almost believe she was a virgin again.

Most evenings she stole ten minutes before supper to look through her scraps. She had a tiny piece of everything she'd worked on so far: champagne satin from Mrs Tanner's night robe, green watered tabby from Miss Partridge's pleated petticoat, and a dozen others besides. Now she knew what good cloth felt like, she realised what nasty rubbish was most of the stuff hidden in her bag under the bed. The fabric was no good, to start with: dull-napped and limp, with cheap dye that faded in sunlight or after one wash. That open robe with the salmon scalloped petticoat she'd thought so fine when she found it on a stall on Mercer Street – she fingered its patchy sheen now and blushed to think she'd paid four shillings for the thing. The royal blue had seeped off the back of her jacket-bodice already. Trash. And as for the cut of most of her dresses, it appalled her to think she'd been strolling round for so long with all her seams slightly askew.

Her new scraps were only leftovers, slipped into her pocket at the end of the day; Mrs Jones never even seemed to notice they were gone. But already Mary had sewn herself a handkerchief from six triangles of best white cambric, with an edge of blue ribbon, and some evenings she took a half-inch of candle up to her room after dinner and worked on a little scarf, from a strip off the end of that silvery gauze they were using for Miss Fortune's overskirt. Not that she had any call for finery, in her present life, but someday—

It was still Mary's firm belief that service was a fool's game, and no way to make a living. But for the moment she couldn't seem to think of another. Her old trade seemed inconceivable. The Seven Dials life sounded like a lurid drama, acted out with puppets against a black sheet.

In the back of Mary's mind was one tiny anxiety: surely

somebody in the house would wonder why she didn't have
monthly courses like other girls. She even thought of getting
hold of some pig's blood to wrap up in rags. But one day as
she passed Mrs Jones in the narrow hall, each carrying a bale
of cloth, the mistress rested a hand on the girl's shoulder and
murmured that she knew Mary was only a young thing yet.

Mary gave her a puzzled smile.

'And I didn't start till my seventeenth year, myself. But
whenever your time comes on you . . . if you should ever find
your small-clothes *stained*,' the older woman said in her ear, 'just
you come to me at once.'

Mary kept her face straight. 'Yes,' was all she whispered.

'At such times,' said Mrs Jones, 'a girl needs a mother.'

Mary watched her out of sight. She felt giddy with swallowed
laughter. To think that she'd got the belly business over and done
with at fourteen, down in Ma Slattery's reeking cellar, but in
this house she was considered a chit of a girl who hadn't
even begun!

Suddenly she wanted to weep.

Deceiving the Joneses was all too simple. *Easy as pissing the
bed*, as Doll used to say. Decent people only saw what they were
expecting to see. She was reminded of a purse-snatch called Mary
Young who'd had a pair of artificial arms, or so the story went.
Young used to sit in church with her straw-filled gloves folded
demurely in her lap, while her real hands were busy picking
pockets left and right. She'd had a good long career before they
carted her off to Tyburn.

Even Hetta trusted Mary. She was always asking for a splash
of the maid's Hungary water on her dimpled wrists, and she
begged to learn the clapping games that London children played.
At dinner, Hetta often wriggled over to stand beside Mary, till the
maid gave in and lifted her on to her lap. Why the child had taken

a liking to her she couldn't tell, except that anyone would be a relief after that old poison ivy of a nurse.

These days Mary went about her duties like someone who'd never been out past midnight. A little sharp-tongued, perhaps, but a good girl on the whole. The marks of her old trade didn't show on the outside, it seemed. Some days she even forgot that her lies weren't the truth. She almost began to be convinced by her own story of a wandering orphan, bereaved of the best of mothers.

One day at the afternoon tea table, Mrs Jones and her patrons were full of veiled allusions to someone called Sally Mole.

'You never met her,' said Mrs Jones afterwards.

'Who is she, though?' asked Mary.

'Was.' The mistress sighed, shaking her head over her tiny perfect stitches. 'She's dead now, poor wretch. Complications.'

'What sort of complications?'

Mrs Jones rolled her eyes. 'You're a terrible one for the questions, Mary Saunders. If you must know—'

'Yes?'

'Sally Mole . . . she was a local girl. Known to go with men. Strangers.' Mrs Jones covered her mouth with her hand. 'It makes a body's skin crawl.'

And indeed Mary, sitting there beside her mistress, did feel shame rise like a sickness inside her. *Strangers*, she thought. *A body's skin*. Heat scalded her cheeks.

'See, now, I've made you blush!' Mrs Jones reproached herself. 'It's not fitting, at your age, to hear such foul things.'

So Mary dipped her head and attended to her hemming.

Nance Ash had been keeping an eye on the Londoner for a while. Well, somebody had to be vigilant. She'd questioned her own judgement, at first. Could it be that she disliked Mary Saunders simply because of her youth and vigour? Certainly, it galled her to see such a stripling playing tig in the hallway with Hetta, the two of them charging about like dogs and crashing into the furniture. And then, Mary Saunders had a habit of questioning the nurse's authority in apparently tiny things – the choice of a word, a prediction about trade or weather – as a way of undermining her in greater matters. The new maid was in very thick with the mistress, these days; there was much talk of *her mother's hands*, and *such a genius for the needle*. As if sewing a few flowers was real work, deserving of gratitude. As if it could compare with the endless burden of raising a girl child, and a brattish one like Hetta at that.

So Mrs Ash had continued to pray to the Lord for understanding and patience to enable her to bear sharing a house with Mary Saunders. Only gradually, over the weeks, had she let herself become convinced that the Londoner was rotten through and through.

It was not a matter of hard evidence yet, just a sort of vapour that hung about the girl. But it was only a matter of time before the corruption burst out and revealed itself. Mrs Ash comforted herself with the Book of Job:

> *How oft is the candle of the wicked put out!*
> *They are as stubble before the wind,*
> *and as chaff that the storm carrieth away.*

'There's something not right about her, don't you think?' she remarked to Daffy one morning as he was sanding a miniature wooden sailboat for Hetta in the yard.

'Who?' He looked up, startled.

'The Londoner, of course.'

'Oh, do you still call her that?'

'I think she rouges. Those lips aren't a natural shade.'

'They look all right to me,' he said lightly.

Mrs Ash gave him a stern stare. Surely the Saunders creature hadn't got her claws into him already? 'And it wouldn't surprise me if she turned out to be a thief,' she added. 'It's said the big city's full of them.'

'You're a bit hard on the girl,' said Daffy, his wig slipping as he bent over the toy, sanding vigorously.

'You know you must tell the mistress if you catch her out in any dishonesty, though,' remarked Mrs Ash. 'It's our Christian duty.'

'It seems to me', muttered Daffy, 'that our Christian duty is to mind our own business.'

The nurse went purple to her cheekbones. The manservant had never given her such a back-answer before, in the year since he'd come to live on Inch Lane. So much was clear to her: Mary Saunders was spreading seeds of rebellion wherever she turned.

One morning when the girl was out at market, Mrs Ash climbed the creaking stairs to the little attic room where the two maids slept. And there she found her proof at last. The mattress was scattered with colour: strips and corners of silks and taffetas, a curl of silver thread and a length of lace wound round a bit of paper torn out of a book. All spread across the thin brown blanket like a miniature pageant of the vices – Vanity, Idleness, and their bastard child, Theft.

Mrs Ash hoarded the knowledge for a few hours. But when she passed the girl in the hallway, later in the morning, she held up one flat hand to stop her in her tracks. 'I know your crime,' she said, with no preamble.

Mary Saunders went a sickly kind of white.

'Shall I inform the mistress,' the nurse went on almost civilly, 'or would you rather make your own confession?'

The girl's jaw was jutting out. 'What have I got to confess?' Her voice shook with guilt.

Mrs Ash stepped some inches closer. 'I know you despise us as peasants who've seen nothing of the world. You think yourself our better because you come from the City. As if we'd soil our shoes on the streets of that Gomorrah!' She found she was almost spitting; she paused for a second and licked her lips dry. 'But we're not so ignorant down here that we don't know the laws of the land.'

Mary tried to push past.

'*Thou shalt not steal*,' said Mrs Ash in the voice of Moses.

The girl froze, and stared at her. 'Steal?' she repeated.

As if she didn't know that's what it was called! 'Doesn't the Scrap Act call it plain theft, to keep the odds and ends of any trade, whether for misuse or for sale? These' – and with a flourish Mrs Ash dragged a fistful of bright fabrics out of the depths of her pocket – 'these items belong to your masters, and well you know it. Silk, this is,' she said, flapping a triangle of bright blue, 'I know that much, and you can't pretend otherwise!'

The Londoner did something very odd, then. She didn't try to snatch the bits of cloth; she made no denials. Instead a look crossed her face that was something like relief. She put her head back and laughed like a girl who had no cares in the world. She had all her teeth, and they shone.

Mrs Ash was left alone in the passage, her hands clenched as if with cramp.

In the wavering light of the candle, that night after supper, Mary's needle seemed to wink in and out of existence. Spots wandered across the worn linen, and for a moment Mary thought they were bloodstains. In the deep yellow candlelight an infinity opened between her eyes and the needle, and she couldn't remember which side of the cloth was up. To shake off this vertigo, she leapt to her feet to trim the wicks. She liked to do this before Mrs Jones reminded her to. It gave her a flickering sense of being needed.

There was a knot deep down in her stomach. Nothing had been said about the scraps yet. She'd never heard of that wretched law – if it wasn't the nurse's malign invention. Had Mrs Ash decided not to tell the mistress, or was she just biding her time, planning to expose Mary in front of the whole family? Mary could feel the nurse's eyes sweep over her, every now and then.

Mr Jones read a paper in his shabby brown wing-chair; his eyelids fluttered. Mary watched him from beneath the edge of her mob-cap. He sat so straight, so much like any other man might sit with his legs crossed, that it seemed to Mary not so much that his leg was gone as that it was invisible, tucked out of sight somehow. Her sore eyes felt tricked as they searched for the line missing from the picture. His muscled arms bulged at the cuffs.

Which bits of a man were necessary, she wondered? Mr Jones seemed a whole man as he was, but what if he had no legs at all? Or no arms? If only his trunk remained, propped up on the couch, would he still be Mr Jones? How much could a man lose and still be himself? What about his yard, she wondered; what would he be without that?

His eyes lifted to hers.

Hot-faced, Mary looked back at the candle she was trimming.

Mr Jones cleared his throat with a great rumble and turned a page. 'These trading posts we're fighting the Frenchies for – I must admit I'm hard put to it to tell one from the other. *Quebec*, for instance; I wonder, is that one in India?'

'Such heathenish names,' muttered Mrs Ash.

'And I see here the Prime Minister has warned the American

colonists that if they push the Redskins any further west it will come to blows in the end.'

'Imagine,' said Mrs Jones vaguely, her eyes on her needle.

'There's news of a great fire in London, Mary,' the master added, peering at the bottom of the page. 'A street called the Strand; do you know it?'

It was all Mary could do to keep from crying out. She imagined the great porticoes, three times the size of anything in Monmouth, blackened by flame, and the Misses racing along the gutters, their light skirts pocked with ash. 'I do,' she said faintly.

Mrs Jones looked up from her needle, blinking. 'What's London like, then, Mary?'

Where to begin? 'Well, all the streets are lit up, all the time,' Mary told her mistress. She knew she was exaggerating, but she had to, or she'd miss the truth by a mile.

Mrs Jones grinned as if she'd heard a very good joke.

'Such a waste of candles,' said Mrs Ash severely from her corner.

Mary didn't turn her head. 'No, they're oil lamps on poles,' she boasted. 'And the flames are every colour of the rainbow.'

'They can't be,' observed Daffy.

'Well, they are,' she said cheekily. 'Have you been there, that you know so much about it?'

'No,' said Daffy, very calm, 'but I'd wager I know more than you about the chemical processes of combustion.'

Mary rolled her eyes. Did he hope to dazzle her with syllables? What a curious fellow he was. They'd shared a house for more than a month, and had it ever occurred to him to so much as kiss her? Not that she'd have let him, but it did seem strange that he hadn't tried. Mary still wasn't used to being around men who showed no sign of wanting from her what all the others had wanted.

Mrs Jones was still marvelling over the street lamps. 'Just to think of it!' Her small pupils held pinpricks of light.

Mary's lies got wilder after Daffy had gone off to his basement room with *Botanical Curiosities of the Island of Britain* and half an inch of candle. The others would never know the difference, she decided, so she could tell them anything. She had the impression she was conjuring London out of the hot musty air of the little parlour. She claimed, among other things, that the streets were so choked with Dutchmen, Mohammedans and Indian princes that you could walk for half a day and never see a plain English face.

'Mohammedans, really?' asked Mr Jones with interest.

'Thousands of them!' Mary added that fine ladies wore trains ten yards long, with spaniels taught how to carry them in their mouths. Fighting bucks duelled every hour of the day in St James's Park, so the air rang loud with their steel, and the grass was dark with blood. She even did the street cries for the family's entertainment, in her best Cockney accent: 'Noo great cockles, sprats, lamprils!'

'Foyne warsh-ball, come buoy!'

'Cherry roype, red pippins!'

''Ave ye any corns on y'toes?'

She made them laugh, all except Mrs Ash, who'd gone off to bed in the middle of Mary's description.

'London's not half such a place in my romances, though,' said Mrs Jones, puzzled. 'There it's all paying calls and buying gloves.'

Mary gave her a startled glance. She should have remembered Mrs Jones was a novel-reader. Lying about her past had become such a habit, Mary found it hard to stop. She let out a contemptuous puff of breath. 'Pugh! Authors!' she said. 'They don't see the half of it, cooped up with their pens all day.'

'Very true,' said Mrs Jones, nodding. 'I can almost see why your father and mother took themselves off to London. It must have been a thrilling sort of life, at times.'

Mary almost wanted to slap her for her foolishness. Why did the woman believe everything she was told?

She tried to imagine them together, her grim-faced mother and this woman whose voice was always rippling up and down, whose small pointed face never stopped moving. But for that Mary would have needed to picture them before their lives had split like two paths in a wood. To see her mother as she'd been when she was a girl called Su Rhys, before anything and everything had gone wrong, before the fool she'd married had lost his eleven days.

'Oh, Mary, before I forget,' murmured Mrs Jones, digging in the pocket that hung inside her skirt. She produced a handful of shiny scraps of fabric, and leaned over.

The girl received them in her cupped hands. The very same ones that Mrs Ash had confiscated; not a thread missing! She stared at her mistress.

'It's only natural for a girl to have a liking for odds and ends,' said Mrs Jones lightly, 'and I can't do much with them myself. Next time, ask me, and I'll see, can I spare enough for a little cape.'

Mary's eyes were prickling. 'You're too good,' she said, very low.

Mrs Jones waved the thanks away as if it were a fly, and returned to her sewing. Then she let out a genteel burp, and remarked, 'I can't seem to stomach that last batch of beer.'

'Some good cider, that's what you need,' said her husband.

'Why, yes, that would be more wholesome, I believe.'

'Daffy,' said Mr Jones a minute later, when the manservant came in with an armful of sticks for the fire, 'you might go down to the Crow's Nest to fetch the mistress a pint of cider.'

Daffy stopped in his tracks.

'Go on,' said Mr Jones mildly, 'it's late already.'

The manservant cleared his throat. 'The King's Arms is not much farther.'

Mrs Jones laid a small hand on her husband's wrist ruffle. 'My dear—'

'Now, Daffy, enough of this nonsense,' he said, his voice booming in the little parlour. 'The Crow's Nest is the nearest and the cheapest, and it's high time you mended this foolish quarrel with your father—'

Mary stood up. 'I'll go.'

Her master and mistress stared at her.

'I'd be glad to get a breath of air,' she said with a yawn. 'I'll just fetch my cloak.'

Daffy gave Mary a smile so grateful it took her by surprise. The fellow thought she was doing him a favour!

Mr Jones's forehead was creased. He applied to his wife: 'I don't know; should the girl be out so late?'

'Ach, it's only round the corner. If she kept herself safe on the streets of London, Thomas, I think she can go as far as the edge of the Meadow. Just go straight down Grinder Street, Mary, and tell Cadwaladyr to put it on the slate.'

Everything was just around the corner in this town.

Mary's lantern shed a weak circle as she picked her way down Grinder Street to where there was a gap in the houses. The chill air wormed under her cloak. She turned towards the Meadow, which was a sea of black earth. There was the Crow's Nest. She'd been expecting a painted sign, but the crow's nest hanging above the bright doorway of the alehouse was real; it still held a few fragments of eggshell. Some of its twigs hung loose, twitching in the cool wind. She blew out her lantern.

Though the only light inside came from a pair of fires, Mary winced at the brightness as she came in out of the night. There was a reek of old beer and straw. She worked her way through a knot of old men, knuckling dice on the beaten earth floor; when one of them accosted her in a mumble, she took no notice. She kept her cloak fastened in spite of the blast of heat from the fire. So this was what Daffy had left behind him, she noted curiously; a low, shabby sort of place.

In the corner behind the barrels the drawer-boy straightened up. He couldn't have been more than ten. 'Sup of perry, lass?' he asked cockily.

'Cider. For Mrs Jones. And draw it fresh,' Mary told him, handing over the tankard.

'Always,' sighed the boy, pulling the spigot from a barrel.

When he handed over the pint, she gripped it and turned to go.

'Penny halfpenny,' called the boy, louder than he needed to.

Heads turned through the smoke. Mary began to flush. 'Mrs Jones said to put it on the slate.'

'Not bloody likely. Pay the reckoning or give the cider back.'

What an insufferable boy. She turned on her heel, and behind her he shouted, 'Cadwaladyr!'

The landlord emerged from the back, his leather apron rolling. 'What's this?'

Mary interrupted the drawer-boy. 'I'm maid to Mrs Jones the dressmaker, sir, and she sent me . . .' But by then she had recognised Daffy's father. Fright gripped her by the throat and cut off her breath. She'd never known the man's name, but how well she remembered the eyebrows like white flames, and the weight of him on top of her, in that dirty inn at Coleford.

Devil take the man! Disappearing and turning up again like some kind of spectre. She hadn't caught a glimpse of him since they'd both got down from Niblett's wagon in the first week of

January. Now here he was, landlord of the nearest tavern – and he knew her too, though she dropped her eyes at once and turned her face into her dark hood. Cadwaladyr's gaze burned against her cheek.

'She won't pay for the cider,' said the boy.

'Mark it down on the slate,' his master told him.

'I weren't to know *which* Mrs Jones, was I?' he grumbled.

But Cadwaladyr shoved him away. 'There's a spill wants mopping in the cellar.'

Mary kept her eyes on the floor. All she could hear was the click of bone dice above the dull chatter.

Cadwaladyr stepped nearer as soon as the boy was gone. 'I know you, don't I?' he said very quietly.

She decided to go on the offensive. 'To my cost,' she said miserably.

The landlord leaned close, till his broad nose was only a few inches from her chin. His whisper was wet. 'No use playing the innocent with me, Miss. Not a week after Coleford but I came down with the clap!'

She looked back blankly. Her heart scrabbled like a rat in a cage. So it was true what Doll once said, then, that you could spread it long after your own symptoms were gone. 'Mr Cadwaladyr, I have no notion—'

'You have something, though, because you set me afire with it,' he said in a rumble. 'I think you must be as arrant a poxy slut as ever walked the Strand.'

He couldn't know how close he'd hit. Mary's eyes scurried. She could have cursed this so-called clergyman for a lecher who'd deserved no better than he'd got, but she didn't dare provoke him. If he raised his voice to denounce her, she was ruined in this town. Already some drinkers were casting curious glances.

'That's a pound you owe me, for starters,' he added, a little louder.

Mary let her face pucker; her eyes glittered with tears. Frantically she searched for something that would make them spill over. She thought of Ma Slattery's cellar; of Doll, rotting in the alley. But still the water hovered behind her eyelids, as if these memories were only stories, horrors that had happened to some other girl. Until she thought of a night long ago, and said in the silence of her mind, *Mother*. Then tears slid down Mary's cheeks.

Her voice was choked; she leaned on the bar and spoke low in Cadwaladyr's ear. 'How dare you make such insinuations, after what you did to a friendless girl?'

She grabbed the tankard of cider and spun around before he could answer. She was out of the door and halfway down the lane before she remembered her lantern was unlit. The night was black as tar; she had to fumble her way like a blind woman.

Her mind raced. Now Cadwaladyr knew that the girl who'd tricked and clapped him was living as a servant in Monmouth, surely he'd choose to speak out and ruin her? Perhaps the Welshman was passing on the story already, entertaining the bumpkins. Word would travel like plague in a primitive crow town like Monmouth, where there was rarely anything to talk about. The Joneses would probably get the news from the milkmonger, first thing in the morning.

Damn, damn, damn the man.

She could lose her job, and worse. On the curate's word she could end up in the gaol on the outskirts of town, just for whoring.

If ever there was a time to run away, this was it. She knew she should have left with the first thaw. Now she'd have to pack her bag as soon as she got home, and slip out before morning to take the first cart going to Bristol. Time to start all over again.

Her feet were numb under the muddy hem of her cloak. A reluctance of the bones. Something weighed her legs down like a lead skirt; something quailed in her at the prospect of the journey ahead. Had her vision contracted that much, in the mere two months she'd lived in Monmouth? Had she lost her nerve?

It shocked Mary, what she thought then. What she discovered, as she picked her way across the cobbles by the muddy radiance of the stars, was that she wanted to stay.

Every morning that week Mrs Jones and Mary embroidered Mrs Morgan's white velvet slammerkin, while the light was good and their eyes were fresh. The mistress had decided not to put the girl to help Abi with the housework, any more; Mary's hands were too good to wear out on the back of a scrubbing brush. When the pair of them were working away side by side, hour after hour, Mrs Jones had the curious sensation that they were not mistress and maid but equal helpmeets, almost.

Already they had their customary exchanges, their small jokes. 'Wherever did I put that needle, Mary?'

'In the waist of your apron, madam.'

'That's right!' Mrs Jones plucked it out as if she'd never seen it before. 'What would I do without you, Mary?'

'Sit on a needle, madam.'

She said things to Mary that she'd never have thought suitable if she'd stopped to consider the matter. 'It was our neighbour Sal Belter told me how to get a boy,' she confided one morning.

'Didn't you get him the usual way, then?'

'Oh you cheeky thing.' Mrs Jones felt herself going pink to the sharp tip of her nose. 'What am I doing, talking of such matters to a green girl?'

Mary kept her head down, making minute, regular stitches.

'I lay on my right side, look you now,' the mistress went on in a murmur, 'and I made Thomas lie on his left, and so the child was begot in the right-hand chamber and was a boy.'

Mary frowned at her sceptically. 'Did you not do that for Hetta, then?'

'Oh, I did indeed. I did it for them all,' Mrs Jones assured her, 'when I remembered, any rate. Three of the others were boys.' She heard her own voice go bright and thin, like glass. 'At least I think it was three; one of them, you know, it was too early to tell. The first of our boys lived till he was six,' she added briskly.

'He did?'

'Then he caught a fever in the coal pit.'

'Where's that?' asked Mary after a minute.

'In the forest, beyond the pastures. Maybe I shouldn't have named him Orlando. It was a burdensome name for a wee boy.' Mrs Jones stared at the point where her needle pierced the deep softness of the velvet. 'But Thomas blamed the bad air in the pit. That's why he never let our Grandison out to work. We'd lost all the others by then, you understand. Thomas said Grandison would be different,' she said, a little wildly. 'He would learn his lessons and preserve his health and grow up to be a gentleman and a credit to his family.' She was shaking slightly now, like a post in a high wind.

Mary kept on sewing, but looked up at her mistress after every other stitch. She reached out one hand and rested it on Mrs Jones's skirt.

Mrs Jones squeezed the girl's slim fingers. She looked at her with brimming eyes, and gave her a twisted smile. 'Don't mind me,' she said under her breath. 'I'm a fond and foolish woman.'

Mary changed the subject now, giving Mrs Jones a chance to get hold of herself. 'What sort of a man is Daffy's father?' she asked casually.

'Cadwaladyr? Oh, I couldn't say.'

'I thought you knew him?'

'I do, Mary; that's why it's hard to sum him up in a phrase. Poor Joe,' she said with a little sigh. 'He's looking jowlish these days. Never had anyone to look after him, see. He didn't marry till he was past thirty – some woman from beyond Abergavenny, a stranger to us all – and then didn't she die in childbed the very first year! They had to cut the boy out of her, I heard,' she added with horrified relish.

'So Daffy never had a mother?'

Mrs Jones shook her head. 'He and his father had to knock along together, though I did what I could for the mite, and had him in to play in the shop many a time. I fear that's where he got a taste for the business.'

'Ah,' said the girl. Mrs Jones could see the rapid intelligence in her dark eyes. 'So when he grew up—'

'He announced he wasn't going to bide alongside his father in any smelly old tavern; he meant to work for Thomas Jones.'

The girl's white teeth flashed in a grin. 'War broke out?'

'You can't imagine! He's a skilful fellow, though, is Daffy; that must be said. He's got a knack with the knife and the needle. Thomas couldn't manage without him.'

Mary worked on beside Mrs Jones for a minute, her glossy head bent over her sewing. 'Nowadays, though,' she asked, 'has Cadwaladyr any . . . do you think he might ever take a second wife?'

'Not at all.' Mrs Jones was amused at the idea.

'Or would he ever . . .' The girl blushed faintly. 'You know, go with a bad woman. Like Sally Mole, while she was alive.'

Mrs Jones gave her maid a stern look. 'Mary, how can you say such a thing of our curate, a man of God!'

'I just wondered,' said the girl a little sulkily.

'You can tell just by looking at Joe Cadwaladyr, the thing's impossible,' said Mrs Jones, more gently. 'The whiff of loneliness comes off him like . . . onion.'

The maid nodded thoughtfully. Then, with one of those swerving changes of subject, she said, 'There's something I must admit to you, madam.'

'What is it?' asked Mrs Jones, concerned.

'When I came away from London in such a hurry, I left . . . something owing.'

'Debts, Mary?' Mrs Jones's hand froze over the velvet hem.

'Just one,' said the girl rapidly. 'Rent ... . In her sickness, you know, my mother couldn't help but run into arrears, and our landlady at Charing Cross . . .' Her voice trailed off.

'You mean she wouldn't forgive the debt of a dying woman?' asked Mrs Jones, appalled.

Mary shook her head slowly.

'How much is it, child?'

'Near a pound.' It came out in a whisper. 'I knew it was wicked to rush off without paying, but I couldn't think where else to turn but to you. Only, now the sum is preying on my mind—'

'Of course,' murmured Mrs Jones.

'—or, I mean to say, on my conscience. I can't rest till I send it back to the landlady.'

What a jewel this girl was, thought the mistress. Just fifteen years old, but the wisdom of twice that.

Mary's voice was faltering. 'So I wondered if you might possibly . . . advance it on my wages?'

'Well, now,' dithered Mrs Jones. 'It's not the usual thing, you know, Mary. Nothing till the end of the year, is the rule. I don't know what Thomas would say.'

The girl nodded miserably.

Delight bubbled up in Mrs Jones; she knew what she was going to do. She leaned closer and murmured in the girl's ear. 'But I have a little fund for emergencies, look you, and if I advanced you the money out of that, there'd be no need to trouble Thomas with the matter at all, would there?'

A smile flashed, quick as a fish.

'That's what we'll do, then, Mary. You won't need to fret any more. It'll be our wee secret.'

The girl grabbed Mrs Jones's fingertips and kissed them. Her mouth was hot and soft as a child's.

This time Mary told the drawer-boy at the Crow's Nest to fetch his master and no dawdling. As soon as Cadwaladyr stepped up to the bar, she moved into the light. Yes, it was true, she thought, examining his tired eyes; apart from her, he probably hadn't touched a woman in twenty years. Which meant that if he had indeed picked up an itch, it was from her, and there was no point bluffing.

'So it's you again,' he said, 'the innocent maiden.' His vowels stretched with contempt.

Mary wet her lips with her tongue and said, in a murmur that was barely audible, 'We both did what we oughtn't, Reverend.'

'I'm only Reverend on Sundays,' he said warningly, drawing his tufted eyebrows together; 'here I'm the Master.'

'Well, any rate,' she said soothingly, 'it's not a bad clap you've got; it's the kind that cures itself pretty fast. So I'll say nothing if you'll swear to the same,' she suggested.

At that the man smiled grimly, and leaned on his fists on the bar. 'Our cases aren't alike. My parishioners must already know that I'm a man of flesh and blood. Do your masters know you're a whore?'

Mary shut her eyes for a second. The word winded her; it had been so long since she'd even heard it.

His voice came closer; his breath smelled of strong beer. 'Jane

Jones, of all the women in the world you might have taken advantage of! How would she like to know what kind of slut she's let into her home?'

Anger came up in Mary's chest like heartburn; if she'd had a knife in her pocket, it would have been in her hand by now. But she opened her eyes and saw how old this man was. How much he needed to punish her: not for the clap, nor the money, but for the night on a stinking mattress in Coleford when she'd played the virgin and fooled him into feeling young and dangerous again. 'Please, sir,' she said with difficulty. 'Please. I need to keep my place.'

He folded his arms more tightly. 'I've thought of a way you could repay me,' he offered.

'Yes?' she asked, curious. Maybe she would get to hold on to the money in her pocket after all.

He nodded towards a little group of drinkers in the darkest corner of the inn. 'There was a traveller asking for a girl, tonight, and I told him there was no one since Sally Mole.'

Mary met his level gaze, waiting for it.

'Sally used to take them to a room over the stable.' He jerked his head. 'The stairs are round the back.'

He just wanted to humiliate her. She should have known.

'A shilling a go to you, the same to me,' he added lightly. 'At that rate it wouldn't take you too many nights to pay off the pound you owe me.'

Mary allowed her lip to curl. She took enormous pleasure in scooping the coins out of her hanging pocket and sliding them across the sticky bar. 'You're too kind, but there's no need. Here's your money, Reverend.'

His eyes went wide with surprise. She picked up her lantern and Mrs Jones's cider and stalked out.

Daffy was leaning against a post with his hands in his pockets. He watched Mary emerge from the tavern; the door banged shut behind her. Her colour was up; it must have been the heat from the fire.

When she caught sight of him she leapt, and almost spilled the cider. 'My God, man, what are you doing skulking about here?'

'Waiting for you,' he said, slightly offended. 'It's a dark night; I thought you could do with company home.' He took the lantern from her and opened the glass to trim the flame.

'Why, thank you, then,' said Mary, almost meekly. She took his elbow before he offered it, and they set off up Grinder Street.

He tried to think of an interesting topic of conversation to propose, but for once his mind was entirely blank.

'That's not a bad alehouse your father runs,' Mary remarked.

Daffy let out an inarticulate puff of contempt.

'You don't think so?'

When the words came they were like a swarm. 'It's the same as it was in my grandfather's day, and his granda's before him,' he told her. 'The man hasn't expanded, or improved, or so much as whitewashed the place in twenty years!'

'Would you?'

She had a way of cutting to the meat of things that took him aback. He thought for a moment, then said, 'Probably not. Pulling pints is a low business, whitewash it or not.'

'Lower than being a manservant?'

He flashed her a look, but she was only teasing. 'That's my father's argument,' he told her. 'He still thinks I'm going to crawl home in the hopes of someday owning that sodden barn. He says no son and heir of his should follow another man's orders. But what he doesn't see,' Daffy added eagerly, 'is that my aims are high.' The girl's smile was wide and shiny. He felt tempted to go on. 'I'm more an apprentice to Mr Jones than a mere servant, you know; I made most of that last pair of stays for the Widow Vaughan myself.'

'Did you really?'

'And I've done a couple of very plain pairs for a Quaker family. Besides, trade will expand with the town, it's sure to. We get more visitors of quality every winter; Monmouth is becoming the regular stopping-place after Bath. I tell you, Mary, one of these years there'll be a sign hung up that says, *Davyd Cadwaladyr, Master Staymaker*!'

She was laughing, a low gurgle in her throat. He flung her arm away from him as if it were a snake. She stopped in her tracks, there, at the corner of Inch Lane.

'Mock all you like,' he said, his voice ragged.

'Oh, Daffy, I wasn't laughing at you,' the girl said, soft and serious. 'Only at your . . . passion.'

He shrugged, then folded his arms. 'My future is a matter of some importance to me,' he said stiffly. 'What else should I spend my passion on?'

In the lantern light, her mouth was pursed up like a tight little rosebud. 'On Gwyneth, for instance.'

'Ah. No,' he said, finding it surprisingly easy to bring out the words. 'We're not to marry, after all.'

Mary's eyebrows shot up. 'But the mistress told me you've been walking out for years.'

'Well, my cousin is promised to a pig-gelder now,' he said, 'and there's an end to the matter.' As he said it, he almost believed it.

'No!' she said, narrowing her black eyes at him.

'I don't blame the girl,' he said lightly. 'Her family can barely feed themselves, and I'm in no position to marry yet. Who could blame her for trying for a better life?'

They turned down Wye Street in silence. The moon was

enormous, and bright blossoms loomed out of the darkness. On a tree, narrow buds like fingernails clutched the sky; Daffy reached for one, and it pricked like a needle. It seemed to him that there was some urgency in the air, but then he always felt like that in February: a sense of something breaking out through his skin.

On Inch Lane Mary stopped, with her hand on the front door, and said, 'Truthfully, you know, I wasn't mocking your ambitions.'

He nodded in acknowledgement.

'I have a few of my own,' she added.

Her tone was curiously discreet; not one he'd ever heard from her before. Daffy craned his neck to watch as she disappeared up the narrow stairs.

'Go on, do it today,' Mary told Abi as they were dressing that morning.

'Don't know.'

'What are you so afraid of?' asked Mary, lacing up the older woman's leather stays at the back.

Abi shrugged. 'You trouble,' she murmured as she climbed into the brown holland skirt that Mary had reversed and hemmed for her. The girl let out a roar of laughter.

Abi had spent a fortnight thinking about it, but it still made her break out in a sweat along her hairline as she stood kneading bread on the kitchen table. All she knew was that to ask for something was to show a weakness: a back bared to the whip.

'Mistress,' she said quietly as Mrs Jones bustled out of the pantry, wiping her hands on her apron.

Mrs Jones spoke distractedly. 'Those meat dumplings are quite dried up, Abi, I fear we must throw them out.'

'Yes, mistress. But please?'

'What is it, then, Abi?'

The maid-of-all-work looked down at her hands, covered in dough to the wrist. She spoke through a tightened throat. 'I think. Wonder. I hear—' And then she broke off. She couldn't mention Mary's name; that would be tale-bearing of the worst kind. On the plantation, you could end up with your throat cut in your sleep for that.

'Come now, tell me what's the matter,' said the mistress with gentle impatience. 'Is it about the dumplings?'

Abi shook her head. 'Some say—' she began again. And then, with a sudden bluntness, 'I want wages.'

'Oh, my dear.' Mrs Jones blinked at her. A long pause stretched between them. 'This is unexpected, Abi. After all the years you've been with us. Are you not content in our family?'

Abi made a painful shrug.

'What is it you lack? Tell me. Is it a new dress you'd like, for Easter? I never thought you cared about such things.'

She shook her head violently. 'Wages,' she repeated, as if it were a magic word.

'But what for, exactly? I mean, to buy what with?' Getting no answer, Mrs Jones rushed on: 'You know you're still not used to our money, my dear. Remember that time you got tricked out of a whole shilling for that old slice of salt pork?'

Abi bit down on her lip. She knew it: all she'd brought down on herself was disaster. That whoreson of a butcher, she remembered him now. It was her first year in Monmouth, and when she'd asked for her change he'd denied she'd given him any more than thruppence. 'I said sorry.'

'Indeed you did, and it's all long gone and forgotten,' Mrs Jones told her, patting Abi's floury elbow.

The maid's voice was hoarse with frustration. 'I just want some wages.'

'Well, now.' She could see the mistress's face change, withdraw into itself. 'I must discuss this with the master, of course. But I fear I know what he'll say: we haven't a penny to spare at the moment. We have such heavy expenses, and you've been with us long enough to know how the quality are about paying their bills, Abi!'

The maid stared back at her, refusing to nod.

'But maybe at Christmas, if our affairs are in a better state,' Mrs Jones finished in a rush. 'Yes, that's a better notion. Not so much a wage as a sort of Christmas present. To reward you for all the years you've been part of the family.' Nodding, as if she had resolved the matter to everyone's satisfaction, the mistress made her escape.

Abi stared after her. For eight years she had thought of Mrs Jones as a good woman: the kindest mistress she'd had, anyway. But today she could see right into the woman's heart, to its kernel of cowardice.

She stretched the dough apart in her hands, ripping it like flesh.

The first Sunday in March, and the light was the shocking yellow of daffodils. After dinner the servants had their afternoon off, and Daffy slipped away as usual. But half a mile outside town on the Abergavenny road, he turned and folded his arms over his waistcoat. 'What do you want with me, Mary Saunders?'

'A body's got a right to walk where they please.' She stepped out of the shadow of a cherry tree on which the first few blossoms had opened.

'Well, the next time you follow someone on the sly, take off those clacking heels of yours. You couldn't track a deaf rabbit.'

Mary gave him one of her unexpected red smiles. 'Is that all you do on your days off, then, go a-rabbiting?'

Daffy shook his head.

'How do you pass the time out here, then?'

He shrugged. 'I look. I try', he said sarcastically, 'to enjoy the quiet.'

'What's there to look at?' asked Mary.

'Plenty.'

Farther up the hill he was pleasantly warm from exertion, and Mary was panting like an old dog, with her ridiculous pocket-hoops bouncing from side to side. He shortened his stride a little. To be fair to the girl, she didn't give up easily. They passed thin lambs; he pointed out the traces of their wool caught on the rough skin of the blackthorn trees. He paused for a minute, to watch a hare scudding across a field, and to let Mary catch her breath.

The faint path wound between dried discs of cow dung, like dark clouds in the grass, holding tiny blue lakes from the last rain. It got very stony, then, and he heard a sudden skid of gravel behind him. Mary was down on one knee, and there was a muddy tear in her skirt, but she hadn't cried out. A laugh escaped from his mouth.

'Pox on you,' she growled.

'It's only a wee rip.'

'It's only my best blue gown.'

'Well, why'd you come out rambling after me in it?' Daffy gave her his hand to help her up, and again when they had to scramble over a pile of stones. 'This is the Kymin,' he told her.

'I never climbed a mountain before,' puffed Mary.

He let out another roar. It had been a long time since he'd found anything that funny. 'This isn't a mountain, girl! The Kymin's barely a hill. Now that,' he said, pointing over the skinny spires of Monmouth and far beyond, 'is a mountain.'

Green upon green, and the smuts of sheep speckling the land.

He waited for her eyes to find the long spine of the mountain, and the sharp drop where it ended. Blue-grey stone, almost transparent from this distance. 'Only a small one, mind, but she's a beauty,' he added.

'What's it called?'

'The Skyrrid. They're the three sleeping beasts: the Sugar Loaf, the Blorenge, and the Skyrrid.'

'Have you climbed it?'

'The Skyrrid? I have.'

Mary shaded her eyes. 'I wonder why you'd claw your way up a vast rock, only to scramble down the other side again.'

'So that you'd know you had,' said Daffy.

Mary gave him a dubious glance.

'The slopes were all covered in moss and whortleberries. When at last I got up on to the bare ridge, I thought I'd burst with the terror of it,' he told her. 'It was no wider across than a bed,' he hurried on, aware of her mocking eyes, 'but I walked all the way along it.'

Her eyebrows hunched together. 'Whatever for?'

'I wanted some soil from where the chapel used to be. It's considered a holy mountain.'

'And did you get some?'

'I have a bagful in my trunk,' he confided. 'It's said to ward off disease if you sprinkle it under the bed, and to put a soul to rest, if you scatter it on a coffin.'

Mary's lips were pursed up with amusement. 'So even you, a rational fellow, are given over to superstition!'

He shrugged, grinning uneasily. 'I don't exactly believe it, but I like to hedge my bets. And the mountain does have a holy feel to it. You can see nine counties from the top,' he added.

He thought she might ask him to name them, but she only stared around her critically. 'Why are there fences round some fields, but not all of them?' she asked.

'Ah,' said Daffy, 'that's the tide of history you're looking at.' He liked the phrase, but Mary slid him a scornful glance. 'By the time we die, you and I,' he hurried on, 'every inch of green in Britain will be parcelled up for farming, and there'll be no more common land. That's how Gwyn's family came down in the world,' he added; 'they used to keep pigs on the common down at Chepstow, till the lord had it enclosed.'

'So it's an evil, then, this fencing?'

He shrugged ruefully. 'I couldn't say. Progress depends on it; we can't stand in the way of the times.'

Mary nodded abstractedly.

'I could lend you a very good book on this very question.'

'When do I get time to read books?' she asked him, her lips twisting with amusement.

'Now there you show your ignorance,' he reproached her. 'So-called female education is shockingly insufficient. You have an exceptional mind, I've noticed—'

'Exactly,' said Mary, her black eyes mocking him. 'So I can do my own thinking instead of parroting from books!' A crow flapped overhead; she lifted her chin to watch.

'*Brân*,' said Daffy, savouring the sound.

'Beg your pardon?'

'That's how we say crow, in Welsh.'

'Oh, that gibberish,' said Mary with scorn. 'Get that from a book, did you?'

'No, from my grandam.'

Mary stared at the bedraggled bird, which had settled on a bush. 'It's not much to look at, is it?'

'Ah, but your crow is a thoughtful and witty bird,' he told her.

'Dirty nuisances.'

He shook his head, once more amazed by how little the girl knew. 'I grant you they'll steal anything that shines, but they've a fine sense of humour, and they know things.'

'What things?'

'When it's going to rain, for instance.'

The girl rolled her eyes.

'And they're said to tell the future. Not that I credit that,' Daffy added. 'But I did read of one that lived to be a hundred years old.'

'Books are full of lies,' Mary told him, laughing deep down in her throat.

The crow flew closer, as if to hear its praises. It gripped a fence, claiming it for its own. There was a gloss like ice on its thick bristling coat. It let out a hoarse cry, its beak gaping to release the sound.

'You must never kill a crow, by the way,' Daffy warned her.

'The farmers do, don't they?'

'Sometimes,' he said doubtfully, 'but it's bad luck. It might come back when you're asleep and peck out your eyes.'

Mary laughed again, but he could hear an edge of fright in her voice. 'It's nothing to a vulture. I saw vultures at the Tower in London. Huge crooked-beaked frights.'

'*You forget I'm from London, fellow*,' he quoted in a whinge, just as she'd put it on her first day in Monmouth. It was hard to make this girl flush, but Daffy thought he could detect a darkening along the cheekbone.

'If you've spent your whole life in the back end of nowhere,' she told him loftily, 'you can hardly be expected to understand what you're missing. In London,' she went on before he could answer, 'there are things you wouldn't even know the words for, despite all your book-learning! The walls of rooms are hung with silks and satins of such beauty you couldn't imagine.'

Daffy bent down suddenly, and picked a small startled white flower. 'Anemone,' he said, handing it over; he made her repeat the word until she had it right. 'Find me a silk to match that.'

Mary rolled her eyes. 'Mrs Jones and I can cover skirts in glorious flowers, without any need to go out in the mud to see them.'

'Pugh!' he said rudely. 'Little neat stunted things, you embroider, all the same shape, and flat as thread. That's not nature.'

She shrugged, her collarbone moving like cream in the gap where her kerchief had loosened.

Daffy ran to and fro, picking flowers to fill her apron. Red campion, which wasn't red at all, he explained, but pink like the inside of a lip. Bugle, which sounded like music but was made up of little spikes of purple blue. After hooded vetch came a small pale thing he called cuckooflower, though some said lady's smock, and others, milkmaids.

'What need has it for three names?' she asked.

'What need have you for three dresses?'

'You mock me.' Mary walked along, staring down into her apron. 'Nine,' she said finally.

'Flowers?'

'Dresses. That's if I count a bodice and a skirt as one.'

He let out a whistle, mildly impressed. 'How did you amass such a fortune?'

She went a little pink. 'I got most of them very cheap, in London.'

'And why do you need all those dresses,' he teased, 'when the plants of the field have none?'

'Ach,' she said scornfully – it was a sound she had picked up from her mistress, he noticed – 'we'd be poor paltry creatures if we walked naked.'

For an instant he let himself consider the image: Mary Saunders, walking buck naked across the top of the Kymin. Then he shook his head to clear it.

'Now the Master,' said Mary, 'he doesn't even need two legs.'

'Mr Jones is a great man,' Daffy told her seriously. 'To overcome such a hindrance when he was only a boy – well, that's my idea of spirit.'

'Is he a model to you, then?' asked Mary in her teasing voice. 'Are you going to grow up to be a one-legged staymaker and marry a dressmaker, too?'

Daffy could feel a blush rise from his neckerchief, though he didn't quite know why. 'Mrs Jones is . . . the best of women. When I was a child, and my father was such a blunderer, she was the saving of us. She used to come by our filthy house with a basket of potted pears and clean linens, and my father's face would light up as if she were the Angel Gabriel.'

'Had he a yearning for her, do you think?' asked the girl. 'He speaks very highly of her,' she added slyly.

Daffy stopped short, disconcerted. 'You mean – when he was first widowed?'

'Or even before that, when they were all young together. Cadwaladyr didn't marry till late, did he? Long after Mrs Jones did. And he never took another wife after your mother died, though he could have done with the help, it sounds like.'

'That's true,' said Daffy unwillingly.

'And if your father did have a longing for the mistress,' Mary went on with animation, as if telling a story, 'that would explain why he so resented your coming to work for Mr Jones.'

'That wasn't it at all,' objected Daffy, his mind moving like mud. 'My father thinks the tavern—'

'Damn the tavern!' Mary's dark eyes glittered. 'It's jealousy, pure and simple. He can't bear to see you in service to the man who stole the woman he wanted!'

Daffy shook his head as if to get rid of a troublesome fly. 'You've read too many romances,' he said pointedly. 'You should try an encyclopaedia.'

'Romances are more educational,' she called back. She was almost dancing, now, circling ahead of him across the green back of the hill.

'They are not. They've misled you. Not all motives are low,' he insisted sternly. 'The human heart is not such a gutter as you think it.'

'Daffy,' she said, coming up very close to him and speaking softly. 'Take my word for this. I know more about the human heart than you'll find in all your encyclopaedias.'

Something in her eyes like bitterness, or sorrow. It shocked him. What had happened to these eyes, in only fifteen years of living? He wanted to reach out and shut them with his callused palm. He wanted to kiss Mary Saunders till the mountains wheeled around them.

She turned away, as if she could read his mind. 'What's the master's leg like, tell me?' she asked after a minute, as breezy as ever.

'What?' asked Daffy, dizzy.

'The leg he hasn't got. What's it like?'

Daffy wrestled with the metaphysics of this.

'I mean the bit of it he has, before it stops,' she said impatiently. 'Is it jagged, then? Can you see the teeth marks of the saw?'

'I've never seen it.'

'You must have.'

Daffy shook his head again.

She walked a little closer to him, and whispered: 'Is there anything else missing?'

This was a most forward and peculiar girl. His face was hot. He turned to face into the cool breeze and stared down into the valley. 'That's the Sugar Loaf,' he remarked after a minute. 'And there's Glamorganshire. They speak no English there.'

Mary gazed down on the foreign country. After a few minutes, she spoke as if continuing a silent conversation. 'You could do better.'

He glanced at her, bewildered.

'That Gwyn. She doesn't sound like she was much of a match, anyway. And first cousins shouldn't marry, I've heard; they have queer babies. I'm sure you could do better.'

He didn't know what to say. He felt like laughing, but no sound emerged.

Mary pointed to a flower with a big white head. 'What's that one?'

'Ah, yes,' he said. 'Ramsons, it's called. Rub it on your wrists for perfume.'

She obeyed, unguarded. A reek rose from her.

Daffy laughed aloud. 'Some call it wild garlic.'

She threw the crushed stems in his face and ran down the hill.

Mr Jones had never made a bigger set: fat old Widow Tanner would need sixty bonings for her new Easter stays. Well, if he finished them by Good Friday he was going to charge her double, and defy her to query it! Mary Saunders held an arc of whalebone for him while he backstitched it into place. Her hands were sure; they never trembled.

'I'll name no names, Mary,' he murmured, tugging the thread taut, 'but some staymakers do no more than slot the bones into tucks in the cloth, so they ride about as they will.'

The girl sucked in her breath as if shocked at the very idea.

He knew she was making fun of him; he didn't take offence. His eyes focused on the skeleton of boning in its skin of dull linen. It would take three more days of work before he could start adding the sets of laces – front, back and side – that Mrs Tanner's vast flesh would require.

'Will this pair be silk?'

He gave the girl an amused glance. He'd never known anyone to take such a relish in fine fabric. 'The cover will be. But that matters little, Mary. Any set of stays can look well on the outside, even if there's shoddy work within.' He moved the girl's cold hands infinitesimally, to change the angle of tension. 'It's the bones that matter.'

'I know that,' she said, a little bored. 'But the new green paduasoy is so much handsomer than that old brocade you used on Mrs Pringle's stays.'

Mr Jones's mouth curled up at both ends. 'Ah, well now, beauty. Beauty demands sacrifice, Mary.'

'Sacrifice?'

'The French have never understood that,' he pronounced. 'Their lovelies are loose; all they care for is a row of glossy bows, and a plump *décolletage*. But here in England we make the most unyielding stays in the world. *Upright in body*,' he quoted, '*upright in soul*. English ladies' sides are straight and narrow beyond anything nature can produce.'

'Stays hurt though, sometimes. You should try them,' she remarked under her breath.

He let that bit of pertness go. 'There's a universal worship of beauty which the tender sex cannot escape. Did you ever see the Misses Gunning, Mary?'

She shook her head.

'No, of course not, you must have been a child,' he corrected himself. 'Well. They were the most famous beauties of their day, Miss Maria and Miss Susanna. Can you guess how Miss Maria died?'

Another impatient shake.

'Paint,' he said with grim satisfaction. 'She used a powder to make her face pale and smooth, and it poisoned her in the end.'

Mary gave a little shudder. 'So will you be making Hetta a pair of stays?' she asked after a minute.

He glanced at her curiously.

'Haven't you heard her asking for them?'

'The child's not six years old,' he murmured, pushing his long needle through the linen.

'So, in the case of your own daughter, you admit they might do harm?'

This girl had a dreadfully teasing manner, sometimes. Mr Jones bit down on a smile. 'Hetta might do well enough with a little pair in canvas, kept loose. I have always discouraged my wife from lacing too tight.'

Mary Saunders glanced down at herself. His eyes followed hers. Under her blue bodice her chest was as taut as a sapling. For fifteen, she was a full-figured woman. 'Where did you get that pair?' Mr Jones asked professionally.

'London.'

'But what shop?'

Her dark eyes clouded over. What had he said? 'A friend left them to me,' Mary answered finally, 'when she died.'

He returned his eyes to his work. 'It's a simple set,' he said briskly, 'not much force to them, but the line is true.' His hands dithered over the white fragments of whalebone, then seized the one he wanted. 'You're not the kind of customer I like, though,' he muttered under his breath.

'No?' asked Mary.

'Not enough needs fixing,' he said neutrally. 'A girl like you might as well wear a sack.'

He didn't look up, in case she was blushing.

'So you prefer ugliness?' she asked a little hoarsely.

'In a sense,' Mr Jones told her. 'That set of stays I made for Mrs Leech, for instance – now there was a challenge. You realise, Mary, I can mould the female form into whatever I like. I aim for an effect of harmonious symmetry, much like the architectural designs of Mr Adam, I like to think.' He thought this allusion was probably wasted on the girl. 'I might go so far as to call myself a maker of women,' he explained.

'So you improve on the work of the Maker?' she asked cheekily.

His blade slowed as he pondered this remark. 'Continue it, rather. I use what He has provided us with to bring His creations to the height of perfection.' Mr Jones lifted a curved slip of white bone up to his eyes for inspection. 'But I have a liking for stays themselves, quite apart from fitting them to their wearers. The intricacy of them, you know; the strength.'

'Yes?'

'How they hold everything in place.'

Mary Saunders smiled. Her mouth was really too wide, her master decided. Her lips had too much blood in them. What was that old rhyme?

> *Men's Tools according to their Noses grow;*
> *Large as their Mouths are Women too below.*

Head bent, he blushed faintly over his work.

The manservant came in then, with a stack of boxes. He brought a faint tang of the outdoors with him; the smell of hard work in the fresh air.

Mr Jones glanced up just then, to ask Daffy something, and saw the manservant standing there, arms by his sides, looking at the maid, and the maid staring back at him. *Mary and Daffy*, the master said to himself, turning away; *Daffy and Mary*. Like an old rhyme.

He heard Hetta squeal in the passage, and Mrs Ash's stern tones, drowning her out. He waited for the quick steps that meant his wife, and her voice, soothing the child and the nurse too.

What Mr Jones had seen had locked his throat, and made him turn a little sick. His hand was shaking, so he laid down the blade. He felt old, and crippled. A pain started up in the leg he'd lost a quarter of a century ago.

Nance Ash woke with a sense of weight on her hands and face. After a few seconds, she remembered that this was Easter Sunday. *The Lord is risen*. She waited to feel her spirits lift, but nothing happened.

Easter was her favourite festival, as a rule. It had few of the frivolities of Christmas. It was concerned with pain, and the purposes of pain, and pain's triumph and consolation. But this morning her heart was shut up like a tomb, and the great stone was too heavy to move aside.

On the floor below she could hear the quick steps of her mistress. A woman of whom Nance Ash would have to say that she was fond, even if Mrs Jones had thwarted her on many occasions over the years (most recently and disgracefully in the matter of those cloth scraps), and had an unfortunate tendency to place her trust in false friends such as Mary Saunders. A kind enough mistress; better than many, no worse than some. Not noticeably godly, but not quite godless either. A woman who had come up from nothing – Back Lane, Mrs Ash added mentally, which was worse than nothing – by means of some skill with a needle and marriage to a hardworking man. *The Lord maketh poor and maketh rich*. God had seen fit to place Mrs Jones at the head of a family, secure in the love of a fine upstanding husband, for reasons best known to Himself. And Mrs Ash He had put under this woman as a servant.

It would never occur to Nance Ash to question His will. He had given her masters who had kept her on long after her milk had dried up, out of charity. The word was a dry crust in the mouth, but then, what else had she to swallow? For the thousandth time, Nance Ash steeled herself to obey. *And the Angel of the Lord said unto Hagar, Return to thy Mistress, and submit thyself under her Hands*.

All this could be borne. Worse than this could be endured. In hopes of a resurrection in the end.

She dressed the same way as she had every day of her life. Dolling herself up for Easter would hardly impress the Risen God. On a turn of the stairs she almost ran into the Londoner and the manservant, who were standing deep in conversation. Their faces were not a foot apart. At the sight of Mrs Ash they backed off. Guilt on the air, like dust motes catching the light.

'Good morning, Mrs Ash,' said Daffy, very sprightly. 'May I be the first to offer the felicitations of the day?'

'The resurrection of our Lord is not a carnival,' she told him, brushing past. She didn't look behind her to see the girl's face; she knew just what mixture of impudence and lasciviousness it held. The cheek of her, to come into this household and set herself to distract a young man from his duties! It seemed to Mrs Ash now that Daffy had been an excellent fellow until Mary Saunders fixed her dark eyes on him.

Well, they had better be careful, the pair of them. She wasn't going to turn a blind eye to smuttiness in corners, whatever others did. What they were feeling – oh, Nance Ash remembered it well enough from the days of her engagement, that unholy knot of excitement in the stomach – it could bring them down like a hurricane in the end.

For Easter dinner the Joneses were going to have hare pie, thanks to Daffy, who'd come home with two of the creatures over his shoulder. Mrs Jones smiled to herself as she brushed egg across the pastry lid. The Lenten days were over.

That was twice recently that Mrs Morgan had commented on their absence from church; it was time for the whole family to make an appearance. At St Mary's, the women sat in a row at the back of the right-hand pews, packed in like fish. Mrs Jones had put her teeth in, for the occasion, so she was trying to remember not to smile too wide, for fear the pewter settings would catch the light of the candelabra. On her left was Mrs Ash, down on her knees from the moment she'd entered the church, head on her hands; her mistress swallowed a wave of irritation. Out of the corner of her eye she could see her husband and Daffy, over on the men's side. Daffy was looking up at the ceiling as if something miraculous were happening among the spiders there. Her husband had his hands knotted in his lap in a perfectly orthodox fashion. No one would guess his conviction that, as he'd put it to her only the other night, the Church of England was as corrupt as a dead dog, and not at all a suitable place for addressing the Divine.

Mrs Jones took a long breath and began to enjoy herself, despite the feeling of too many teeth in her mouth, eating her up. All around her she recognised clothes she'd sewn herself. She elbowed Mary when Miss Theodosia Fortune went by in that taffeta cape with the festooned hem that had caused them so much trouble. Then she craned to see past Mrs Halfpenny, asleep in her butterfly cap, delicate snores rising. Over the other side of the church, Mrs Halfpenny's husband, the town clerk, had got something tucked inside his prayer book, she noticed; his lips moved as he read.

Mrs Jones toyed with the notion that the ladies of Monmouth were her puppets: walking advertisements for her handiwork. The vainer ones flicked their heads from side to side like pigeons, to check that no one was wearing more ruffles than themselves. With all the coloured skirts and plumed straw hats, and the old stained glass behind them, the little church was as bright as a fruit bowl. Even Cadwaladyr's vestments were as vivid as a bruise.

The curate's sermon was on dress. 'Are the fair sex empty vessels,' intoned Cadwaladyr gloomily, 'that they must make such a fuss of their outsides?'

Mrs Halfpenny had woken up now. Beside her, plumes twitching in annoyance, sat the stately Mrs Morris of Chepstow, who owed five guineas at the Joneses and God knows what elsewhere.

'The waste of time and money on mere attire will surely reduce this nation to beggary,' complained the curate. 'Unless' – his reddened finger moved along their pews – 'the ladies turn of their own will from proud vanity to sober economy.'

There were rustles and creaks all around. 'And this from a seller of spirituous liquors!' hissed Mrs Halfpenny.

'The fellow is trying to ruin our trade,' murmured Mrs Jones mischievously in Mary's ear. She'd never heard ladies rebuked to their faces before.

But Cadwaladyr must have realised by now that he'd gone too far. Midstream, his sermon changed direction. Neatness without could signify neatness within; he went so far as to admit that the Creator was gratified by beauty in his creatures. 'But above all, what He demands is transparency of heart,' the curate went on, his voice rising: 'that His people should be what they appear to be.'

Beside Mrs Jones her maid sat with her jaw jutting out. She

seemed to have taken against the man. What an unpredictable girl Su Rhys's daughter was. Not that Su had been entirely free from moods and megrims herself, good woman that she was.

St Mary's was as hot as an oven by the time the sermon was over. Under the weight of incense and pomade, Mrs Jones registered the sweat of outrage. And another smell she didn't recognise, dark and vegetative. Only on the way out, shuffling to the back of the church behind the vast arcs of skirts and the odd dress sword, did she remember what it must be. Behind the pews the church was floored with the gravestones of the great families. In one corner the pavement had been dug up, and earth piled high, smothered in flowers and leaves. It must have been a winter burial; the greenery had rotted to the slime of February, and it all smelled rampantly alive.

'Sometimes,' Daffy said dreamily, 'when I have a whole day off, I walk right down the Vale to the old abbey at Tintern. There's never a soul there. I like to stretch out in the long grass and count the windows. I never end up with the same number twice!'

Mary lay with her face six inches from his, in Chippenham Meadow at eight in the evening of the mildest day of April. She could feel Daffy's hot breath on her cheek. He was one of those people who gave off a sort of cloud of heat in every direction, even through his double-layered winter jacket.

'The sky is so blue through those old stone pillars, Mary. It looks as if a giant wandered by and lifted off the roof to see what was inside. Maybe I'll take you down to Tintern someday, in the summer?' he suggested. 'It's a long enough walk, but you're stronger than you know.'

She nodded, not listening. Her head was propped on her fist; she glanced down at the tops of her breasts, creamy as fresh butter.

Now he was rambling on about the crows, pointing as they

wheeled from tree to tree at the darkening horizon. 'They each go off to search for food alone, at twilight,' he said eagerly, 'but then the leader calls them home. They chase each other, for sport, but they all end up asleep together in one great roost. Strength in numbers, you see.'

Mary yawned and stretched, inched a fraction closer, as if she didn't know what she was doing. She could see the front of Daffy's breeches tautening. Power pulsed in her like water in a spring. She told herself that she could make this man stand up like an ear of wheat.

Oh, it was delicious, this moment before the demand, before the rebuff. Because of course she would say no. She had no intention of risking her new life for a roll in the grass with Daffy Cadwaladyr.

He'd better not try it. He'd better not take a single liberty. Mary wouldn't even need to speak, in fact; she would simply push him off her, the moment he stopped talking and climbed on top of her. Because every man came to a moment like that. Young or old, civil or boorish, they all reached a point where what was happening in their heads was rendered irrelevant by what was happening in their breeches. Even the gallantest gentleman, when he was all talked out, would take hold of a girl and crush her against him as if she were no more than a mattress. They couldn't help it; it was their low nature. It wasn't worth getting upset over. What was it Doll used to say, cackling all the while? *They'd fuck a goat if they couldn't find a woman, dearie. They'd fuck a hole in the wall!*

Daffy had stopped talking, without her noticing. It was as if he'd run out of words. He did a peculiar thing, then; he reached out and touched Mary's cheekbone; lightly, as if he were brushing away a speck of coal dust. She thought of Doll, that first morning, wiping mud out of the lost child's eyes.

Her throat hurt, all at once, as if she were swallowing a stone.

She wished the two of them could stay for ever frozen in this moment, hidden in the grass, as the setting sun slid across the fields of Monmouth. Before any asking, any refusal. While this strange, tame young man was still looking at her as if she were worth any price.

It all came down to the market in the end, she reminded herself. When corn was plentiful, the price of bread would fall. Whatever a woman gave away, she cheapened. Men wanted what they couldn't afford. For all Daffy's book-learning, Mary knew he'd turn out to be the same as every other man, in the end; for all his soft talk, she knew exactly what he needed from her. *A hole in the wall.*

Mary Saunders had never given anything away for free, and she wasn't about to start now. She let his hard fingertips move across her mouth, for a long second, while she gathered all her powers of refusal.

'Marry me,' he said simply.

She sat up so fast she scraped her elbow. The black world spun round her. 'What?'

'Didn't you hear me?' he asked, blushing red.

Sick with dizziness, Mary started laughing. It was all she could think to do.

Daffy put his hand over her mouth, as if to seal it up. 'Let me speak,' he said hurriedly. 'Give me a minute. It's a very sensible plan.'

'It's a nonsense!'

'No,' he gabbled, 'no, listen. I'm a cautious man—'

'You're a fool with swollen breeches!'

He blinked at her, startled. Very well; let him know how coarse she could be. Let him realise what an impossibility he was asking.

Daffy got up on one knee, and knotted his hands together.

'I swear,' he began, 'I swear it's not just a matter of . . . amorousness. It seems to me – it has seemed to me for some time now,' he corrected himself, 'that you and I have much in common.'

Mary let her mouth twist into a smile. Was that what he called it?

'I mean,' he added hastily, 'we neither of us seem to have any immediate prospects of bettering ourselves, but when we consider the matter closely, we're both in a position to profit from our experience.'

'Daffy, man, what are you talking about?'

He cleared his throat with a donkey's bray and rushed on. 'I know you're fond of the family, as am I, but they can't expect us to stay for ever. What I mean to say is, by the end of the year I'll be ready to set up my own sign as a staymaker. And you – you're almost qualified for dressmaking, and millinery, and such, aren't you? Mrs Jones is always saying how quick a learner you are. And so before too long it might be possible for us to . . .'

'Marry?' she asked in the long silence.

Daffy nodded so hard she thought his head might crack off. 'I'd wish,' he said, straining for the words, 'to be the kind of husband who's as much . . . friend as lover. Do you understand me? What I'm offering is a – a partnership, in all things.'

Mary's mind scurried like a rat. The man liked her, wanted her, was her match in hard work and ambition; was that such a small fortune? What had the Joneses, when they'd started out, but a mutual fondness, a few skills, and a wish to rise in the world?

'I know you're still very young,' he rushed on, 'and if you liked we could wait. But not too long, I hope. I mean, if you say yes.'

Mary let herself down into the grass. Her heart lurched in its cage of ribs.

'Please,' he added. 'I meant to say, please. I've thought it all through. I've thought of nothing else. I haven't read a book in weeks!'

That made her laugh again, in triumph. She let her eyes rest on his blue liquid ones. 'What about Gwyn?' she asked, for the pleasure of hearing the answer.

His cheeks were dark with all the blood in them. His wig was slipping off. 'I never felt like this before,' he said simply. 'I didn't think to ever feel like this.'

What would life be like with such a man? Nothing Mary had ever bothered to imagine, in her dreams of a glittering future. It would be a chance to shed her old self, once and for all. She would be an ordinary girl again, then an ordinary wife. This was the town all roads seemed to lead to. The ending to every story she'd ever read.

'Maybe,' she breathed.

'Yes?' His voice was harsh, like a soldier's in battle.

'Maybe yes.'

Chapter Six

Bloom Fall

'Don't forget the rowan.'

'Rowan?' repeated Mary, mending the handle of her basket with a bit of old twine.

'For nailing up over the door,' said Mrs Jones patiently. 'To keep out witches.'

Mary stared at Mrs Jones over the kitchen table, and gave a helpless shrug. 'Whatever you say.'

It was May Eve, and Mrs Jones had released Mary from the endless hem of Mrs Vaughan's muslin cape and sent her off to the woods to go blossoming. 'It brings the summer in,' Mrs Jones explained, half-laughing. 'If we don't hang blossoms up by May Morning, nothing will bear fruit.'

And indeed, thought Mary, the world was full of strange things and stranger people, so what harm could it do to nail up a few branches of blossom?

In the warm evening the river was cluttered with swans and gulls. The trees shuddered with roosting crows. There were purple bunches Mary didn't recognise till she got up close, and breathed in, and remembered the baskets in Covent Garden: lilacs. How the scent of them used to swim above the stink of the discarded fruit underfoot. She walked deeper into the wood now. An old tree, slumped under its rolls of bark, was turning green all over;

through cracks in its sides the fresh twigs were breaking out, hungry for the light.

In a clearing Mary passed half a dozen locals hacking branches off a fallen birch that was the length of four men. Jarrett the Smith looked up and wiped the sweat and insects off his forehead. 'How d'you like our Maypole, Mary Saunders?'

She gave him a quick smile.

'Long enough for you, is it?' And a sly guffaw from another fellow.

Who'd said that? Maybe the red-haired man at the back, one of the ones whose names she didn't know. But they all knew her, evidently. She walked on faster. Her heart was thumping in her chest. Would they have spoken that way to any female passing through the woods today, given that it was the season of rising sap and dirty jokes?

She was safe, Mary reminded herself. She was not yet sixteen, a virgin without a history. Her only secret was that she was engaged to be married to Daffy Cadwaladyr, a respectable manservant of twenty.

Nothing was impossible.

She wasn't sure which bush was rowan, but she started to fill her basket with white tangled blossom; if she brought home a bit of everything, she'd be all right.

The creak of a breaking branch, and she spun around. But it was only Daffy, his face lit up with a smile like a Roman candle. 'Sneaking after me, were you?' she asked, trying to be stern.

'Mrs Jones sent me to carry your basket.'

'She didn't!'

'She did!'

'She knows, then,' Mary told him, letting him press his throat against her wide red mouth. 'She's such a romantic.'

'She can't know,' he said, troubled. 'I haven't said a word yet. We agreed, not a word till after Christmas.'

'The woman's got eyes in her head, hasn't she?' murmured Mary. 'And she can smell it on the air. Every bird and plant in this wood is getting mated. It's the season.'

Not a word from Daffy; he'd loosed her long dark hair from its starched cap and dipped his face into it. His breath was a live creature at the nape of her neck. And suddenly for the first time in her life Mary felt it. A flickering in her stomach; a thrill as sharp as a blackbird's note. It occurred to her that this must be what Doll had had with her journeyman: what ordinary women felt at the hands of ordinary men.

Was it indeed due to the season, the ripening on all sides? Or was it because of the seriousness of this man's fingers? Mary's body shook behind her rigid stays. There was no time to waste. When she ripped open Daffy's breeches, a button fell into the ivy. His eyes were startled, huge. 'Wait—' he stuttered.

Mary didn't bother answering. Hair hung damp in her eyes. She didn't care if she was giving herself away by such forwardness, or if her hands had the practised ease of a harlot. What mattered was to catch hold of this tiny feeling before it disappeared for ever.

She was on top of him, then he was on top of her. There were twigs in his wig. Her heel was caught in a loop of ivy. All round them the scent of crushed blossoms went up. Daffy's lips moved as if drinking Canary wine from an invisible bottle. His legs thrashed like flames.

She slid him into her, swallowed him up. Daffy's whole body went as stiff as a corpse. It was then that Mary realised he'd never done this before in his life. He was much too new at it to realise she was no virgin. She was touched; she was appalled. His bliss was so close she could nearly taste it. She waited for it to spread into her body, fill it up.

But the fact was, the act felt the same as it always had. A necessary conjunction. A temporary occupation. She was numb. She was a million miles away. *Not half so big as his father, is he*? remarked Doll in her head.

Mary squeezed her eyes shut. Her own thoughts repelled her.

It was all over in minutes. 'Oh, Mary,' Daffy cried in her ear, 'oh, Mary, oh, Mary,' till it became a sound that had no meaning.

His dead weight on her was the same as any other man's; the same crumpled feeling, the same stickiness, cooling as fast in the twilight. She wanted more than anything to shove him off her, and had only mercy enough to lie still.

When he raised his head she saw his eyes were wet. 'This is the happiest hour of my life,' he whispered huskily.

She strained her neck up to kiss one of his eyelids. The whole thing was impossible.

Kneeling up, searching in the foliage for his missing button, Daffy spoke more calmly. 'Let's come back here, to this very spot, every May Eve,' he said, 'for the rest of our lives.'

Mary stopped brushing leaves off her skirt, and stared at him. 'But Daffy,' she began warily, 'we won't be in Monmouth *always*.'

'Where else will we be?'

A watchman's wooden rattle started up in Mary's head. 'There won't be enough room for us here.'

'But Monmouth is growing apace,' he told her cheerfully. 'I believe it could soon bear two staymakers, and two dressmakers. We may need to begin in another town in the Marches, but it won't be long until we come home.'

Home. The word was bitter in her mouth. This was where the trap lay, she saw now. 'London's that,' she said, almost gruffly. 'My home is nowhere else. I'm a London girl.'

Daffy shook his head gently, as if at a child. 'Not any more, my sweetling. If you could see how much you've changed—'

Anger made spots behind Mary's eyes. 'I'm the same as I ever was. And as for you, I thought you claimed to have ambition!' she spat at him. 'I didn't know you planned to eke out your days in a miserable crow town.'

His face went white. 'If it's good enough for the Joneses—'

'Pox on the Joneses!' she roared. 'I want more from life than to end up a poor man's Mrs Jones.'

Daffy's hands were twined together like wet rope. He wore the painful expression of someone trying to recall the second verse of a song. 'Mary, Mary,' he remonstrated, 'all else aside, how could we think of bringing up our children in the big city?'

She stared at him. For a moment she'd forgotten how little he knew about her. He had no idea who she really was: a barren, raddled whore. His innocence repelled her as much as her own deceit.

She and he were too unlike, she saw now; they could no more combine than oil and water. They wanted different things in life and had different plans for getting them. Mary's path and Daffy's had briefly crossed in this blossoming wood before snaking away in opposite directions. The old happy ending had no place in this particular story. How could she have been such a fool?

'I've made a mistake,' she said quietly, and turned to pick up her basket.

'What do you mean?'

'I can't marry you.'

'Not quite yet, I know,' Daffy blundered on, 'but in good time—'

How could she ever have thought of mating herself to such a plodding, ordinary man? 'Never,' said Mary, walking out of the wood.

John Niblett the coach driver brought news that the war with France was over at last after seven years, and the Government had ordered public rejoicings in every town. But Mr Jones spent the evening poring over the *Bristol Mercury*, and announced over griddle cakes at supper that this so-called peace was a disgrace. 'We beat the dogs fair and square, and now we're handing them back Guadaloupe and Martinique!'

Mary would have liked to stroll down to the bonfire on Chippenham Meadow – they said there was going to be dancing – but she feared to meet Daffy there. The man's eyes were as red as a rash these days. He kept hovering in her vicinity, as if he had some grand, decisive declaration to make. But she made sure never to be alone with him. Nothing he could say would make any difference.

Within a few weeks the blooming trees were scraggy again. Mrs Jones said bloom fall was the season that always made her sad; it came on so quickly. The blossoms nailed to the walls of the house faded and curled after a few weeks, but their smell grew stronger.

To Abi, they always seemed to have a tang of rot. Late one warm May night she lay on her side of the bed and stared out of the tiny window. The shutter had been left wide open to catch some air. There was nothing to see but an indigo sky. Beside her, Mary Saunders let out a long breath between her teeth.

'You fight with your fellow?' asked Abi.

Mary's head turned towards her as quickly as a bird's. 'What fellow?'

Abi snorted mildly. As if the way Daffy had been looking at Mary recently wasn't enough to spark tinder.

Mary turned her back and spoke very low into the darkness. 'He's not my fellow.'

That meant yes. A bad fight. Abi waited; sometimes silence was the loudest question.

'Besides,' said Mary, flouncing on to her back and staring up at the low ceiling, 'I wager I'll get farther on my own than if I harness myself to such a dumb ox.'

'Where you going to?'

'Never you mind.'

Again, Abi waited. She had learned not to be hurt by such automatic rebuffs. This girl had to be handled like a sharp-clawed cat.

'London, where else?' said Mary at last, as if the darkness were squeezing the words out of her.

'When?'

'Not any time soon, but someday. There's no use going back till I have good clothes and money. Turn up empty-handed in the city,' said Mary scornfully, 'you might as well lie down in the road for the carthorses to trample.'

Abi shut her eyes and suddenly was back in Bristol, the day the ship from Barbados came in to port, nine years ago, in the chilliest rain she'd ever known. Her skin where the brass collar had been was naked, raw. The streets were no wider than outstretched arms, as crammed with faces as a trash heap with rats, and every face was white. While Abi had been waiting for the doctor to collect all his trunks, an enormous rattling cart had borne down on her, and it had occurred to her to step in front of it. What had stopped her, she wondered now? Cowardice? Or fear that her spirit, set loose in those tangled streets, would never find its way home to Africa?

'I ask for wages, like you said,' she mentioned.

'Why, I never thought you'd dare,' said Mary, animated. 'And?'

Abi shook her head mutely.

Mary let out a puff of contemptuous breath. 'A girl I used to know in London, she once told me, masters are like cullies.'

'Cullies?'

'You know,' the girl said hastily, 'men that go to whores. Masters are like that to servants; they use you up and toss you aside like paper. What did he say, when you asked?'

'She,' Abi corrected her. 'Was the mistress.'

A tiny pause, while Mary registered this. 'Oh,' she said at last, 'I thought it would have been the master. Still, Mrs Jones can't go against his word, can she? When it comes down it,' she added bitterly, 'a wife's only a kind of upper servant.'

'She say maybe give me present, at Christmas.' Abi heard the flatness of her own words.

She found her hand being pulled along the sheet and held very tight. It was a curious sensation, mildly uncomfortable, but also comforting. She tried to remember the last time any-one had held her hand like that: without trying to make it do anything.

Mary's narrow fingers traced the scar that went right through Abi's hand, from back to palm. 'What happened here?' she whispered. 'I know it was a knife, but what really happened? Was it long ago?'

Abi let out a tiny sigh. For a while she didn't say anything; long enough that she thought the girl might have drifted off. But the grip on her ragged palm never loosened. 'I come into house—' Abi began at last.

'This house?'

'No, no. Big estate in Barbados. Was house slave by then. Easier. Saved my life, you know? Wouldn't lasted half as long in the fields.'

'Go on.'

She squirmed a little. She'd never put words to this memory before, let alone English. 'So that day the door standing open.'

'Yes?'

'And master, he there on the floor, all bloody.'

Mary gave a little whistle of excitement.

'There was big knife,' Abi went on, 'stick up out of his eye. It look so bad.'

'What did you do?'

'Try take it out, but it stuck fast.'

'Ugh!'

Abi let out a little painful laugh. 'So then neighbour men run in, and find me with blood.'

'On your hands?'

'All over.'

'And they think you've done it?' asked Mary, leaning up on one elbow.

'They sure,' Abi corrected her, 'because of blood. And they want – what you call it? After killing.'

'A trial?'

Abi cleared her throat in frustration. 'A yes. Yes to killing.'

'A confession?'

'That the word. But I won't give no yes. Won't say I done nothing. Not me.'

'So they let you go?'

Abi stared up at the dark ceiling. What was the point of relating the facts when this girl just didn't understand what it was like, back on the island?

'Go on,' whispered Mary, like a child cheated of her bedtime story.

'So they put me on kitchen table,' said Abi weightily, 'tell me they going stick the knife into one bit and another bit till I say yes, then after they going kill me quick.'

The attic was quiet. 'My God.'

'They start with this hand here,' said Abi, tugging it out of Mary's grasp.

'So what stopped them from going on?'

'Another neighbour come in then, say they catched the man with blood on his shirt.'

'Which man?' asked Mary, bewildered.

'The killing one. He got master's moneybag in pocket.'

'Just in time for you!'

Abi let out a small snort. 'You don't know nothing.'

'Well, tell me, then!'

'Then the neighbours take me to auction, sell me for pay for master's funeral.'

'How much did you fetch?'

'Twenty pound,' Abi told her. Was the girl impressed by this figure, she wondered, or did she consider it trifling? 'It would be more,' she added a little defensively, 'except for my hand bleeding.'

Mary lay very still beside her.

All in all, Abi was glad she'd told this old story. It made it smaller, she found, to wrap it in words and fold it away. She rolled over now and pushed her face under the pillow, waiting for sleep.

On Mary's birthday, it so happened that Mr Channing came back to Monmouth from the horse races and paid nine months of tailoring bills in full. Mr Jones told his wife to bring the best port up from its hiding place in the scullery, for a double celebration. Mr Channing rode off after a single glass, but Mr Jones sat up after dinner toasting his king and country, his patrons, and all his family. 'To our maid Mary, the best of young women, with heartiest felicitations on completing her sixteenth year!'

They raised their glasses.

'To Henrietta Jones,' he declared next, 'the Belle of the West!'

'Why am I a bell?' Hetta demanded, tugging at her father's cuff-ruffle as he drank.

'Because you make so much noise,' suggested Mrs Ash without looking up from her Bible.

'No, my dear,' he said, lifting her on to his lap, 'it's a different kind of bell, that means beautiful lady.' And indeed as he looked down at her snow-white head, it did seem to him that Hetta was all he could ask for in a daughter. And for some men, that would be enough; some men wouldn't wake up in the middle of the night from dreams of driving in a carriage beside their fine handsome son.

She bounced violently on his knee and started up the old game. 'Fafa, where did your leg go?'

'Did I never tell you?' His eyes widened. 'One night I was fast asleep and a big rat chewed it off.'

'He didn't!' Her voice was delicious with fear.

'He did. Has he never woken you up nibbling your toes?'

'Don't scare the child,' laughed Mrs Jones, looking up from her work.

On his ninth glass of port, her husband sensed a delightful cloudiness about his head. His throat opened, and words spilled out; he even insisted on wetting Hetta's lips with port, 'to give her a taste for the best'. After his wife had gone off with Mrs Ash to put the child to bed, Mr Jones couldn't seem to move from his chair. It was so very comfortable; the liquor had fitted every curve of horsehair to his body. At last only his maid Mary remained by the bottle, her head resting on one fist, listening.

'Oh, indeed, great plans, great plans. In a few years, Mary, I shall buy up a draper's business to combine with ours. The Joneses of Monmouth will be known as the most complete purveyors of sartorial goods west of Bristol.' He relished the genteel ring of the words.

'How many years are a few?' asked Mary.

Mr Jones shrugged, insouciant. 'Certainly by the time our next boy is born.' He could see the girl come alert at the phrase, but he went on. 'My intelligencers tell me that our trade is likely to have tripled in value by then.'

'Really, sir.'

Did she disbelieve him? There was a dry edge to the girl's answers sometimes. Like her mother Su Rhys before her. What Mr Jones didn't let himself remember in his wife's presence was that he'd never much liked her best friend. 'Hetta will go to a school for young ladies,' he hurried on, 'and my son will become a gentleman.'

'How can you be sure?' Mary asked.

'I shall send him to the best tutors—'

'No, but,' she hesitated, clearly struggling for tact, 'how do you know you will have another child?'

Mr Jones beamed down at her. The port was singing in his veins. 'My wife is young yet. God will provide.' He leaned his elbows on the table until his face was a foot from hers. 'He owes me,' he whispered, too loudly.

Mary Saunders leaned back a little.

'Don't you see?' Mr Jones had never explained his conviction to anyone. He'd tried to tell his wife once, but she had covered her ears and called it sacrilegious talk. 'It's a sort of . . . *bargain.*'

The girl watched him warily.

'The way I see it, Mary,' he went on, slurring just a little, 'the Maker owes me the price of a leg.'

His grin elicited a tiny one from her.

'It'll be worth it in the end.' He glanced down at the sharp fold of his velvet breeches. 'Every time it aches where there's no flesh to ache, I've reminded myself of that. I shall have a son who'll live to make me proud, with an income to support him in style. He'll grow up to be a lawyer, maybe, or a physician,' he said, his voice booming in the little parlour. 'He'll drive a coach and six, and his footmen will wear livery. He'll write Esquire after his name!' Mr Jones was laughing helplessly, but he'd never been more serious. 'He shall, Mary, I tell you he shall. Was not the celebrated versifier a plain linen-draper's son?'

Her forehead wrinkled up.

'You know the man. Pott. Post. Mr Pond? The poet.' His brains were getting fuzzy.

'Pope?'

'That's it, good girl. A little frayed scrap of a man with a hump, no taller than Hetta.'

'Was he?' she asked doubtfully.

'He was,' said Mr Jones. 'And has that diminished his fame? Not at all.' A vast yawn cracked his face now. 'What about you, my girl, on this festive day of yours?' he asked benevolently, tilting his cup to get the last few drops of liquor.

'Me?'

'What are your own . . . aspirations, if you have any?' He bent forward now to look more closely into Mary's pale face. She'd be quite a beauty, it occurred to him, if only she'd smile more often. 'Sixteen is still young, but in time you may hope to marry, raise a family.' He leaned closer. 'Will you set your cap at some strapping Welshman, eh?'

'No.' Her answer was chilly.

He'd already decided he must have been mistaken about her and Daffy; certainly, the way they were skulking from room to room these days suggested that they couldn't stand the sight of each other. 'Still, you never know what might happen,' he said pleasantly. 'I'll tell you a strange story, now, about a gentleman of my acquaintance. On his travels in Africa a few years ago he captured this black, you see, and brought him home to the village of Dolgellau. Didn't he teach the fellow English and Welsh, and call him John Ystunllyn, and the black is said to be able to pronounce his own name as perfect as a Welshman! The fellow's both gardener and steward there now, on a good wage, and courting one of the maids, last I heard.'

The girl looked blankly back at him.

'So you see, Mary, you might think at first that your lot here is a lowly one, but if you bear patiently and do your best, you might rise a degree in the end.'

She shook her head. 'I'll go back to London,' she said flatly.

'In whose service?' he asked.

Mary looked away, and nibbled on her thumb. 'I could be an actress, maybe.'

'An actress?' His mouth began to curl in shock and amusement.

'Or a rich man's wife. Something that lets me wear silk all day. Something to lift me above the mob.'

Her master found that his good humour had evaporated all at once. He sat up straight; his head was vibrating and there was a sour taste in his mouth. 'Girl, your words grieve me.'

Her eyes were as dark as pebbles on the road.

'Did that mother of yours never teach you to mind your station?'

Mary stared back at him. She looked half-witted sometimes.

'All that embroidery has gone to your head, or perhaps this port is too rich for your blood. You make your future sound like a game of dress-up.'

'It won't be a game.'

He tried to infuse kindness into his words. 'You are in service, now, my dear girl. And in some kind of service you will remain, in all likelihood, married or not, one way or another, for the length of your days.'

'Have you not read the letters of Pamela Andrews, then?' Mary asked shrilly. 'She was nothing but a maid, and she got a lord in the end.'

Mr Jones let out a little puff of laughter. 'Mary, Mary, that was only a story.'

She turned her face away, as if she didn't believe him. Was the girl crying? His voice softened and he reached out and took hold of her sleeve. The warmth of her skin came though the thin cloth. 'My dear, it's like . . . a great river.'

When her face came round to meet him it was dry. 'What is?'

'Society.' Mr Jones tried to catch hold of his train of thought. He'd heard it in a sermon once, from Joe Cadwaladyr most likely. He wished he was sober enough to be sure of getting it right. 'Some float along on the surface, you see. Catching the sunlight, I mean, and spreading themselves, as it were. Others, like my own family, the middle sort,' he went on more fluently, 'begin down in the dark—'

'On Back Lane, you mean?'

He winced. 'Yes, for instance. But through the Divine Plan,' he went on more confidently, 'we move up through the water, towards the light, if no obstacle blocks our way.'

'And where am I, then?' Her voice was dangerous.

'On the riverbed, I suppose,' he said, disconcerted. Was that right? Was there no kinder way to put it? 'You and your kind form the rock our whole society rests on,' he went on.

One thick eyebrow went up slightly.

'But consider the comforts of your lot, Mary,' he said cheeringly. 'You've no family of your own to provide for, no name to maintain; you're free from all the anxieties of your betters.'

'Are you better than me, then, Mr Jones?'

Her eyes didn't turn away. He could have slapped her for such cheek, but he wouldn't. Besides, it was a fair question. 'Probably not, Mary,' he admitted, his tongue cleaning the rim of his cup, 'but I have been placed over you.' After a long minute, he added, 'I've no wish to quarrel, especially on your birthday.'

'Nor I, sir.'

'I know you're a good girl, really.'

The smile she gave him was most peculiar.

His head was spinning. He hauled himself up, then. 'Shall I leave the lantern?'

'No need.'

He took it, then, and hopped off to bed, the circles of light lapping the walls. The last he saw of Mary Saunders, she was still by the parlour window, looking out at the waning moon.

The next evening, after supper, Mrs Jones looked very faint and queasy. She pressed her apron to her mouth.

'Is the beer disagreeing with you again, my dear?' her husband asked.

Mary saw her chance and stood up so fast the table shook. 'I could fetch you some fresh cider, madam,' she said.

Mrs Jones blinked at her. 'Would you mind, Mary? I do believe it would settle my stomach.'

Halfway down Grinder Street, Mary slowed her pace. It wouldn't do to call attention to herself. She was a respectable maid going on a respectable errand on a fine summer evening. Her chemise was wet with sweat under her arms.

Feet thudded behind her. When she saw who it was she turned her face away and walked faster.

'For mercy's sake,' said Daffy, 'why won't you speak to me?'

'There's nothing to say.'

'Is it because of what we did, in the wood?' His voice was strangled. 'I never meant to take advantage. When I look at Mrs Jones, and think how disappointed in me she'd be—'

'She knows nothing,' said Mary coldly.

Daffy nodded, very stiff, as if his neck was made of wood. 'Then what is it? Is it London?' His tone turned desperate. 'I might – I would consider coming to the city, you know, but only for a year or two. Only till the first child.'

'Forget it,' she said through closed teeth. 'Forget me.'

'How can I?' he almost roared. 'We sleep in the same house.'

'We wouldn't suit,' she told him, turning to show him her stony face. She would have liked to speak softly to him, but it would only have prolonged his pain. 'I'm not like Gwyn, you know.'

'Is that it?' Daffy asked, his voice harsh with hope. 'Do you not like to take another woman's leavings? Because if that's your fear—'

She shook her head and almost smiled. 'I'm not what you need.'

He opened his mouth to protest.

'Trust me on this,' Mary told him, dead serious. 'You wouldn't want me if you knew me better.' Then she turned on her heel and set off towards the Crow's Nest as fast as she could. She kept one ear out for Daffy's steps behind her, but heard nothing.

Her mind was made up. Mr Jones's drunken lecture on society had convinced her of something that she'd long suspected. She was never going to get where she wanted by being nothing but a maid. As fast as she might climb that ladder, it would sink into the mud, or somebody one rung up would stamp on her hands. Nor would she be able to make enough money to go back to London in style, except by resuming her old trade. After all, what was the sense in signing yourself over to one master for life, when you could rent yourself out to many? She'd thought she could escape her former self, but she'd been daydreaming. *When in doubt*, said Doll in her head, *stick to what you know*.

Cadwaladyr drew the pint of cider himself, tonight. He waited for Mary to speak. There were two boys within earshot, playing shove ha'penny. 'Have you any, ah, fresh cod in tonight?' she asked softly, her eyes flicking to the drinkers in the corner.

A long pause. She half-expected him to laugh in her face. 'Might have,' he murmured at last.

'Is it still a shilling each?'

Cadwaladyr nodded, his face blank under his tufted eyebrows.

All round Mary rose the wet stench of the dung heaps. No stars out tonight, and the moon wasn't up over the Meadow yet, thank the Maker. She set the tankard of cider down on a brick and moved farther into the dark shadows along the back wall of the inn. She reached the rickety staircase and laid her hand on it. Her stomach growled.

Here he lurched at last round the side of the building, the traveller, his inflamed face hanging like an udder. His coats swayed open, lined with curling lengths of colour. A ribbon pedlar; Mary felt the sourness in her mouth, and almost laughed.

She stood and faced him for a moment. Here was her old life coming to suck her in again. Time was a loop, not a line. She was fourteen again, walking up to the St Giles ribbon man, and there was no way out.

Mary turned and climbed the thin wooden stairs; they were slick with moss. The pedlar hiccuped delightedly and followed her. All the room held was a straw mattress and some packing-crates. Everything stank of beer; the walls seemed to sweat it out. She wasted no time; she bunched up her skirts around her waist and lay face-down on the mattress. That way she wouldn't have to look at him.

After some fumbling the man was up to the hilt. Her ribs jerked against the rough mattress. Her insides tightened automatically. *Like dancing a jig*, Doll said behind her eyes; *the body never forgets*. The cully panted tiredly but ploughed on. How the beast in a man kept him going! Mary thought of the staked birds she'd seen in Market Square on Shrove Tuesday, staggering about in their own blood till the laughing cocksquailers clubbed them down. 'Why do the men do that?' asked Hetta, and all Mary could tell her was 'Because they like to.'

This was going to take a while; the pedlar was past his prime. Mary's thighs were aching. She began to squeeze with all her force, though her back hurt from hours of smoothing Mrs Harding's new petticoats with the charcoal iron. To encourage the fellow, she made a sound in the back of her throat; not a cry of pleasure, which she knew from experience could put some men off their stride, but a mild grunt of pain.

She was horrified to hear the church bell strike ten. Even Mrs Jones would never believe it took this long to fetch a cup of cider. Panic began to rise in Mary's throat. Oh, merciful providence, let them not send Daffy back down to look for her . . .

She was tempted to buck the pedlar off into the straw and make a run for it, but then she'd never see her shilling, though he'd had the use of her for a quarter of an hour. Hands pressed against the bristling straw, Mary took the weight of the man's desperate thrusts. What was that rhyme they'd taught her at school?

As the worms that work the soil,
Man was made for constant toil.

Finally she remembered a line she used to save for such occasions, when an ageing cully seemed to be taking all night. 'Why you hurt me,' she complained, turning her head so she could feel the pedlar's hot wheezing in her ear. 'You're too big.' He thrust harder. After another minute, Mary added a whimper: 'You'll tear me in two!' She could almost feel the words crowding together in the man's head, quickening his pulse, stiffening his guilty resolve.

A moment later it was all over, and his foam soaked the tops of her stockings.

Scurrying up Inch Lane with a small *clink-clink* in her pocket, Mary rehearsed her lines. Shame pulled on her sticky legs like a ball and chain.

In the parlour, the fire was almost out and Mrs Jones snoozed alone over her darning. 'A pedlar jostled me in the lane, madam,' Mary said breathlessly, 'and your cider spilled. I had to go all the way back for more.'

'Never mind, Mary,' yawned Mrs Jones, taking a sip. 'You're a good girl to go out so late. Oh, that's very tasty. That's very settling stuff.'

The bald moon had slid through the shutters of the attic room. Abi's shape was a long shadow in the bed. A great weight bore down on Mary's shoulders as she bent to prise her shoes off.

She was a greasy harlot, that's what she was. Had always been and ever would be and had been a cretin ever to imagine otherwise. Had Mary been marked as a whore by the midwife who pulled her out, head first into the draughty world? Did she bear some tiny invisible brand? To think she'd come all that way across the country, only to find herself face-down under a dirty cully again. Like Doll's old joke: *A yard's the same length anywhere.*

Sticky in her palm, twelve pennies, her half share of the fee. Not enough, not half enough for a bandy-legged pedlar. Then again, when was it ever enough? When had Mary ever walked away from a cully and felt fairly rewarded?

She peered through the moon-striped dark. The maid-of-all-work was flat in the bed like a tomb sculpture; light caught her glossy brown cheekbone. 'Abi?' whispered Mary warily.

No answer. Silence covered the sleeper like a blanket.

Mary's bag was under the bed; she pulled it out, slowly, making only a faint scrape on the boards. She knew the contents of her stocking without looking inside. She added the pennies, one by one.

You couldn't call it a plan. It was more like a hunger, starting up inside her sour stomach. Cadwaladyr was doing her a favour, really. The ten pounds a year the Joneses allowed her was only the beginning of what she needed. If she stayed here in Monmouth, where she never had to spend a shilling, she could build up a little stock against poverty by making the same trade she'd made all her grown life. That way when she went back to London – as early as next spring, maybe – it wouldn't be the same way she left it. She could drive back with unpatched linen, some fine new dresses, and a fat weight of coins in her pocket, heavy against her leg, to ward off all danger.

Lying still in bed, she spared a thought for Daffy. Was he asleep, or lying awake cursing her? How her life might have changed all at once with the slip of a syllable, a simple *yes*. To be a wife and a mother in a small country town was the life millions led and other millions prayed for. What gave Mary the right to resent the dull round of domestic duties, to demand a life of silks and gold? What was the tapeworm in her stomach that always made her hunger for more?

Mrs Partridge hadn't yet made her toilette, Mrs Jones and her maid were told when they called at Monnow House. The building rebuked them; three storeys high, it drew its skirts back from the muddy thoroughfare. Mary stared up at the glinting windows and savoured the thought of being so rich you could sleep in till half past eleven. Mrs Jones dipped her knee to the liveried footman and asked permission to call again at noon.

To Mary it seemed strangely illicit to dawdle under the church-yard yews in the middle of the day; it was the first time she'd ever seen her mistress wander without work in her hands. The May air was light and the trees smelt sharply green.

Mrs Jones led the way across the north side of the churchyard. There were no stones marking the bumpy green turf. 'Why is no one buried here?' Mary asked.

'Oh, they are, my dear. Unbaptised babies, don't you know, and paupers from another parish.' Round the corner of the church, Mrs Jones passed two truant boys who were playing leap-frog over the soft-edged tombstones. She didn't say a word to them, only smiled. On the worn white wall of St Mary's was a carving. 'Are they soldiers, fighting?' asked Mary.

Her mistress peered at it. 'I think it's Adam and Eve. It was clearer in my grandmother's day.' Then she stepped back and pointed upwards. 'Look at that, now. Our great spire is said to be two hundred feet high.'

Mary nodded as if impressed. How could she explain the grandeur of St Paul's to this woman who'd never been beyond Cheltenham? And then the breeze turned and the golden bird at the top wheeled round, just like the one on St Giles, the morning she'd run away. The tail glinted, taunting her.

For distraction she turned to the nearest headstone.

From earth my body first arose,
But here to earth again it goes,
I never desire to have it more
To plague me as it did before.

She thought of her body: the rubbery dampness of it. How it served her. How it wearied her.

'Very true, that one,' said Mrs Jones enjoyably. 'Read me some more; my eyes are tired this morning.'

Mary recited the epitaphs of various Lucases, Prossers, Lloyds and Adamses. '*In Memory of his Wife who Bore Him 2 Sons and 1 Daughter and Died in Childbed June 1713 Aged 38.*'

Mrs Jones gave a little shiver. 'Jessie Adams, that was; she was a friend of my grandma's.'

Mary moved on to the next, which was still bare of moss. '*Sacred to the memory of Grandison Jones—*' Her voice dried up all at once.

'—*son of Thomas Jones, of Monmouth, and his wife Jane.*' The older woman's tone was gentle.

The girl couldn't think what to say.

'Now Delmont, our third,' said Mrs Jones, pointing to the name farther down the headstone. 'I got that name out of a story by Mrs Haywood. Even if she was a bit of a hussy!'

Mary counted the names. It was a small square, lightly scored with letters; she tried to guess its cost.

'Maybe Thomas would be better off with a young girl who could give him half a dozen boys,' Mrs Jones went on, as if remarking on the weather.

Mary stared at her.

'But who could suit him or know his ways as I do? Besides,' murmured Mrs Jones, moving on to the next grave, 'I've not quite given up yet.'

Something in her tone alerted the girl. Could it be? Surely not. A tiny laugh in the mistress's breath, as she smoothed her plain black bodice over her stomach.

'You're not—'

'Did I say so?' asked Mrs Jones innocently.

Mary gave her a wide grin. 'I thought—' Then she stopped herself before the insult slipped out.

'You thought I was too old. Yes,' said Mrs Jones meditatively, 'I was afraid I might be.'

They walked on a little way. Mary stooped to read an epitaph so old its letters were almost worn away.

We all must die, there is no doubt;
Your glass is running – mine is out.

Mrs Jones slid her arm into Mary's as they moved on towards the river. 'I've not told Thomas, mind,' she murmured.

'Why?' asked Mary. At the thought that she was the first to know, she felt delight like a chip of sugar in her mouth.

'Oh, I mustn't raise his hopes yet. I used to tell him every time I had the least expectation, but then he was sorely disappointed when it came to grief. And he was so very broken in his spirit when Grandison was taken last year. Mind you, it comes to all of us, rich or poor,' Mrs Jones added, looking back at Monnow House, the highest in the line of creamy buildings. 'Madam in there's been brought to bed ten times, and not a one living.'

Mary tried to imagine it. Something like Ma Slattery's cellar, but ten times over; all your ambitions amounting to blood in a pail.

As they neared the river, she was startled by a glimpse of its blue. Though there was no visible sun, the Monnow shone like a broken sword cutting its way through the countryside. It held a slice of sky, that was what it was; Mary looked up and saw the bright blue, tucked between the clouds. At the end of the lane the cottages ran out and there was only muddy meadow.

She and Mrs Jones picked their way carefully, so as not to ruin their shoes.

The earth crumbled softly at the river edge, fraying into the water. Mary watched the ripples advancing. Then she pointed in puzzlement. 'I thought it ran the other way, down to Chepstow?'

'Oh, it does,' said Mrs Jones placidly. 'Look closer.'

Mary bent over the water and saw how she'd been tricked. The ripples were only on the surface, carved by the breeze.

'If you watch that twig, and those leaves coming down to us,' said Mrs Jones, 'you'll see its true path, hidden under the ripples.'

The bell told them it was noon already. They turned to hurry back to Monnow House.

Mr Jones was totting up the books. Meaning, he leant one elbow on the edge of the little polished desk and looked over the shoulder of Mary Saunders, who was quicker at calculations. 'Hmm,' he said every now and then, in a judicious tone.

He spent his time fretting.

He had read all the right literature. He had paid good money for volumes with titles like *Aristotle's Masterpiece* and *Conjugal Love*; he kept them in a locked drawer in this very desk, so as not to cause scandal among the servants. Between their covers he had gleaned much wisdom, such as: never perform your duty on an empty stomach. Or, a woman who lies on top will give birth to a dwarf. Thomas Jones considered himself a conscientious husband. He watched his wife for the sure signs of pregnancy: thickened ankles and a swollen vein under the eye. He did his best to give her pleasure, because without it, he knew, a woman never conceived.

But these days he had the feeling she was lost to him.

Mary Saunders had been making little stifled exclamations for some time. Now she jabbed at the ledger with her stubby quill. 'Twenty-two pounds, five and sixpence!'

He leant over to read the total. 'Ah. The Morgans.'

'They haven't paid you a penny in fourteen months.'

Mr Jones licked his lips. 'Is it so long? Well, the Honourable Member is a busy man.'

'His wife swans in here every month.'

'Mary.' He sighed. 'You don't seem to realise the difficulty of our position. Such patrons must not be pressed.'

'Are you a worm under their boots?'

Mr Jones gave her a very cold look, and she bit her lip. He tapped the ledger to indicate that she should carry on with the accounts.

He wondered where his wife was now. Sewing away in the shop, no doubt, her needle moving as fast as a swallow. She always let him know when she was going out to a patron's house, and informed him of what she'd told Abi to serve for dinner. And whenever he asked after her health, she would say, 'Very well, thank you, my dear', or mention some trivial face-ache or stye. But for a long time now she hadn't told him anything that mattered. Above all, she didn't explain why she always seemed to fall asleep between the hour they retired to their room and the moment he climbed into bed after her.

Mr Jones was not an excessively demanding man. Not as far as he knew. In the old days, for instance, whenever his wife was pregnant, he'd quite understood the importance of refraining, so the child wouldn't be shaken in the womb. Those had been burdensome times, but at least he had felt that he and Jane were at one, conspirators in a thrilling enterprise; their eyes might meet above the tea-kettle, and he would take a long scalding drink and know that all this self-command would be worth it in the end. After they'd lost Grandison last year, they had tried again at once, but it came to nothing, and then he hadn't wanted to put Jane to the trial again so soon. But the months had gone by, and still she didn't turn to him in bed, or so rarely that he hardly even remembered the last time. He didn't want to press her, but considering her age, their time was running out. And to wait, as he now did, without knowing when or why, was more than he could stand.

A terrible thought struck him. Had it not, in fact, been understood between them that they did indeed mean to try again? Perhaps Jane was worn out. Perhaps she had given up, without ever saying the words. And who was he to oblige her to hope again? What did he know of the dreadful disappointments of a woman's body?

He could hear Hetta in the passageway, bumping into something over and over, and laughing. Heaven knew, he was grateful for her. But a daughter, no matter how devoted to her parents, was only theirs for a time; she would marry into another family and bear children with another name. Was it presumptuous to long also for one single son? A son that would inherit the business, and support his parents when they were too old to work? It was a lot to ask, but he asked it. It was part of his quiet bargain with the Maker. It was the triumphant future for which the boy Thomas had swapped his leg.

Mary Saunders breathed heavily over the books. 'Do they balance?' he asked.

'Not yet.'

She was at her most handsome when she was concentrating, her lips pursed and dark from biting, her eyes on her work. His wife assured him the girl was not even a woman yet, which he found hard to credit, but she believed that grief, such as Mary's for her dead mother, might well delay the matter. He hoped she wouldn't leave them for a good ten years, for all her daft ambitions about going on the stage or catching a rich husband. Some local journeyman would marry the girl in the end, perhaps, or even a glover or stockinger. Women should not spend all their very best years in service, drying into spinsterhood. Look at poor Mrs Ash; who would believe she was four years younger than his wife?

His eyes throbbed as he tried to follow the figures under Mary's pen. They would never add up. Drapers charged early, and patrons paid late, or never, and even in good months there was a scarcity of coin, which was all the fault of the Dutch. Sometimes he was amazed there was dinner on the table every night. His wife was such a capable manager, she never complained. She never told him her troubles any more; not for months now. Instead she entrusted them to this chit of a girl. He heard the two of them murmuring like bees over their work in the shop, but if he walked in he could never tell what they were talking about. The chosen confidante was a stranger to the family who had none of his experience of the world, who could offer no comfort – who, above all, didn't love Jane Jones as he did.

What was it that women had between them that made the words flow as easy as milk? What was it that his wife couldn't say to him?

One afternoon, by bad luck, Mrs Harding and Mr Valentine Morris both sent their carriages to Inch Lane with last year's suits, demanding an inch let out here and two inches there, and could Mrs Jones kindly give the collar a more modish cut, and have the whole pressed and returned in time for the May Ball? Mr Morris's German valet and Mrs Harding's French maid swore at each other in the narrow hall.

'I don't know at all, Mary, it's a whirling world,' said Mrs Jones, letting her head sink back against the wall of the shop for a moment. Her heart was thudding, and she felt as heavy as oak, though her shape hadn't changed at all yet. 'New patterns every year, stitches so tiny I can hardly see them, names of stuffs I can't so much as pronounce . . . Is there no end to it all?'

'Haven't fashions always come and gone?' said Mary Saunders.

Mrs Jones shrugged her shoulders to ease their ache. 'It seems faster, these days. Sometimes I think of what my grandchildren will wear to church, and I might not even know the words for it.' Her hand rested on her belly, still flat, and she gave the girl a tiny smile.

Hetta was fractious; she insisted on playing with the needle box, and after Mrs Ash had come into the shop three times to tell her she'd drop it, finally she did. The nurse took the child out of the room by the ear, muttering, 'This is what comes of having a name out of a storybook,' which of course was aimed at the mother. Mrs Jones got down on her knees beside Mary to pick up the tiny needles.

'Hetta hates her,' whispered Mary conversationally, 'and do you wonder at it?'

'Oh, Mary.' Mrs Jones dropped the needles back in the box. 'If you could find it in your heart to be a little kinder to poor Mrs Ash . . . She won't be here for ever, you know.'

The girl's eyes widened. 'You mean—'

'This time is different, isn't it?' murmured Mrs Jones, glancing down at herself. 'We'll be needing a wet-nurse, see.'

Mary nodded delightedly. 'So Mrs Ash will have to go.'

'Well,' said the mistress helplessly, 'I must start looking out for a place for her, that's all I mean.'

'I hear they need females in Virginia . . .'

'Mary Saunders!' She smacked the girl on the wrist, swallowing her smile. It faintly troubled Mrs Jones that she couldn't make herself feel very sorry at the prospect of losing Mrs Ash after all these years of faithful service. Nothing much mattered these days except what was happening inside her: like a blast of trumpets on a soundless day.

Sometimes when she glanced up from her sewing it was as if twenty years had rolled up like a carpet and she was a girl again, doing her darning with Su. She talked to her old friend sometimes; more and more these last months, ever since she'd begun to suspect her condition. *Su*, she said in her head, *thank you for your daughter. I only wish you could have seen mine.* There was an infinitesimal hint of a curve below her ribs, but not enough to show, yet. She shut her eyes and wished hard that this one would be a boy. One who would live.

Her husband was looking hangdog these days. In bed at night, his eyes rested on the ceiling; he never guessed that his future was sprouting like a seed beside him. She would have comforted him in the best way she knew how, except that it might endanger the child. Time was she used to tell Thomas everything, but that was years ago, before their family grew and shrank again, before any of the necessary secrets. She longed to give him the good news, but something laid a chill hand on her and said to wait. Just a little longer. It mightn't be true. It mightn't last; it mightn't live. So for now she kept the secret hidden in her mouth like a pearl. She sat and stood and walked as if her skirts were lined with silver, but nobody noticed except Mary.

Now the two of them were laughing over some bit of nonsense when Daffy came into the shop to deposit a stack of trunks. Mary's laughter cut off as if a door had slammed shut. Mrs Jones looked up from her needle, and noticed that the two servants both looked everywhere in the room except at each other. 'Mary,' she quietly, a few minutes after Daffy had left, 'is there anything you wish to tell me?'

The girl shook her head, eyes on her sewing.

'I mean to say, I did once think – that is, I know how young you are, but I once imagined that you and Daffy might be beginning to have . . . a fondness for each other. Was I wrong?'

'No,' muttered Mary.

'These things do often occur, in a household,' said Mrs Jones vaguely. 'It's only natural.'

Finally the girl looked up, her cheeks flushed. 'The truth is – he asked me to marry him.'

'At sixteen!' said Mrs Jones, her mouth puckered with shock.

'He wanted to marry me and take me away from here, and I said no.'

'Mary!' exclaimed Mrs Jones, her eyes brimming over at the thought of it. 'My poor girl. My poor good girl.' The maid smiled a little, shyly, while the mistress searched in all her pockets for a handkerchief. 'Don't mind my foolishness,' Mrs Jones stammered through her tears. 'It's only my condition.'

Mary handed over a clean folded handkerchief, and Mrs Jones mopped her eyes with it. How glad she was; how blessed by such loyalty. To know there was someone who cared about her too much to leave her service, who would stand by her through all trials!

'Cider's ever so strengthening in the early months, I've heard,' Mary told her mistress, and frequently offered to go down to fetch her some from the Crow's Nest after dinner. Mr Jones was all in favour of whatever could restore a bit of colour to his wife's cheeks.

Mary's life was folded over like a hem. There was a day side and a night side, and to look at one you'd never guess the other. She wasn't too sure which Mary was the real one. It was strange, but it was how it was.

Hidden in her bag under the bed, her single gold-clocked stocking was getting heavier, the coins mounting up. Grubby ones, shiny ones, a few with edges clipped off by coiners, and a whole crown a sozzled lawyer from Edinburgh had dropped between her breasts for a tip, probably thinking it was a penny. Cadwaladyr was civil, these days, apart from his mocking eyebrows; he always gave her a few minutes to get round the back and out of sight in the little room above the stable, before sending the cullies out to her. *Sukie* – his own invention – was the name he gave her. 'Tell Sukie I sent you,' was what he said to the cullies. They were always travellers, passing through, on their way to Bristol or the North, for a job or a sale or a bargain; Mary had told Cadwaladyr from the start that she wouldn't touch a Marcherman, for fear of starting talk in the town.

Most nights she found it effortless, being Sukie. It was strange to be dressed so respectably and have an unpainted face, and to work so fast and so surreptitiously round the back of the inn, but otherwise the trade was as familiar as an old glove. Once she was greeted by a queue of three Yorkshiremen outside the stable, quarrelling over who'd go first. Another night, a drunken Cornishman wanted to do it standing up but fell down on her and got mud all over her blue holland gown.

She offered no preliminary toying, unless the cullies needed it. It wasn't like the old times in London, when she had taken some sort of pride in pleasing, in luring customers back for more. No, these days she was in a hurry and all she wanted was her half of the two shillings it cost these men to get relief in the wilds of the Marches. Sometimes they grabbed her by the breasts, exclaiming over them. If she was face-on, she had to smell the men's beery breath; one lout even tried to kiss her, but she moved her mouth away. Mary preferred to lie face-down on the straw mattress and think about other things, such as the diamonded petticoat she was embroidering for Miss Lucy Allen, but which she would look much handsomer in herself.

Right at the end, when a cully was weakened, she sometimes put her mouth to his ear and told him that if he gossiped about Sukie to a soul in Monmouth, she'd come after him with a knife and make an opera singer of him.

She was always careful. As far as the drinkers at the Crow's Nest knew, she was just a maid who popped in for a pint of cider for her mistress every few nights, and never lingered to flirt or play dice. She never went round the back to the stables if there was anyone there to see her. And Cadwaladyr wouldn't blab, would he? Not as long as she kept paying him his poundage? But then Mary remembered his face, that first night he'd recognised Jane Jones's new maid as the girl who'd tricked him at Coleford: his eyes under their thick white brows, standing out with rage.

One cold evening an Irishman who stank of baccy, with a little worm of a yard, tried to bargain her down: 'Sixpence for you and the same for the innkeeper.'

'Why,' she asked, 'because you're only half-sized?'

He made her nose bleed. She walked home empty-handed, with some story of getting a sudden nosebleed in the lane.

'Did you see a black rabbit?' asked Mrs Jones wisely.

Mary shook her head, and another red drop escaped her handkerchief.

'Ach, it's always the black rabbits that bring on bloody noses, don't you know?'

That was the only time Mary went unpaid. Most nights she was home in a quarter of an hour with a shilling or two in her pocket. 'What a good lass you are,' Mrs Jones would say, taking a mouthful of her cider.

In the attic room, Abi was dreaming of plantation food: slithery mackerel, pumpkin and pigeon-peas, a gulp of rum if you were lucky. Coocoo, sapadillo, jambalaya: even the words warmed her mouth.

She floated up from sleep to find Mary Saunders stepping out of her petticoats by the light of a thin tallow candle. It was late. She caught a waft from the girl, and it reminded her of something. 'You been with a man?' she asked curiously.

Mary jumped, and turned on her. 'Of course not!'

'Only asking,' muttered Abi, putting her face in the pillow.

The girl continued folding her clothes across the chair as if they were royal robes.

Who could he be, Abi wondered? Not Daffy Cadwaladyr; he was going round with a face sealed up like wax these days, and spent every spare moment deep in *An Historical Account of the Hebridean Isles*, as if nothing was real unless it was written in a book. Could the girl have found herself another lover among the whey-faced men of Monmouth?

As Mary climbed into bed, Abi held on to the hem of the blanket. She heard a faint clink: a chain, or a necklace, or a coin on another coin? Then the soft scraping of a bag being shoved back under the bed, and Mary lay down flat again.

Finally Abi understood, and all at once was overcome with sorrow.

She'd known a few slave girls who got hired out by their plantation masters to make a bit of cash when times were hard, but she'd never before met a woman who sold her body of her own choosing. Not one who had a job, and food, and a roof over her head. It crushed her spirits to realise that even Mary – the bold, the careless Mary Saunders, the Londoner with high ambitions – wasn't a free woman.

She decided to risk asking. 'Mary. You do it for money?'

There was a terrible silence. Abi wished she'd kept her mouth shut. Then she heard a delicate letting out of breath and Mary said, 'I don't know any other good reason.'

Abi couldn't answer that. She hadn't lain with a man in so long she could barely remember what it felt like. The last must have been the doctor who'd brought her to England, she supposed. He'd woken up hard on the ship every morning and ridden her first thing, with the sea rolling past their cabin porthole like a green monster. One day he had peered at her cunny afterwards, calling it *most interesting*; he said English women were not shaped so. He had even made a drawing of it to put in a book he was writing. Abi's legs had shaken with cold, but the doctor had told her to hold still for the sake of science. After days of labour he had proudly shown her the drawing, and she had howled in panic. There was no face, no body, just a fruit axed open, leaking across the page.

'You won't tell a soul?' asked Mary in the darkness.

Abi answered that with a contemptuous puff of breath, which seemed to reassure the girl. 'After I come live on Inch Lane,' said Abi reflectively after a minute, 'I lay wake up here, waited for master to send for me.'

'What, Mr Jones?' said Mary with a tight giggle.

The woman shrugged. 'Masters are like that with house girls. Then after while I thought maybe Mr Jones lose more than leg.'

Mary's laughter rose and filled the air.

'Now I think things just different in this country.'

They lay side by side, silent. 'Do you miss the business?' asked Mary at last.

This was hard for Abi to answer. 'Maybe the end bit,' she admitted at last. She thought of heat and wet cupped inside her, those times she'd been put to breeding with the big field slave, though it had come to nothing. 'All peaceful,' she said, remembering, 'no more noise, no more jigging about.' Nothing more being asked of her, nothing she'd done wrong, nothing to guess at or say sorry for.

On Saturday night Mrs Jones went to bed early, complaining of backache again. Her husband wondered if that was just another excuse for going to sleep before him. He sat up over his *Bristol Mercury*, the words almost indistinguishable in the candlelight, till everyone else had gone to bed too. He was restless tonight; the May air coming through the window was scented with flowers. For the first time in years, he felt like going to a tavern. He reached for his crutches.

By the time he reached the inn by the Meadow where the crow's nest stirred in the mild breeze, his bladder was troubling him. He hopped around the back of the building. And there, of all people, was Mary Saunders, leaning against the stable wall.

'Mary?' he said blankly. 'I thought you were abed.'

Her hand shot up to hide her face, then fell. Her eyes were tarnished coins on white leather. Mr Jones wondered, was the girl sick, or astray in her wits? 'Mary?' he repeated, making sure she was the same person who'd sat next to him at supper. 'Whatever's the matter?'

'Nothing, sir.' Her voice was salty and peculiar.

'But what in Heaven are you doing here so late?'

'I don't know, sir.'

What a fool you are, me old muck-mate! How quick you lose your head in a tight spot! Mary thought she could hear Doll Higgins open her throat and laugh. There were so many lies she could have told her master, if she hadn't been so shocked to see him. That she was stretching her legs while Cadwaladyr filled Mrs Jones's jug, for instance. Or that she had felt queasy in the alehouse and had stepped out for some air. She could have claimed she wanted a look at the moon, even – only the moon was dark this week. The stars, then; there was the Plough, shovelling away all night.

But her mouth was sealed shut now, after that one stupid phrase: 'I don't know.' Mr Jones swung his crutches and moved closer to her. His face was shifting; she watched suspicion fill up the lines. She couldn't think of a word to say. Disaster was about to fall on the two of them.

Heavy steps: Sukie's cully at last. Like an ill-timed actor he shambled round the corner, steadying himself with a hand on the sooty bricks. His bearded face was lit with anticipation. Mary stared at the sky. Surely, seeing a man and a woman in conversation, this fellow would simply piss against the wall and go back to the inn.

'Where be the whore then?' he called.

Mary squeezed her eyes shut.

'I beg your pardon?' Mr Jones was hoarse with surprise.

'Landlord said there'd be a young trull above the stables that'd do it for two shilling.' The man peered into the shadows, where Mary was standing. 'I'll bide my turn,' he told Mr Jones amiably, 'but I can't stop long.'

Mary tried to summon up a shocked expression. All she managed was a grimace, guilt written on her skin.

Mr Jones took in a noisy breath. 'Go about your business, fellow.'

'My shillings be as good as yourn, an't they?'

'Be off or I'll fetch the constable,' barked Mr Jones with a cold wheeze of breath, hoisting his crutch and waving it at the fellow.

Mary watched the cully's mud-marked breeches lumber round the side of the building. There she stood beside her master, all her muscles locked. Eventually he lowered his crutch. If he'd been going to beat her with it, she thought, he'd have started by now.

Like a pair of genteel strangers, each of them waited for the other to speak. Mary tried to think of a convincing explanation, but her mind was moving like treacle. Her body thought faster. She fell on her knees before Mr Jones and felt a sharp pebble enter her shin. Flinging her arms around her master's hips, she pressed her head against him. Sudden tears soaked into the thinned velvet of his breeches. The mannish smell of him filled her nostrils.

Mary didn't know it before, but she was in fact sorry. Strangely sorry for all she was and ever would be, for all she'd done and left undone and never would do. For the way she'd been given a second chance at ordinary life and had crushed it underfoot. What was it she needed from this man? Punishment or forgiveness, hard words or a soft hand on her cap? Complicity, above all.

He didn't say a word.

Her hot face nuzzled into Mr Jones's buttoned flap. *Any sign of life in the basement?* as Doll used to chuckle. Heavy hands landed on her shoulders and tried to push her back, but she clung on. Far above her she heard the clearing of his throat. She lifted her chin and pressed harder against the velvet with her eyes, her nose, her wet cheeks.

Ah. Ahah! All wasn't lost. She mouthed encouragement into the stirring cloth. Her master attempted to back away, and almost lost his balance, but Mary moved with him and held him fast, gripping his nervous buttocks through the brocade of his coat. She could feel where his left leg ended, the neat fold buttoned up behind. He staggered, almost toppled, but she clung on.

'If you please, sir,' she whispered without looking up, as a sort of incantation. Words were a risk; they might win her a crack across the eyes with a crutch, and lose her the only place she had in the world. 'Please, sir, I'm good, sir,' Mary repeated like a child. She hardly knew what she was saying. 'Please, sir, for free, whatever you like, if you please, sir.'

The creature curled up in her master's breeches heard that, woke fully and stretched. Mary's lips reached for it through the hot fabric. All she heard from above was a guttural kind of sound. Her knees were starting to ache so badly she could think of little else. If she let go, Mr Jones might still back away, yet if she stayed on her knees they'd surely put down roots into the mud. There was no use waiting for a word; whatever the man did, he wouldn't be able to give his yes to it.

Mary staggered to her feet. She didn't attempt to meet Mr Jones's eyes. Instead she turned to the wall, planted her feet securely, hoisted her skirts as high as they'd go, and waited.

Over the long moments that followed, the absurdity of the scene did strike her. She imagined her white buttocks gleaming through the night like the missing moon. Damp air invaded her; all her muscles contracted. Her steel hoops weighed heavy on her wrists. Her stockings, laden with mud, were beginning to slip below her knees. Maybe not the most appetising sight for a man in two minds. She'd gladly have wriggled, or murmured something lewd, if she'd had any confidence it would improve her chances. Instead she rested her cheek against the cool brick and shut her eyes. She stood there for longer than seemed possible. Perhaps Mr Jones was lifting his crutch to deliver one mighty blow. Or else he might be turning to go home, to hurl her possessions out of the window into a puddle in the yard. How long was she going to stand there before admitting that her time was up?

Behind her, the light crash of the crutches. Her head whipped round to see if the man had fallen, but he was right behind her.

What Mr Jones told himself was that he was going to pull down the girl's skirts and cover her shame. Any minute now all this would be over. He was not such a weak sinner as to be overpowered by mere nakedness.

He wouldn't so much as touch her white skin. He'd keep his

breeches done up. He wouldn't push his shaking fingers into her; he wouldn't find her wet fire. He was not a man who'd let the basest part of himself rear up in a dark alley. He wouldn't take his own maidservant against a dirty wall. He'd have nothing to do with such foul delight. He wouldn't feel the O of her terrible muscle lock around him as she drew him into the hot black cave at the heart of the night.

Thank the Maker for his infinite mercy, as Matron Butler used to say, thought Mary. Only the bricks of the wall could see her dirty smile. Mr Jones held her by the stays; the whalebone creaked as he lunged back and forwards. His heat within her filled her up. She squeezed as tight as she could. If she made it very good for him, would that save her? Might this wild card pay off?

He was hurrying now, no trace of the gentleman about him.

Did the Joneses do this every night, after tying on their linen caps, she wondered, or hardly once a year? Was it a long struggle with his wife, she being no novelty, or a shortcut to pleasure, since she had to know by now what would work for her husband? Did he move in his wife just the same way as he moved in her maid? Mary thought about this very same piece of flesh entering the privates of her mistress, and a profound shiver ran through her.

Mr Jones would stagger home tonight still sticky from Mary. He'd stain the marriage bed with their servant's uncouth juices. Would Mrs Jones emerge from sleep, and recognise that scent? Would the smell of rutting make her want some for herself? Would she spread her sleepy legs and spur her husband on, no matter if he said he was worn out? Would the thought of Mary, her tight-laced flesh bruised against the rough wall of the Crow's Nest, make the man rise again? Would he spend his very last drop in his wife tonight? Would he plant the maid's seed inside the body of the mistress, smearing their juices, mingling their scents together?

Mary stood stock still and a lightning went through her, forking and slicing, every toe, every fingernail, every hair on her head. What in all the seven hells—

Afterwards she gripped the bricks for fear of falling. The world seemed to spin, and nothing was what it had been before.

A little later, she was dimly aware that Mr Jones had slid out, flooding down her leg. 'Thank you, sir,' said Mary mechanically, dropping her skirts.

She left him with his head against the wall.

Mr Jones had finally lost his balance. His one leg wobbled; his crutches had fallen in the caked mud. Such a weakness that had come over him; the girl had drained him dry.

He'd never done it standing up before. He'd never done it anywhere but in his bed. He'd never touched a woman who wasn't his wife. Not since the death of his last son had he known such grief.

At breakfast, Mary kept her face blank. No one would know, to look at this girl in her starched neckerchief, that anything had ever happened to her. Her mind ticked like a watch as she made her calculations. She watched Mr Jones's hands on his knife and spoon, and remembered how his fingers had closed on the hard sides of her stays. All her triumph and excitement had given way to shame. Neither met the other's eyes. Mary nibbled her toast and tried to remember to breathe. She considered what hold this man had over her, and she over him.

Maybe he'd send his wife an anonymous letter, Seven-Dials style: *Yore mades a hor. You ony have to look at her*. But Mary was quite prepared to burst into tears and confess that the master had been forcing her since the very first night she came to this house. Would that save her? Who would Mrs Jones believe? Would she trust her beloved Su's daughter over her husband? Maybe she would side with him anyway, not much caring about a dalliance with a servant: men would be men, after all.

Mary could only hope that inside her master, guilt, confusion and lust had stirred up such a thick soup that he'd say and do nothing at all.

At mid-morning she was embroidering alone in the shop. She had a question about the colour of a thread, and she couldn't find the mistress anywhere, so finally she went upstairs and knocked on the Jones's chamber door.

A sound from behind the wood; like a bird in a trap. Mary knocked again, then pushed the door open.

Mrs Jones was alone, crouching on the floor. Sweat patched her face. Mary shut the door and leaned against it. Her mistress looked up and made an attempt to speak. Had she found out, was that it? Did she know what her husband and Mary Saunders had done last night? Could she smell betrayal on the air, and was it breaking her heart?

'Are you ill?'

No words.

'Mistress! Shall I fetch Mrs Ash?'

A violent shake of the head. And then the older woman's face seemed to crack like a bowl, and tears leaked out of every line.

Mary knelt beside her mistress, holding her up. She tried to pull her towards the bed, but Mrs Jones clung to the ground, her petticoats weighing like tents. 'Blood.' The mistress's narrow wet mouth formed the word again. 'Blood in the pot.'

'Perhaps it's only a little,' said Mary doubtfully, and she reached under Mrs Jones's skirts to pull the pot out.

Dark blood ran along the floorboards, pooled in a knot of wood. In the overflowing pot, something that wasn't blood. Mary pressed her mistress's face to her own shoulder, not so much to comfort as to blind her. Mrs Jones began to shake now, her shudderings made no noise.

Oh Christ, had Mary somehow brought this on? Was this the Maker's wrath? But if so, the wrong woman was being punished. In her mind, Mary was back in Ma Slattery's cellar, with Doll gripping her wrists, and the red worm in the basin. At least she'd been glad to be rid of it. But to Mrs Jones the same swimming shape was more precious than all the gold in creation. Mary crushed the weeping face harder against her collarbone.

Words came up, muffled; she released the woman. 'All that's over now,' said Mrs Jones.

'No,' said Mary, and again, faster, 'no. You've time yet, surely.'

'I am forty-three years old,' said Mrs Jones, her voice flat and formal. 'I have no son to give my husband.' Then she got to her feet with one sickening lurch and picked up the chamber-pot.

Mary took it from her, as on any other day; she had to pull a little to make Mrs Jones's hands release it. She covered it with a cloth. 'I'll come back up with water,' she said. 'For the floor.'

'Very good.'

'Will you go to bed now, madam?'

Mrs Jones was still hunched over. She wiped her face on her sleeve. 'No, Mary, there's work to be done.'

They turned away from each other, as if embarrassed.

At the door, the girl was stopped by a word.

'Mary?'

She turned her head.

'I'm glad you were here.'

Guilt like a splinter in her heart. The girl's vision blurred with tears. 'Yes.'

'Oh, and Mary. No one needs to know.'

She nodded once, slowly.

As she went downstairs with a cloth over the pot, she felt a curious sensation like fetters around her ankles. She passed Mrs Ash on the stairs, and had to hold the pot high and casually, as if it contained the usual leavings.

The weather turned cold again in the last week of May, as if the year were reversing itself.

Stiff-faced, Daffy made a note of this unseasonable weather in the back of his coverless *Curiosities of Monmouthshire*, and never looked up from the page if he could help it. Abi wore two extra shawls she'd borrowed from Mary, and huddled into herself. To Mrs Ash, watching from her upstairs window as she stuffed paper into the cracked frame, the occasional soft flakes of snow seemed another of the plagues sent down to warn sinners. Waste; milk spilling across the landscape.

Mary remembered a big storm from her first winter on the streets, the elms broken down in Hyde Park, the drifts that blotted out doors and windows, the family that starved to death on Bedford Street before they were dug out. And the smell of chestnuts, hot in her hands, as she and Doll thudded along the frozen banks of the Thames.

These days her master and she looked anywhere but at each other. He hadn't told yet, she was sure of that, but it could mean he was busy preparing his story. The mistress would surely have noticed something was wrong with him except that she herself was a walking ghost. It felt to Mary as if winter were knotting itself around them all again, and wouldn't be shaken off.

On the last evening in May, when Mr Jones had gone out to his tradesmen's club, Hetta begged for the Queen story. 'But that's a winter tale, my love,' said her mother mechanically.

'It's cold enough for winter, Muda,' objected Hetta, squatting by the fire.

So Mrs Jones shut her prickling eyes and conjured up the details. 'The Queen of Scots wore a black velvet dress,' she recited as if from her own memory, 'all buttoned up with jet acorns, set with pearl.'

Darning beside her, Mary nodded with professional appreciation.

'Her veil was long,' Mrs Jones told her listeners, 'and lace-edged like a bride's.' It soothed her to think of it, she found.

'White?' asked the child, from Mrs Ash's bony knee.

'What else would a bride wear?' Mrs Jones smiled at her daughter. 'Her shoes were of black Spanish leather, her stockings were clocked with silver, and her garters were green silk.'

'How do you know?' asked Daffy suddenly.

Mrs Jones stared at her manservant.

'I mean to say,' he explained in some confusion, 'how could – how was it possible for – for anyone to see her garters?'

A snigger from Mary. Mrs Ash made a choking sound. 'Shouldn't the fellow sit in the kitchen?'

'He means no harm,' said Mrs Jones.

'Such a question to ask!' hissed the nurse.

'The garters are a matter of public record,' Mrs Jones hurried on, gathering her forces. 'Perhaps her ladies wrote everything down afterwards. Well now. They disrobed the Queen when she reached the centre of the hall, don't you know. She stood there in her petticoat – crimson velvet, with a crimson satin bodice, and red sleeves they tied on her to match.'

'The colour of blood,' said Mary.

'Indeed.' Mrs Jones flicked an uneasy smile at the girl. 'And after the Queen had forgiven her executioner – and paid him too – she blindfolded herself with a white cloth embroidered in gold, and she covered up all her auburn hair.' She paused for a moment, so they could imagine the fiery hair being snuffed out. Mrs Ash, Scriptures open on her lap, was pretending not to listen. Mrs Jones's voice gathered force. 'Then the good lady knelt down, didn't she, keeping her back straight as a rod, and she placed her little white hands on the wood for a moment to get her balance.'

'Was it all gory?'

'Was what, Mary?'

'The wood. After the last person.'

'Would you let the woman tell the story?' barked Daffy from his corner.

'That's all right, Daffy. I suppose the wood must have been a little stained.' Mrs Jones stared into the embers, imagining the stains.

'Go on, Muda,' said Hetta. 'What did Queen Mary do next?'

'You know this bit,' said the mother with a faint laugh. 'Show us.'

The girl slipped away from her nurse's side. She flung her head forward and her arms back, making the shape of an arrow.

'Just so,' said Mrs Jones approvingly. What a sharp girl her child was growing up to be. Gratitude, that was what was called for now. She wasn't childless, was she? Many had been taken but one had been spared.

Hetta crouched at her mother's feet. One milky curl had come out of her cap; Mrs Jones took it between her fingers for a moment before tucking it away.

'Did they really chop off her head, then, Muda?'

'It took three blows,' said Mrs Jones, nodding seriously. Some said you should protect children from such knowledge, but in a world as cruel as this one they had to find out about such things sooner or later. 'And then the strangest thing happened,' she said, digging up a forgotten detail. 'The executioner threw her cap off and held her head up by the hair, and the next thing it was bouncing on the floor, but the hair was still in his hand.'

Mary shuddered and turned her face away.

'Her head fell out of her hair?' asked Hetta, her voice rising to a squeak. 'You never said that before.'

'It was a wig, don't you see, *cariad*? A fine red wig to hide her poor head, which had lost its hair after all those years in prison.' Mrs Jones could feel her voice break with the sudden sorrow of it. After all that, to end up bald!

'I read in a history that they picked her head up again,' said Daffy quietly, 'and her lips kept moving for a quarter of an hour, but no one could tell what she was saying.'

Mrs Jones had never heard that before. The image disturbed her; those regal lips reduced to miming gibberish. 'All I know', she said, 'is that Queen Mary went to the axe with grace.'

'Like the first King Charles,' suggested Mary, 'wearing two shirts so as not to shiver on the scaffold.'

'Exactly, my dear.' Mrs Jones reached out for the girl's cold hand and squeezed it.

'That Queen of Scots was a Papist, though,' objected Mrs Ash.

'Well, she was a brave lady, for all that,' said Mrs Jones uncomfortably. 'And it's all a long time past now,' she added after a minute.

'It was a bad cause she died for,' said the nurse under her breath.

Sometimes Mrs Jones couldn't imagine how she'd lived with this harridan for so long. 'To my way of thinking, Mrs Ash,' she said quietly, 'the manner of her death is a lesson to us all to keep our heads high in times of trouble. Especially you, Mary Saunders,' she said, taking up the girl's chilly fingers again. 'When disaster comes you must remember your namesake.'

'Which disaster?' asked the girl, a little nervously.

'Ah, it comes to us all,' Mrs Jones told her, with a little wheeze of laughter. 'It's only a matter of when.'

When the mistress stood up she felt grief settle over her again like a cloak of lead. She went to close the parlour shutters and found it had been snowing all evening. As she watched, the air came apart, splitting into small diamonds which spiralled down as if glad to have loosed their bonds. For a few seconds each flake was unique and free, before it settled on to another and became part of the blanket of white the field was drawing up over itself. Every outline of an ungainly fence or rusting plough was smoothed over; every morass of mud and cinders was blotted out. Even the ruts John Niblett's wagon left on Grinder Street had turned ornamental; the snow picked them out like curls.

That night in bed Mrs Jones lay dreaming of snow. In this dream, all her work was done, and she lifted the latch of the kitchen door, letting herself out so quietly that not an ear pricked after her. She left her slippers behind; her bare feet were exhilarated by the snow, it sharpened their edges. Her new glass soles took her down the garden, following no path but the eddy and shift of the falling flakes. She paused to pluck a frozen apple from the tree; she ate it, filling herself up with sweet cold.

Then she was sleepy and lay down behind the tree where every surface was cushion and sheet, pillow and blanket, below and above and around her all at once. She could feel veil after veil alight on her, weightless, sealing her in. Sleep burned along her arms and legs. She had never felt so pristine, so safe. Now she could sleep.

In a little while, snow would have filled up her footprints; she'd left no trace. And this was the part Mrs Jones wouldn't let herself remember in the morning, no matter how often she had this dream. It was morning and they were looking for her everywhere; everywhere a woman might be, but they didn't think to look at the bottom of the garden, where the snow was deepest behind the apple trees, where it had formed into drifts curving like white breasts out of the field.

Chapter Seven

Punishment

That last freakish snow of May melted away overnight, and June came in warm and humid. At the Morgans' select card-party for the King's twenty-fifth birthday, it was said the ices melted to slop before they were served.

All through June the weather was hot and still. Mary Saunders stayed at home every evening and waited for the end.

What was there to stay for, in this wretched town, she asked herself? Daffy hated the sight of her. Mrs Ash always had. Mr Jones was wearing a face like a dented shield, and any day now he might break down and tell his wife what kind of girl Sue Rhys's daughter really was. Mary's nerves jangled in dreadful anticipation, and several times a day she thought of packing her bag and running away.

But she found she couldn't do it. For one thing, she had nowhere else in the world to go. Absurd though it was, the fact remained that this was the nearest she had to a family. For another, she couldn't walk off of her own free will, not since she'd found Mrs Jones down on her knees, bleeding out her last hope into a chamberpot. The woman was thinner these days, almost translucent. She needed Mary more than ever.

As the weeks went by, Mary gradually let herself conclude that her master hadn't breathed a word, and wasn't going to.

Whatever had happened between him and his maid, that night, he was evidently determined to forget it. He wouldn't be the first man who could wipe his memory clean of such things. But in any case Mary was unspeakably relieved.

'Cider,' she reminded her white-faced mistress; 'you need some strengthening now or you'll be no use to your family.' So Mary went down to the Crow's Nest almost every night. There were plenty of travellers in summertime who wanted a quarter of an hour with Sukie in the room above the stables. The stocking under her bed was growing as heavy as a skull.

For the whole month she and Mrs Jones worked away on Mrs Morgan's velvet slammerkin, trying not to stain it with their sweaty fingers. The silver thread glittered on the white, forming tiny hard apples and convoluted snakes. 'Wherever did she find the pattern?' asked Mary. 'I never saw anything like it.'

'Oh, it's my own,' said Mrs Jones easily. 'Mrs Morgan asked for something on the theme of Paradise.'

That afternoon Mrs Partridge sent her footman down to say she had to have her paduasoy bodice and sleeves reversed and freshly ribboned in time for Midsummer.

'But that's Wednesday, isn't it?' Mary asked Mrs Jones. She wiped her forehead with the back of her hand, careful not to wet the needle. 'However will we finish the quilling on Miss Fortune's new petticoat too?'

Her mistress's face was as pale as the belly of a fish these days, but she let out a faint laugh. Her thin hand lifted to rest against Mary's cheek for a moment. 'That's city time, my girl. You're still thinking like a Londoner. In the Marches we reckon our dates by the Old Style, which means true Midsummer's not for a fortnight yet.'

Mary stared at her. 'You mean . . . it didn't happen here?'

'What didn't?'

'The change,' she said in confusion. 'The new calendar. When I was a child—'

'Oh, that,' interrupted Mrs Jones with a mild contempt. 'Yes, the dates were moved about right enough, as the Government ordered. But you can't change time.'

Her eyes were on her tiny stitches, and the silver thread winking round her finger. She didn't see Mary's strained smile. The girl spoke to Cob Saunders in her head: *So, Father, I've found your eleven days. They were here all along.*

It was black night by the time the men started lighting the Midsummer Fire on the Kymin. The Joneses and Mary watched from lower down on the hill; Mary stood beside her master and mistress, holding Hetta, who had insisted on coming to see what her nurse called *heathen nonsense*.

'It's to bring on a good harvest. The spark to start the bonfire has to come from oak twigs rubbed together,' Mrs Jones told Mary excitedly. 'The men use nine different kinds of kindling!'

Mary nodded, jogging the heavy child on her hip. She watched the first banner of smoke rise and waver around the ears of the crude wicker giant. He was propped up on the mass of old wood and animal bones at the very heart of the fire. The girl was very aware of Mr Jones standing behind her, looking the other way, down into the town.

How red the flames were in the small heart of the bonfire; redder than they ever got to be in the little hearth at home. Flame shouldn't be contained in a little grate, Mary thought; it should always be lit on a hill. Let the giant stretch and uncurl all his arms, now. Let the many-headed dragon lick herself awake.

Around the shoulders of the wicker man the white smoke billowed, caught on the wind. Hetta coughed and yelped in delight. 'He's burning!'

'That's right,' said Mary.

The fire seemed to want to fly away with the smoke; flames broke off and floated for a second until they lost their wings and disappeared. It was as if the flames couldn't remember how to burn without the bonfire, without the branches and old bones anchoring them down. The wind shifted, the clouds reddened and Mary's eyes stung in the massive heat. She had a craving to leap into the fire's embrace and let it turn her all colours.

'Look you now!' said Mrs Jones, jogging her elbow and pointing. The woven giant was burning grandly, his huge head engulfed in fire, leaning back at a reckless angle on the heap of flaming rafters. His neck must have burnt away, because suddenly his head came loose and fell. Mr Jones seized Mary by the sleeve; she jumped at his touch, almost dropping Hetta. He jerked them out of the way as the ball of fire rolled past them, down the hill, spitting out sparks.

'Thank you, sir,' Mary muttered, but her words were drowned out. The cider-scented crowd were cheering madly; it was as if some invisible St George had beheaded the monster. The head moved brokenly now, setting the long grass on fire in places; three men ran forward to stamp it out. If they weren't careful the whole hill might go up, thought Mary. Now there'd be a fine sight. She imagined every withered blade of grass lighting its taper at the next, till the whole Kymin was one glorious flaming mound, a beacon that could be seen all the way to London.

The drums had taken up the pipe's rhythm. Despite everything Mary felt a wild happiness rise up inside her; she began to jig on the spot. Hetta whooped with pleasure. 'Dance! Dance!'

Mr Jones's crutches dug a purchase in the soft grass of the hill as he moved up to his wife. His face was set in a rather ghastly grin. He dropped the crutches and began to hop in time to the drums, graceful as a hare. Mary watched him with wide eyes.

Mrs Jones let out a laugh without any mockery in it. She took his hands into her own and bobbed on the spot. 'Aye,' she called to Hetta, 'your Fafa was always a good dancer.'

Hetta flung out her arms to her parents. Mary moved over and set the child down. She took her mistress's hand, which was soft and damp from exertion. They were all dancing like a chalk circle round the child, keeping the night at bay. Mary took a chance and reached for Mr Jones's free hand. She stopped when she saw his eyes, raging red in the firelight. All of a sudden he stopped dancing and bent down to pick up Hetta with one hand and his crutches with the other. He embraced her as if she were treasure. 'Time this child was in bed,' he said gruffly.

'Oh, but Thomas, it's only once a year—'

'Stay,' he told his wife. 'I'll take her home.' And without another word he was off down the hill, oddly graceless on one splayed crutch. Hetta clung round her father's neck, and stared almost drunkenly over his shoulder.

Mrs Jones stared after him, troubled. 'I do think the child might have stayed up a little longer.'

Beside her, Mary stood with her face in her hands. Her teeth were chattering as if with cold. What had she done to this family?

'Mary, sweetheart, what is it? What ails you?'

'I – I have to tell you,' the girl said all in a rush, sobbing.

'Yes?'

But confession was impossible, Mary discovered between one breath and the next. There was nothing she could say that wouldn't hurt her mistress worse than anything she'd already done. 'I'm not the girl you think me,' was all she could come out with, hoarsely.

Mrs Jones's narrow face was entirely innocent. The bonfire crackled and roared behind her.

'My mother . . . I fought with my mother,' blurted Mary, improvising. 'Before she died. She never liked me. She never loved me,' she went on, a tear dripping into her collar. 'I wasn't the daughter she wanted.'

'Oh, Mary.' The woman's face screwed up and Mary thought perhaps she was shocked, but then Mrs Jones started to laugh, in a weak sort of way, holding her stomach as if it still hurt her, as if she was still bleeding inside. 'Oh, Mary, my love. We all fight with our mothers before they die.'

'Do we?' she asked stupidly.

'Of course. We only remember the fight because of the dying, see?'

Mary's face was wet with misery.

Mrs Jones pulled the girl into her arms on the smoky hillside. 'There, there, *cariad*. Look now, I'll tell you a secret to make you laugh, will I?' she whispered into her ear.

In this embrace Mary felt entirely safe.

'Something not even Thomas knows?'

The girl nodded, her face against Mrs Jones's cool neckerchief.

'Cob Saunders – your father – courted me long before he ever looked at your mother.'

Mary looked up in shock.

Mrs Jones was wearing a little shamed smile. Her hand almost covered her mouth. 'He was all for marrying me and sweeping me off to the great city – but I was fearful. For all Cob was a charming fellow, you couldn't be sure of him. And when I let myself think of all that dirt and noise, and the thousands and thousands of strangers' faces—' Her spiralling voice broke off.

Mary shrugged, wiping her eyes on the back of her hand. 'London's just a place like any other.'

'Well, I'm only glad it wasn't me who went. Because while I was dithering, you see, didn't Cob take up with Su!'

The girl let herself think about that. Was there no friendship in the world without treachery hidden at the heart of it?

'I won't say I didn't mind at first,' Mrs Jones went on, nodding judiciously, 'and I had quite a quarrel with Su over it, but it was true I'd had my chance with Cob before she ever stepped in, and besides, what was the use in harking back on maybes? And then not two years later, Thomas came home from Bristol, a master tailor, and we were married in a month. The gossips called me *another man's leavings*, but Thomas never thought there was anything in it.'

'But were you still—'

'Oh, I forgot your father fast enough. After Thomas and I set up the shop, I was too busy to fret about anything. I may have had moments of regret in my life, but you know, they wouldn't add up to an hour.'

Mary was letting herself think about the other ways the story might have run. Tears stood out in her eyes.

'What is it now, child?'

'It means—' She spoke with difficulty; her throat felt swollen. 'You could have been my mother.' She let the tears fall, flowing faster now. She was gathered to Mrs Jones's soft bosom again, and the muslin neckerchief soaked up the salt water.

'Hush,' her mistress was murmuring in her ear. 'Don't cry, *cariad*, never you cry.'

The girl let grief rise up in her like a well. Such luxury.

Mrs Jones rocked her, stroked her hair, whispered in her ear. 'Amn't I a mother to you now?'

Alone in the kitchen one hot Sunday morning in July while the Joneses were gone to service at St Mary's, Abi felt the house close in on her. In one corner stood a great pile of breakfast dishes to be scoured with sand; in another, a half-jar of butter going sour. Only the surreptitious scratchings of the mice interrupted the silence.

A minute later she was halfway down Monnow Street, heading away from the sound of the church bells and the town ladies with their enormous skirts and hard faces. Abi rarely went out of the house, and when she did she always remembered why she didn't. A child stopped across the street, open-mouthed. A bigger one, behind him, scooped up a handful of last year's leaves. 'Blackie,' he shrieked as he threw them. The warm wind arced the leaves back into his face.

Abi walked on, faster. The ground slid away under her feet. She had the impression that now she'd started she'd never stop. She'd walk across the world and no one would stand in her way. She might even reach the sun – the real sun, not the watery image of it that hovered over this country. She remembered Sundays on the Island, lying in the shade of the huts, too tired to move, with music like a dream of fever on the air.

'If the mistress won't listen to talk of wages, you could always try the Quakers,' Mary Saunders had said a few nights ago, casually.

'Why?'

'It's well known, that's all,' said Mary with a huge yawn; 'they've a liking for blacks.'

All Abi knew about the handful of townspeople known as Quakers was that they were freakish folk who wore grey and went hatless. How they might help improve her condition, she could hardly imagine. As she filled the irons with hot charcoal, or stirred the lettuce soup, she fretted over what that phrase might mean: *a liking for blacks*. Was it the sort of liking that men had for Mary, the men who paid her all those coins she hid under the bed when she thought Abi was asleep?

Sometimes Abi wished Mary Saunders had never come to the house on Inch Lane, never shaken Abi out of her long somnolence, never said words like *wages,* or *liberty.*

It was the sticky restlessness in the air today that was prompting her to seek out the Quakers. Mary had said she thought they met upstairs at the Robin Hood, at the end of Monnow Street. The landlord cast Abi a curious glance now, as she crossed the sawdust-clotted floor of the Robin Hood, but he didn't say a word to stop her. The stairs creaked under her shoes. She put an ear to the door at the top, to hear what was going on, but there wasn't a sound. At first she thought the meeting was over. Then she heard a throat clearing, and another. It was as if the people behind the door were all waiting for someone important to speak. She stayed there, her ear pressed damply against the wood, for what felt like an hour, but nothing broke the silence.

When at last she heard chairs being pushed back, Abi fled. She wasn't going to be discovered on the stairs, like some kind of spy. She waited under a tree across from the Robin Hood for another long stretch of time. Leaning on the parapet of the bridge she stared down into the hurry of the water. She didn't care if there was trouble when she got home. It was good to have empty hands, at least; to have nothing to fold or cook or wash, just for an hour.

Finally grey-frocked figures began to emerge in twos and threes from the side door of the Robin Hood. Abi's heart pounded. She waited for one of them to look up or catch her eye, but their heads were all bent. At last the trickle of people died away, and she knew she'd missed her chance. Then she cursed herself for a snivelling coward who deserved the life she'd got.

One more: an elderly wigless gentleman with a thick file of papers under his arm. Abi shook off her paralysis and shot down the street after him. She followed him all the way across Chippenham Meadow, but he never looked back; he seemed unaware of her steps behind his. She hadn't moved this fast in longer than she could remember. On Quay Street there was no one else within earshot, and 'Sir?' she cried, 'Sir?', hoarsely.

He turned, his forehead creased. 'Why do you call me that?'

She backed away. The man was offended that she'd dared to speak to him.

But then he took a step towards her. 'Do I know you?'

Abi shook her head, very fast. 'No, sir. I mean, no,' she corrected herself.

'Don't be alarmed, sister,' he said, coming up close and speaking softly. 'I'm only a plain human soul like yourself; my name is Daniel Flyte. What need have we of titles?'

Abi's eyes narrowed to cracks. This was a very strange sort of Englishman. He wore his own hair, grey and thin. His buttons were made of horn. His coat, his shirt, his breeches, were all one grey, as if he'd been bleached in a sheep dip. But his face was brown from the sun and his eyes were bright.

'What can I do for you?' he prompted her.

She didn't know how to begin.

'Will you go along with me?' He resumed his brisk walk.

'My name Abi,' she said all at once, stumbling along beside him.

'Abi what?'

She was at a loss. 'That's all.' She stopped herself from saying *sir*, that time.

'Have you no surname?'

'Some say Abi Jones,' she admitted.

'Well, then,' he said patiently, as if to a child.

'But the Joneses not my family,' she blurted. 'They my owners.'

This, evidently, was the key to unlock Daniel Flyte. He stopped in his tracks, and his face came to life, all furrowed with distress. 'Sister,' he said, taking her by the wrist, 'no one owns you.'

Sometimes it was best to agree with whatever white folk said. Abi shrugged.

'You belong to your Maker, but your soul is free,' Daniel Flyte assured her. 'No man can hold another as property.'

'Well, the Joneses my masters, anywhichway,' Abi told him glumly. 'We live on Inch Lane.'

'You receive no remuneration?'

She blinked at him.

'Pay, that is? Wages?'

'No, sir.' She remembered his resentment of the title. 'I mean—'

'Never mind,' said Daniel Flyte with a wintry smile. 'Call me what you will.' His smile fell away and he tightened his grip on her arm. 'So these people, these Joneses, hold you in forced servitude?'

'I suppose,' said Abi.

The old man shook his head violently as if in pain. 'I belong to a Society of Friends,' he told her, 'who believe all men and women are worth the same, because they each have a bit of the same light in them. Do you see?'

She stared at him.

'A little fragment of light, hidden in each of our hearts. You follow me?'

She nodded, wary.

'Do you know what it says in the Bible about slavery?'

She shook her head, as he seemed to expect it.

Daniel Flyte's voice took on a fervent resonance. 'It says that masters must give fair wages to their servants, because they too have a master in heaven. It says, *You shall eat the fruit of the labour of your hands*. It says furthermore, *Do not submit to a yoke of slavery!*' His cheeks quivered with emotion; his lips were wet.

Abi was losing her grip on this conversation. She had to ask him, before they were interrupted. 'So I wonder,' she whispered, stepping closer, 'I wonder if you come, maybe. Come speak to my masters.'

'Ah.' Daniel Flyte let go of her wrist, then, and covered his mouth with his blunt-nailed hand as if he had just remembered something. 'Now therein lies a difficulty. I must tell you, sister, that our Society is a small and generally ill-liked one in these parts.' His voice had shrunk. 'Our policy is not to . . . intervene directly. In private families, that is to say. The risks are such – the delicacy of our position with regard to our neighbours—'

Abi felt her strength drain away through her feet. When he came to a pause in his speech she muttered, 'Must go now. Mustn't be late.' She turned and walked away.

'But, sister, if you come to our Meeting—'

She kept walking. Well, that was what you got for talking to strangers: less than nothing. The man in grey didn't attempt to stop her. She turned her head once, and he was standing with his hands by his sides, watching her.

Despite the disappointment, something he'd said hung in her mind as she hurried home: *the fruit of the labour of your hands.* She thought of all the fruit she hadn't seen since Barbados: plum, breadfruit, mango. She let herself imagine fruit, filling up her mouth.

That day Mrs Ash began to reap her harvest. It had been slow work, often tedious, but it had borne great fruit in the end. How many hours had she wasted in idle, worldly chit-chat with her neighbours, listening out for the name of Mary Saunders? But yesterday, by glorious accident, she'd been standing in the queue at the apothecary's, when who did she fall into conversation with but the drawer from the Crow's Nest? He was a very helpful lad, most articulate, especially after Mrs Ash agreed to lend him a shilling. He told her so much about the girl known as *Sukie* that Mrs Ash had to send Hetta to stand outside so her ears wouldn't be polluted.

To think of it, God's own curate in Monmouth was a pimp for that whorish girl! Now Mrs Ash came to think of it, Cadwaladyr's sermons had always lacked rigour, smacked a little too much of the world.

She'd slept on it till today, Sunday; she'd wanted to do the Lord's work on the Lord's day. She sat at supper, dipping her barley bread in her soup and taking tiny bites, watching the London girl. All evening Mrs Ash waited. She put Hetta to bed early and would accept no pleas for stories. She said nothing and did nothing when Mrs Jones sent her pet down the road to fetch her a pint of liquor. Mrs Ash simply went up to the last flight of stairs, leading to the attic, and sat there three steps from the top, as quiet as a cat at a hole.

When she heard Mary Saunders coming up through the silent house, she got to her feet. Her shadow slithered down the bare wood. The girl flinched when she saw her. *No peace for the wicked.*

'What kept you so long, Miss, down at the Crow's Nest?' Mrs Ash began civilly.

The girl stared up at her, blank-faced. 'Nothing. The cider takes a while to draw.'

'Is that so?' The silence lengthened. Mrs Ash knew the girl wouldn't be able to resist answering.

'Don't you believe me, then?' said Mary, chin up.

The nursemaid folded her arms like snakes. 'All I know is what I hear.'

'What d'you hear, then?'

'That you've been seen,' said Mrs Ash, savouring the sounds.
'Where?'

She threw the words out like trash. 'Round the back of the
stinking alehouse, with all manner of men!'

Mary was silent, as if with astonishment. 'Who says?' she
asked.

Mrs Ash shrugged, as if to suggest that her informants were
the elements themselves.

'Well, it's not true,' hissed Mary. 'None of it! I don't know what
kind of troublemakers you've been talking to, but it's perjury, the
lot of it.'

The nurse let the girl's blustering words hang in the air till they
faded. She wanted to remember every sweet moment of this.

Mary inhaled heavily and walked upstairs. Mrs Ash grabbed
the girl's skirt as she passed. She rifled the folds feverishly,
though the girl struggled. Yes, there it was, a wet mark, as big
as her hand. She stretched out the blue cloth to display the stain.
'What's that, then?'

'I must have sat on something,' said the girl, faltering.

The nurse let out a snort of derision.

'Would you call me a liar?' Mary went on, shrilly.

'No, that's not what I'd call you, *Sukie*,' said Mrs Ash delib-
erately.

The girl's face was white with guilt. It was as if the house were
beginning to shake under their feet.

'*Yea*,' Mrs Ash declaimed, '*you have polluted the land with
your whoredoms and sorceries.*'

Mary stared at her crazily.

'Filthy harlot! *The Lord shall smite thee with a consumption*,'
quoted Mrs Ash triumphantly, '*and with a fever, and with an
inflammation, and with an extreme burning, and with the sword,*

and with mildew; and they shall pursue thee till thou perish.' It was as if the words had been stored up in her head all her life, just for this moment.

'Get away from me,' said Mary Saunders. She struggled up the stairs, but Mrs Ash was still holding her by the skirt, so she floundered like a boat in high seas.

'*And the Lord shall smite thee with madness,*' hissed the nurse, '*and blindness, and astonishment of heart.*'

Was the girl going to cry? Her eyes were burning holes in her pale face as she turned. '*Judge not,*' she told Mrs Ash in a shaking voice, 'that's what the Good Book says too. *Judge not, lest ye—*'

But before she could summon up the rest, she'd been interrupted. Mrs Ash's sharp fingertips almost met in the girl's soft arm. 'You dare to quote Scripture at me, you poxy little drab!'

Mary shook her off with one violent motion. In the girl's eyes, Mrs Ash could see a change, as Mary registered the fact that there was no use in further denials. The serpent shed her disguise. 'At least men pay good money for me,' Mary spat over her shoulder as she went up the last few steps. 'You'd have to pay them yourself.'

Mrs Ash's ears were ringing like church bells. She made a last grab.

'Take your hands off my dress!'

There was an appalling rip. The dirty white shift showed through the cloth of Mary's skirt. The girl reached down and gave the nurse a shove hard enough to send her down five steps.

Mrs Ash landed against the wall. She dusted herself with trembling hands. Her breath was loud with panic and outrage. 'Very well,' she gasped, 'I'll trouble you no further. I'll just go and wake the Joneses now, if they're not awake already. You'd best be packing your bags.'

'You wouldn't.' The girl's tone was doubtful.

Mrs Ash could suddenly see how young this creature was. She'd never felt such power before. It swelled like yeast in her mouth: 'See if I don't.'

Now it was Mary's turn to crouch down on the steps. 'Please.'

'Please what, you godless whore? What can you say for yourself?'

The girl was silent.

Mrs Ash put her hands on her hips, and looked up at her. 'Did you think you could bring your sluttish ways into a respectable town like this and no one would notice? Turning our own curate into a filthy-pawed pimp? How dare you serve a good mistress by day and go trulling round town by night, dragging this whole household down into the dirt with you!'

'Don't tell the mistress.' The girl was beginning to sob, but her cheeks were still dry. 'She'll turn me out of doors.'

'Good enough for you.'

Mary's eyes were glittering when she raised her head. 'I've nowhere else to go. Please, Mrs Ash. I'm sorry for what I said. Please don't tell. I was driven to do what I did, at the Crow's Nest,' said the girl finally, the words spilling out. 'It was only a couple of times. I needed the money.'

'For what?'

'Old debts.'

That came out a little too glibly; was the girl lying? Mrs Ash peered up at her, trying to read her pale face.

'It was the only way I could think of to pay them off,' Mary rushed on. Then her voice turned a little wheedling. 'You know yourself, madam, what it's like to be so reduced in your circumstances, that . . .'

'That what?' asked the nurse, dangerously.

'That you have to make a . . . a trade of your body.'

Mrs Ash was rooted to the spot. She let herself imagine smashing this girl's head against the wall. 'It is hardly the same,' she said icily.

'No. Not at all.' With another sob: 'Forgive me.'

The nurse stared up at the harlot. Her triumph was suddenly mixed with exhaustion. She knew she wouldn't go and wake Mrs Jones. Not tonight, not just yet. She would hold on to this moment as long as she liked. Maybe a day, maybe a month. Such a gorgeous sensation, might and mercy mixed. And the girl abased on the steps and weeping like a baby, knowing that it was in the older woman's power to ruin her, any hour of any day. 'I'm going to my bed now,' Mrs Ash told her with the gravity of a queen.

Mary, watching the dark figure disappear in the stairwell below, blinked the tears back into her sockets. She stood up and examined the damage; the seam was ripped all along her waist. The old bitch would pay for that, somehow, she promised herself. The hypocrisy of the woman, too – not to admit that they'd both lived by renting themselves out. Cunny or tit, what was the difference?

In her own room, Mary sat on the edge of the bed, softly. Her heart was still crashing around from rib to rib. Now there in Mrs Ash, thought Mary, was an example of a woman who had risked nothing and ended up with nothing. That's what you got for being a servant of no ambition: a shrunken life, hung up like a gibbet as a warning to others.

Abi was face down in the pillow; how tired she must have been to have slept through all that racket outside the door. Mary bent and pulled her bag out from under the bed. Her stocking was full, voluptuous with weight. She spilled the coins into her lap, very gently. They covered the width of her dress. The scaly heft of them gratified her hands.

Mary tried not to think of Mrs Jones's face, if Mrs Ash did

decide to tell. Instead she concentrated on the coins beneath her hands. If all else failed, she had this: some kind of future, spread out in her lap. A few coins were dull, others gleaming, and they all bore different faces. Funny how she couldn't tell, now, whether any one of them had been purchased with a week's hard labour with her needle or a quarter-hour behind a tavern. She rubbed a few coins between the ruffles at her elbows, to polish them. She'd tested them all by biting, as soon as she got them, but tonight she was haunted by the idea that in her absence they might somehow have been replaced with counterfeits, or rusted away. She chose one and closed her teeth on it, despite a pang from a rotten molar. She'd like to eat the coin, she thought. To swallow them all, and keep them safe in the gilded cavern of her body.

Abi couldn't stay still any longer. When Mary had slid the bag under the bed and slipped between the sheets, Abi went up on her elbow and whispered, 'Mary.'

'What is it?'

'Talked to a Quaker man today.'

'Did you?' Absently. 'So will he come speak to the mistress?'

'No,' said Abi bleakly.

Mary turned her head towards her. 'You should run away,' she said, on impulse.

Abi curled her lip. What kind of nonsense was that?

'I mean it,' said the girl with animation. 'You wouldn't stand for such treatment if you'd a spark of spirit in you.'

Resentment flared up in the maid-of-all-work. She flung back the blanket and hauled her nightshirt up to the top of her thigh. She put her finger to the old brand.

'What's that?' asked Mary, staring. 'Another master's name?'

'Look close,' said Abi gruffly.

Mary brought the wavering candle near enough to the skin to make out the letter R, stamped in black.

'That means Runaway,' Abi told her before she could ask. 'Means I done it before, in Barbados. Means I know running gets you nowhere.'

'Tell me,' said Mary eagerly. 'What happened? Was it long ago?'

Abi wrenched up the blanket and turned on her side. 'Told you enough,' she said through clenched teeth.

'All right then, don't tell me. All I'll say,' added Mary, 'is that your chances are better in this country. If you got as far as London, they'd never find you in the crowds.'

Confusion filled Abi's head, and a sort of grief. Was the girl trying to get rid of her? Did she want the whole bed to herself? Did she not have any need of Abi's company in the long nights? 'What you care, anyway?' she asked hoarsely.

Mary shrugged. 'I just . . . it seems to me that masters shouldn't be allowed to think they own people, that's all.' She leaned over and snuffed out the candle with her fingers.

The maid-of-all-work lay and brooded on this for a minute. Then she spoke up in the darkness. 'If I did.'

'Mm?'

'If I run. You tell me where to go? In London?'

'Of course I could,' said Mary with animation.

'You give me money?'

A cold, prickling silence filled up the bed.

'Mary?'

'What money?' came the answer, almost formal.

Abi was suddenly sick of these games. 'You think I deaf?' She didn't care if her voice could be heard in the room below. 'You think I don't know what money sounds?'

'It's none of your business.'

'You got a stocking full!'

'I earned it.'

'I need some. I never get away without some money.'

Mary lay as stiff as wood.

'Please!'

'I'm sorry for you, Abi, but no. As a friend of mine used to say, *Every girl for herself.*'

It occurred to Abi now how easy it would be to pick up the pillow and press it down on this girl's haughty face.

'Oh, and by the way, I know how much I have, down to the last ha'penny,' Mary threatened softly. 'And you know I'd be able to smell your hands on it if you ever so much as touched it.'

Abi's fingers were full of murder. She put them in her mouth and bit down.

In the dog days of August, hives walked their way up Mary's ribs; her sleeves stuck to the crooks of her elbows. The air was full of dust from the hay harvest. For the first time in months Mary missed London, found herself pining for all the worst things about it, even the reek of the Thames lying low.

Trade was slack. There was a spinster called Rhona Davies who'd recently set up as a dressmaker over on Wye Street; she offered nothing fancy, but her low prices were tempting old customers away from the Joneses. At the house on Inch Lane, Mary sweated over the accounts, while Mrs Jones nibbled her thumbnail. Missing sums, outstanding bills, bad debts. Everything depended on the Morgans, that was about the sum of it. If Mrs Jones – rather than some smooth Bristol dressmaker, or even, God forbid, a London firm – got the commission for young Miss Anna's coming-out trousseau, the family on Inch Lane would be eating good beef all winter. Most of their other patrons were off taking the waters or shut up in their houses with gigantic paper fans; nobody was in a paying humour.

Over breakfast, dinner and supper, on the stairs and in the yard, Mary felt herself being watched by Mrs Ash like a Recording Angel. Any day, on a whim, this woman could choose to bring down destruction on her head. That was what tortured Mary: the not knowing whether or when. She kept her eyes low and did nothing to provoke the nurse. When one morning Hetta clung to Mary's skirts and said she wanted to learn to embroider, Mary had to push her off: 'Go back to Mrs Ash.'

The child heard the hint of poison in the maid's voice, and clearly thought it was for herself; her lip hung down. But what could she do, Mary asked herself? Mrs Ash smiled placidly and held out her hand for Hetta.

The girl never went near the Crow's Nest, in case Mrs Ash ever came to hear of it; she got Mrs Jones's cider from the Green Oak instead, and told her mistress it was much fresher. On the rare occasions when she saw the Reverend Cadwaladyr, at market or in the church porch after service, she looked away. Her hoard of coins had stopped growing. They stuck to her palms when she counted them. They were all she had, but they weren't enough.

She and Abi shared a room without meeting each other's eyes; at night they lay rigid, inches apart.

The air reeked of fermentation from the cider brewing. Mary's forehead bore a permanent crease. 'Whatever's the matter with you these days?' Mrs Jones asked one afternoon when they were down in the kitchen, pressing sheets.

'Blame the heat,' said Mary shortly.

Right through August, storms blew up every few days; no sooner was washing pinned up on the line than it was soaked through again. The farmers complained of mildew in the corn.

Mary had a sense of waiting, but for what? These days all she was doing was killing time.

Mrs Morgan walked in on the first of September for the final fitting of her velvet slammerkin. For all the heat, she was still swathed in her black fur-edged cape. Reverently Mrs Jones lifted down the snowy velvet dress and spread it in Mrs Morgan's lap to show how the snakes and apples on its train caught the light. 'Just think how the silver thread will set off madam's hair!' she said.

Meaning, thought Mary, bored, that Mrs Morgan was as grey as an old dog.

'How this will eclipse them all at Bath!' trilled Mrs Jones.

Yes, even if a mule wore it, thought Mary. Her hives were driving her demented. To distract herself from the itch, she stroked the nap of the velvet slammerkin with one pin-callused finger.

'It's fine work,' the Honourable Member's wife conceded at last. 'Well done, Mrs Jones.'

The dressmaker bobbed gratefully.

'For the winter, I think I'll have you make me a riding-habit, as well as three complete suits of clothes for my daughter's first season. And your husband might fit us both for some dress stays.'

Mrs Jones nodded, glowing. Mary could tell she was too excited to speak. Their eyes met over Mrs Morgan's shoulder, and Mrs Jones gave the girl a tiny wink, as if to say that their worries were over. The dressmaker picked up the dress, and Mary rushed to help her hold it like a cloud of white over Mrs Morgan's head so madam could worm her way into it.

Mary stood back and considered. What an almighty waste of a year's embroidery! Inside her silver-veined splendour, the woman looked plainer than ever. Stretched over the gigantic hoop and layers of petticoats, the slammerkin seemed to fill the room, bobbing against the trunks and almost knocking over a chair. It was magnificent, in this humble setting, but it was also quite ridiculous. Mary itched to try it on. How much better she would carry it off than Mrs Morgan. Mary's breasts were twice the size, for starters. A laugh bubbled up in her throat.

'Why is your maid looking at me so insolently, Mrs Jones?'

Mary blinked, and looked down at her hands. She'd forgotten to be careful.

'Was she, madam?' Mrs Jones, breathless.

'Indeed she was.'

The girl had turned her back, now. She pretended to be sorting through some jackets hanging from the ceiling; she buried her head among them and bit her lips to stop the laugh from coming out.

'Well, Miss, what have you to say for yourself?'

Mrs Morgan's voice, tight as a chicken's, increased Mary's merriment. She pressed her face against a train of cool satin. 'I'm sorry, I'm sure.' Her words came out muffled.

'You will look at me when you address me!'

Mary turned, with a face as rigid as china.

'High time you learned some respect for your betters.'

The word hung in the air between them. Mary kept her mouth sealed shut. But she couldn't prevent one eyebrow lifting. A gesture that whispered, *You, my better?*

Now her mistress's eyes flicked between the two of them in panic.

'I beg your pardon, madam,' Mary said to Mrs Morgan, adding a deep curtsy, to be on the safe side.

'She meant no harm.' Mrs Jones gave her patron a paralysed smile.

Mrs Morgan sighed and turned aside to examine her profile in the long mirror. 'I would not keep a girl so pert, myself,' she remarked.

'No, madam,' said the dressmaker. 'She's not generally so. It's the heat, I do believe.'

'I doubt she would have reached such a height of impudence without some encouragement, Mrs Jones.'

No answer to that.

The Honourable Member's wife lifted her arms resignedly to indicate that Mrs Jones should begin undoing the slammerkin. 'The neckline a quarter-inch lower, I think.'

'Very good, madam.'

She stood there like a doll with her arms in the air. And Mary, watching from under her lowered lids, realised all at once that the rich were useless. The more servants they depended on, the feebler they grew. Parasites!

But she went over to help her mistress with a perfect humility of manner. She meant to behave herself for the rest of the fitting. And all was well until, in the struggle to hoist the narrow bodice off over her head, Mrs Morgan's shift fell open and her left breast flopped over the edge of her stays. It resembled nothing so much as a lightly fried egg, livid and elongated, quivering on the edge of the plate. Mary had never seen anything so funny in her life. She looked up and saw the Honourable Member's wife, who had noticed what the girl was looking at. A huge and terrible laugh spilled out of Mary's mouth before she even knew it was coming. She clamped a hand over her lips, but it was too late.

What Mary remembered afterwards, as she stood in the hall, against the closed door – with her heart banging almost loud enough to drown out Mrs Morgan's shouts: 'By Christ, I say she laughed at me! I tell you, the slut guffawed in my face!' – was not Mrs Morgan's face, but Mrs Jones's. Lost, dreading, like a child in a wood.

Mrs Jones couldn't eat a bite of supper. Afterwards, she waited till she was alone with her husband.

'Jane?'

She looked up, startled at the first name.

Mr Jones laid a warm hand over hers. 'You're not yourself this evening.'

She blinked at him with grateful tears. 'It's nothing.'

'Has the child been tiring you?'

How she would have liked to nod, to blame it all on the petty exhaustions of an ordinary day. It wouldn't be the first time she'd kept something from Thomas, after all. She had had bigger secrets, lies of omission.

But she shook her head regretfully. 'It's only – Mary. She was . . . pert. With Mrs Morgan.'

His forehead drew into a knot. 'Pert?'

'She meant no real harm – she only laughed—'

'Laughed? At what?' he interrupted, his face dark.

'Nothing,' said Mrs Jones unconvincingly. Somehow she couldn't bear to describe the incident, the breast in all its pallid limpness. She was half afraid she might laugh herself.

'And what of the commission?'

His wife squirmed. 'That's what's worrying me. That's why I've brought it up at all. When she first came in today, Mrs Morgan asked me to undertake three sets of clothes for her daughter—'

'And now it seems Mary Saunders has caused an utter breach in our relations with our most prominent patron!' He pronounced the words as if in a court of law.

His wife flinched. 'I don't know about that, Thomas. Mrs Morgan left in such a hurry—'

His hand thumped the table. 'We'll be lucky', he growled, 'if any member of that family ever steps into our shop again.'

Mrs Jones put her face in her hands.

'As for the girl, I'll give her *pert*,' he roared. 'I'll give her *no harm*. Bring the chit down this minute and I'll whip the smile off her face.'

His wife could feel her face stiffen into a mask of horror. 'But my dear, consider—'

'Bring her down for a round dozen this minute, I say. Her kind can't be reasoned with.'

'Thomas.' Mrs Jones tried to gather her forces. 'We've never resorted to such punishment in our family. I cannot agree—'

'You cannot?' The vein on his nose stood out. 'Well, what matter if you can agree or not? I hope we'll have no petticoat government in this house!'

In the whole length of their marriage, through money troubles and domestic disputes, she'd never seen her husband's face so distorted, so beyond her reach. It was as if, by some piece of girlish foolishness, Mary Saunders had ruined her master's life.

Mr Jones pushed his chair back; it made a dreadful squeal. Every nerve in his wife's body strained away from him, but she stayed where she was. He stood, breathing heavily. Something was softening his face – not kindness, it seemed to her, but some obscure doubt. As he scrabbled for his crutches, he mumbled something, so low she barely caught it.

'I beg your pardon?' she whispered.

'You do it. More seemly.' And with that he'd lurched out of the room.

'Abi said I was wanted.'

When Mary came in, the mistress was standing in the parlour like a thief, red-eyed, her hands behind her. 'Mary,' she said very fast, 'Mr Jones – that is, we – have decided, my husband and I, that you deserve a whipping for your conduct today.' A birch rod emerged from behind her skirts. She toyed with it, as if it was some fashionable accessory she didn't know how to use.

Mary looked at her mistress very hard. They waited in a dull silence. Mary couldn't quite believe it. She hadn't been whipped since she was thirteen years old, and lost the penny through a hole in her pocket.

Mrs Jones's words squeezed out painfully: 'What you did was very bad.'

'What did I do, exactly?'

The older woman's lips trembled. 'You laughed at Mrs Morgan.'

'I meant nothing by it. I said I was sorry.'

Her mistress put her hand up to cover her mouth. Realising it still held the birch, she put it down again. 'It was the way you looked at her, when you were laughing.'

'I'm not responsible for my face, madam!'

But Mary knew this was bluster. When she had accepted the advance on her wages, back in the spring, she'd as good as signed herself over. Her back, her hands, her words, every muscle in her face.

'Your behaviour deeply offended Mrs Morgan. It has probably lost us the year's most important business.'

'Well, she shouldn't have been so touchy,' muttered the girl.

'Oh, Mary,' said Mrs Jones helplessly, 'what lady could bear to be looked at in that way, at such a moment?'

At this Mary couldn't prevent her mouth from forming into a tiny smirk.

'If you prove yourself to be a child,' Mrs Jones said, in a stiff and borrowed voice, 'I must treat you like one.' She shouted loud enough to startle them both: 'Come in, Abi!'

Only when the maid-of-all-work came in, expressionless, and stooped over, did Mary understand. She was to undo the laces of her stays and bare her back, then put her wrists in Abi's hands and lean her body against the curve of Abi's spine and give herself over to be whipped like a common convict. When all she'd done was laugh at the wrong moment! When the order had clearly come down from Mr Jones, who wanted her punished not for today, but for the night when she'd lifted her skirts to him.

Mary didn't have to stand for this. All she had to do now was walk upstairs and pack her bag. She had more than enough money to take Niblett's wagon to London and make a new start.

But something held her. Maybe the habit of servitude. Maybe the stillness of the three women, like masked actors in a play. Or the look in her mistress's unfocused eyes that said, *Help me, Mary*?

Mr Jones stood with his ear pressed against the door, hard enough to make it tingle. As each blow fell in the little parlour he seemed to feel the wood shake. Nobody inside the room spoke a word or let out a cry of pain. His wife was not shirking the job, he could tell, even though she couldn't know he was listening. Whatever Jane set herself to do, he thought with appalled love, she did to the best of her ability. Even if the choice was not hers to make.

The strokes came hard and regular. At the tenth, there was a hiatus, as if Mrs Jones had lost count, or more likely, he imagined, as if she was shaken by the sight of a speck of blood leaking through the girl's shift. But then came the eleventh, and finally the twelfth. The silence was a dreadful relief.

It was he who needed a whipping. Mr Jones did know that, now he had calmed a little. It should have been him in there, baring himself to his wife's birch rod and begging her to lift the skin off him. He should have knelt at her feet and said, *I broke our marriage vows with a dirty whore, one you think of as a daughter*. And then he should have asked, *What can I do to repay you? What bargain must we make so we can go on?*

Gall makes a poor supper. That's how Mary's mother used to put it. And tonight Mary could taste bitterness going down like a nut, settling in her stomach. It planted itself, put down roots, and began to grow, nourished on her dark blood.

Alone in the attic room, she shifted position on the bed now. The pain forced a little gasp out of her. She reached behind her with shaking hands and started to undo her bodice. The stays took longer to come away. But she was damned if she'd cry.

What was it Doll had said once, waking out of a deep drunkenness on a winter's night? *No use getting fond of folk. They'll always let you down in the end.* Mary reached under the bed, wincing at the bruises and weals along her back. She scrabbled for her stocking, the little worm that contained all her hopes. She spilled its riches across the rough blanket, faintly cheered by their ring and shine. This was all that stood between her and all the other girls out there. This was all she could rely on: gold and silver and brass, firmer than steak between her teeth. She arranged her hoard in piles and made letters and numbers from them. They all spelled freedom.

The candle was down to half an inch. She was tired to the bone. Pain moved back and forth across her back, like lines scribbled through a sketch to strike it out. All at once Mary couldn't keep her eyes open. She let herself sink down on the bed, embracing her dragon's hoard. She wondered, would she wake with a heart turned to stone?

Mrs Jones stood still. Not a sound from behind the door; barely a wink of light through the keyhole. She raised her hand to knock, but it was shaking. Her fingers still smarted from wielding the birch.

She pushed the door open, and for a split second before the draught snuffed out the candle she saw Mary Saunders, slumped across the bed in her shift, like a child who'd fallen asleep unawares. The small light glossed her dark hair before it went out.

Mrs Jones heard a clink, and a half curse, and the scrabble of a tinder-box. 'No, please, my dear,' she began, 'I'm sorry—'

'Wait,' ordered the girl in the darkness.

When the candle had been lit again, Mrs Jones stepped forward and sat on the very edge of the bed. There was a thin pillow between them.

'I thought it was Abi,' said the girl, very cold.

'No.' Mrs Jones's voice was hoarse. 'Abi's to sleep with Mrs Ash tonight. I thought you might rest easier with the bed to yourself.' She looked down at her closed fist. 'There's something I must say, my dear. Can you not guess what it is?'

Those eyes, like scorch marks on a sheet.

'It wasn't my own wish to punish you in that way. I know you meant no malice, with Mrs Morgan . . .' She cleared her throat; the noise was deafening in the little attic. 'Well,' she said, very low, 'we have the same master, you and me both.'

That bold eyebrow, inching up again, putting a question mark after everything.

'Aren't we all servants, one way or another, Mary?' pleaded her mistress.

The girl put her hands down on the pillow and leaned very close to Mrs Jones. 'Maybe so, madam. But some get whipped,' she whispered with hot breath, 'and some do the whipping.'

The older woman felt her eyes flood. She was blinded. She looked into her own heart, dusty as charcoal.

She opened her hand, after a time, and offered the girl a tiny pot with a paper cover. 'Ointment. For your back. May I put it on for you?'

She thought for a moment that Mary might throw it back in her face. But the girl turned away, and started lifting her shift. Her shoulders were creamy in the candlelight, as far down as the first red stripe. Mrs Jones edged nearer on the bed. The pillow between them made a curious clinking sound. Mary froze, and it was that, more than the sound, that alerted her mistress. She lifted up the pillow and saw coins leaking across the narrow bed.

'What's this?' Mrs Jones's words were simple with surprise. Then she began to count. Her hand shuddered as it turned over the bigger coins as if they were stones in a puddle. Finally, she asked: 'How much is here?'

The maid turned to look down at the money as if she had never seen it before. 'Eleven pounds, three shillings and tuppence ha'penny,' she said.

Mrs Jones's mouth repeated the words without a sound. Her hands laid the pillow flat in her lap, and pressed down. For a moment she was tempted to get to her feet and walk away, and forget she'd ever climbed up the stairs to the attic tonight. Then she found her voice. 'Mary Saunders!' It was an accusation, a denunciation, but also a plea.

'What?'

'Where did you get this money?'

'It's mine,' said Mary.

'But how can it be?'

Mary stared back at her, as blankly as a cat.

Mrs Jones's voice gathered strength and momentum. 'I know you lied to me about your old debts. But how can a maid in your position *possibly* have amassed such a fortune?'

That eyebrow again.

'Would you not call it a fortune, then?' asked the mistress, weakly. 'Eleven pounds!'

The girl's wide lips were sealed.

Mrs Jones shut her eyes for a moment. She had to take control of this conversation. 'What matters is not how much it is,' she said more quietly, 'but where you got it.'

'That's my business,' snapped Mary.

Her mistress's mouth became a horrified O as the terrible thought occurred to her. 'I'll have no thievery in this house.'

'I've thieved nothing.'

'You must have. You must have robbed things from our patrons. You couldn't have got it any other way, if you hadn't a penny when you came to us,' said Mrs Jones, panic hitting her like a wave going over her head. 'Tell me whose it is,' she insisted. 'The Misses Roberts's?'

The girl shook her head.

'Not Mrs Morgan's, surely?'

Another weary shake.

A dreadful thought occurred to Mrs Jones. 'From us, was it? Would you stoop to that? Did you steal things from your own family to sell? For we are your family, you know; we're all you've got.'

The girl stared back in furious denial. Were those tears in her eyes, or just the shimmer of candlelight? 'I stole nothing. It's mine, I swear,' she said shrilly. 'Every penny of it.'

'But where did it come from?'

'What does it matter?' Mary's voice rose to a shriek. 'Money always comes from somewhere. From everywhere, more like. Think how many pockets these coins have lain in. What matters is that I earned it.'

'Honestly?'

A long pause. 'Yes.'

'You're a liar,' said Mrs Jones. Bile in her throat; she swallowed it down. 'I don't know what else you are. I don't think I want to know.'

Mary shrugged again, mechanically.

With a few desperate sweeps, Mrs Jones shovelled the coins into her apron. Mary's hand reached out, and Mrs Jones slapped it out of the way, without thinking. The girl's fingers stung from the touch. 'Do you know the law of this land, Mary Saunders?' She paused to strain for a breath; her apron sagged, heavy with coin. 'You'll hang if you're proved to have stolen so much as a handkerchief.'

'I'm not a thief,' said the girl through her teeth.

Mrs Jones ran to the door, hunched over her apron. She turned once, her voice shaking, to say: 'Say your prayers.'

The door cracked shut behind her.

Morning came in Mary's window as on any other day.

She fitted her stays on over her bruised back, pulling them so tight she hissed with pain.

All day she worked in the shop, with her eyes low, sweating through the September heat. All the movements of her body seemed to say, *Remember. Remember what a good maid I am. Remember your promise to treat me as a mother.*

Mrs Jones's face was waxy. There was no chit-chat over their sewing today; they didn't exchange a word except to ask for the scissors or thread. All their intimacy was turned to stone. Mary's hand shook as she worked. She felt perpetually on the verge of tears. Her thoughts went out like arrows: *Trust me. I can't tell you where the money came from. But trust me anyway.*

They put the last stitches in the lowered neckline of Mrs Morgan's white velvet slammerkin without a word.

By dinner time Mary's head was tolling like a bell. She pushed her food around her plate. Her thoughts moved sluggishly. She knew she was being a fool. She could hear Doll nagging, somewhere behind her eyes. *Own up to whoring, my dear, and all you'll get is a whipping at the cart's tail or a spell in the lock-up at worst. But if this mistress of yours turns you in for thievery, it's the hempen halter for you, girl.*

There was something Doll wouldn't understand, though: how much Mary wanted to stay. Here, in the stuffy clutter of a small sewing room in the Joneses' house on Inch Lane in the town of Monmouth in England or Wales or somewhere in between. Despite the iciness of her mistress's eyes; despite everything that had happened. Till this endless afternoon, Mary had never quite known the truth: this was home.

And how could she stay, if she ever said those words? *Men*, and *Crow's Nest*, and *a shilling a go*. There was no nice way to put it. Once those words were spoken, all was lost. Mrs Jones would have had to be a different woman to bear the sound of those words. There was no room for a whore in this family.

That Sunday Mary went to church with the Joneses, even though her skin was mottled with heat and there were spots in front of her eyes. She kneeled meekly, remembering the pose from the Magdalen. The sermon was on patience. The Reverend Cadwaladyr gripped his pulpit with sweaty hands and exhorted each of his parishioners to temper their misfortunes by meek and Christian resignation. 'If your schemes have come to nothing, if your plans have gone awry,' he urged, 'trust in the Almighty.'

For a moment Mary tried to believe the man – despite all she knew about his profound hypocrisy. Would the Almighty save her from the thief's noose? Would the Mighty Master force Mrs Jones to give Mary her money back and care for her again, in the old way? Would the Maker let Mary tell her mistress the truth and the sky not fall in?

'Be like the reed,' said the curate, 'that bends and is not broken, in the same wind that uproots the tall cedar.'

Mary thought of a high wind, of its teeth stripping leaves from branches that crashed down all around her. Now her heart was banging round her ribs like a rat in a trap. She felt nausea rise inside her and begin to spiral. Cadwaladyr's words had retreated to a great distance.

'Mary?' A tiny whisper from Mrs Jones.

She would have liked to answer, but she was too far away. Her head whirled. She swayed on her knees. Her throat moved; she bit her lips to seal them shut.

A soft arm around her, another on her face, the fingers cool as water. Mary was violently sick into her mistress's hand.

Mary woke in the middle of a sweat-soaked night. A hand was pressing a cool cloth to her chest; she clutched it in her own. A small squeeze of the fingers.

'I won't be sick much longer,' Mary croaked after a while. 'I swear it.'

'Hush now, *cariad*.'

'Don't turn me out.' Hot water ran from Mary's eyes, into her ears, down her neck.

'Hush, child. Sure, you're one of the family, I've told you.'

'I'll be a good girl if you'll only let me stay,' she sobbed.

'I know you will.' The woman's voice was light as down.

'Let me stay. I'm sorry. I'm so sorry.' Mary couldn't remember what for.

'I know, I know.'

Then it came to her, the awful thing. 'I'll never do it again, Mother. It was only for the ribbon.'

'Shh.' The cool hand put the cloth to her forehead. 'There's no ribbon.'

Mary panicked, tried to sit up. 'Where's it gone?'

Her mother was pressing her down on the pillow, and kissing her on the forehead. So heavy, so soft. 'It's put away safe.'

She let herself subside. 'Doll had one first.'

'Doll?' The voice sounded bewildered. 'Who's Doll?'

Mary turned her hot face into the pillow. 'Doll's in the alley.' She was plummeting back into the darkness.

When she woke again there was a man leaning over her with a knife. She knew his devilish eyebrows. She screamed so hard she made him jump.

'I'll hold her, Joseph, and let you try again.' That soft voice, that wasn't her mother, Mary realised. It was Mrs Jones, of course.

She spat in the man's face. 'I know you!' she shrieked. 'With your big knife and your robes. That'll be ten guineas to you, sir!'

'Shush, now, Mary,' said Mrs Jones. 'Cadwaladyr's kindly come to help with the bloodletting.'

Mary began to buck and kick against the sheets that bound her.

'You'll feel the better for it, my dear,' her mistress promised. 'It's the only thing to break a fever.'

'There was blood on the sheet already,' she roared at the man. 'It was only wine!'

Cadwaladyr had retreated to the corner of the room, his arms folded, the great knife sticking up. Mrs Jones beckoned to him. 'Come back, do, Joseph. It's the fever talking.'

Mary tried to spit again but her mouth had turned to ashes.

Then the woman held Mary down while the man cut a line down the side of her neck. Mary said nothing, she only listened to the blood as it fell into the tin pail. Dimly she was aware that the woman was crying. 'We would save your life, Mary. We wouldn't do it except to save your life.'

Mrs Jones came downstairs with blood all over her apron. Her husband stood in the parlour and watched her walk about. He wanted to open his arms to her, but they were locked by his sides. 'How is the girl?' he asked softly.

A violent shrug.

'Is the fever easing?'

His wife sat down at the table and rested her jaw on her fists. 'It comes and goes.'

He nodded, like a puppet. If the girl died, he knew his wife would never forgive him.

Then she looked up at him and said, 'I know you've no liking for Mary. You always hated her mother, didn't you?'

He blinked in astonishment. 'Hated? Su Rhys? Not at all. How could I have hated the poor woman? I will admit,' he stammered, 'I do think . . . I didn't think her quite worthy of your friendship, once you were grown women.'

His wife's eyes were small bits of glass. 'You thought she made a bad choice, when she married Cob Saunders, and she deserved her punishment.'

He didn't know what to say.

'But sometimes, Thomas, sometimes punishment just happens.'

All of a sudden her face was running with tears. In two leaps he was there; he was wrapped around her like ivy. 'What is it, my love?' he kept saying, as her whole body shook with her sobs. 'What is it?'

'The baby.'

He thought he must have misheard. He put his ear closer to her mouth. 'Which baby?'

'The last one.'

He held her in his grip while she cried and cried. He waited. Eventually Jane Jones sat up and wiped her cheeks with the heels of her hands. She made a face that was supposed to be a smile, he imagined. She held in her sobs and kept her voice low. 'I lost it in May,' she said. 'I'm sorry now I didn't tell you.'

All the air was punched out of him.

'It only lasted a few months, this time. I don't know if it would have been a boy or a girl.'

Her husband found himself kneeling on her skirt, gripping her elbows. 'We must try again,' he said very fast. 'The Maker will reward us in the end. We must trust in his justice.'

She shook her head over and over. 'Thomas,' she whispered, and then, more firmly, 'Thomas. We have a daughter.' She stopped, as if to gather her strength. 'We have each other.' Another pause for breath. 'That's our lot.'

They stayed pressed together in that awkward shape. His solitary leg went numb under him, and then his arms, until at last he couldn't tell his body from hers.

The church of St Mary's was empty. Mrs Jones knelt at the back and offered up a prayer of thanks for the recovery of her maid.

In her pocket, dragging her down on one side, a stockingful of coins. She'd counted it again this morning. She flushed as her fingers sorted out the gold and silver. Her heart was clanging like a horseshoe on an anvil. *Where in the world?* was all she could think. *Where in the world did the girl get it?*

Now Mrs Jones pressed her head against the cool back of the pew. Her mind was moving in tight little circles; confusion was like a fog across the road. To make someone confess a crime, she'd read somewhere, you cut the tongue from a living frog and laid it on them when they were sleeping; they'd speak up in their sleep as honest as a child.

Nonsense. She should simply have demanded of Mary Saunders

where she'd got the money, asked the question over and over during her fever and her convalescence, till she'd got her answer. But she hadn't dared. There was so much she didn't want to know. Whatever the truth turned out to be, at the very least she'd have to throw Mary Saunders out into the bare countryside. Mrs Jones's heart quailed at the thought. She'd come to rely on Mary – too much, she quite saw that now. She'd been weak. She'd made an intimate of a servant, a half-grown girl. She'd confided things to her maid that should only have been said to her husband. She'd trusted herself to a deceiver.

Well, she knew what to do with the money, at least. She'd brought it here to slip it into the Poor Box. Charity was the highest virtue, wasn't that what Cadwaladyr was always saying in his sermons? *Blessed are those who give.* Mrs Jones could do with some blessing.

Cadwaladyr would never know where the eleven-odd pounds in the Poor Box came from; he'd marvel at such goodness, and wonder which of the local rich had made such a gesture. Then afterwards, if anyone ever asked about money found in Mary Saunders's room, Mrs Jones could deny all knowledge. It was dirty money, to her, until it went into the Box. At least now it could feed some of the town's landless and jobless unfortunates for a few months, or pay for a dozen paupers' funerals.

As Mrs Jones stood up she felt the weight of it against her leg. Temptation ran through her like a wave of desire. It occurred to her for the first time that she could very easily keep the money. It could slip into her private savings that she kept in a box in the bottom of her wardrobe. It could recompense the family for the loss of the Morgans's commission. It could form another wall to shield them from disaster, in case all their plans of advancement went awry. No one need ever know.

She felt quite faint with the idea of it. Money from nowhere:

not worked for, not sweated! Mrs Jones stood motionless, for a moment; anyone who saw her would have thought she was praying. And she was, in a way. *Judgement*, was the word she was mouthing to herself. *Remember the Day of Judgement.*

She glanced around: no one in sight. Then she pulled the stocking out of her pocket and rushed over to the Poor Box on the wall. Her hands came up full of coins; she stuffed them into the slot.

The air cooled a little in the second week of September. Down by the river, Jennett the Gelder was cutting the boars; their incredulous squeals rang through the town. Mary walked home with a basket of malt for the winter brewing. Her legs trembled under her; her breath was shallow. The fields were newly seeded with rye. She saw a small child racing at the birds to scare them away. How many days would it take him to earn a penny? Her eyes stung. Ever since the fever broke she'd been ready to cry over nothing.

But she hadn't been entirely idle, during her convalescence. She'd come up with a good story at last: so simple, Mary cursed herself for not having thought of it before. The money, she was ready to confide in Mrs Jones, was a secret legacy from her mother. *Tell no one you have it, Mother said to me on her deathbed. Keep it hidden away for hard times. For your old age.* Mary had been rehearsing this story all week, till it sounded like Gospel truth.

There was something black hanging from a fence by the bridge into town. Mary's eyes were weak and blurry still from the fever; she went up close. A dead crow, hung by its feet, its wings sagging wide as if it were flying downwards, about to hit the ground. It swayed on the wind. Mary picked up the smell coming off the body, dark and musky.

She hurried home.

She knew if she watched and waited, the right moment would come, and it had.

'How do you feel in yourself, now, Mary?' asked her mistress.

'Quite well.' It was only a little lie. Her vision was only slightly blurred. She could stop her hands shaking if she remembered to.

Mr Jones was out at his club, where he went more and more, these evenings. Mrs Ash was upstairs mumbling over her Scripture. Daffy had gone walking by the river on his own. Even Abi was out for a taste of the mild evening air.

If Mary didn't speak up now, she might never get the chance. 'I was wondering,' she began, 'now that I'm in my health again . . .'

'Yes?' said her mistress.

'Can I have my money back?'

That bright, loving face disintegrated all at once. Mrs Jones's breath seeped away. 'Oh, Mary.'

'I'm ready to tell you, now, where I got it,' the girl said with what she hoped looked like an innocent smile. 'I should have—'

Mrs Jones shook her head and interrupted. 'No need, no need.'

'But I want to tell you,' Mary insisted. 'I want to set your mind at rest. I can trust you with what I've never told a soul.'

'Mary.' Mrs Jones put her fingertips against her maid's lips to hush her. After a long moment, she went on, almost in a whisper, 'It's gone.'

Mary's face went stiff. 'Gone?'

Mrs Jones licked her lips nervously. 'I did what was best.'

The girl waited.

'I put it in the Poor Box.'

Mary heard the words, but she could make no sense of them. The thing was impossible.

'You see, my dear,' said her mistress in a rush, 'I know you did wrong – though I don't know what, exactly – but I feel sure in my heart that you're not a wicked girl. This way, the money is put to good use and you're cleansed of it. Do you see? It'll go to paupers, and orphans.'

'Orphans?' repeated Mary hoarsely.

'Yes, poor creatures, orphaned just as you were.'

Mary's mind raced. Then let them work for their bread, just as she had!

'You can put it out of your mind, now,' gabbled Mrs Jones, watching her face. 'You can make a fresh start. We won't speak of it again.' She leaned over and patted Mary's hand. She let out a breath of relief. 'Now I think I'll step out for a little air, too, the evening's so close.' She hurried to the door.

The silence of the house closed in around Mary Saunders, and she stayed sitting there like an unfinished statue. It was all a great puzzle and bewilderment. Her mind was tired from the fever still, that had to be it. Any minute now she'd understand.

Then outrage swept through her veins, intoxicating her like gin. Charity, that was what they called it.

Grateful we must always be
For the gifts of charity.

But what about the thefts of charity? The sins of charity? The arrogance of a woman who confiscated another's whole hard-earned fortune and dropped it in the Poor Box? Who made herself a Lady Bountiful with another woman's sweat, with the proceeds of a hundred nights round the back of the Crow's Nest?

With one bound Mary reached the stairs. Time to pay herself back. In the Joneses' room she went straight for the wardrobe. The box was locked, but that wouldn't stop her. Mary ran downstairs, her heart pounding like a drum. In the empty kitchen she picked up the first thing she could find, a cleaver with smears of mutton fat on its blade. On the way back upstairs she heard herself panting like a wolf. With the back of the cleaver she smashed the lock of the box till it came clean off. The lid opened with one loud crack.

She counted, and counted again, sure her eyes were cheating her. There was only five pounds, three and sixpence. Mrs Jones's puny, private store. For a moment Mary almost pitied her mistress.

Then she remembered the Poor Box, and rage began to bubble up in her again. This fury was bigger than the fever. It moved like a great wind that sucked up everything in its path. It astonished her. Rage at every cully Mary had ever serviced, every disapproving woman's face, her mother, even Doll – everyone who'd ever judged her and tutted over her and thought they knew best and let her down in the end. Kicked her out or left her, one or the other or both, always and everywhere. All Mary's old griefs welled up now, but rage swallowed them as fast as they could come. Her mouth was bitter, her legs were locked, her hands were sharp. *The bitch is going to get what she deserves.*

First Mary filled her pocket with the contents of the smashed box. She'd be damned if she was going back to London without some money to start a new life. Then she went to her room and rouged her mouth and her cheekbones. She ran downstairs again; nothing could tire her now. She used the cleaver to whack open the store cupboard. She had the strength of ten women. She ripped the cork out of a bottle of best Canary and drank it right off, though its harshness made her cough. She took another bottle into the shop.

If she went back to London without fine clothes, Mary thought blurrily, she'd be nothing but a beast of the field, a vagabond, shooed along from parish to parish till she ended up in the workhouse with her feet chained to the wall. Time seemed to have slowed down now. The long mirror tempted her, so she shucked off her plain brown dress and climbed into Mrs Morgan's white velvet slammerkin *A loose dress for a loose woman, you sleezy slut of a slammerkin*, laughed Doll in her head. It was hard to fasten the dress on her own with fingers made clumsy by the drink, but she managed. She filled the dress as if it had been made for her. The little silver snakes were wriggling on their long train. Mary stood and twirled in front of the mirror, and the whole world seemed to turn. Enraptured, she grabbed the bottle of wine and toasted herself, from her endless train to her scarlet lips. She'd never seen anything more beautiful.

It was hard to decide what else to take. Her mind was gliding along as if on ice. Her future might depend on the cut of a neckline, she knew that. Miss Theodosia Fortune's new red cape, of course, and Mrs Partridge's green paduasoy sack gown, and she couldn't think of leaving that pink bodice she'd quilled for old Miss Elizabeth Roberts. It was too young for Miss Roberts, anyway, thought Mary; no use primping in the grave! She crushed taffetas and piled slithery satins high in her arms; she propped a pair of Pompadour heels under her chin. There was no limit to what she could carry. She'd made these dresses, sewn her sweat into them. She'd wear them. They were hers.

'Mary?'

Her limbs froze. The wine swirled in her head. She turned

at last, like a packhorse under her load. She stumbled on her snowy train.

'Mary!'

She'd never heard her mistress shout before. Startled, she lost her grip on the dresses, and they slid to the floor.

Mrs Jones's face was deformed. 'Take that off at once.'

Mary looked down at herself, the white velvet river of her body, and all of a sudden she was stone-cold sober.

This was where the road petered out. Where could she run to, this time? In a minute, she knew, Mrs Jones would call for the constable and have her maid taken away as a thief. Mary could be hanged for this; they would hang her by the neck till she was dead for the theft of so much as a single lace-edged handkerchief, let alone two armfuls of the best dresses west of Bristol. *This woman has all the power*, thought Mary with absolute clarity. *I live or die by her word. She said I was her daughter, but she could have me killed.*

'Don't talk to me that way,' she said at last. The sounds came out slowly, thick as mud. 'You don't even know me.'

'I know very well who you are,' said Mrs Jones. 'You're my servant.'

So much for love. Mary gathered all the bile in her mouth and spat in her mistress's face.

The older woman, petrified to stone, looked back at her. There was spit on her cheek.

'I'm no orphan, by the way, for starters,' remarked Mary. 'My mother's alive and well and hates my guts. Every word I've ever said to you was a lie.'

All the colour had drained from Mrs Jones's face.

'I'm a whore; hadn't you guessed it yet? You're not the sharpest knife in the box, are you, Mrs Jones? That money you stole, I earned it with my own crack. I've had every stranger that's passed through this miserable excuse for a town.'

Pain like lightning across the woman's forehead.

'Why, I've had your own husband up against a wall!'

Only a blankness about the mouth.

Then Mary couldn't think of anything else to say. She was emptied out, hollow. She waited for Mrs Jones to bend under the weight of all those words. She would have liked to see her weep.

Instead, the mistress cleared her throat and said, almost sedately, 'Get out of my house.'

Mary began to drift towards the door, light as air.

'And take off that dress before you soil it.'

She froze on the spot. The strange thing was that she could feel the mistress's words coming true. Her skin soured, leaking poison through every pore, contaminating every stitch of the silver embroidery. The velvet hung on her like a snakeskin. She couldn't peel it off now; there'd be nothing left of her. Unable to speak, she shook her head.

Mrs Jones held out her hand. When Mary didn't move, the mistress made a peremptory little movement of the fingertips.

The meat cleaver was on the sewing table where she'd left it. She picked it up now; its weight was delicious against her fingers. This was the hand she'd always wanted, the hand no one could shake off, no one could ignore. Now Mary had come into her own. Now she was the Queen.

Mrs Jones didn't seem to notice this transformation. She stepped up to Mary and wrenched at the sleeve of the white velvet slammerkin. They both heard it rip.

Mary stared at her skinny shoulder, laid bare in the gap, like the bone of an animal. Everything was spoilt now. There was nothing left clean in the world.

The first blow was so easy. It happened before Mary knew it

– as if the cleaver had taken its own simple revenge on behalf of the dress. Mary didn't know what had happened until she saw blood make a fine spray across her milky-white bodice.

Spoiled, all spoiled.

So then she took a firmer grip on the slippery cleaver and struck again. This time the thick blade lodged in Mrs Jones's neck. She was on the floor. Blood rose like a fountain, like a firework.

Mary met her mistress's eyes, and now she couldn't tell who was falling, who was bleeding. It all seemed like some peculiar play. Mrs Jones tried to speak. Mary tried to answer. Their lips barely moved. They addressed each other like beasts in a language neither understood.

The dying woman saw her maid drop to her knees in front of her, saw her lips open, but all she could hear was a great roaring. There was no pain, only a blurring of the lines. Mrs Jones couldn't comprehend what had happened; she knew only that something was very wrong. There was puzzlement and sorrow and the candle going black. Something she'd forgotten to say or to ask, and where were the children? What was it that she had to remember to do before nightfall? There was red everywhere, and who was to clean it up? She couldn't go to sleep yet. She couldn't let go of the day until everything was done.

Mary had no idea which was the moment of death. The small eyes never did shut. Hours seemed to pass. She couldn't measure time except by the spreading of the tide of blood towards the place where she squatted. When her hem was heavy with red, she staggered to her feet.

The mistress's eyes were staring. Mary leaned across the darkening pool and shut one with her finger. It left a streak of blood from eyebrow to cheek; a mummer painted up for Twelfth Night. Mary stared down at her dress, polka-dotted with scarlet. *Cold water, and a rub of lemon, Mary; that's what it needs.* She couldn't bear to touch the other eye. It watched her as she backed away across the floorboards. She feared to turn her back, as if on royalty, or a demon.

She grabbed an armful of clothes at random, without looking at them. Her feet left sticky patches on the floor in the passage. She moved too slowly; she fumbled with the latch. With a tiny fragment of her mind Mary knew she was an outlaw now. But she couldn't really believe that there was anyone left alive in the world.

'Mistress?'

When Abi opened the door to the shop the breath was shocked out of her.

She stood at a careful distance so the pool of blood wouldn't mark her. But then she saw it on her arm, a long smear of red. From the door, maybe? She began to shake. She backed out of the room without a sound.

Waiting in the passage, Abi shut her eyes, tried to unsee what she'd seen. She felt nothing for the dead woman, yet; she was too busy making plans. How was she to prove that she hadn't been here? Who could bear witness? She could run away now, this minute, to the other end of town, but what if someone saw her go?

For weeks now Abi had been haunted by Barbados. When she'd been called in to hold Mary Saunders for her whipping, that was what had started it. Not that any of the mistress's blows had fallen on Abi, but as she'd held the wrists of the so-called friend who had betrayed her, and borne her weight, and as the strokes of the birch had resounded through the girl's body into Abi's – she'd felt terror rise in her mouth like bile. She was back in Barbados, and not the sunlit, heavy-fruited island of her deceptive memory, but the place where she'd sweated away nearly twenty years of her life, and never felt safe from a blow, never for one moment.

And now, watching the pool of darkness spread from Mrs Jones's cleft neck, Abi knew that her world had cracked apart all over again. Last time a master of hers had died, she'd got a knife stuck through her hand for punishment. What would they do to her this time?

Behind her, the crash of the front door. Daffy's whistle, a snatch of some dancing air.

Abi opened her mouth and began to scream. Screaming was what the innocent did, wasn't it? She did it mechanically, as if scaring off birds. Now she should run for the neighbours, that would look like proper behaviour for an innocent woman. She pushed past Daffy in the narrow passage and didn't stop to explain. She raced round the corner and down Grinder Street to the nearest tavern, to where the crow's nest swung and creaked in the September breeze.

It was like a procession, but much faster. Something ancient and costumed, with rules and rituals no one understood, Daffy thought, as he cantered up Stepney Street after the shifting lights of the older men. He was gaining on them. Their shouts echoed like fragments from an obscure festival that hadn't been celebrated in their lifetimes.

'Stop her,' bawled one.

'Hold her,' screeched another.

Daffy saved his breath for running. Monnow Street stretched like a worm, all the way to the moonlit river. At the head of the weaving chase he could see his father, his wig slipping off, running faster than any of them. Daffy's feet pounded the pavement, and slipped briefly on a bit of old fruit. Ahead of them all, Mary Saunders reeled like a drunkard. Her white gleaming train dragged in the mud. She squeezed a load to her chest like a baby; a flap of lace fell down, and she bent to save it from the dirt.

On the long straight street their movement seemed preordained. There was nowhere else to go. The street was empty but for the quarry and the hunt and a few startled faces at windows. The girl ran straight for the bridge, its stone gap narrowing to the eye of a needle. Cadwaladyr was the length of a man behind her. No, she wasn't going to jump in the river, realised Daffy. She still imagined she'd get away.

Chapter Eight

As the Crow Flies

All night Thomas Jones was in the kitchen with his wife. He had her in his lap. When the door started to creak open, and Mrs Ash slid her head through the gap, he cursed her with a Welsh phrase he thought he'd forgotten.

But the weather was warm for September. The burial couldn't be put off.

Mr Jones came out of his house in the glare of noon and walked down to bang on Dai Carpenter's door. His breeches were rusty with blood. His crutches weaved and scraped through the dust. In his pocket he had coins amounting to two guineas – part of the moneybag recovered from the prisoner – for a good beech coffin.

Afterwards he did something he'd never done in his life: he climbed upstairs in the middle of the day and lay down. Lay on his back in the empty bed and had no idea where he was; the world whirlpooled around him. If he stopped thinking, there'd be silence, and that would be the worst thing. So he asked himself questions, loudly enough to fill his head, like a child throwing stones at a sleeping dog. When would he find the time to finish that pair of satin stays for Mrs Greer? Had Mr Jenkins ever paid the last shilling on his summer cloak? How much sausage was left in the pantry, or had it gone off?

Grief was a pricey business. Before darkness he knew he would have to go down to Rhona Davies on Wye Street – the town's only dressmaker, now – to order mourning weeds for himself and the child, and the servants too. Then the house would have to be filled with drink and meat for the Watch. Not that he had any desire to invite the neighbours in to gawk all night at his wife's body, but that was how these things were done.

Pain, obscure and tentative, in his leg. Not his real leg but the one the barber had cut off forty years ago. What had they done with that blackened limb, Thomas wondered now? Was it buried somewhere, maybe in the vegetable patch behind the old house on Back Lane? What he remembered was the sound of the saw skidding against the bone. And his boy's mind racing, then as now, full of plans and queries: *What trade could I follow that doesn't need two legs? How will I make up for what I lack?* And, ticking away in his childish heart, the real question: *Oh Lord, how will you repay me?*

After dinner, when Abi had taken away his untouched plate, Mr Jones let his eyes meet his daughter's for the first time. In her soft fat face, her eyes were so like her mother's. How could he never have noticed?

'Fafa,' she said warily, 'where did Muda go?'

The silence pulled them all together like a net. 'To heaven, child.' His words came out heavy with breath.

A pause, as Hetta pressed her finger to a crumb and swallowed it. Mrs Ash stared into her lap. Daffy scraped back his chair as if to leave the table. Then Hetta asked, 'Did she fall in the river?'

The nurse took a sharp breath, as if to rebuke the child, but the master's answer came smoothly. 'No.'

A longer pause. The three adults stared at the child as if she were a thundercloud coming their way.

'Did a big rat eat her up?' she asked, playing the dreadful game.

Mrs Ash's hand shot out to cover Hetta's mouth, but her father got there first. His elbows strained against the tablecloth; he held her tiny face between his hands. His nose was almost touching hers. 'No, it wasn't a rat.'

Hetta tried to nod. Her cheeks were squashed.

'It was Mary Saunders killed her. Do you follow, child?'

Mrs Ash stirred in her chair as if her stomach pained her. 'Mr Jones—'

'Child?' he repeated. He had to be sure Hetta understood. Right now he didn't care if it appalled her; he needed to hear the truth spoken, and be sure his daughter knew it.

'Our maid Mary?' asked Hetta, tears shuddering in her eyes.

'That's right. Mary Saunders killed your mother dead.'

And the child's face collapsed as if he'd punched it.

'Tell us this, and quickly, did the black have a hand in it?'

'No,' said Mary, before she understood what the constable meant.

'The black claimed she found the body. She had a stain on her sleeve.'

Mary caught a glimpse of escape. The lie that might save her; the syllable her life might hang on. Temptation opened like a chasm, dizzying. How easy it would be to give them what they wanted, to let them believe that Abi was at the back of it all . . .

She was suddenly repelled by herself. Wasn't one killing enough for her? 'No,' she said, more firmly than before.

The constable shook Mary like a rag. 'You'll get no benefit from shielding the heathen.'

'I'm not. I'm not shielding anyone.'

'Was it not the black's idea, at least?'

'Abi did nothing. Said nothing.' Mary's words came out like gasps. 'I swear. She knew nothing. No one's to blame but me.'

'A girl of sixteen?'

'I've got the woman's blood all over me,' she shrieked then, flapping her heavy skirt at him. Blood browned to the colour of mud, in great arcs and puddles across the white velvet, the silver snakes and apples. 'What more proof do you fools need?'

Mary thought it would all be over quickly, after that. But as she waited in the basement of the courthouse, stripped down to her shift and a blanket, she came to realise her mistake. By the end of the morning she'd been committed for trial at the yearly assizes, but no one thought to tell her when that would be. There was no hurry, after all; she understood that now. She was not important.

She'd never been out to Monmouth Gaol before; she'd never had cause. It was away up the Hereford Road. The constables took her in a wagon, with her elbows roped behind her. The wind made a tear run from her left eye. Her face itched. The wagon crawled past a few solidly built new houses, a couple of cottages. Then the town of Monmouth ran out, and there was nothing but bare land. Mary had the impression she was going into the wilderness, crossing into a country beyond time.

And after all, what did it matter where she was taken? Her path had run out. Her story was told. What she thought of as her life had ended and there was nothing to take its place.

The funeral was on the third day. There was a tremendous turnout that afternoon; Inch Lane was clogged with mourners. The Morgans sent their carriage to park at the corner of St Mary's Street, as a mark of respect – though they didn't take the trouble to come in person, Mr Jones noted bitterly. When the men had hoisted the coffin out of the narrow house, they put it down on the ground and set out beer and bread on it. It was Dai the Grinder who drew the short straw from Mr Jones's clenched fist, and had to be the Sin Eater. He took a mouthful of the dry bread and washed it down with beer. Mr Jones tossed him a sixpence; Dai picked it out of the mud. Then they all moved in to spit at him, and he pushed through the knotted crowd and shambled away. 'All my wife's sins go with the Sin Eater,' announced Mr Jones loudly. He hoped the Devil could hear him. He hoped it was true.

And who was to take away his own sins? What he couldn't forget, what he couldn't tell a soul in the world, was that May night behind the Crow's Nest, where he let his breeches down and gave in to the monster that lurked in the belly of every man. His mouth was full of dust now. Without his wife, what was Thomas Jones but an ageing cripple, a one-legged buffoon, the dupe of a skinny young whore?

No one could stop him lifting his corner of the coffin, along with his wife's three cousins and a nephew. He shed one crutch, and flattened his shoulder against the smooth beech. He knew he was impeding their progress. Every time he leaned on his crutch and swung forward, the coffin leaped as if something live was trying to get out. Sweat formed a spiked crown around the edge of Mr Jones's wig. He'd lost all trust in his senses; he couldn't tell if the sky impaled on the spike of St Mary's was grey or the earth underfoot was brown.

The mort bell was tied to a yew outside the church. The Reverend Cadwaladyr was clanging it wildly, as if warning of invasion. His face looked like raw meat. Had he been crying? He'd always been soft on Jane, her widower remembered.

Chrysanthemums, dried to brown around their edges; the south corner of the churchyard was strewn with papery flowers from the last burial. There was little room left in the Jones plot on top

of all the children's coffins. The men filed to the left now, the
women to the right, just as they did in church. Mr Jones took
up his position like a pillar, beside the headstone, which had a
freshly chiselled verse.

Here lie the bones
of Jane Jones,
murdered.

He'd wanted something more than that. Something to begin to
describe her: *virtuous wife and beloved mother*, or *deeply mourned
by all who knew her*, or *who by her uniformly estimable actions
has earned eternal rest*. Maybe even *whose untimely death calls
out to heaven for vengeance*. But there wasn't much room on
the stone, and every letter had its price, and Mrs Ash had
persuaded him that his wife wouldn't have liked extravagance.
He had insisted, though, on having her trade emblems carved on
– bobbin, bodkin and shears – for all the mason had grumbled
that it wasn't customary in the case of a woman.

A chill breeze moved through the trees; the first whiff of
autumn. 'Oh God,' recited Cadwaladyr gruffly from his broken-
backed prayer book, 'I believe that for just and wise reasons thou
hast allotted to mankind very different states and circumstances
of life, and that all the temporal evils which have at any time
happened unto us, are designed by thee for our benefit.'

Mr Jones heard the words, as he had many times before, and
suddenly didn't believe them. What benefit to anyone was this
particular temporal evil, this incongruous death? He fumbled in
the recesses of his mind for his faith, but it was gone. He no longer
believed that his Maker would recompense him for all his losses.
The bank was empty.

'*Then the weary are at rest*,' read Cadwaladyr, his dark circled eyes glancing up from the page, '*and the servant is free from his master.*'

But Jane was gone to the master from whom no one was ever set free, thought her widower. All round him, the people of Monmouth were joining in the old familiar prayers, but he was calling God new names, and not holy ones.

Villain.

Whoreson.

Turd.

The holy bargain made as the saw bit through the boy's leg had been broken.

Then again, how could he prove that there'd ever been any such bargain? The Maker didn't speak, not in words. Not forty years ago, not now. What a fool that boy Thomas had been, to have mistaken God's silence for assent.

The air roared in Mr Jones's ears. The coffin was lowered now, all the way down, bumping against the others. He stepped up with the first handful of dirt. He threw it down hard, as if to wake his wife, or his Maker, or anyone at all to answer him.

Poor man, thought Mrs Ash. Pity was sugar under her tongue.

It wasn't that she lacked feeling. She'd been crying on and off for three days and nights, ever since she first saw that purpled body on the kitchen floor. Her heartbeat was still rapid with the shock of the sight. To think of it! *We know neither the day nor the hour.* Of course she grieved for Mrs Jones, who hadn't been the worst of mistresses, not by any means; the house would sound hollow without the light movement of her feet.

What gall the Reverend Cadwaladyr had, standing up there as pious as a monk, when the shillings in his pocket came from pimping for a murderess! Nance Ash had trekked the five miles to the vicar's house yesterday, to tell him about his curate's shameful connection with the girl who'd killed Mrs Jones. But to her mortification he'd told her that Cadwaladyr's actions as master of the Crow's Nest were not under the aegis of the Church – and that the case was bad enough without her meddling.

But how comforting the curate's prayers were, still.

For we must needs die,
and are as water spilt on the ground,
which cannot be gathered up again;
neither does God respect any person.

Nance Ash nodded her head at a pious angle. There was a hidden pattern, a reason for all this horror, even if most mortals were too blind to distinguish it.

Behind her ribs was joy. A tiny, parched kernel, but joy nonetheless. Now was it come, the hour of her redemption? Now would the servant be granted her just reward?

Well, Mr Jones would need looking after, she argued with herself. The man would really have to marry again, for his own sake as well as the child's. A virtuous woman, someone old enough to share his burdens. But still young enough, perhaps, to bear his son.

Nance Ash's heart was thumping. She was only half-ashamed to allow these thoughts so soon. She cradled them to her breast. Head bowed, she prayed that good might come out of evil. She cast a glance at Mr Jones, and nibbled her lips to make them redder.

The gravediggers stood by the door for spade money. The mourners, filing out, gave more than they could afford, as a mark of respect.

Daffy hung back till everyone was gone, fingering the little paper bag in his pocket. He shivered in the chill of the empty church. For three days he'd felt as if he had a fever. To have had connection with a murderess – to have come within a whisker of marrying a monster— Once more he shut his eyes and thanked his Maker.

The Skyrrid soil in the bag was damp. He scattered a handful on the coffin in the open grave, so his poor mistress would rest easy. Not all of it, mind; he saved a good sprinkle, in case his cough came back this winter. You should always hold a little in reserve, he knew; you never could be sure what evils lay ahead.

Outside in the sun, he was brushing the mountain dust off his hands when he sensed someone walking by his side. Blonde hair, pink freckled skin. He stared at his cousin Gwyn. It had been months since they'd exchanged a word.

'Daffy,' she murmured.

'Gwyneth. A fine crowd,' he added, to get them past the awkward silence.

Her knotted hair was full of light. She nodded, her pale eyes low. 'She was well thought of, your mistress.'

'I never served a better,' said Daffy.

After a little silence, Gwyn said, 'They caught the girl, I heard.'

'Aye.' His walk slowed; he felt sick.

'You must have known her as well as anyone,' said his cousin, letting her curiosity show.

He gave a small, exhausted shrug.

'Would you ever have thought it of her?' she asked, eyes shining.

Daffy started to shake his head, then stopped. 'Now I think of it,' he said unwillingly, 'there was always something about her.'

Gwyn's sky-blue eyes widened. 'Vicious?'

'No, no.' He considered the matter as he walked a little nearer to the girl's side. 'But something more than a maid needs. She was . . . troublesome.'

Gwyn allowed the pause to lengthen. 'I heard a thing,' she murmured.

'Oh?'

'That she'd, you know, more than one way of turning a penny.'

'I never heard that,' said Daffy, his eyes on the crowd that stretched ahead of them. Then he turned and looked at his cousin hard. 'What do you mean, exactly?'

She went the loveliest shade of salmon pink. 'I don't know any details.' He could always tell when she was lying. 'But something to do with a tavern. And travellers.'

Daffy shut his eyes for a second and suddenly could see her, Mary Saunders, cider tankard in hand, going down the Crow's Nest every other night in all weathers to do Mrs Jones a favour. Her black eyes, her long stride. Of course. His skin burned with embarrassment. For all the books in his possession, he still failed to read the stories written plain as day in the faces of the people around him.

It didn't matter now. He had to change the subject before he gave himself away. He turned his eyes on Gwyn, her mild curves in her patched lavender gown. He might as well take his last good look now, before Jennett the Gelder got his stinking hands on her. 'So. Is your day set?' he asked, as civilly as he could manage.

'My day?'

Like a child with a scab, he knew he should leave it alone. But he went on. 'The date of – of your—'

She interrupted him before he had to say the word. 'Oh, no.'

'No?' he repeated, his voice high and bewildered.

'That's all off,' said Gwyn.

Daffy stopped dead.

Her cheeks were burning pink again. 'Jennett's off to Norwich,' she said, 'to marry a widow with a bakery.'

Daffy nodded in what he hoped was a sympathetic manner. A spark landed on the kindling of his heart, rested and glowed. He felt inflammable. He felt as if any minute now he might fall down in the street with excitement.

Without risking any more words, they walked together up the street as far as the Joneses', where Daffy's master stood like a lightning-struck tree, accepting condolences from neighbours.

Abi didn't attend the funeral. When Rhona Davies had arrived to measure the family for mourning weeds, Abi had stayed in her room and wouldn't come down. So now she watched the procession from the attic window.

She'd heard Mr Jones talk to Hetta of heaven, but those stories were for children. What would happen was, Mrs Jones would be put in a hole in the churchyard and her spirit would go into the mud. When Abi died, on the other hand, she knew she'd be going back to her own country. Sometimes she longed for it: the bright heat, the wet colours. Always supposing her spirit would be able to find its way.

In the lane behind the house, men were killing a pig; Abi waited for the screeching to end. Every year this sound told her that the long winter was coming and the stock had to be cut down. When she breathed in she caught a waft of the tanning pits in the back lane; fresh pig skins were beginning their slow decay to leather. Meat had to be salted for the fasting season. Soon the birds would be circling overhead, preparing their flight.

Time to go.

Just as Mr Jones stumbled into his house and shut the front door on the crowd, Abi was slipping out the back way. Under her left arm she held the bag Mary Saunders had left behind her in their bedroom, filled with bright and gauzy clothes that Abi had never seen Mary in; she thought they must be what women wore in London.

Hidden down her leather stays was the five pounds in silver the Quakers had given her, after considering the matter in silence during a month of meetings. She'd asked Daniel Flyte when he and his Society would expect to be paid back, and he had smiled peculiarly, and said, 'Not in this life.'

Terror tightened now like a brass collar round her neck.

Would she be pursued? She couldn't tell. It all depended on Mr Jones. He might be too slumped in mourning to think about anything but his wife – but then again, he might take Abi's desertion as another treachery, and call in the professional slave-catchers from Bristol to bring her back in fetters. If there were pursuers, she thought they would probably expect her to take John Niblett's wagon to London. Instead she was going to catch a boat at Chepstow, go down the Severn and around the coast. She had prepared all the sentences she'd need to say. *I go on master's business. Passage to London, please. I have money here.* The Quakers had drawn her a map; she couldn't read the words on it, but she could point to the right roads.

Daniel Flyte had assured her that she'd be safer in London, but she was to look out for the slave-catchers, especially if there was a hue and cry printed about her. He had read her one or two from the newspapers, his voice shaking with indignation. *Run away from her master on the 15th of September*, hers might go, *one Abi Jones, about 30 years of age, with a scar through her left hand. Whoever brings word of her to Mr Thomas Jones by the Robin Hood tavern in Monmouth, shall have 2 guineas reward for his pains.*

But there would be other black faces in the big city, she knew, and the generality of white folk couldn't tell the black ones apart. Daniel Flyte had given her some addresses of houses that might take her in for the night, sympathisers with what he called *the cause*.

Abi had no idea what she would find in London. At every turn she expected to be robbed, raped, left for dead. But she knew this much: there was nothing to stay here for now. A voice in her head shouted, *Run*.

Mary's dress was a ragged brown thing they'd given her when she'd first arrived at Monmouth Gaol. She wondered where it came from; some woman who'd sold it for the price of a drink, or died in it, maybe? Clothes outlived people, she knew that. Clothes were more of a sure thing. She wondered what they'd done with the white velvet slammerkin. There was good stuff in it, too good to throw away. Had someone tried to wash the blood out of it, or at least to cut good unstained scraps of embroidered velvet out of the train for salvage?

The wet air of autumn blew right through the day cell: in one window and out the other. There was no time, up here above the town, only weather. Mary overheard the odd mention of dates, and remembered what they used to mean, but the calendar was only a childhood story to her now. At Hallowe'en, bonfires scented the air. On the day of All Souls, Mary pictured the people of Monmouth piling new evergreens on all the graves at the back of the church. Mrs Jones's grave would look almost like the others by now. Was the point of the All Souls ritual to hide the dead away under moss and slime, to speed up the process of forgetting, until memory was only a marsh and all hard things were buried and smoothed over in the wet ground?

She tried not to remember things, but there was nothing else to do. Her whole short past came running at her, the day the purse-snatch tried to take her red ribbon. During the day she could look out of the window, at least. The fields had turned rusty with the coming of winter; she'd never seen earth this colour before. Had her crime stained the whole world?

Images waited for Mary in the night room, where all the prisoners were packed in like bruised fruit and the darkness was absolute. There were no rules here at all. Even survival wasn't obligatory. Those who wanted to might turn their faces to the wall. Sometimes when she woke in the darkness and smelt the bodies all around her, she was briefly deceived into thinking she was back in the Rookery, waiting for Doll to come home. She had found her old self again, the lawless one. She couldn't imagine ever having been clean, or ever having been part of a family; those chains were broken for good.

She stood beside the window of the day room and listened to the crows. One bird sounded harsh, like a crack in the sky. Five together were restless, circling. But more than ten, and the sounds smoothened out in the distance, until the twilight air began to shimmer and vibrate. Finally Mary was coming to understand why the crows cried so unceasingly: to prove they were here.

Two forgers were gaoled in December. They offered to give Mary a great belly, so she'd escape the noose. She told them she was barren, but they weren't listening. They took her on the floor, with a bit of coal sticking into her back. She wondered why anyone would want to enter a body like hers, a tomb of flesh.

She didn't know when, but she knew she was going to die, either with her face against the floor of the night room or swinging from a rope in the market square. It didn't occur to her to protest. She was farther away from the living than the dead, and she couldn't remember the way back. On the worst days, all she longed for was to skim right over this winter like a stone on a lake. A vague wish for time to leap forward – as in her father's last year on earth – and for it to be all at once the day of her death.

Mary found herself talking to her father a lot in the night. It was suddenly easy to do what she'd never done before: forgive Cob Saunders. For his madness, his outrageous demands, the way he'd laid down his life for the sake of eleven stolen days. Mary knew now that death moved through the crowd wearing the face of an ordinary stranger, and tapped you on the shoulder with no warning. Better to run into his embrace.

It was not that she wanted, with any great passion, to die. She still breathed in what air there was and ate the little she could scrounge, though mostly for something to do. It was more that she no longer thought of herself as truly living, or as having anything left in the world to lose. Everyone she'd ever loved had left her, and always through her own fault. She had broken her mother's heart, abandoned Doll, and killed the mistress who loved her. This made it hard for Mary to imagine a future worth staying alive for.

Late on Twelfth Night, darkness covered the whole sky like spilled pitch. The guards were drunk; they still hadn't come to bring the prisoners up to the night room. Mary was standing by the window, wrapped in half a blanket against the cold. The only light came from a lantern in the corner of the cell where prisoners were crammed around a game of dice. The yellow radiance spilled into the night and was lost. Mary couldn't feel her fingers; one hand was knotted in her blanket, the other was wound in and out of the bars. If she stayed here any longer the guards would have to tear her away like ivy, her brittle fingers snapping as they were pulled free.

She became aware at last that what she thought was the sound of sheep outside the town was a chorus of voices, almost erased by the wind. She heard men's voices, coming nearer, but couldn't make out a word of their song. Then the music broke off, and for a moment there was nothing but the shuffling of feet on the cold road below the gaol. Mary pressed her head against the bars, but couldn't see a thing in the darkness. The sky pushed against her eyes. There was a thumping on the door below.

What reared up in front of the window was a nightmare Mary had never had before. The horse was pure white, clothed not in hair but bone. Its teeth were bared in fathomless delight. Its body was a cloud, rippling in the night breeze. So it had come for her at last, thought Mary, the white horse in her dreams of riding triumphant through a crowd. The great jaw opened and shut with a clang of bone.

She must have screamed without hearing herself, because all of a sudden the window was full of prisoners, jostling for a view. Mary was crushed against the bars, her ribs registering their print. She bent her foot against the wall, but the crowd wouldn't give. Her body swayed back and forward with each surge and shove. Barely an arm's length from her, the horse's glittering sockets held her gaze.

'It's the Mari,' cried an old man behind her.

And then the song rang out and was carolled back again, from behind her this time, all around her, in the hoarse voices of condemned men, and Mary could hear the bells and tambourines from below, the answering chorus. She didn't understand a word of it. It was as meaningless as the crunch of bone when the horse's jaw lifted and fell – on a stick, she saw now. Beneath the great beast's paper ears, green ribbons swung like reins, and its eye sockets were full of broken glass. It began to prance; suddenly she could distinguish the man inside it, his feet like an insect's beneath the bleached sheet trailing in the mud. He was surrounded by his fellows, mud-faced, bawling louder now, one with a fiddle, another dressed as a hag, all of them dancing in spirals like men pursued by bees.

When the song ended the mummers held up their caps, and

pennies began to rain down from the prison's tiny window. Soon enough the singers drifted away. The crowd thinned and started moving back towards the town; the fiddle dwindled to a far-off squeak.

Behind Mary, the old man was pressing his head into her blanket. She turned and shook him off. His face was a riverbed of tears. He spoke to nobody in particular. 'Never thought it,' he whispered. 'Never thought I'd live to see them taking out the Mari again.'

Then the guards came to herd them into the night room.

The Saunders trial was set for the first day of the Monmouth Assizes in March of 1764. Mary hadn't been outdoors in almost six months; on the cart that brought her from the gaol into town, she kept her eyes screwed up against the white spring light. She hadn't slept or eaten for a few days; consequently she felt nothing but a numbness. The grass was wet under the rattling wheels. What was that prayer she'd learned at school?

Oh Lord who can all things renew,
Scatter my sins as morning dew.

Spring slid into Mary's nostrils; the fields were spread with dung.

The courthouse on Market Square echoed with voices and shuffling steps. When all the benches were full of respectable townspeople, the guards had to bolt the doors to keep out the rabble. Mary limped into court between two guards.

Only when she heard him did her head go up. Mr Jones, on his feet, shrieking higher than a woman, his fingers pointing like icicles: 'Killer! Killer!'

The judge's hammer had no effect.

'Killer!'

The guards had to muscle him out. Mary watched mutely, but felt a spark of life start up in her chest. To be hated so much, that reminded you that you existed. She could hear Mr Jones's screams leaking from the passageway.

The lawyers were most interested in the details of what they called *this most horrid crime*. Injuries on the neck of the deceased consistent with the infliction of two, three, or four blows? Five pounds, three and sixpence, confiscated from the prisoner; in what coinage?

Only late in the day did they get around to asking why. 'Turning now from means to motive,' said the judge on the right, clearing his throat with a phlegmy rattle. 'Mary Saunders, have you any justification whatsoever to offer for your heinous actions?'

Save yourself, you silly bitch, urged Doll in her head. So Mary's mouth opened and she began to rant like a madwoman. 'Yes, sir. I do, sir. I am a poor miserable abused creature, sir.'

One white eyebrow went up.

She told the court that Mrs Jones was the cruellest of mistresses; she'd whipped Mary raw, stuck needles under her fingernails and stolen her dead mother's legacy. Mr Jones had forced her to lie with him every night, given her a foul disease, and threatened to chop her into pieces. Mary shrieked and wailed, telling the court about all the horrors that went on behind closed doors on Inch Lane.

The crowd ooed and ahhd, but she could tell no one believed a word of it.

At last Mary sank back into numbness. She had nothing more to say.

The judge on the left suddenly woke up and rubbed his watery eyes to peer at her. 'Is there any respectable person of property to testify to the prisoner's character in court?'

She shook her head.

'Has the prisoner shown penitence?'

Mary knew this was her last chance. It was like Petition Day at the Magdalen. These men didn't want truth, they just wanted a sob story. But when they wrote down your life in their books, the terms were always theirs.

'Any shame, or remorse?'

Mary chewed her lips.

'Do you not hang your head and weep?' the judge asked her fretfully.

She cleared her throat. 'Sometimes.'

That was evidently not the right answer.

'When you weep,' he prompted, 'is it with true regret, or merely pity for yourself?'

'Regret.'

'What do you regret, then?'

Mary's neck hurt from looking up at him. She knew from gaol gossip that if you could only make them feel sorry enough for you, they might just commute your sentence to transportation to the Americas. But when she tried to imagine such a country, her mind went blank. She thought of Abi, bent double in the noonday sun, bundling canes. Her breath was shallow now. She spoke honestly, as if to herself. 'The slammerkin.'

'Speak up!'

'I regret the gown.'

'Which gown?'

'A white velvet slammerkin, with embroidery in silver thread,' said Mary slowly, pedantically.

'The one you were wearing when arrested? The one belonging to Mrs Morgan?' asked one of the lawyers.

'Belonging to me.'

'How so? How so, belonging to you, prisoner?' he repeated.

'I embroidered it.' Her words ground themselves out slowly. 'I earned it.'

'You killed your employer for the sake of a garment?'

A long hiss went up from the crowd. Mary tried to remember the moment when Mrs Jones had ripped the dress from her shoulder. She shrugged, suddenly too tired to explain.

'Was it for the money it would fetch?'

Her head was spinning from the bright lights of the candles on every wall. The lawyer blurred before her eyes. She was melting, draining away. He didn't understand. None of these moneyed men did. Their robes were trimmed with the finest fur and they didn't even notice. Mary hadn't spoken so many words in a row in months. She cleared her throat and made one last attempt, speaking gruffly: 'She shouldn't have tried to take what was mine.'

'Who is this person you speak of?'

Mary tried to say the name of the dead woman, but her throat closed on it. All she could repeat was, 'It was mine.'

Their faces were blank as coins. The lawyers and judges in their dusty black cloaks asked her no more questions. They squabbled like birds.

'Surely no one will dispute, gentlemen,' one began, 'that if a priest kills his bishop, or a wife her husband, or a servant his master, then the crime is accounted by natural law as a sort of treason, insofar as it reverses the natural order of authority. Thus the girl must burn.'

'But Mrs Jones being not the master,' another objected, 'but only the wife of the master, the crime is simple murder, and the girl should merely hang.'

A yawn; the judge on the left had woken up again. A conciliatory voice emerged from a mass of chins. 'Gentlemen, what if she were to be hanged first, and then burnt?'

Judicious nods all round.

Mrs Ash kept a tight hold of Hetta's hand, so as not to lose her
in the crowd that was forming in Market Square on the morning
of the execution. The child's fingers wriggled, but her nurse
gripped them all the harder. She smiled tightly as she watched
the narrow mouth of Stepney Street for the cart that would bring
the prisoner down from the gaol. Mrs Ash's lips moved in time
with the Divine Word:

> *Her end is bitter as wormwood,*
> *sharp as a two-edged sword.*
> *Her feet go down to death;*
> *her steps take hold on hell.*

At least this death would have a meaning, unlike so many others,
she thought. Its message would be spelled out as clear as the
bold-print moral in a book of fables: justice was always done in
the end.

The nurse's back was tired. The family had been waiting
in Market Square since dawn. The family, meaning, what
was left of them: herself, Hetta and Mr Jones. Daffy the
manservant had got himself another position with indecent
haste, and Abi the slave had run off without the least Christian
compunction. In Mrs Ash's view they should have published
a hue and cry for her, but Mr Jones couldn't be persuaded
to take the trouble. 'Let her go,' he'd mumbled; 'let them
all go.'

What was left of the family would wait the whole day if they
needed to, so long as they saw the girl hanged in the end. Waiting
was Nance Ash's strength. During the six months that had passed
since her mistress's death – a time of shocks and losses – she
had kept the little flame of hope burning. At least now she was

waiting for a question to be asked, after so many years of simply waiting.

Under her sparse lashes, she looked up at the man beside her. Mr Jones stood as rigid as a post; his crutches seemed to be leaning on him, instead of him on them. The child waited between the two adults. They formed a perfect triangle.

The words were very near, Mrs Ash was convinced of it. They were building up, as if behind a membrane. Any day now Mr Jones would put the question. It might come bluntly, or as a delicate hint; it might sound flat, or bring tears of relief to her scratchy eyes, but surely she'd recognise it when she heard it.

Or should she begin, she wondered? Men were such cowards.

Hetta wrenched her small hand out of the nurse's sticky grip and hid behind her father's leg. Mr Jones glanced down, absently.

'She needs a mother,' remarked Mrs Ash, seeing her chance.

Pain ran across the man's face like a lizard.

Briefly she regretted causing it, then pressed on. 'I'd not intrude on your grief, my dear Mr Jones, but have you ever considered . . .'

Had he considered her? Ever? Had he for one moment of the years they had lived under one roof truly considered Nance Ash, noted her many inestimable qualities, her worth, beyond rubies?

She ploughed on. 'For the sake of your child. Of your children,' she faltered, 'not yet born.'

He stared at her, the skin around his eyes almost black. 'You think I should take another wife, Mrs Ash?' he said, his tone indecipherable.

She nodded deeply. She couldn't let herself seem too enthusiastic. 'That may be God's hidden plan.'

Mr Jones shrugged, as if his Maker's views were neither here nor there. His eyes had returned to the carpenter on the scaffold; he lifted Hetta high on to his shoulders to give her a better view. After a minute, he said, 'All I know is, I'm no good alone.'

Mrs Ash's mouth curved into a smile, then she swallowed it. 'Have you given any thought – have you met with any woman who has the qualities you seek?'

Now. It had to come now. *The labourer deserves the fruit of his toil.*

'As it happens, yes.'

A pause, a lifetime long.

'I've spoken to Rhona Davies. The dressmaker, you know,' said Mr Jones flatly, his eyes on the scaffold. 'We're to wed in June.'

A sword in the heart.

Mrs Ash turned her face away so he wouldn't see it break. Hetta stared down blankly.

Our days on the earth are as a shadow, and there is none abiding.

'Hush now, Hetta,' he told his restless daughter, letting her down for a minute and giving her another bit of gingerbread. Blinded by the crowd, she stumbled as they pushed against her, and gripped her father's crutch for support. Mrs Ash, her face in her hands, didn't seem to notice. Surely she wasn't weeping for Mary Saunders? How strange, Mr Jones thought: such misapplied tenderness in a dry old peapod like her.

Hetta still clung to his birch crutch, smoothing the wood with her thumb. Without this small sticky-faced child, he thought, there would be no purpose to anything, and he might as well go down to the banks of the Wye. It would be quite deserted; everyone was here in the Square this morning. He could let himself fall into the rushing river, let the weed drag him under the current.

Mr Jones put that thought to one side and went back to making plans. He considered certain incontrovertible facts. Rhona Davies was twenty-seven years old, and a perfectly good seamstress, though not known for fine embroidery. She would in all likelihood make a perfectly good wife. It couldn't be easy for a woman to run a business on her own, he supposed; certainly she had jumped at the chance of a partnership with the widowed staymaker, said yes with no coyness or prevarication.

She would be kind to Hetta, he knew. She would sit in his dead wife's chair, using her workbag, mending his twice-darned stockings, pouring tea from his China kettle. (He had thought of smashing it, that first night, just for something to break, but Jane wouldn't have approved.) This second marriage would feel like a mummery and a mockery at first, but perhaps he'd get used to it. He and Rhona Davies might have half a lifetime ahead of them; twenty years of chances to produce a son, or several children, even; children with nothing of Jane Jones about them.

He cringed at the thought.

There was nothing wrong with Rhona Davies. She was strong and sturdy, though with rather more sharpness of wit than he liked in a woman. Just a little like Mary Saunders, he thought, and felt hatred rise up to swamp him.

He stared at the fresh white scaffold, and the coil of rope on the platform. He must watch carefully and commit the coming scene to his mind's eye: the witch squatting in her cart, the noose of justice hoisting her into the air. His memory was not what it used to be; already the details of his life with Jane were beginning to fray around the edges. Already he couldn't see his wife's face as it had been, only the clammy mask she left behind her, edged with brown blood. Surely the coming scene was not one he'd ever lose, though? Every bone in his body cried out for the girl's death. Surely when Mary Saunders's body was burnt to ash, some trapped nerve in him would be relieved, some hole in the world sealed up?

Just about every prisoner in Monmouth Gaol offered Mary a swig from his bottle; it was a tradition. She was soused by the time she climbed on to the cart outside the gaol. She felt no fear.

She held her hands out with a child's obedience, and the hangman tied her wrists in front of her. His mask hid all his features but a shock of red hair and a weak chin; she didn't know him. He was no Thomas Turlis, Master of Tyburn, that much was clear. This fellow was probably a farmer; maybe the only things he had killed before were pigs and foxes. She hoped he knew how to hang a girl.

The spires and roofs of Monmouth caught the first rays of light and bent them. For a moment, as she lurched along, the wheel of the year seemed to have rolled back and Mary was a stranger, newly come to town in John Niblett's wagon. A pretty enough place, she thought idly. She could be happy here . . .

She wasn't too drunk to know where the cart was taking her, this fine spring morning, but she was just drunk enough to convince herself she didn't care. Unaccustomed to motion, she thought she might be sick over the side of the cart. But the Queen of Scots would never have done that on her way to execution, Mary told herself, making her mistress's little cluck of disapproval.

It wasn't far at all: Hereford Road, Monk Street, Whitecross Street, Stepney Street. When they turned the last corner, the cart lurched into a hole, and a splinter pricked Mary's knee. She pulled away, and with her bound hands she managed to tuck her skirt around her, between her legs and the harsh wood. Only then did it strike her as peculiar to be cosetting a body that would be dead before noon.

The Market Square was choked with people. For a moment,

Mary, staring over the edge of the wagon, wondered if today was some festival; had Easter come early this year? Then a tentative roar went up at the sight of the cart and she realised, with a peculiar thrill, that they were all there for her.

The good people of Monmouth needed to see her hang, even if it cost them a day's pay. Their faces were tense with anticipation. They looked at her as if they'd never seen her before. She recognised a handful of servants she knew to talk to, and quite a few of the patrons – Mr and Mrs Jenkins, and the two old Misses Roberts in their sedan chairs, even. And a lot of strangers, besides, who must have travelled here for the day. But it wasn't like a Tyburn crowd, full of whores and tourists so used to the sight that it barely made them laugh. Mary would have laid a bet that most of these folks in Monmouth Square had never seen anyone swing before.

When the driver got down, the crowd engulfed the cart. A small girl on her father's shoulders grinned up at the prisoner. Mary could smell orange peel and hot spice cakes and an open barrel of ale. Everyone was dressed in their best; hats were bright with ribbons. The mood wasn't one of revelry, though; most faces looked tense, unsatisfied.

There's something in you that'll never be satisfied till you swing, Mary.

Her mother's voice, clear in her head. Could Susan Digot have got word of the death of her old friend Jane, by now? Would she find out the name of the girl who'd done the killing? It would take a lot to surprise her.

A shameful death like your father's.

It came to Mary now that her mother had been right, after all: Mary had been born for this. In sixteen years she'd shot along the shortest route she could find between life and death, as the crow flew.

None of this was real. It was a story, come to life in a crude woodcut.

'But what kind of a girl was she?' Gwyneth went up on the balls of her feet to see across the square.

Daffy looked away and shrugged a little. How could he speak of Mary Saunders in the past tense, when she was sitting on that cart not a hundred feet away, with those ink-blot eyes and the sharp profile he still saw in his nightmares, even after all these months? He was trying not to look at the scaffold behind her, the snakish hang of the rope. It had been a bad idea to come today.

There was his father, twenty feet away, scanning the crowd as if searching for pickpockets. His face was set in the lines of an old man, Daffy thought. He caught Cadwaladyr's eye without meaning to. He gave a slight nod. Nothing too deferential; no hint of apology.

But Cadwaladyr nodded back, and pushed his way through the crowd. 'Davyd.'

'Father.' The first words they'd exchanged in a year and a half.

'Gwyneth, how are you?'

'Very well, sir,' she said, blushing as she bobbed on the spot.

Then there seemed nothing more to say. Cadwaladyr looked down and brushed a leaf off one worn shoe with the toe of the other.

Daffy cleared his throat. 'Mrs Jones would have been glad it was you that officiated at her funeral, I think.'

His father lifted one eyebrow. The white hairs were tangled like briars.

To fill the silence, Daffy added, 'She was a good woman.'

'Have all your books taught you no stronger words than that, boy?' Cadwaladyr's voice came out like a roar. 'Jane Jones was the best woman in this godforsaken country.'

And with that he was gone, absorbed into the crowd.

Gwyn gave Daffy a weak little smile of encouragement. Her hand slid through the crook of his elbow, like a worm through soft earth. 'I am glad you left that house on Inch Lane, though, Daff. No good could have come of staying.'

'I don't know,' he said, his head beginning to pound. 'I feel sorry for the master.'

'It's a cursed building,' she told him, holding on tighter. 'You're better off at the Misses Roberts's.' She kept her eyes on the cart where the prisoner sat as if daydreaming.

Daffy shut his eyes and concentrated on the warmth of Gwyn's arm in his. This was all he needed. If she did marry him in the end – as she'd promised on the Scriptures, this time – then he'd never hold the long hiatus against her. To marry a good woman he loved was more than a fool like him deserved; more than his father had ever had. And if the image of the Londoner did lurk in his dreams, well, many a man had to live with a ghost or two.

He looked over at the girl on the cart again; he couldn't help it. She had the whitest face in the Square. Suddenly he was rocked by pity, deep down in his bowels. Sixteen years old was all she was. Last summer Mary Saunders had been rolling round on May blossoms with him, and today she was facing her death, with a faintly haughty expression.

It came to Daffy then, how easily the worst in oneself could rise up and strike a blow. How even the most enlightened man had little power over his own darkness.

Abi was lost in the streets of London. The map she carried was meaningless. The houses were crowded together like toes in a boot.

She spared a thought for Mary Saunders. *Are you dead yet, poor bitch?* She needed a guide, someone like Mary who knew how this swirling city worked. Abi couldn't believe the filth, the colour-soaked fury of it all, the smells spilling from coffee-houses and fish-shops. She looked up and saw a golden bird spinning in the wind. 'Where's this?' she asked a passing boy.

He spat black on the cobbles. 'St Giles,' he said, 'where else?'

The crowd seemed to part for a second and there was a black man, but not like any Abi had ever known. His face had the sheen that came from eating fresh butter, and above it sat a wig as big and glossy as a cloud. His white velvet jacket stretched across his shoulders, and his smooth stockinged calves were massive. He was an emperor among men. It seemed anything was possible in this topsyturvy city.

Abi smiled straight at him; she couldn't help herself. But his eyes slid past her, as if she were no more than a stone in the road. She remembered that she was not young and not handsome. As the black man walked on by, she saw what made his coat flare over his hip: stuck through his belt, a knife big enough to chop off her head.

Stepping sideways, she almost tripped into the gutter. She staggered, but regained her balance. Strangers barely turned their heads. She wondered whether her skin had turned white overnight, or become quite invisible. This place would do, she thought with a sudden surge of hope; no one would ever find her here.

All at once the bells of St Giles began to ring, deafening her. The sound ricocheted off the buildings; Abi thought it would never stop till the end of the world.

So many eyes on Mary Saunders in the Market Square, greedy for details. Fame at last! So this was the moment she had so often dreamed of, when a crowd gathered to watch her ride past. Mary stared down at her foul and ragged skirt, which was hardly what she used to imagine she'd be wearing. For bracelets, two narrow rusty chains, locking her wrists together. For a necklace, the noose the hangman had just dropped over her head. The rough rope rested against her collarbone. So ordinary, a simple O, an idly open mouth to swallow her up. The long tail of hemp pooled in the cart at her feet.

Dai Carpenter was still working on the scaffold, hammering in the last nails. Beside him stood the red-haired hangman, scratching behind his mask. In her drunken haze, Mary felt a wash of pity for the man. When she'd done her own killing, the cleaver had moved in her hand so quickly that she'd hardly had time to feel its weight. But this man had to carry his tools with him; his work was marked by an awful decorum. The night before a killing, he knew exactly what would be demanded of him the next day – and without any rage or madness to help him, either. And the night after, he had to pull off his mask, scrub his hands, and sleep.

Her thoughts moved turgidly. What would the hangman do with her afterwards, she wondered? All bodies were worth something, in the end. In London they were sent to Surgeon's Hall for dissection, she remembered, as a further punishment. Would a young surgeon of Monmouth pay half a crown for Mary's body, to learn his trade on? Would he lay her on his slab tonight, this last hasty cully of hers? And what would he find inside? Would there be some mark, a smear, a little knot of evil?

But no, the drink was making her forgetful: they were going to burn her afterwards. If she craned her neck sideways, she could just see the enormous pile of wood. Now her heart began to hammer. Her body was going to make a bigger glow than Midsummer Night on Kymin Hill where the family from Inch Lane had had their last dance. The women to whom Mary had served tea for a year would warm their bony fingers at her bonfire tonight. They'd say good riddance to her, and whisper darkly about poor Mrs Jones: *It could have happened to any of us!*

Mary looked away from the stack of splintered wood. Her eye fell on Daffy Cadwaladyr. He was too far away for her to tell if he was looking at her. But then, why else was he here if not to watch her be punished? It occurred to her then that if she'd married him, she might have had someone to mourn for her. She might have had an existence worth mourning. After all, how else was the value of a life to be measured but in the tears shed at its close? Daffy had been her best chance, she saw now, and she'd thrown him away like a scrap of paper.

And then she saw his head bend towards the woman beside him, and she recognised the stray blonde curl: his beloved Gwyneth. For some people, she thought, trials were only temporary; they sailed towards happiness through the roughest weather.

Bile filled Mary's mouth. Her drunkenness was wearing off. She jabbed her nail into the soft crook of her elbow, as a test; the pain came through sharp and clear. It occurred to her that this was no story, but the last hour of her real life. And now she started to shake.

It would have been better, she thought frantically, if the neighbours had struck her down at once, as soon as they'd caught her. Cadwaladyr's thick hands had certainly closed round her neck, when he'd caught up with her that night on the bridge, and it had taken five men to pull him off. Yes, it would have been better if Cadwaladyr had dragged her back to Inch Lane and pushed her face into a basin of Mrs Jones's cooling blood and drowned her there and then on the kitchen floor. Then frenzy would have been paid with frenzy, instead of this cold retribution. It made her nauseous, to think of all the stately preparations for this event. Why, she wondered, had the authorities fed and housed her all winter, if they longed to see her thrash in the air today? Why did the men of law pretend to be so much loftier than other murderers?

Killing was killing, when you came down to it. Punishment had no rhyme nor reason; it fell like hail.

Mary glanced again at the pile of wood in the corner of the square. She gripped one twitching wrist in the other hand and told herself not to waste time being afraid. She wouldn't be alive to feel the scorch of her feet, would she? It was the people of Monmouth who'd have to recognise that smell. It was men like Daffy Cadwaladyr who'd have to remember it always.

A lanky boy climbed on to the cart for a moment. Mary stared back at him, waiting for the insult. But he blew a loud kiss, and thrust a paper into her lap. Before the breeze could lift it, she gripped it in her bound hands. The inky words were still wet. *The Confession and last Dying-Words of Mary Saunders.*

Confusion seized her. Who was this guilty namesake? Then she understood, and almost laughed out loud. It was her, a heroine in print. This was her free copy. Some scribbling hack had made it all up, every word of it.

Mary's father, it seemed from the *Confession and last Dying-Words*, was a Herefordshire labourer who'd earned his living by the sweat of his brow, until he died of grief upon hearing of her arrest. She also had a sister near Bristol to whom she'd recently written, *Alas! honest Poverty is better than Riches iniquitously obtained. I now bid you adieu for ever in this world!* The fictional Mary Saunders rode in true sorrow to answer for her sins before God wearing a light camblet gown, a silk handkerchief, and a black bonnet.

Mary shut her eyes for a moment and saw this other self, pristine and penitent, riding into the noonday sun. What was it she'd told Daffy, that day on the Kymin? *Books are full of lies.*

The paper shook in the breeze. Mary looked about her on the cart for somewhere to put it, and only then remembered that she wouldn't have a chance to read it – or indeed anything – again. She opened her hands and let it flutter away. It brushed the red cheek of a small boy sitting on his father's hip, and then it was lost to view.

What did it matter what was written or not written on some smeared broadsheet, she told herself, when soon enough everyone would forget the details? Strangers might remember a trip to Monmouth to see a girl hang, but who would spare a thought, in time to come, for the whos and hows and whys? Children might remember the taste of the oranges, and the greedy breathings in and out of the crowd, but nothing else. Not her name.

The thought made Mary bite her lip with distress. Nameless-ness. Oblivion. Unless her obscure and brutal story survived in some form, what proof was there that she had ever lived at all?

Mr Jones was standing not three lengths from her, like a spider glued to his web. She flinched. His hands held tight to his crutches. There was a stain on his black coat: egg, or broth?

Vinegar might shift it, Mary, or a rub of salt.

Her mistress's voice. Mary's pulse was suspended for a second.

The master's eyes rested not on her but on the cart. He didn't shout out, this time. It was as if he couldn't see her, wouldn't see her, until he saw her dead.

He had hoisted his daughter on to his shoulders for a better view, Mary saw. This was one lesson the child wouldn't be taught in school. Mary looked away, for fear of meeting Hetta's eyes. *Do you really have no mother?* the child had asked her, in her first week in the house on Inch Lane, her pupils full of astonished sympathy.

Afterwards, Mary supposed, the father and daughter would

walk home hand in hand, and Mr Jones would never let the name of Mary Saunders be said in his house again. From now on, thought Mary, the child would assume this was the way of the world. She'd always expect the people she loved to kill each other.

It was Hetta's eyes, more than anything else, that made the salt tears start to fall. They rushed down Mary's face, blinding her.

The crowd swayed round Mr Jones like waves against a rock; the people of Monmouth were tired of waiting for the spectacle to begin. Mary stared blurrily down at her filthy shift. Would they burn it too, she wondered, or sell it scrap by scrap for souvenirs? She knew it was a petty matter, but she would have given anything to be hanged in black satin. How vanity endured to the end! Clothes being no protection, she told herself, folks might as well cast them off and go naked across the world.

Terror squeezed her like a rag.

Halfway down her stays, Mary's bound hands found the ribbon. Faded to the colour of beetroot, Doll's red ribbon. She wound it round her numb fingers, tight enough to hurt. Nothing could have scared Doll, not even a gallows. *Chin high, me old muck-mate*.

All at once she remembered the way out. If you were about to hang and you had no friend in the world to haul on your feet, then there was only one way to escape a slow strangulation: *jump*. She remembered the Metyard woman at Tyburn, who'd cheated the crowd; that stony face, that leap into space. How innocent Mary had been in those days; she'd thought the people who committed murder were a different species. She'd assumed that they hated the people they killed, if they were capable of emotion at all. She would never have guessed that such things could happen as easily as sickness, or weather, or love.

Her thighs tensed like branches in a high wind now. She had to bide her time; she mustn't show her intentions. She had to wait till she knew the end of the rope was knotted to the scaffold. Till the hangman pulled the white bag over her face, and climbed down from the cart, and slapped the horse's rump. That would be her cue to jump. If she tried too early, she'd make a mess of it, and they'd haul her back into the cart.

Mary's heart was smashing against her ribs with fear and excitement. She felt the rope around her neck begin to move; her head whipped round, but the hangman was only unwinding the coils, heaving the end over the scaffold, like any sailor about to make for open sea. He pulled the knot tight around the wood. A scattering of applause.

He came up to the cart, then, the little white bag in his hand. He swung himself up like a child playing on a fence. 'Forgive me,' he muttered formally to Mary.

Her last chance for a touch of human skin. She obeyed her impulse and kissed the man on one bristly cheek, below the mask. His skin was warm. He jerked a little, but didn't shudder or wipe it off. He lifted the white bag, and dropped it over her head.

The light was blotted out. The cart shook as he jumped down.

Sackcloth, coarse against Mary's nose; her temples itched. She'd never thought to take a last look at the world. She should have stared up at the sky while it was still there. A little light filtered through the floury cloth. Mary gathered all her forces and waited to hear the hangman slap the horse's rump. What if the noise of the crowd drowned the little sound out? What if the next thing she knew was the slow mauling of the rope, lugging her by the throat into the air? Terror, now, knocking on her ribs like a debt collector who wouldn't wait any longer.

In times of trouble remember your namesake, Mary. That voice in her head, mild as milk. The girl could almost believe it was Mrs Jones. She could almost feel her mistress's soft hand in hers.

Let the Queen of Scots be a lesson to you to keep your head high.

She would. She'd jump higher than the spire of St Mary's Church.

Come along now, girl.

The townsfolk would cover their faces and gasp, to see her swing like a dark angel.

It's time, my dear.

Soon she would be rid of the whole business; soon she'd have left this messy and cumbersome self behind.

Mary. This way.

The hangman's whistle, almost merry. The cry of a child, tugged out of the way.

Mary?

That sound of the hangman's hand on his horse's rump, so intimate, so familiar.

Coming, mistress, she said in her head.

Mary staggered to her feet on the jolting cart as the noose tightened its kiss on her neck. She leaped into space, high, higher than she'd ever been in her life. She came down with a clean snap, and the crowd scattered like birds from the swing of her feet.

Note

Slammerkin is a fiction, inspired by the surviving facts of the real Mary Saunders' life, which are disputed and few. She was a servant in the employment of one Mrs Jones in – or just outside – the town of Monmouth, which at the time was in England but now is in Wales. On 13 September 1763 she killed Mrs Jones with a cleaver. She was held in Monmouth Gaol until the Assizes on 7 March 1764, when she was convicted of murder. On 21 March 1764, at the age of sixteen or seventeen, she was either hanged, or burned, or both.

Some other real people make brief appearances in this novel: Mrs Farrel, who squeezed a fortune out of her twenty lodging houses in St Giles; the Metyards, a mother and daughter who killed their apprentice Nanny Nailor and were executed by Thomas Turlis on 19 July 1762; James Boswell and Samuel Johnson; the prostitutes Alice Gibbs, Elizabeth Parker, and Ann Pullen (alias Rawlinson) who was charged with stealing her mistress's clothes in January 1763; at the Magdalen Hospital, Matron Elizabeth Butler, and the Reverend William Dodds, who went on to be hanged in 1777 for forging Lord Chesterfield's name.

Doll Higgins is an invention, but several women were found starved and frozen to death in London in the terrible winter of 1762–63. The character of Abi is inspired by the case of an anonymous woman who was enslaved in Angola and brought to Barbados, then Bristol, and whose genitals were displayed in a fold-out engraving in a book published by Dr James Parsons.

What little contemporary commentary there was about the murder of Mrs Jones suggested various motives. *The Gentleman's Magazine* claimed that Mary Saunders had planned the crime carefully in order to get hold of her mistress's savings. But, according to a broadsheet, *The Confession and last Dying-Words of Mary Saunders*, the girl did it because she longed for 'fine clothes'.